Lindsay Buroker

This is a work of fiction. Names, characters, places and incidents are products of the author's imagination or are used fictitiously and are not to be construed as real. Any resemblance to actual events, locales, organizations or persons, living or dead, is entirely coincidental.

Editor: Shelley Holloway
Cover and Interior: www.streetlightgraphics.com

PROLOGUE

Tikaya Komitopis slid one finger down the encrypted message while she translated the plain text letters onto a fresh page. She smiled. Her new key was working.

As she revealed more lines, giddiness stirred in her belly. She forced herself not to rush, not to get ahead of herself. Finish translating the message, then read it.

Tikaya tuned out the susurrus of voices in the war room. She ignored the sweat moistening her freckled hands and the mugginess of the salty air that failed to stir the leaves in the palm trees outside the window. A wisp of blonde hair escaped her long braid and dangled before her spectacles, but she ignored it too.

Only after she copied the Turgonian admiral's signature did she grab the paper with both hands, devouring the message.

Tikaya shoved her bamboo chair back so quickly it toppled to the floor. She glanced about the desk-filled room. Everyone had stopped work to watch the door where her supervisor stood with the president. Their graying heads tilted toward each other, some discussion on their lips.

She blinked. When had the president arrived?

Then elation sent her racing across the room, sandals slapping the wood floor. Perfect. He should know first.

"Mr. President?" she called, though he was already looking her way. "I have—"

Her hip rammed the corner of a desk. She flailed for balance, tripped over her own feet, and pitched forward. The president caught her in an awkward embrace. Mortified, she lurched backward and found her feet as heat swarmed her cheeks.

"Professor Komitopis," he said gently, amusement in his blue eyes. "Do you surf?"

Tikaya stared at him in bewilderment, then over his head and out the open door. In the bay, a steamer rumbled toward the docks while a few students straddled surfboards near the beach.

"No, sir," she said, letting puzzlement into her tone.

"Don't start," the president said.

Her supervisor snickered. Oh. She was being teased for her clumsiness. The men's eyes held no spite, but that did little to abate the heat plaguing her cheeks. It was bad enough she stood two inches taller than either man; she had to stumble around like a drunken sea lion in front of them too?

"You have a message?" the president asked.

The importance of the note flooded back to her. "Yes, yes. The war, sir. It's over."

The president's eyes widened.

"Or it will be in a couple weeks," Tikaya said. "Listen: 'Admiral Dufakt, by his Ancestrally Ordained Imperial Highness Emperor Raumesys's order'—I love it when they use that long title in their encrypted communications. You don't even need frequency analysis when you've got such an obvious key phrase. Every time they—"

"Tikaya," her supervisor whispered. "The message."

"Oh, pardon, sirs. The Turgonian emperor says, 'warships are to stand ready to facilitate troop removal and diplomat transportation for treaty negotiations.'" She tapped the page. "That's the official part that went out fleet wide, and this second paragraph came on another page. I believe it's a personal message between admirals.

"'That's it Dufakt. With Fleet Admiral Starcrest's death, we've gone from dominating the Nurian forces to scrambling to survive encounters with those ancestors-cursed wizard ships. Having the Kyattese cryptanalyst hand over so many of our decrypted missives to the Nurian government exacerbated our problems. How an island full of scientists managed to steal so many of our correspondences, I'll never know, but I do wish Starcrest had lived to punish them, especially since taking over their piddling nation was his idea. We'll recoup and get the Nurians next time. Send along your recommendations for promotions. Signed Acting Fleet Admiral Mourncrest.'"

"Good news, yes, indeed," the president said.

His head tilted to the side, eyes far away for a moment, and Tikaya recalled he was a telepath. He must be getting a message from some aide back in his office. Or maybe his wife wanted him to stop for groceries on the way home. Tikaya had never studied the mental sciences and did not know how likely that was, but she smirked at the thought of the president popping into the market for sugar and bananas.

When his eyes focused on Tikaya again, concern hooded them, and her amusement evaporated. His tone turned grim when he spoke: "Step outside with me, please, Professor."

Tikaya handed the note to her supervisor, and an uneasy flutter vexed her stomach as she trailed the president.

A breeze wafted in from the ocean, making it feel cooler outside despite the sun radiating off the sidewalk. Seagulls squawked in response to a steam horn blasting in the bay. The president stopped in the shade of a jackfruit tree.

"The work you've done for us this last two years has been phenomenal, Tikaya. I'm grateful, and if our nation knew about it they would be too."

She shrugged, embarrassed by the praise, and prodded a fallen jackfruit with her toe. "Thank you, sir, but I've just been hunkered in a room, playing with symbols. It was different from my regular work but similar. A fun challenge." The president's eyebrows twitched, and she winced. She should not call anything related to the war fun. Too many had died. "The men and women who risked their lives to obtain the missives are the heroes."

"I'm grateful to them, too, but their names aren't the ones starting to show up in Turgonian naval orders."

"My name isn't..." She froze. The Kyattese cryptanalyst. That had been in the message, not for the first time. The Turgonians seemed to believe a single person responsible. Her. The humid air did nothing to stifle the chill that raised the hair on the back of her neck.

"If they find out who you are," the president said, "your life will be in danger."

"They won't figure it out," she croaked, mouth dry. "They won't. They'll be looking for a cryptanalyst, not a philology professor buried in a back room at the Polytechnic, deciphering dead languages on dusty scrolls and tablets." Why did she sound like she was trying to convince herself? "We don't even study cryptography on the islands; surely they'll think it was some Nurian who worked with us."

"I hope that's true, but...I hear you're good with a bow."

For a moment, the topic shift befuddled her. Then realization dawned and made her shake her head. "In the field in the back of my parents' house, yes, sir. But I couldn't shoot anyone."

"I suggest you keep up your practice in the months ahead."

Tikaya closed her eyes and drew in a deep breath. She did not even like hunting. That had always been her brother and her father's domain. She shot because she found the repetitive, mechanical task conducive to thinking, to problem solving. She had worked out many language puzzles while plunking arrows into the straw targets on her parents' plantation.

"I hope you understand that I cannot regret bringing you into this," the president said, "not when you've been so pivotal to our people retaining their freedom. But I do...owe you a great debt. I will do everything possible to deflect foreign questions about your involvement, and I will pray for your safety in the months and years ahead."

"I understand, sir. If anything does happen, I don't hold you responsible. I had to do this. I wouldn't enjoy living under imperial rule." She sensed his grimness and wanted to reassure him. "Those warmongers probably make their professors wear swords to class, and, given how easily I can trip over my own feet, that'd be a death sentence for sure."

The president smiled, but it did not reach his eyes.

"Something else, sir?" she asked.

He sighed, gaze toward the sea. "Yes, the reason I called you out here... I just learned the bad news. It's about your fiancé."

Fear tightened Tikaya's chest. "Parkonis?"

"I'm sorry. The Turgonians sank the Eagle's Spirit off the coast of the northern island. There were no survivors."

"They sank—" Her voice cracked. "No, they wouldn't have... The *Spirit* is an archaeology vessel! It doesn't even have a cannon." She gripped the tree for support.

The president placed a hand on her shoulder. "I know."

Tikaya sank to the grass and buried her face in her lap. She did not want to believe Parkonis was dead, but hot tears streaked down her cheeks and dampened her dress.

The war was over, but she had nothing to celebrate.

CHAPTER 1

Moisture slicked the handle of Tikaya's machete, and sweat saturated her hemp dress. Her blade rang as she scraped leaves free from a stalk of sugar cane.

Sunset approached, and she had yet to cut a hand, leg, or other notable appendage. Maybe she was finally growing competent with the machete. The hilt slipped in her damp palm, and she nicked her thumb. Maybe not.

She lifted her spectacles to wipe moisture out of her eyes. A reflection in the glass made her jump.

Machete in hand, she whirled toward the cleared area behind her. A man towered a few paces away, a dagger and cutlass at his belt, and a muzzle-loading rifle crooked in his arms. His bronze skin and dark hair would have marked him a foreigner even if the black military uniform with its fine factory weave did not. It was a uniform she had not seen in a year, not since the war ended, but she had not forgotten its significance: Turgonian marine.

Several paces lay between her and the wagon where her bow rested on the driver's seat. She had kept it within reach the first couple months after the treaty signing, but time had dulled her vigilance. Swallowing, she shifted her gaze left and right, hoping to spot a couple of the seasonal laborers her father hired to harvest the cane. But the day grew late, and she had worked herself into a private corner of the field. The house stood hundreds of meters away. No one would hear her yell.

The marine said nothing, though his dark eyes followed her darting gaze. Running would confirm she had a reason to hide; maybe she could trick him into thinking she was no one of consequence. Not that being an innocent would necessarily make her safe from a Turgonian.

"If you're looking for rum," she said, his language sliding off her tongue automatically, "my brother's working in the distillery. He can sell you enough for your entire ship at a fair price."

The marine's eyes widened, and a satisfied—no, triumphant—smile stretched across his face.

Dread curled through her belly. They knew who she was, what her role had been in the war. Addressing him in his language had been a mistake, a confirmation that they had found the right person. She eyed the rifle, noticed it was loaded and cocked. A huge mistake.

"I'm not here for rum," the marine said. "I seek the cryptomancer, and I believe you are she."

Tikaya did not have to feign surprise. "The what?"

"The one who broke our codes during the war. The one who thwarted our best cryptographers. The one who—" his jaw tightened and a muscle in his cheek jumped, "—gave our decrypted messages to the Nurians. That meddling cost us a dozen ironclads and thousands of men."

"Your people tried to take over our islands to serve as a strategic outpost." Her hand flexed on the machete. "You sank *more* than a dozen of our ships, including a peaceful archaeology vessel with my—" She stopped herself. She might have every right to condemn this man, but it was stupid to do so when he stood across from her holding a rifle. "We wanted no part of your war. We did what we had to do to protect our freedom. I don't know who your cryptomancer is, but I am certainly not that person. I am a simple plantation worker, helping my family grow sugar cane and make rum."

"A simple plantation worker who speaks flawless Turgonian," the marine said.

She stifled a grimace. If those thoughtless first moments were her undoing... "The Kyatt Islands are in the middle of many nations' trade routes. Our children study several languages in school, and many of our people are polyglots. You'll find the true experts working at the Polytechnic." A place and job she had not returned to since losing Parkonis.

For the first time, a hint of uncertainty lurked in the marine's dark eyes. She held her breath, willing him to believe her.

He eyed her up and down, and she shifted her weight, abruptly aware how the dampness of her dress pronounced her curves. There were more things to fear from a strange man than being shot. She tried to ease backward, but dense cane blocked her.

The marine reached for his belt, and she crouched, brandishing the machete in both hands.

"If you touch me, I'll cut off your..." Tikaya knew the Turgonian word for penis, but some cursed ancestor with a sense of humor momentarily sucked it from her mind. "Man part," she finished feebly.

The marine's eyebrows lifted. His hand had unclasped not his belt buckle but an ammo pouch, and he pulled out a scrap of paper. "You're not my type, and if that's what you people call a fighting stance, it's amazing you can even defeat the sugar cane."

She should have felt nothing but relief, but embarrassment flushed her cheeks. The marine approached, the paper extended. Though he did not act as threatening as he might, her muscles tensed. The Turgonians had slain hundreds of her people, including the one who mattered most.

Tikaya wanted to tell him to take his note and leave, but curiosity kept her silent. What could he possibly have come all this way to show her?

He stopped a pace away from her, holding out the paper. Reluctant to close the final distance, she did not move for a long moment. He waited. Mosquitoes whined, reminding her that darkness approached. Tikaya lowered the machete and accepted the note. Even with her suntanned skin, his fingers were dark next to hers.

Though he did not try to touch her, she sidled away to study the paper. It was not a note at all but a page of symbols. Someone had painstakingly copied complex symmetrical markings interlinked in small groupings. Her teeth caught her lip. She had seen many languages, but she had never seen this one, if it even was a language. It could be anything.

"Where did you get this?" she asked, gaze stuck to the paper. After a moment, she realized she had asked in her own tongue instead of his and switched, repeating the question.

"My commanding officer."

"No, I mean..."

"My commanding officer," he said again.

Tikaya snorted. "Is it a language or..." She stopped herself from saying substitution cipher. If she hoped to plead ignorance of this cryptomancer, she had best not say anything related to cryptography.

"You tell me."

"I've never seen anything like it, and I've seen—" She caught herself again, this time short of admitting she had studied dozens of languages, living and dead. "We see a number of languages here on the island."

Tikaya tried to watch him, to gauge his reaction, but the symbols kept drawing her eyes back, demanding her attention. What if it *was* a previously undiscovered language? Something from ruins the Turgonians had dug up on their continent? They were not a people known for archaeology, nor sharing secrets. If she were to translate a new language and bring awareness of it to the global scientific community, it would assure her a place in the history books. A tempting thought, that.

"Does it mean anything to you?" the marine asked.

"No, I don't even know if this is logographic or syllabic or alpha..." Great Grandmother's eyeteeth, she was saying too much again.

Indeed, the soldier watched her through narrowed eyes. Time to end this conversation and get out of these fields before darkness fell and he changed his mind about her being his type.

Tikaya held the paper out for him. "I don't recognize it. I can't help you. You should try at the Polytechnic."

He stared at her, face unreadable. Cicadas began droning, and a bead of sweat slithered down her spine. Then he took the paper, returned it to his pouch, and walked away.

* * * * *

A pair of whale-oil lamps burned on either side of double doors marking the front of a large grassy mound. The earthen-walled structure held her family's distillery and processing equipment, and the clank-thunk of machinery echoed from within. Tikaya paused to prop her bow against the door frame as she entered the chamber. Cool, dry air offered a reprieve from the muggy evening heat, and her steaming body welcomed it after the run from the fields.

She almost tripped over a passel of laughing, sandy-haired toddlers throwing wads of bagasse at each other. Running into her nephews and nieces usually made her smile, but now she froze, mid-step, thinking of the marine. His presence represented a threat not only to her, but to her whole family, a family big enough that they joked how it was impossible to be lonely any place on the plantation. That was why she had returned this past year. The flat she shared with Parkonis near the Polytechnic had been too empty after his death, but now she feared she had endangered them all.

"Tikaya," her brother, Kytaer, called. He stood before a press, feeding sugar cane into the rollers. The long stalks cracked and flattened, and juice flowed into a collection bin below. "Glad you stopped by so I could warn you."

She tore her gaze from the tussling children. Warn her? Had the Turgonian already been here?

"Professor Meilika is in the house," Ky said. "She's joining us for dinner. She and Mother have been conspiring all afternoon. About you. How to get you back deciphering runes on broken tablets and potsherds and all that."

Tikaya exhaled slowly. Nothing new. Good. That meant the marine had not been by. She still had time to warn everyone and figure out what to do. No, she knew what she had to do. She had to pack. She could not stay here. If any of her family came to harm because of the role she accepted during the war, the guilt would torment her forever.

One of her nephews bumped into her leg and fell on his bottom. She picked him up before he could decide if the tumble was a big enough calamity to cry over. She swiped bagasse off his dusty trousers and directed him back into the game with a playful swat on the backside. A lump sprang into her throat at the idea of leaving them indefinitely. But for fate, she might have had little ones of her own by now.

"Children, time to wash up for dinner!" That was Ky's wife, calling from the path, somewhere between the house and the processing plant.

The youngsters trundled out, voicing mutters of "aw" and "do we have to?"

"You're looking particularly glum and thoughtful," Ky said when he and Tikaya were alone. "Did Mother and Father already talk to you?"

Tikaya had seen neither of her parents since early morning, so she arched her eyebrows and joined him at the press. Like their father, Ky shared her uncommon height. For him, though, it had always been an advantage, making him a boyhood star at swimming and running. For her... Well, at least she could reach the high book shelves in the library without a ladder.

"I heard them talking," Ky explained. "You're getting the wasting-the-talent-Akahe-gave-you lecture again soon. I know Father appreciates an extra hand during the harvest, but he's worried you've been here moping too long. And Mother...wants you living in town again where you can find a 'nice young man to make babies with.'"

Tikaya winced at the familiar words. Ky patted her on the shoulder.

"Sorry," he said. "Are you all right? You look preoccupied. If you were puzzling over some ancient runes, I'd know why, but I can't imagine the mysteries of the cane fields are putting those thoughtful creases between your eyebrows."

16

"I ran into a Turgonian marine," Tikaya said to hush her brother's garrulousness. She usually found it endearing, but tonight his chatter grated.

Her words did the job. He gaped for a long moment before saying, "Where? When? You haven't been to town for—"

"Here. Just now. In the north field."

Still staring at her, Ky shoved the lever that turned off the press, and the clank-thunks faded.

"He was looking for the cryptanalyst from the war," Tikaya went on, voice sounding loud in the new silence. She lowered it. "I think I persuaded him I wasn't that person, but I'd be surprised if their research doesn't lead them back to me again. Tomorrow morning—"

A clank sounded near the entrance, and a metallic canister rolled across the cement floor. Smoke billowed, and acrid fumes stung Tikaya's eyes. Oh, Akahe, she did not have until tomorrow morning.

"What is—" Ky started.

She grabbed his arm and yanked him deeper into the distillery even as another canister clinked through the doorway. Smoke hazed the entrance, but she glimpsed men slipping inside. They did not know the layout of the distillery; that ought to be an advantage.

She led her brother past the press and around two massive molasses vats.

Ky gripped her shoulder and whispered, "Turgonians?"

"I assume so." Tikaya tugged to keep him moving. The earthen back doors had grass growing on them; she hoped the soldiers had not recognized them as an entrance and posted guards.

They eased past copper pipes and the towering stills, and she crooked her toes to keep her sandals from slapping against the hard floor. Smoke curled into her nostrils and tickled her throat. She dared not cough.

She thought of her bow, still propped by the front door. Blighted banyan sprites, why had she even bothered carrying the thing around the last year?

In the back, rows of rum barrels lined the walls, and the double doors came into sight. She froze. They already stood open. Beyond them, in the fading light, grass swayed under a soft breeze.

"I didn't leave the doors open," Ky whispered.

If men waited outside, Tikaya could not see them, but that meant little. Perhaps they were crouched beside the doors, ready to pounce. Maybe they were already in the house, threatening her family. Or worse. If anything happened to her kin, it was her fault. She swallowed. She had to make sure the soldiers focused on her.

"I'll run," she whispered. "They should only want me."

Even as she put a hand down to push herself to her feet, Ky grabbed her arm. "No."

A shadow moved behind him. She opened her mouth to yell a warning, but she was too late. The butt of a rifle thudded against his head, and he slumped to the floor.

Tikaya turned to run and crashed into a broad chest. Hands clasped her arms. She twisted, trying to free herself, but the steel grip held her fast.

She screamed. A hand clapped across her mouth. She tried to bite it, but the grip smothered her with its power.

A damp rag pressed over her nose. Terror roiled in her belly. She sucked in a deep breath, thinking they meant to suffocate her, but a sweet insidious odor flooded her nostrils.

Fuzziness encroached on her mind, and her thoughts scattered. Blackness tunneled her vision, and a moment later, the world faded away.

CHAPTER 2

The ground was vibrating. No, Tikaya realized as awareness returned, not the ground, the floor. Cold, textured metal chilled her bare calves and seeped through the back of her dress. A rocking rise and fall accompanied the vibrations.

She opened her eyes to a dim, fuzzy cell. Her spectacles were missing. Unimaginative gray steel surrounded her. The monotone color marked the bulkheads and even the sturdy gate dividing her from a corridor. No portholes allowed a view of the outside, but the swells of the sea and the reverberations of a nearby engine told the story: she was locked in the bowels of a Turgonian warship.

And her brother—had the marines brought him too? She remembered the sickening thud of that rifle butt striking his head. She prayed they had left him alive, where her family could tend him, but a selfish part of her wished he was in the brig with her. The idea of being alone on a ship full of hostile marines...

She shuddered.

Tikaya rolled onto her belly. No pain lanced through her body, but stiff muscles suggested she had lain on the deck for hours.

Across the corridor, a second gate marked another cell, though darkness—and her poor vision—shrouded the interior. She stood and pressed her face between the bars. A blurry lantern burned at the base of a ship's ladder leading up. No guards stood within sight.

She probed the small lock set in her gate. She could not even get a fingernail into the fine hole. Alas, picking locks was not a typical course in the Kyattese school system.

"Wonderful day." Tikaya realized she had probably been on the floor throughout the night and amended the last word: "week."

Chains clanked in the cell across the way, and Tikaya jumped.

"Hello?" she asked in her tongue.

Maybe her brother was there, or others of her people had been taken. Maybe she was not alone against the Turgonians after all. The clanks stilled, leaving only the rumbling of the engine.

"Hello?" she asked again, this time in Turgonian and this time with less hope.

Silence.

Tikaya peered into the cell. Was that a human form slumped in the back corner? She tried other languages from the islands and coastal nations on the Eerathu Sea. Nothing elicited a response.

A hatch thudded open, catching her trying yet another greeting. Boots rang on the ladder, and a pair of marines strode toward her.

"Don't poke the grimbal, girl." The tall man in the lead jerked a nose sharper than Herdoctan potsherds at the opposite cell.

"Grimbal?" Tikaya frowned.

"Giant shaggy predators up on our northern frontier. They're probably the most irritable beasts in the empire, and they'll sink their teeth into you if you get anywhere near their territory."

Tikaya stopped herself from saying she had heard of the creature and the expression—if she hoped to deny she was their cryptomancer, she ought not appear too worldly. It was curiosity about the other prisoner that had prompted her query. Her shoulders, and her hope of denying anything, slumped when the second marine drew close enough for her to identify without her spectacles: the man from the cane fields. No doubt he had arranged her capture when she failed to convince him she was no one of consequence.

She squinted to read the name sewn on his jacket: Agarik. He stood, hands clasped behind his back, watching the other marine, his superior, she assumed, though she did not know what ranks the pins on their collars denoted.

"How're the accommodations, Five?" The speaker—his jacket read Ottotark—rapped a baton against the mystery prisoner's gate. "A lot better than what you're used to of late, eh?"

There was no response, not even a tinkle of chains rattling. Despite the silence, Ottotark chuckled at his own wit. He turned his attention to Tikaya and when his gaze lingered on her breasts, she forced herself not to step back.

"Where is my brother?" she asked. "Is he..."

"We left him in the distillery," Agarik said. "He's alive."

"Thank you," she murmured, hoping she could trust his word.

"So, the source of so many of our troubles. A woman." Ottotark shook his head. "Seems strange you'd be involved in military matters."

Tikaya bit back a response about how it was hard to remain uninvolved when invaders were trying to take over one's whole island chain.

"I reckon you just sat in an office on a beach," Ottotark continued, "and someone brought our messages to you. Is that how it worked?" The lamplight glinting off Ottotark's dark eyes did nothing to warm them, and a challenge hardened his voice. He resented her. Every Turgonian she encountered probably would.

She lifted her chin. "What are you going to do with me?"

"For the trouble you caused us? We're going to kill you, of course."

Tikaya swallowed, or tried to. Her throat constricted, and her mouth was too dry.

"Sergeant..." Agarik frowned at the other man.

Ottotark bent over, hands on his knees, and laughed. The raucous noise echoed from the metal bulkheads. "I jest—we're not killing you. Not now anyway. We need you to translate something for us first."

Tikaya barely kept from snorting. After what the Turgonians had done to her people—to *her*—she would not even help them tie their shoes.

Ottotark fished a keychain out of his pocket. "Time for you to visit the captain."

While Ottotark unlocked the door, Agarik slipped Tikaya's spectacles through the gate. She blinked in surprise and met his gaze as she accepted them. Nothing so friendly as a wink or a smile suggested she had a secret ally, but he seemed someone who treated people, even prisoners, with respect.

She had barely hooked the spectacles over her ears when Ottotark grabbed her upper arm and jerked her into the corridor so she fell against him. The amusement on his face, however crude, was gone now. He grabbed her breast, even as his other arm snaked around her waist to keep her jammed against him.

Tikaya shoved a hand against his chest and tried to thrust a knee into his groin, but his strong embrace left no space to maneuver.

His lips curled into a snarl. "We may need you, but you deserve a lot of pain for the deaths you caused."

Ottotark's fingers gouged her breast, and she gritted her teeth at the pain, determined not to gasp or cry out, though fear surged through her body. She craned her neck toward Agarik, hoping he might step in. Though his clenched jaw made tendons bulge on his neck, he made no move against his superior.

"What's the matter with your sergeant, Corporal Agarik?" a deep voice spoke from the other cell. Though quiet, it cut through Ottotark's angry lust, and he jumped, relaxing his grip. "Doesn't he know the Kyattese are sorcerers as well as scholars? In another second, she'll probably cast a spell to shrivel his testicles into wrinkled, rotten walnuts."

Ottotark frowned into the cell. "Nobody wants to hear you speak, Five." Still, he released Tikaya, shoving her toward the corporal.

Agarik was gaping at the dim cell, but he recovered enough to take her arm. Under his firm, professional grip, the heartbeats hammering in her ears slowed.

Tikaya watched over her shoulder as the guards led her away, but the unseen man did not speak again. The trek took her up to the main deck, where they marched past two long rows of cannons. The sharp tang of gun oil competed with the briny scent of the ocean roaring past beneath them. She peered through an open cannon port, hoping to glimpse her islands. If they had not sailed too far, maybe she could escape to a lifeboat—if the Turgonians had lifeboats. With that warmongering culture, one never knew. They had idiotic notions about glory in dying a warrior's death, so they might condemn their men to go down with the vessel.

Dozens of marines occupied the deck, some sparring in a makeshift arena in the middle and some cleaning rifles, pistols, and cutlasses at tables folded down from the wall space between the massive guns. The men slanted her looks ranging from openmouthed bewilderment to sneering hostility, by which she assumed some knew who she was and some were not in the need-to-know camp. The empire did not employ women in their armed forces, which likely meant she was the only one on board. Not a comforting thought. More than one man arranged to bump or jostle her as paths crossed. Unlike at home, everyone she passed was as tall or taller than she, and their wayward elbows and shoulders battered her with the force of falling coconuts.

Past the galley, aft deck, the loitering marines thinned. Tikaya's guards stopped her in front of a whitewashed door. A bronze sword-shaped name plaque read: Captain Bocrest.

Sergeant Ottotark thumped his baton against the wood planks, eliciting a barked, "Enter."

Inside, a bare-chested man performed pushups on a polar bear rug stretched before a desk. Though his short hair ran the same color as the plethora of steel comprising the ship, the defined muscles of his broad torso promised him hale. Arms like pistons in a steam engine, he pumped through another fifty pushups, while Tikaya stood and waited. The space was large, as one would expect of the captain's cabin, but spartan with nothing so frivolous as curtains for the portholes or cloth for the dining table.

The captain finished his pushups, jumped to his feet, and faced Tikaya. Her eyes were level with his nose, but he probably weighed sixty pounds more than she.

"Dismissed," he told the guards without looking away from her.

Evidently, he was not worried about her walnut-ifying his balls. He was probably not worried about much. The collection of dented and scratched daggers, swords, pistols, crossbows, and rifles on the wall beside his desk did not appear decorative.

"Sit." The captain jerked his thumb toward an uncomfortable-looking wood stool and strode around the desk to his own chair.

Tikaya wanted to cross her arms and stare defiantly, but suspected he would force her into complying. And, like Sergeant Pissed and Horny, he might like it. She perched on the edge of the seat.

"Tikaya Komitopis." He gripped the sides of his desk, his eyes intent. "Daughter of Loilon and Mela. Three siblings. You grew up on your parents' plantation and showed a gift for languages at a young age. You studied them at your university where you went on to teach for four years until the Western Sea Conflict, which involved your island. Your people chose to fight against—"

"Against becoming slaves to Turgonia, like everyone else you've conquered in the last seven hundred years."

"—Turgonia," he continued as if he had not heard her. "You were recruited by your government to break our ciphers, which, despite having no background in cryptography, you did. Repeatedly. And then your people handed our decrypted messages to our enemies." His eyes narrowed, his knuckles whitened where he clenched the desk. Powerful arm and chest muscles twitched beneath his bare bronze skin. "You cost us our victory. Your dishonorable tactics forced us into a stalemate with those cursed Nurians, and we ended up losing tens of thousands of men for terms no better than we started with. Is there anything pertinent that I don't know about you?"

"I like coconut shrimp and my favorite color is blue." Antagonizing him was probably stupid, but she would rather burn her favorite books than ingratiate herself with these people.

His eyes narrowed further. "We were researching you in order to identify and kill you for your crimes against the empire, but there's been... an incident. We need something translated and our languages experts are taking too much time."

That probably meant they were stupefied and stumped. How desperate did the empire have to be to ask a foreigner for help?

"Time?" Tikaya asked.

"There isn't much of it." He unlocked a drawer and withdrew the paper she had already seen along with two rubbings.

He laid them on the desk, and she started to lean forward, despite her intent to remain aloof. She caught herself and forced herself to sit back. Yes, the symbols interested her, but what could she do without the reference texts in the Polytechnic? Even at home, she would likely be stymied if nothing like the Tekdar Tablet existed: a bilingual source that said the same thing in two languages, one already known.

"Why is time a factor?" she asked.

"You don't need to know."

"Where did the symbols come from?"

"You don't need to know."

She tamped down irritation. "Is it ciphertext? Or a language?" She lifted her hand. "And, yes, I *do* need to know that."

"We believe it's a language. An ancient language. We need you to decipher it and compile a dictionary. Our team can handle the rest."

She snorted, both at the idea of being able to simply look at these rubbings and produce a dictionary and because she would not hand anything to their 'team' even if she could. "You mean your people can take my work, hide it from the rest of the world, and keep whatever knowledge it affords you to yourselves."

"That's none of your concern," he bit out, fingers still rigid where they gripped the table.

"If you're not going to tell me anything, then I'll have to guess. I figure you've found some ancient ruins guarding some fabled treasure and you've gotten your people in trouble trying to extricate the goods without knowing who or what you're dealing with. You need to know what the writing says so you can get at whatever it is you're after, hoard it from the rest of the world, and no doubt shoot the foreign translator who helped you. You people are—"

The captain leapt around the desk so quickly she did not have time to brace herself. He grabbed her by the neck and thrust her against the wall. Swords and pistols clattered to the deck. Her feet dangled above them, and she grabbed his bare forearms, scrabbling to loosen his grip.

She gasped, tried to suck in air. His fingers dug deeper into her windpipe. Though a rational part of her mind said they needed her and would not seriously damage her, pain and terror pumped uncertainty through her heart.

"Everyone on this ship wants you dead," the captain growled, breath hot against her cheek, chest heaving with rage, "and I'd like nothing more than to snap your neck right now."

Tikaya barely heard him. She clawed at his wrists and wheezed for air.

Idiot, she cursed herself. Why had she goaded him? She knew what they were, what atrocities they had committed during the war. Blackness encroached on her vision.

"But my orders say to get that language translated, and you *will* do exactly that. We know where your family lives. If you don't help, your parents and your siblings will be sacrificed. Your help or their lives. You choose."

The captain dropped her abruptly, and she collapsed before she could get her feet under her. She bit her lip, and blood tainted her mouth. He hauled her to her feet, his hand digging bruises into her arm. He took the papers, smashed them into her palm, and shoved her so hard she crashed into the door, cracking her shoulder against the unyielding metal. Tears stung her eyes, and she dashed them away. She would never let these people see her cry.

He pushed her aside to open the door. "Get out of my office."

Tikaya, rigid back to him, walked out. Corporal Agarik and Sergeant Ottotark waited outside. Agarik spotted the blood running down her chin and gave her a sympathetic frown. Perhaps it was her imagination, but it seemed that guilt lurked in his eyes.

"Pampered librarian," the captain muttered before his door slammed shut.

Unsurprisingly, the sergeant eyed Tikaya with lasciviousness and went out of his way to rub against her on the way back. She clenched her jaw, determined not to react. When they locked her into her cell, she willed them to go away. Alone, she would not have to maintain the stalwart facade.

Before they left, the corporal pressed a kerchief into her hand. After the hatch clanged shut, she staunched the blood trickling from her lip.

She threw the notes on the floor and paced circles around the confining cell. That bastard wanted the impossible. And he was going to kill everyone she loved if he didn't get it. How was she supposed to translate a dead language with nothing more than a couple rubbings of runes?

Tikaya slammed her hands against the hard metal wall. Her short, fast breaths rasped in her ears. She forced herself to take deeper ones. Panicking would not help. She needed to escape and get her family to safety. Yes, that was the best plan.

She eyed the cell across the way. An ally would make escape easier.

"Five?" she said. "Thanks for the help earlier."

She waited several moments, but no answer came. Maybe he had been taken from his cell. Maybe he was sleeping. Or—she grimaced at the idea—maybe he would not talk to her because he hated her as much as everyone else on the ship. Just because he had not wanted to see a woman manhandled did not make him a devotee. Though it did suggest he was decent, maybe worth the effort of bringing around.

"I now know why I'm here," Tikaya said. "Sort of. I'll tell you about it if you tell me why you're here. And why you have a number instead of a name."

She stepped close to the gate, propping her elbows on the cold metal bars, and peered into his cell. Her eyes had adjusted to the gloom, and she made out his form in the deep shadows of the back corner. He sat, slumped against the walls, and, though she could only guess at his height, she had the impression of a big man.

"Are you a crew member being punished for something? Or are you a prisoner too?"

He had only voiced the single sentence, but that rich baritone had sounded native Turgonian. Of course, *she* spoke the language like a native and was not one. Maybe he was another linguist brought in to help. And they had chained him because... Why? He was more dangerous than she? She snorted. Who wasn't?

Neither her questions nor mental musings stirred him to answer, and only silence came from his cell. For now, she would have to plot an escape on her own. She ticked the bars with a fingernail. As long as she remained in the cell, she would not have a chance. Reluctantly, she allowed that cooperating with the captain, or at least *appearing* to cooperate, might be the only way to get herself moved to less secure lodgings.

Tikaya slid the rubbings through the gate and laid them on the floor. The single lantern burning in the corridor provided wan illumination, and she had to squint to read.

"I wish I knew where these rubbings had been taken. I can't even assume it's the Turgonian continent, because the empire's ships troll the world. This is a short sample, but some of the symbols do repeat." She spoke out loud and in Turgonian for the benefit of her neighbor, just in case hearing her voice might bestir him to comment on something, but she soon lost herself in contemplation and forgot him, the poor lighting, and even that she was on a ship full of marines.

"If it's alphabetic, it's a large alphabet," she murmured. "I'm more inclined to believe we're dealing with a logographic or logophonetic script. In that case, there could be thousands of symbols in the lexicon." She sighed, daunted at the prospect, but she tingled a bit too. It had been over a year since anything challenged her like this. "As far as I can tell, the symbols are abstract, not like Jutgu Hieroglyphs where so many are ideograms that represent ideas or physical things. That would have been useful." She tapped a page. "That glyph reminds me of the Aracha vowels, but I suspect it's just a coincidence. This is far more complex. The way the symbols are clustered and linked is unique. I'd guess the groupings represent words, or maybe sentences or concepts. Some are quite large. Seventeen in that series. Eleven, two, seven, seventeen again."

"Prime numbers."

Tikaya had forgotten her silent neighbor, so she cracked her forehead on the gate in surprise when he spoke. She grunted and rubbed the nascent bump. "What?"

"Are all the groupings prime?" It was the same deep, mellow voice he had used to speak to the guards, though a note of curiosity had entered it.

Tikaya recovered and bent over the rubbings again. She almost asked him to come forward and have a look, but remembered the clink of chains. He was probably shackled in the back specifically so he could not reach the gate and any passing guards.

"Huh," she said after a moment. "They are. The highest grouping, which appears only once in these samples, is twenty-nine."

She gazed thoughtfully into her neighbor's dark cell. She would have noticed the prime number commonality eventually, especially if she had been scribbling notes, but that his mind went right to that gave her an inkling that she was sharing the brig with someone more than an average thug.

"You're sure you're working on a language?" His chains rattled, and his dark form changed position. She could make out little, but guessed he had shifted to face her.

"I'm not, no. That's what the captain told me. An ancient language that he wants me to decipher. Though I don't think he knows much or he'd understand there's no hope of translating a text by looking at a sheet of symbols. I'm guessing he was just parroting what someone higher up told him."

"Likely." Was that an amused note in his voice?

"I'm not sure how much stock to put in his claim of 'ancient' either. The Turgonians don't use the mental sciences and can only rely on the relative dating method for judging age. Even that's questionable, since they've only been on their continent seven hundred years, and I'm not sure how much, if any, documentation they did of the existing cultures before they assimilated them. Or killed them off. Brutes."

Her neighbor—Five, she reminded herself—said nothing at that, and she winced, recalling he might be Turgonian himself. She rubbed her lips, annoyed at her mouth's proclivity for blurting things out without lacing in any tact.

"Erm, anyway," she said, "all primes between two and twenty-nine are represented in these samples." Casually, hoping she could draw him out, she added, "Supposing this is a language, do you have any thoughts as to what might be the significance of incorporating primes in the core structure?" The first thing her mind flashed to was that each number might signify a different part of speech, but using seventeen symbols to represent a verb seemed like overkill.

His chains rattled. A shrug? "I'm sure you already know prime numbers are the building blocks of natural numbers. They can only be divided evenly by one and themselves, and anything that's not a prime number is made up of prime numbers."

"Building blocks," she mused. "Like letters are the building blocks of my language, perhaps. Though in this case the numbers are the wrappers, not the content." She stood and stretched, wishing the cell afforded her more room to pace.

"You are Kyattese, is that correct?"

Tikaya stilled, realizing he did not know who she was to the marines. If he *was* a Turgonian, her chances of turning him into an ally might plummet if he found out she was their cryptomancer.

"Yes," she said carefully.

"Did your president survive the war?"

Surprise and then suspicion flooded her, and she regarded him through narrowed eyes. "Yes, why wouldn't he have?"

"Is he...a good man? Good for your people?"

Tikaya did not know what to make of this line of questioning and responded only with another clipped, "Yes."

She folded her arms across her chest and decided not to answer anything further about her people or her nation, especially not anything the Turgonians might use against them. Fortunately, Five asked no more.

"Why don't you answer a question for me since I'm answering yours?" she suggested.

He did not respond.

"I'll settle for one," she said. "Will you answer me one question?"

His soft snort hinted at amusement. Tikaya decided to take it for consideration.

"What's your name?" she asked.

A sigh mingled with the hum of the engines. "Not that question. Ask another."

"Why not that?"

"You're replacing your one allotted question with that one?" A hint of dryness infused his tone.

"Yes."

Another sigh. "They took my rank and my name as punishment. Five was my number on the penal boat going to Krychek Island, and, as far as the empire cares, it's the only identification I have now."

"Krychek Island," Tikaya breathed. "Isn't that where they send criminals so vile they're afraid to execute them outright? Out of fear their spirits will linger in the area and afflict the living? So they send you to the island with no food, no weapons, no resources, the assumption being you'll kill each other off far from anyone worth haunting? They say those few who do survive turn into animals, bestial and deranged and cannibalistic and..." She caught her lip between her teeth. There she went again, probably offending the only person on this ship who had stood up for her.

"Glad our penal island is renowned even amongst foreigners." Five's dryness held a bitter edge this time.

She sighed. She *had* offended him. And she had a new concern. If he was that much of a criminal, dare she side with him? What could he have done to merit such a harsh punishment? Brutality seemed bred into the Turgonian culture, so she struggled to imagine someone who fit their definition of vile. Five sounded normal—pleasant—but perhaps it was a facade. He had to be shackled for a reason, though Captain Bocrest's current problems must trump that reason, or why else would Five be here?

"But the captain came to pick you up? Isn't Krychek Island usually a permanent residence?" she asked, wanting to be sure. "Its location is even secret, isn't it? So families can't make rescue attempts?"

"Correct." Tension riddled that one clipped word, and she hesitated before asking the next question, but she had to know if he was likely to be a threat to her.

"What was your crime?"

Clothing rustled and the chains rattled. "No more questions." His voice was muffled, as if he had covered his face. "Please," he added so softly she thought she might have imagined it.

"Of course. Sorry." She meant it. If the place was half as bad as the stories said, she could understand not wanting to discuss it. He was probably lost in his painful memories, and only the puzzle of the language had distracted him. "Uhm, I'll be over here, enjoying the lovely ambiance and pondering these slanted circles, dots, and sideways trees. If you want to talk later, let me know."

She did not expect anything else from him, but he surprised her by asking, "Sideways trees?"

"Well, if trees were symmetrical maybe. Want to see?"

"I can't reach the corridor."

She grabbed one of the rubbings, folded it into a compact stack, and tossed it through his gate. His dark form shifted, so she assumed it fell within his reach, but he said nothing.

"Can you see it?" she asked after a moment. "Is there enough light?"

"Yes. I should have known." He sounded grimmer than a funeral pyre. "I've seen them before."

"Where?"

"Somewhere I never want to go again."

"Where?" she repeated, leaning forward.

He did not answer.

"Five?"

Silence.

CHAPTER 3

Tikaya dozed until the hatch creaked open hours later. The perennial darkness of the cell stole her sense of time, but she guessed it was evening. Her hollow stomach whined for a meal.

Footfalls rang on the metal deck. She eyed the gate warily and let out a sigh of relief when Corporal Agarik came into view—alone. He carried two metal canteens and wooden trenchers narrow enough to slide between the bars. Dried fish, dried fruit, and a couple of hard biscuits soon rested on the floor before Tikaya. Though the meal did not exactly fill the brig with scintillating scents, her mouth watered anyway.

She grabbed a biscuit and gnawed. It had the consistency of sawdust and less flavor. Agarik placed another tray, this one with a larger portion of food, on the floor in Five's cell. He drew his cutlass and used it to push the tray deeper, presumably so the chained prisoner could reach it. Tension marked the corporal's movements—he seemed to fear an attack at any moment—and Tikaya wondered if people had been hurt, or worse, when the marines originally locked Five up. Either that or his reputation was simply enough to instill fear. Even Sergeant Ottotark's bravado had seemed forced. And she wanted to ally with Five? Was she insane? Just desperate, she decided.

Agarik delivered the meal without incident; the chains did not even clank to suggest movement. He sheathed his sword and turned to face her.

"Captain Bocrest wishes to know if you've decided whether to co-operate voluntarily or if more..." he shrugged apologetically, "pressure is required."

What? Threatening families—and windpipes—was not enough to sway most prisoners?

"I'm willing to attempt the translations," she said, "but I have terms. I can't work in these conditions."

"I'll tell him."

"Corporal?" Tikaya asked before he could leave.

He turned back, face guarded. He probably feared she would ask some favor he would be duty-bound to refuse.

"Thank you for your kindnesses," was all she said.

He nodded but said nothing. A bevy of footsteps hammered the deck, the hatch clanked open, and six burly marines clomped into view. Sergeant Ottotark followed, tapping his baton against his thigh as he walked, and Tikaya shrank into the shadows. Now what?

The six marines staggered themselves along the corridor and pointed pistols, not into her cell but into the opposite one. Tikaya stepped forward, afraid they meant to execute her neighbor, but Ottotark rattled the keys.

"Time to visit the captain, Five."

He unlocked the door and waved two of his men inside. They exchanged nervous glances but slid into the cell and stood on either side of the door, pistols never wavering. Ottotark took a deep breath, visibly steeling himself, then walked inside. As yet, the chains had not rattled, and Tikaya half thought Five asleep. Maybe he was just being still, hoping for a chance to escape. Though how he could do so with so many firearms pointed his way, she could not guess.

While all eyes focused on that cell, Tikaya eased forward. She eyed the belts of the men within her reach, hoping to spot a set of keys. Such luck did not favor her.

Corporal Agarik had stepped back when the others marched in, and she caught his knowing gaze on her. She sniffed and stared back. They had kidnapped her; she refused to feel guilty for thinking of escaping.

"Up." Sergeant Ottotark must have unlocked the chains securing the prisoner to the wall. A long still moment passed with no sign of movement in Five's cell. "I said, get up!"

Ottotark lunged into the shadows. Tikaya flinched, expecting the meaty thud of that baton striking flesh. A scuffle and grunt sounded. Someone threw the baton and it clattered against the gate before dropping to the floor. The sergeant growled and drew his arm back, but he halted mid-blow and skittered backward.

Five was on his feet.

"Don't move!" one of the marines inside the cell barked, pistol arm straight and rigid. "We *will* shoot you."

"Doubtful." But Five stopped short of grabbing Ottotark and turned toward the guards, his features still in shadow.

"Cursed bastard, you presume much," Ottotark growled. "We can shoot you without killing you." A speculative note entered his voice, as if he were truly considering it.

Tikaya gripped the bars of her gate, trying to think of something to say to help him. After all, Five had come to her defense.

"Or we can just beat you into oblivion for the rest of the trip." Ottotark hooked a punch into Five's face.

With pistols pointed at his chest, Five could only accept it. Ottotark grabbed his baton and lifted it to deliver more damage.

"I thought Turgonians were supposed to be brave warriors," Tikaya blurted. "Abusing someone who can't fight back is cowardly."

"Sew that yap shut, woman. Nobody wants your opinion." Despite his words, Ottotark lowered the baton and prowled out of the cell. "Let's go, ugly."

Five shambled into the corridor. Thick, tangled black hair hung around his cheeks and half way down his back. A matted beard and mustache engulfed the lower half of his face. Torn, faded trousers with ragged hems reached his calves, and a crudely sewn hide vest covered his torso, leaving muscular but lean—too lean—bare arms visible beneath a layer of grime. Shackles bound his wrists before him, and blood trickled from his nose, adding menace to his already savage appearance. Even slumped, head hanging, he stood a half foot taller than Tikaya.

He glanced at her, almost wincing, and she had the impression his state embarrassed him. She met his eyes with a respectful nod. Criminal or not, he was the most obvious person to turn into an ally.

"Let's go." Ottotark sent two men ahead, then shoved Five after them.

After the group had gone, Agarik nodded to Tikaya's food and water. "Do you need anything else?"

Everything else, she thought, and a trip back home. "Can you tell me who that is I'm sharing the brig with?"

"Nobody knows."

"*Some*body must know."

"The captain," Agarik said. "He doesn't confide in anyone. I don't think Sergeant Ottotark even knows, and he's the captain's adjutant."

"What happens if the captain gets shot and no one else knows the mission?" Tikaya supposed it was uncharitable to enjoy the thought.

"The orders are locked up somewhere. The officers know where to find them."

"Ah." Tikaya pointed to the vacated cell. "Why are your people so careful with him? Is he that dangerous?"

Agarik worked his tongue against his cheek and gazed toward the ladder, perhaps considering whether it would be a breach of duty to answer. "He's a prisoner from Krychek Island, and we lost four men getting him off the beach."

"He killed them?"

"No, the lunatics on the island attacked our party with spears and clubs. Men gone savage. They wanted to escape, and if they couldn't escape they'd kill those who originally brought them there months and years before. Ancestors' wrath, we had to shoot a bunch of them. Seemed they'd rather die than stay there."

"And Five attacked you too?" Tikaya rested her arms on the gate and watched the corporal's face in the flickering light of the single lantern. His gaze had grown thoughtful and distant.

"No, he stood back and watched. You got the sense he didn't want anything to do with us, but he didn't hide either. At first it seemed he'd come along peacefully—he got in the longboat once the captain spotted him and called him over. He didn't give us any trouble rowing back to the ship, but he attacked a guard the first night, got out of his cell, stole a pile of food from the galley, and slipped by everyone on duty." Agarik frowned. "Including myself. Without anyone seeing him, he swiped a sextant, compass, chronometer, nautical almanac, and spare sail, and he was about to drop a lifeboat. He would have been long gone by morning, but Captain Bocrest got an itch, and he was waiting with a loaded rifle."

"So he—Five—surrendered?"

"Not exactly." Agarik rubbed his jaw as if recalling a blow. "Captain threatened to shoot him but didn't, and it took a full squad to wrestle him belowdecks and get him locked up again."

"Where he's been chained ever since."

"Yes, ma'am."

So, whatever the imperials wanted their prisoner for, it seemed he was also too valuable to kill. His first escape might not have worked, but he had that goal in mind too. Good. Two people rowing a longboat would be more efficient than one, and it heartened her that Five had known exactly what to grab. She knew how to sail and navigate in theory but had never been out of sight of her islands.

"One thing's a mite peculiar," Agarik mused.

"Just one?" Everything thus far struck Tikaya as peculiar.

"He didn't take a pen or paper."

"What do you mean?"

"You need to do some figuring to account for the errors and adjustments that come with using a sextant. Not many could do 'em in their head and keep them straight from day to day without a log."

"Maybe he forgot," Tikaya said, though she already had a hunch Five had a background in mathematics. Maybe he could do the calculations in his head and remember the results.

The corporal grunted noncommittally. He seemed as curious about the mystery prisoner as her.

More footfalls rang on the deck. Now who?

"Your duty, Corporal," the captain said, eyes cool as he descended the steps. "It is not here."

"Yes, sir." Agarik ducked his head and trotted away.

This time, Bocrest wore his black uniform jacket with a handful of badges and medals adorning the breast. A fresh bruise swelled on his temple, and dried blood crusted on his chin beneath a swollen split lip. Had someone whaled on him as part of a training session? Or maybe he had already started questioning Five, and it wasn't going well. Either way, the bumps would probably not improve his personality.

Nonetheless, she lifted her chin and met the captain's eyes. Bravado would likely get her further than meekness on this ship.

"Well?" Bocrest asked. "You working with us or are my men taking target practice on your family members?"

It was a moment before she could unclench her jaw. The man had the diplomacy of a stinging jellyfish. "I will help you, captain," she said, forcing a civil tone, "but I can't work in this dark pit, and, surely, if you expected me to translate this language, you brought some basic references and primers. Hodtolk's? Fisher and Grist? Merk's Hieroglyphics Compendium? More samples of this writing would help as well. And I'll certainly need better lighting, paper, pencils, a table. I'll also need the freedom to walk around. That's when I do my best thinking."

Tikaya expected denial, especially over her last request, but after glaring at her for a moment—it seemed his normal way of looking at people—he said, "I'll get you paper and better lighting. You may have one daily exercise period. Beyond that, pace your cell if you need to 'think.'"

He started for the hatch.

"One more question, captain," Tikaya said, wondering if he would answer it honestly or not.

"What?"

"Suppose I succeed in translating this language, in helping you with whatever your problem is. What happens to me then?"

Bocrest eyed her over his shoulder. "If you succeed, your family will not be harmed. You? As far as the emperor and thousands of dead Turgonians are concerned, your deeds during the war condemned you. I suggest you enjoy your last project."

Tikaya leaned against the cold metal wall for support. She wished he had lied.

* * * * *

When Tikaya stepped out of the hatch, the sun made her blink. She stumbled and almost crashed into the guards escorting her outside for her exercise session. Nobody offered a steadying hand.

Wind gusted across the deck, tugging at her braid, and slapping her dress against her legs. When her vision recovered, the sun told her they traveled northeast. Endless sea stretched in all directions, so she could only guess at their position and goal. Though the briny breeze stole the stink of burning coal, the black plumes streaming from two smokestacks suggested the furnaces burned at maximum capacity. Full sails made use of the wind as well, and Tikaya wondered how fast they traveled under the combined power. Perhaps she imagined it, but the sun warming her cheeks felt less intense than back home. Where were the Turgonians taking her?

A pair of marines in gray togs jostled her as they jogged past.

"Stay out of the running lane," one barked without glancing back.

Tikaya sighed and shuffled in the direction the guards indicated. She should have relished the excursion, the chance to stretch and walk, but the lack of company dulled her spirits. She hadn't even been able to speak with Five again. The captain had granted her request for a desk and better illumination by moving her to one of the officers' cabins in the wardroom, which put her on the other side of the ship from the man she wanted to conspire with. And the young private stationed outside her door showed no inclination of allowing her to wander.

The guards led her past masts, smokestacks, and two thirty-foot launches mounted in the center of the deck. She kept her gaze from lingering too long on the big boats. It would take more than two people to get one of those in the water anyway. She stepped past a cannon to glance over the railing. Ah, yes. Smaller cutters were mounted alongside the ship below the gun ports. She and Five could handle one of those. Unfortunately, she needed time with him to make plans.

"Stop gawking." One the guards shoved her.

"I didn't know there was a minimum walking speed up here," Tikaya muttered.

"Exercise is for sweating, not sightseeing."

"You're a pithy people, aren't you?"

That earned another shove.

Tikaya picked up her speed. A heavy gun on brass rails dominated the forecastle, but the area behind it lay open, and a few bare-chested men boxed in a makeshift arena. Racks contained practice weapons, dumbbells, and other exercise equipment. Captain Bocrest and a lieutenant stood on the far side where a temporary archery lane was set up with person-shaped paper targets attached to bales of hay. They practiced with repeating crossbows, though traditional bows also leaned in a rack.

"You going to do anything, woman?" a guard asked.

Feeling self-conscious beneath all the eyes that swiveled to watch her, Tikaya walked over to a pile of sand-filled balls with handles. After a few tries, she found a small one she could lift. She maneuvered through a few exercises, though no one had suggested baths were available, so she was not sure how much of a sweat she wanted to encourage.

"Awkward turtle, isn't she?" one of the guards said.

"Fine by me," the second said. "Makes her melons bounce."

"Hah, and her ass. Bookly thing but I'd mount that in a heartbeat."

Jaw clenched and cheeks flaming, Tikaya turned her back to them.

"Nothing else to mount around here," the conversation continued, "unless you want to crawl into Lieutenant Amn or Corporal Agarik's bunks."

"I reckon they'd be the ones wanting to do the mounting then."

She supposed that explained why she was not Agarik's "type." The marines went back to analyzing her, and, when others joined in, the commentary grew cruder and more explicit. Though the captain stood within earshot, he did nothing to stop the lewd harassment. She wondered if the men would have treated a Turgonian woman this way or if her status as hated-enemy-of-the-empire made it acceptable.

Tikaya gave up the exercises in favor of walking around the training area. She eyed the officers plunking quarrels into the targets, surprised they bothered practicing archery given the power of their rifles.

"How's the *thinking* going, librarian?" Bocrest asked. "You figure anything out yet?"

"I'm working on it. I doubt you have any idea as to the magnitude of the task. People spend years working to translate a newly discovered language, and that's when they're surrounded by libraries full of reference materials."

"Uh huh. Take a few more laps around the ring to inspire my men's fantasies and then go back to work."

"Double or nothing, sir?" The lieutenant hefted his crossbow.

"It's your rum." The captain turned his back on her and loaded a fistful of bolts into his own crossbow.

An idea tickled her mind. "You a betting man, Captain?" she asked before she could talk herself out of it.

Since he had already dismissed Tikaya, he had to turn back to frown at her. "What?"

"Care to make a wager?"

"Like what?"

"I'll bet you there's a weapon here I can best you with."

The snorts and outright laughs around her were no surprise.

"Why would I make a wager with my prisoner?" the captain asked. "What could you have to lose that I would want?"

What indeed?

"Before you offer to warm my toes tonight, know I'm a married man."

The fact that he had a wife—and was faithful to her—left her speechless for a moment.

Bocrest tapped his foot. Tikaya considered the bruises on his face. If she was right and Five had delivered those, maybe she could use that.

"I see Prisoner Five has given you some trouble," she said. "You must need him for something, presumably related to what you need me for. If I lose, I'll persuade him to help you with your mission."

Bocrest laughed. "Why would he listen to the cryptomancer?"

Because Five did not yet know she *was* the cryptomancer. "Because we've established a rapport." If one could call a single shared conversation a rapport.

The laughter ceased, and Bocrest studied her through narrowed eyes. Perhaps that had not been a wise claim to make.

"Fine. What if I lose?" The captain's mouth twisted, showing how unlikely he thought that. "I'm not releasing you or promising anything that would involve breaking orders."

"I want Five to share my exercise periods, an hour each day." The captain was shaking his head before she made it halfway through the sentence, but she pressed on. "I also want you to give him a bath, haircut, shave, and fresh clothing to wear." Tikaya smiled. "Actually, I'll take a bath and fresh clothing too."

"A bath!" the lieutenant roared. "This is a steamer! Water is for pouring into the boiler."

"Surely you could manage a damp washcloth," she said.

"No," the captain said. "No to it all. That's too much extra work for my men. He's too dangerous to have out."

"Why can't these men watch him?" She pointed to the onlookers. "I can't imagine the emperor pays them to stand around and gawk at me. Besides—" the captain's face had grown red, so she patted the air soothingly, "—you don't honestly believe you'll lose our wager, do you?"

He snapped his mouth shut. "No."

The captain stuck his palm out, edge toward her, and she banged her hand against it in the Turgonian gesture for a deal sealed.

"Choose your weapon," he said.

She went straight to the bows. They were designed for tall, burly men, so it took some experimentation to find one she could string and draw. For once her long arms were useful, and her months laboring on the plantation gave her strength she had not possessed during her academic tenure.

"Think she'll even be able to load that?" one man asked.

"Probably shoot her toe off."

"There's no way she'll hit a target."

"Better tell the boys in the rigging to watch out."

"Don't know why my languages instructor bothered teaching me the Turgonian word for encouragement," Tikaya muttered. "Not like they ever use it."

Bow strung, she joined Bocrest.

"Challenger shoots first," he said.

"No practice?"

"No."

"Best of three shots?"

"One shot. Deal's been made. Shoot."

The lieutenant handed her a single arrow.

"I see you're a sporting people." She should have negotiated the rules of the game instead of trying to finagle baths.

Tikaya nocked the arrow and turned sideways, bow held loosely in her left hand as the fingertips of her right curled about the string. Just like on the plantation back home, she told herself.

Except it wasn't. Even on the calm day, the ship rose and fell with the swells, and activity on deck offered distractions. The misty breeze licked her cheeks, and she closed her eyes for a moment, considering the affect it would have on the arrow's flight. She locked her eyes on the red dot in the center of the target and drew the bow, anchoring her fingers in her usual spot against her cheek. The men's ongoing comments disappeared and focus came. She breathed in the tangy air, blew it out, and waited for the quiet moment when her body and the deck were still.

She released the arrow.

It cut through the air and thudded into the red dot. The surrounding men fell silent, mouths hanging open. Tikaya resisted the urge to smile or make any triumphant gesture.

"Your turn," was all she said to the captain.

His expression was less stunned and more dyspeptic. Too late, Tikaya wished she had found a way to make the challenge private. If he did not make as fine a shot, he might lose face in front of his men. And take it out on her.

Bocrest lowered his bow. "A shot that good is worth the prize, for what little reward having that dour bear around will be."

The men grunted in agreement. Good. She recognized the face-saving gesture, but in this case was relieved he had found a solution. After eliciting a promise that Five would join her the next day, she walked a few more laps.

The captain caught up as her guards were about to lead her belowdecks. He clenched her elbow and put his mouth near her ear. "I trust you and Five aren't plotting to escape. If you attempt something that foolish, you *will* be caught, and I'll let Sergeant Ottotark deliver your punishment. He enjoys that sort of work immensely."

CHAPTER 4

Clouds blanketed the sky the next day when Tikaya came out for her exercise session, but the darker weather didn't dampen the curiosity humming through her. Her ally—even if he did not yet know she had dubbed him ally—would join her soon. What would he look like without all that hair and dirt? Would the guards give them enough space to talk privately?

She walked around the outside edge of the exercise area, struggling for patience. The captain was out again, this time trading sword blows with his navigator. Tikaya wondered who ran the ship when these Turgonians spent so much time exercising. Some prisoners of war were probably chained down in the boiler rooms, shoveling coal into the furnaces day and night.

The clamor of crashing steel halted, and Tikaya stopped walking to search for the reason.

If not for the guards surrounding him, she would not have recognized Five. Now clean-shaven with military-short hair, he wore the same boots and black uniform as the marines, though no rank or insignia marked the collars. Taller than the men accompanying him, he strode across the deck, hands clasped behind his back, head up, alert eyes taking in every aspect of the ship.

Tikaya's stomach did an anxious flip. Her putative ally had turned into someone who looked every bit like one of the officers who had tried to take over her islands during the war. Even with no rank on that collar, he seemed more the captain than the sweaty bare-chested Bocrest, who was also staring. A chilling thought gripped her. What if Five *had* been a captain during the war? Someone who fired on her people? Took prisoners? Tortured them.

Five's gaze stopped on the sails nearest the smokestack. A faint sooty black dulled the canvas, and he raised an eyebrow at Captain Bocrest.

For a moment, Bocrest's cheeks flushed, and an excuse seemed on his lips, but he halted it with a scowl. He stalked across the deck, bare chest puffed out, muscles flexed. He barked at anyone foolish enough to cross his path and stopped in front of Five. Bocrest gestured sharply while spitting words out in a low voice.

Tikaya resumed walking, more briskly than earlier, so she could steer close enough to eavesdrop. Before she neared them, the captain thrust his arm out, pointing his index finger at her. She stopped, feeling self-conscious when both men, and everyone else in the area, turned to stare at her.

Only Five's gaze was friendly. The right side of his mouth quirked up in a bemused half smile, and she felt the need to brace herself on a nearby weapons rack.

Bocrest growled, "Convince her," just loud enough for her to hear.

Though Five did not acknowledge the order, those words drove wariness into Tikaya's heart. Presuming Bocrest's relationship with Five was entirely antagonistic may have been a mistake.

He left the captain's side and strolled toward her, his smile widening he approached. A few strands of silver threaded his black hair, laugh lines crinkled the corners of his brown eyes, and a narrow scar bisected one eyebrow, but Tikaya had no doubt women of all ages swooned at his feet. Experience made her stifle her own urge to swoon. Handsome men did not look at her and smile; they looked *through* her, usually not noticing when they bumped her out of the way to close in on some buxom damsel with cleavage like the Inarraska Canyon. Most likely, he had an ulterior reason for that smile.

Tikaya folded her arms across her chest and kept her face neutral as he closed the distance.

Five's first words destroyed her attempt at equanimity. "You're the cryptomancer?"

"What? I, uhm, no. I mean—"

Tikaya winced. Even if he had no ulterior motives, her almost-ally would surely turn against her if he knew. Like the rest of the marines, he would resent her, hate her, glare at her and...

He was staring, not glaring, at her, and not with hatred. Was that—her eyebrows arched—awe?

"It's your people's term," she said, "not what the name plaque on my desk says."

Hoping for nonchalance, Tikaya stuck out a hand to lean casually on the weapons rack, but her focus was on him, and those gold flecks in his brown eyes, and she missed the target. Her fingers clipped the corner and slid off, giving her no support. She pitched sideways with a startled, "Errkt," and would have landed on the deck, but Five lunged and caught her.

Chortles burst from the surrounding marines, and flames torched her cheeks. Five straightened and released her with a pat on the shoulder. She groaned and avoided his eyes. If there had been awe there before, that was surely gone now. In avoiding his gaze, she had a clear view of the marines pointing at her and nudging each other. Even Bocrest's rock-eating jaw flapped with guffaws.

"Walk?" Five suggested gently.

"Dear Akahe, yes."

She departed the scene at a vigorous pace, and Five, with his long legs, easily matched her. His guards fell in behind. At least they proved stolid and silent save for the clatter of gear and synchronized thump of boots on the deck.

"I must thank you for this." Five gestured at himself, encompassing the clean uniform and haircut. "I got the story from Corporal Agarik. It was kind of you to include me in the reward for your wager."

"You're welcome," she muttered, knowing her thinking had not been purely altruistic. "Though I'm surprised the captain let you out, lost bet or not."

"He made me promise not to make trouble during the exercise periods."

"Ah." Interesting that Five's word was enough for the captain to trust him. She glanced at the guards. To some extent anyway.

"It was worth it." He stretched his arms overhead, then windmilled them, something the confines of his cell would make impossible. "I almost feel like a human being again."

It had certainly improved his mood. She thought of the silent, brooding man she had spoken to the first day and could not help but feel pleased her request had lightened his spirit. She gave him a smile and missed a step when he smiled back. Oh, that was nice.

Stop it, Tikaya, she chastised herself. Prisoner or not, he was one of them. That uniform fit him like he had been born into it. Best get some answers from him while he was in an affable mood.

"Given the reception I've gotten here, I'm surprised you aren't..." She watched him sidelong. "Does my wartime hobby not bother you?"

"Actually..." He met her sideways gaze. "It impresses me. A lot."

"Oh," she breathed, then looked away, not sure she wanted him to see her reaction. She had wanted an ally; she had not expected an admirer. She was not sure how to deal with that. Parkonis, though he had loved her personally, had been a little jealous of her professionally. They had worked in the same field, with her discoveries often eclipsing his, and his praise had always sounded grudging.

They passed under men in the rigging, adjusting sails to take advantage of the wind. Only a faint smudge of black wafted from the smokestack today.

"As far as we've heard," Five said, "cryptography isn't taught on Kyatt, so I just assumed what we called the cryptomancer was a team of mathematicians learning as they went. But your specialty is linguistics, right?"

The question sounded casual, but a trickle of wariness returned to her thoughts. Just because he pretended to be an admirer did not make him one. Maybe the Turgonians had simply decided to substitute honey for vinegar, and had talked him into delivering it.

"Yes," she said. "Philology, really. I work with the anthropology and archaeology departments in the Polytechnic."

"Interesting. How many languages do you know?"

"Sixteen modern, and I can read a few dozen dead languages."

"Few *dozen*?" Five halted and gaped at her. "You must be a genius."

The proclamation startled her, and she lurched to a stop beside him, conscious of the guards' gazes on her back. "No, no, trust me I'm not. It's just something I've a knack for."

He lifted a single skeptical eyebrow.

Tikaya shook her head. "A world-exploring uncle gave me a copy of the Tekdar Tablet when I was a child, and I fell in love with solving language puzzles. My parents encouraged it, so I had a head start when I started formally studying in school. That's all."

Five was still standing, gazing at her, and when she met his eyes, she found that admiration there again. It was disarming. Maybe he meant it to be. What had the captain told Five to convince her of?

"Hm." He resumed walking. "My family gave me swords and toy soldiers when I was a boy." Bemusement laced his tone.

"You would have preferred something else?"

"Oh, yes. I kept asking for drawing pads and building materials. I wanted to design a treehouse with a drawbridge to my room and a steam-powered potato launcher for defense."

"Sounds like every boy's dream." Despite her determination to remain chary with him, the change of topic set her at ease. She could not reveal something she shouldn't if he was talking about himself.

"Alas, this was not a paternally approved childhood activity, so I had to find my own building materials." Five scratched his jaw. "I took it upon myself to chop down some of the apple trees in my family's orchard, trees that my great grandfather had grafted from cuttings painstakingly acquired when he was a marine sailing around the world. I, being about eight at the time, was unaware of this bit of history."

"Oh, dear," she murmured.

"Yes. There was a lot of yelling that summer."

She chuckled.

"What *is* engraved on your name plaque?" Five asked as they started on their second lap of the deck.

For a moment, the context of the question eluded her, until she remembered her earlier comment. "You don't know my name?"

He spread his arms apologetically. "Nobody's told me much."

The salty breeze gusted, and water sprayed the deck ahead of them. A lieutenant bellowed at the men aloft.

"Your name for mine," Tikaya offered with a smile. "I can't keep calling you Five forever."

He glanced at the guards trailing them. Maybe, as part of his punishment, he was forbidden from using his old name.

He lowered his voice. "My friends and family, back when I had them..." He grimaced. "They called me Rias."

"Rias?"

Tikaya had a feeling that was a nickname or a truncation. Regardless, it gave her no hints as to his identity. Since she had decrypted all the communications her people had intercepted, she knew most, if not all, of the Turgonian officers with enough rank to command a vessel, and she could not think of any name with those syllables.

"My name is Tikaya," she said. "And, now that we're on a first-name basis, maybe you can tell me what you're supposed to convince me of, Rias."

Their route had taken them to the archery lane. Rias paused by the rack of staves, and the guards tensed, their fingers finding the triggers of their pistols.

"No weapons," the lead man said.

"Captain," Rias called. "May we shoot?"

In the center of the exercise area, Bocrest knelt on a young officer's back, with the man's arm twisted in a lock. The captain scowled over at them.

"May you *shoot*? What is this, the Officers' Club? Perhaps I can get you some brandywine and lobster too?"

"Captain, are you inviting me to dinner?" Rias rested his hand on his chest. "I'm touched."

Red flushed Bocrest's face, and Tikaya wondered at the wisdom of teasing the man. If the captain had a sense of humor, she had not detected it. But he waved a disgusted hand at the guards.

"Let them shoot."

"Sir?" The lead guard's mouth gaped open.

"You heard me," Bocrest barked.

"Yes, sir."

Tikaya eyed Rias. "It seems your word means something to the captain."

"He knows it's all I have left."

Bleakness stripped away his humor, reminding her that pain lurked beneath the facade he was showing her today. He caught her watching and reaffixed his smile.

"Tikaya," he said slowly, trying her name out, then nodding to himself as if he approved. "To answer your question, despite his *threats*—" Rias scowled, "—the captain has doubts about your intentions. He believes I should convince you to help him wholeheartedly with his mission."

She selected the bow she had used the day before. "Why, when he's keeping you chained in the brig, does he think you'd be inclined to speak on his behalf?"

"He believes that my indoctrinated loyalty to the empire will overrule whatever revulsion I feel for him and those who took everything from me."

"They must do a lot of indoctrinating in Turgonian schools."

Rias sighed. "Oh, they do."

"And *do* you think I should help? You recognized something about those symbols when I showed you the rubbing. What was it?"

He did not answer, though she did not think him recalcitrant. His gaze grew far away, his face grim, as if some painful memories had swallowed him and he had forgotten her.

Maybe archery would loosen his mind and unlock his thoughts for sharing. She shot a few times, leaving arrows quivering around the red dot in the target. A stiffer breeze scraped across the deck today.

Rias stirred and selected his own arrows.

"Want to make a wager?" Tikaya asked, thinking she might be able to get him to talk more freely about the symbols if he owed her from a lost bet.

His grimness faded and he slanted her a knowing gaze. "I suspect that would be unwise."

"Captain Bocrest did it."

"Then I'm certain it's unwise."

Tikaya grinned. "Maybe I just got a lucky shot."

"I doubt it."

"Why?" All the marines had been stunned when she hit the target.

He shrugged. "The Kyattese are bow hunters."

"Well..." She smiled and twirled an arrow in the air. "If you're afraid..."

Rias splayed a hand across his chest. "When you were learning our language, did you not also learn that we are a fearless people? I simply don't want to take advantage of you. I studied ballistics in school, and I can't imagine such a martial course being taught at your Polytechnic."

"And did you also study arrogance in school?" Tikaya nocked her arrow, aimed, and plunked it into the bull's-eye.

"Of course." He winked. "I'm Turgonian."

She snorted. Arrogance probably *was* part of their curriculum.

"I even wrote a paper on the ballistics of archery for merit points," he said.

"Less talking, more shooting."

Eyebrows arched, Rias nocked the first arrow, but he paused as a pair of marines strolled past, one munching the remains of an apple. The man lifted his arm to throw the core overboard, but Rias stopped him.

"I'll take that."

The marine shrugged and tossed it to him. Tikaya had an inkling of Rias's intent and did not question him as he readied the bow again. He nocked the arrow and held it against the stave with one hand. With the other, he lobbed the apple core so it arced toward the target. In one swift motion, he drew the bow and fired. The arrow pierced the apple and hammered it to the target right next to Tikaya's bull's-eye.

"Hah." Rias lowered the bow. "After my cocky speech, I feared I'd embarrass myself."

"I hope you got a good grade for that paper," Tikaya said, staring at the impaled apple.

"Me too." He grinned at her raised eyebrows. "It was twenty years ago. I don't remember."

"What was it on?"

"Oh, the usual. Explaining the equations for general ballistic trajectory, horizontal launch, launch velocity, and the like. The fun part was the modeling I did on the different types of bows used throughout imperial history. I analyzed them to show how the design and materials used would define their accuracy, trajectories, distance capabilities, and..." He must have noticed her gaping because he stopped, a sheepish expression on his face. "I'm boring you, aren't I?"

"No!" Tikaya blurted. "I just wasn't expecting you to be so..." Dear ancestors, he sounded just like her when she started talking about languages, and it struck her as hilarious that he could not remember the grade but recalled all the details of the topic. "Uhm, garrulous," she finished.

A blush colored his olive skin. "Sorry. I haven't talked to a woman in two years." He nocked an arrow. "Shall we shoot a few more?"

"Sure, tell me more about your paper."

Rias's fingers fumbled, and the arrow clattered to the deck. "Really?"

"Really." She hid a smile, tickled by his surprise. "The only ballistics experiments I ever partook in involved a wager on who could use a spoon to launch a macadamia nut across the lunch room and into Professor Lehanae's wig."

"Hm, I recall taking part in a similar experiment. Must be a universal education requirement."

They shot while he explained his paper, and Tikaya relaxed for the first time in days. She almost laughed at her earlier guess that he might have been a captain in the war. With that passion for mathematics and those childhood fancies, he had to be an engineer. Probably the chief engineer on one of the big warships. He would have been accustomed to going toe-to-toe with captains to keep his steamer in pristine operating order.

Only after the exercise period ended, and she was again confined in her cabin, did she realize she still did not know what his history was with those symbols and why they stirred dark memories.

* * * * *

The first earsplitting boom yanked Tikaya from sleep. The second made her scramble out of her bunk so quickly she slammed into the fold-out desk. Groaning, she rubbed her hip, took another step, and cracked her toe on the stool.

"No one should wake up this way," she muttered.

More booms drowned her words, this time a whole round that lasted half a minute. The ship trembled with concussions that vibrated her body like a bell. Cannons, she realized, as she groped about to find her spectacles and sandals. She had heard them from afar, but never standing in a cabin under the gun deck. Shouts sounded through the aftermath of the round, though the bulkhead muffled the words. She peered out her tiny porthole. Clouds obscured the stars, and night's darkness smothered the ocean.

Was someone attacking them? Who would be audacious enough to waylay a Turgonian warship? Especially during peacetime? Maybe it was a training exercise. She would not put it past Captain Bocrest to schedule drills in the middle of the night.

A massive jolt rocked the ship, throwing her into the bulkhead. That was no cannon firing. Psi blast. She had a cousin who studied telekinetics and could knock the fronds off a palm tree. Anyone who could damage an ironclad warship was no one she wanted to meet. Still, if this was an attack, maybe she could use the confusion to steal a longboat. She would need to get Rias out of the brig to help. Since he had planned an escape once, he would know where to find the logs and navigation tools they would need.

Shouts rang out and boots pounded, but all the activity seemed to be on the deck above. Tikaya opened the door. Her hopes of escape sank when she spotted her guard standing outside.

The baby-face private noticed her immediately. "Stay inside, ma'am."

"What's going on?"

"I'm not sure yet, but don't worry. It's my duty to protect you."

Yes, but she did not want him to protect her. She wanted him to go away. Still, his earnest eyes said he took his duty seriously, and she managed a "thank you." Though they had rarely spoken, she had placed him in Corporal Agarik's tiny category of People Who Treated Her Like a Human Being.

"Can we go see what's happening?" she asked, though she suspected she knew the answer.

"No, ma'am. Please close the hatch and wait inside." A cabin door slammed open, and a sub-lieutenant struggling to buckle his belt scrambled out, a drunken lurch to his step. He stumbled off, presumably to join the others, and her guard watched wistfully. He did look back at her and add, "I'll let you know what the commotion is about when I find out."

Tikaya shut the door and paced her tiny cabin. Her guard wanted to join the action. Maybe she could nudge him that direction. He was young after all. Maybe—

A scream of agony erupted nearby. Tikaya froze. Though muffled, it sounded like it had come from her deck.

She pressed her ear to the door.

Somewhere down the corridor, a pistol fired, and steel rang. Shrill voices cried out, and her eyes widened. They spoke Nurian, not Turgonian.

"We should go to the brig!"

"I read that marine's thoughts; the woman is up here."

Her insides knotted. They were looking for her.

The Nurians must have found out about whatever the Turgonians had unearthed. Did they want her help too? To beat the imperials to the loot?

A shot cracked right outside her door.

Tikaya could help them find her or she could hide. Though her people had only superficially sided with the Nurians during the war, sharing the messages Tikaya decrypted, it ought to be enough to ensure they would treat her better than the Turgonians.

She eased the door open. The air shimmered as a wave of heat rolled in from the corridor. The invisible force slammed into the private's chest.

She stumbled back and wrapped her arm over her eyes—not quickly enough to miss the agony contorting the guard's face. He screamed and dropped to the deck, writhing. His sword and pistol clattered down beside him. The stench of charred flesh seared the air. In a heartbeat, the marine lay still, skin laid bare to muscle and bone, and bulging eyes frozen open.

Tikaya stared, stunned into immobility. She had never seen death, not like this. She had spent the war in an office, not on battlefields or warships.

"She down there?" someone asked in Nurian.

Tikaya tore her gaze from the downed man and leaned out the door.

Two Nurians crept in her direction. They were shorter than she and darker of skin, like the Turgonians, but they had slanted eyes and wore their long black hair in topknots. One bore twin scimitars in his hands and looked lean and sinewy beneath colorful clothing decorated with bone and beads. The other, wrapped in a flowing black robe, carried nothing. A practitioner and his bodyguard.

The bodyguard pointed a scimitar her direction. "There!"

"Greetings," Tikaya called in their tongue. "My name is Tikaya. Any chance you're here to take me somewhere more pleasant than a Turgonian warship?"

But they were not in the conversation mood. As soon as they spotted her, the practitioner stopped. A glazed trance slackened his face—the sign of someone concentrating on his science. The bodyguard watched her, but also glanced up and down the hall, ensuring no one approached to interrupt his comrade.

Despite the heat lingering in the wardroom, a shiver ran down Tikaya's spine. She ducked into her cabin just as the Nurian lifted his arm. Another wave of energy flared, and the air crackled and wavered against the metal door where her head had been. Heat scorched her face. The hem of her dress burst into flames.

Tikaya cursed, flapping the cloth to put out fire.

Footfalls thundered toward her cabin. She glanced around. Nowhere to hide. The fallen private's sword lay in the doorway. She bent and grabbed it.

The Nurians appeared in the hatchway, shoulder to shoulder. The practitioner's eyes narrowed again. Still crouched on the floor, sword in hand, Tikaya lunged, hoping to surprise them.

She bowled between them, ramming them with her shoulders. Where she might have bounced off burly Turgonians, her size was an advantage here, and she startled the shorter men. Both Nurians pitched opposite ways and fought for their balance.

Tikaya raced through the wardroom and into the corridor.

"Flay her!" the bodyguard called. "She must be killed at all—"

Her instincts prickled again, and Tikaya threw herself into a clumsy roll. Heat crackled overhead.

She jumped to her feet. The bodyguard charged after her. She skidded around the corner at a T intersection. A nook right to the side offered access to a ladder running up and down. She banged a rung with her sword, trusting her pursuers to hear it, then jumped through an open hatch a few cabins down. She dared not stick her head out to look, but their footsteps told her when they charged around the corner. The clatter of swords and shoes clanking in the ladder well said they had fallen for the ruse.

Tikaya could not relax. If there were two Nurians on the ship, there could be more. Cannons continued to blast on the decks above. Perhaps the whole attack was a cover to let practitioners sneak on board to get rid of her. But why? If the Turgonians had unearthed some treasure they wanted to get at, wouldn't the Nurians find her skills of equal use? Wouldn't they want to use her themselves?

"The captain said there was no treasure," she muttered, rubbing sweat from her eyes. She had not believed him, but maybe that had been a mistake. Something about those symbols alarmed Rias, and it hardly seemed that some cheery treasure hunt from his youth would account for it.

More footfalls sounded in the corridor, and Tikaya ducked behind the hatch. Two marines pounded past.

She could not stay there. But where to go? If she headed to the upper deck, she could find the captain. He would protect her from Nurians. He may not like her, but he obviously had orders to keep her alive, at least until she translated the language. Still, going to him and hiding behind his back would eliminate any chance she might have to escape. Better to find Rias and steal a longboat in the commotion.

Her heart lurched. Rias. Locked down in the brig. If the Nurians were after her, might they be after him too? He would have a hard time dodging psi attacks while chained to the deck in a cell.

More marines raced through, and she made her decision. Tikaya glanced both ways, then slipped out. Hoping to avoid the Nurians, she traveled past two more ladders before climbing down to a dark hold on the bottom deck. She groped her way past sea trunks and cargo. Somewhere nearby, engines hummed. The deck trembled with the strokes of massive pistons, while above the cannons continued to roar.

She escaped the hold and found the narrow corridor leading to the brig. As she entered, another wave rocked the ship, and the great ironclad pitched sideways. The ship creaked ominously as she stumbled down the passage.

Nobody guarded the hatch at the end. The Nurians had mentioned the brig, so she advanced with care. She did not think they would expect her to flee this direction, but sweat still pasted her dress to her back, dribbled down her temples, and slicked the sword grip.

The single lantern that usually burned on the wall near the cells had moved. It was hanging—no, being held—a foot above the deck near Rias's door.

She moved closer and, when she spotted him kneeling by the gate, exhaled a breath she did not remember holding. He was still shackled, but the chains that had secured him to the back of the cell lay in a tangled heap next to the broken lantern cover. He held the flame directly beneath the bottom hinge.

Rias smiled when he spotted her, but kept his hands steady. Flames bathed the hinge.

"What are you doing?" Tikaya asked.

His lips shifted into a bemused half smile. "Hoping whoever designed these hinges did not factor in the relatively high coefficient of thermal expansion steel possesses."

"You're going to break out...with the lamp?"

"It worked on the chain bolts." Rias shrugged. "I was fortunate the first attack knocked the lantern off the wall and within reach."

"Yes, those foolish marines should never have left such an obvious tool down here for prisoners to exploit." Tikaya knelt by the door and slid the sword between the hinge and the pin, which surprised her by popping free with minimal effort.

"Indeed." He stood and moved the flame to the upper hinge. "By the way, what are you doing down here with a sword?"

"There are Nurians on board, at least two. They killed my guard. I thought they might want me as a translator as well and I was ready to jump into their arms when they flung a psi wave at me."

Rias's brow furrowed. "Why would the Nurians want to hurt *you*? They ought to be worshipping your people after the help you gave them in the war."

She watched his face, trying to decide if his tone was accusatory, but only puzzlement furrowed his brows. "I don't know. I figured they might be after you, too, though I haven't deduced exactly what your part is in all this yet." Tikaya wriggled her eyebrows to suggest he might share any time. "I decided to come break you out."

Another jolt rocked the ship. Tikaya was not sure how long the flame had to be applied to loosen the bond between hinge and pin but wedged her sword into the crack anyway. It was tighter this time.

"I'm not sure whether to be offended that you'd think Nurian hospitality preferable to Turgonian or tickled that you came down to help me." Rias gave her that lopsided smile again and, despite the cannons thundering above and the threat of Nurians lurking below, she bit her lip to hide a pleased grin.

"I'd think even *you* would prefer Nurian hospitality to Turgonian at this point." She wriggled the sword, and the pin inched upward.

"Not really. I've been in one of their prison camps and—"

Something bowled into her.

Tikaya was rammed into the gate and dragged to the ground. The sword flew from her grip. She launched a clumsy fist at her attacker, but encountered no one.

"Invisibility illusion," she barked.

Metal screeched.

She started to roll to her feet, but her unseen assailant grabbed her hair and yanked her head back. With one hand, she groped for the sword, and with the other clawed for the Nurian. She jerked her head down to protect her neck.

The cell door flew outward, and metal thudded against flesh. Tikaya's invisible attacker grunted. Rias tore the Nurian off her.

She scrambled out of the way. A snap echoed through the brig, and an orange-clad man appeared. He collapsed on the deck. Dead.

Color flashed behind Rias.

"Look out!" Tikaya cried.

He whirled as a woman with scimitar and dagger leaped at him, blades leading. He ducked low and barreled toward her legs. The woman jumped and spun in the air to land facing him.

Knowing Rias was still shackled and had no weapons, Tikaya lunged for the dropped sword. She jumped to her feet, hilt clasped in both hands. Even with her inexperience, she figured she could stab someone in the back, but Rias had closed with the Nurian woman. They grappled briefly, then he released her with a shove. She went down, her own dagger protruding from her chest.

Wordlessly, Tikaya handed him her sword. He would know how to use it whereas she would probably just trip over it.

"You all right?" Rias looked her up and down, brow wrinkled. "Are these the same ones who attacked you above?"

"I'm fine and...no."

He knelt and pulled a pin from the dead woman's hair. "If they can turn invisible, there's no telling how many are on board."

"Comforting." Tikaya watched him probe the lock on his shackles. "How about we use this chaos to escape or find a good hiding place until the ship gets to port?"

His wrist accessories snapped open and dropped to the ground. He pocketed the hairpin. "Let's head above decks and find out what's going on."

Tikaya raised her eyebrows. That was not exactly her plan—her plan had a lot more focus on the word escape.

CHAPTER 5

On the upper deck, Tikaya and Rias crouched behind a funnel venting hot air from the boiler room. Streaks of lightning branched from the cloudy night sky and lanced around the warship, some sizzling harmlessly against the dark waves and others tearing into mast and sail. Agile as monkeys, marines raced through the rigging, beating out conflagrations. Others perched in the fighting tops, rifles firing intermittently. Tikaya hoped they were too busy to look down and notice her and Rias.

Two wooden Nurian ships, decks lit by glowing orbs, trailed slightly behind on either side of the ironclad. Every time they edged too close, an officer on the gun deck barked orders to fire the cannons. The same weather phenomenon setting off the lightning filled the enemy sails with unnatural wind, and, despite the steam-powered propeller adding knots to the warship's speed, the Nurian vessels kept pace. In fact, they could have overtaken the warship, and Tikaya had a feeling they were waiting for something. The assassins to kill her? She grimaced.

"We outman them and outgun them," Rias said. "But wizards always have tricks that make them dangerous. Bocrest has already slagged this, letting them surround us."

At the moment, the invisible assassins were more of a concern for Tikaya. "Let's go to the training area."

Rias tore his gaze from the Nurian ships. "The blades are dulled; real weapons are kept in the armory."

"What I need is over there."

She expected him to question her further, but he simply led her through the shadows. Two marines in the forecastle manned the chaser gun, which was rotated toward one of the Nurian ships and pounded rounds into the night. Open deck lay between the men and the weapons racks, and the intermittent lightning illuminated much.

Tikaya crouched low to approach the backside of the racks, and she sensed rather than heard Rias behind her. The booms of the great gun would have drowned out the approach of howler monkeys.

Much of the exercise gear had been stowed when the ship was cleared for action, and she worried she would not find what she wanted. But, no, there they were. The heavy sand-filled balls sat in the bottom row of a rack.

She slung one to the deck and found Rias's ear. "Sword, please."

He handed her the cutlass, and she sliced open the ball. She stuffed sand into the two hip pockets in her dress until they bulged, then returned the blade.

A fiery projectile the size of her cabin slammed into the side of the ironclad. Ineffective against the metal hull, it bounced into the water, but the energy that had hurled it coursed through the air. Tikaya's skin hummed. She had never been so close to so much power.

Rias tapped her shoulder and they moved away from the forecastle. With an uncanny knack for avoiding the marines running up and down the deck, he led her past masts, funnels, and vents. They rounded the smokestacks, and he headed toward the after bridge. The captain and senior officers relayed orders to the gun deck and barked commands to the men controlling the wheel.

Tikaya grabbed Rias's arm. "Where are you going? We're hiding, re-member? And escaping if possible, right?"

Lightning flashed, revealing him gazing toward the Nurian vessels. "If this ship sinks, we're in trouble too."

"And what would we do to stop that?"

A long moment passed before he said, "All right. We can hide between the launches and still see what's—"

The aft chaser gun blasted, stealing the rest of his words, but she nodded, and Rias led her through the shadows.

Lightning flashed again. Rias ducked between the boats mounted a couple feet above the deck in the center of the ship. The space between them offered a shadowy place to hunker down. The smokestack rose behind them, belching coal plumes and further hemming them in. A determined search would reveal them, but the darkness and chaos offered camouflage—from the marines, anyway. The Nurians had other means of searching for her, but at least lanterns were mounted across the deck from them and would silhouette someone approaching. Assuming that someone wasn't invisible. She touched her bulging dress pocket.

Rias put his back against one of the launches and stood where he could see the movement of the other ships.

"I can hide here alone if you want to find the captain." She hated the idea but could tell Rias felt he could do something.

"No, he wouldn't appreciate my input, and he'd chuck me back in the brig. Besides, the Nurians are looking for you."

"Yes, and I should mention they have ways to find me. They went straight to the wardroom earlier, and I'm sure it wasn't a coincidence they showed up in the brig when I was there." Tikaya looked up at Rias, though darkness hid his face. "It'd probably be a bad idea to be standing next to me if a psi wave is launched in my direction."

"I'll risk it." Rias rested a hand on her shoulder. "Keep your back to me in case they're invisible again."

She sandwiched between him and the other launch, with the smokestack guarding their right side and his sword ready on the left.

"The sand," Rias said, "is for throwing at the invisible attackers? Will it disrupt the spell?"

"Possibly, if I catch them by surprise, and their concentration lapses, but if nothing else it'll outline them for a few seconds until they compensate."

His rumbled, "Ah," sounded pleased.

On the rear horizon, a third Nurian ship floated into view.

"Rust," Rias spit. "He needs to take down one of those ships before the reinforcements arrive. Come on, Bocrest. *Think*. Don't be so stodgy and predictable."

A fiery projectile the size of a cannon ball arced toward them. Tikaya tensed. It clipped the yard closest to their smokestack, and shards of wood rained upon them.

She gulped.

"You all right?" Rias dusted splinters off the top of her head.

"Yes, but it's inconsiderate of these Nurians to muss my hair. I'd at least like to look good when your people toss me on a funeral pyre." Her attempt at nonchalance might have worked if her voice had not cracked on the last word. When she had been fleeing the Nurians, she had been too busy to worry about her mortality. Standing here gave her too much time to think, to wonder if she might very well dodge the assassins only to fall to a random cannonball.

"Don't worry," Rias said. "No funeral pyres at sea. We just wrap your body in your hammock and toss you overboard. Only the fish will judge your hair."

"I'm vastly reassured, thank you."

Rias chuckled.

Oddly, his blasé attitude *did* reassure her. If he was not worried, maybe she did not need to be. She leaned back against him. If not for the guns roaring and the lightning streaking the night, she might have noticed the heat of his chest against her shoulders, the lean hard muscles beneath his clothing, and the gentle breaths stirring her hair. Actually, she noticed them anyway.

"Rias?"

"Yes?"

His murmur was soft, close to her ear, and a thrum warmed her body. Focus, she told herself.

"Do you want to escape or not?" she asked. "If you don't... Well, that's your prerogative, but it'd help me to know. I've mentioned it a couple times tonight, and, even though I chanced upon you breaking out of your cell, you seem to be more interested in what's going on with the battle than getting out of here. I can't help but think that it's handy how we're standing next to a couple boats, and the marines are all preoccupied."

"It'd be suicidal to launch a boat into the middle of the Nurians," he said. "Besides, based on the knots-per-hour average of this ship, the days it's been since you were brought on board at the Kyatt Islands, and our northeasterly direction, I estimate us more than a thousand miles from the mainland. There aren't many archipelagos in this part of the ocean. It's likely we'd die of thirst before making land. Also..."

"What?"

His long exhale tickled the back of her ear. "The fact that the Nurians are trying to kill you makes me believe we really need you."

"We?"

"The empire. Bocrest's family has been personally loyal to the throne for a long time. That Emperor Raumesys picked him over brighter men suggests this is a very sensitive mission. My people may have unearthed something that's put them in danger. If the Nurians have found out, well, they'd be the first to help us on our way to the black eternity."

Tikaya pressed her hand against the cool wooden siding of the launch, dread curling through her gut for a new reason. If the Turgonian emperor had walked onto her plantation and asked for her help, she would have told him to shove sugar cane into his anal orifice. But Rias asking her to stay and help...

She shook her head. She hardly knew him. And he was one of *them*. Surely, she owed him nothing.

"How can the empire's fate even matter to you?" she asked. "After they condemned you and left you to die?"

"Strange, isn't it? By the emperor's decree, I'm dead to my family, my friends, everyone I ever knew, but it was the emperor who cast me out, not them. I still care that they are well, and I'm not sure the orchards where I grew up will ever stop being the place my mind conjures when someone says home."

Tikaya cleared her throat and tried to sound offhand when she asked, "Family?"

"Parents, brothers."

"No children?" No wife?

"My wife didn't want them."

So, there was a wife. The intensity of her disappointment surprised her.

"Ex-wife," Rias said, as if reading her thoughts. "I know you owe nothing to me, Tikaya—in fact, I owe you a couple favors. But if you would stay and decipher the language and help—I can't believe I'm saying this—help Bocrest solve whatever problem my people have gotten themselves into, I'd..."

The request she had dreaded. She swallowed and waited.

"I have nothing I can offer you." He sighed. "Not even my protection since I'm even more a prisoner than you. All I can promise is that I'll do everything possible to ensure you escape and can return to your island afterwards. I imagine you have family you miss, people who are worried about you."

"Yes." If she died out here, would anyone even tell her parents what happened?

"Children?" he asked in the same offhand tone she had used.

"No." Then, feeling the need to lay everything out, she added, "My fiancé was killed on a science vessel that went down near the end of the war."

"Oh." A long beat passed, probably because he did not want to know the answer to the next question, but he asked anyway: "How did it—who sank it?"

"Your people."

She felt his shoulders slump behind her.

"I'm sorry," he said.

A twinge of guilt wound through her; it was not as if he had done it. If he had been on that penal island for two years, he would have missed the last year of the war, the year when things unraveled for the Turgonians and their people stopped paying attention to Kantioch Treaty dictates. Yet she could not bring herself to say it was all right. It wasn't. It never would be.

The attack had slowed, and Tikaya felt a stirring of hope, but then another set of lights appeared on the inky horizon. Another ship, bringing the total to four. The captains had probably just paused to confer—deciding on a final strategy—through communications practitioners. The attack would resume with all four ships joining in, and even the sturdy ironclad would sink under that assault.

"How come none of your people know about this shindig going on in the middle of the ocean?" Tikaya asked.

"I don't know."

A great swirling gust of wind tugged at her dress and whipped loose strands of hair into her mouth. She looked up at the stack. The smoke was not affected, meaning the disturbance was localized.

"Nurian magic!" Rias wrapped his arm around her.

A flash of yellow burned Tikaya's eyes, and vertigo washed over her. A final burst of wind railed at her, her stomach dropped, then silence engulfed her.

She blinked and tried to wipe away the yellow dots swimming before her eyes. Bile churned in her throat, and she forced a swallow. The world came back into focus.

She was belowdecks, not in the ironclad but in a wooden vessel. She stood in a storage space full of Nurians pointing short bows at her, arrows nocked and drawn back. Crates, barrels, and a number of confusing machines, or perhaps practitioners' contraptions, fenced the large hold. Rias still had his arm around her, and he held the sword out before them, but it did not matter with so many weapons pointed their way. A smug woman in black robes smiled in triumph.

"There, that's easier," she said in Nurian.

She lifted a finger toward the bowmen and opened her mouth.

Tikaya scrabbled for something to say, something to sway the woman from giving the kill order.

"Don't tell them," Rias blurted in Turgonian.

Barely, just barely, Tikaya managed to keep the bewildered expression off her face. The practitioner halted, finger still lifted, and frowned at Rias.

"I won't," Tikaya whispered back, also in Turgonian.

"They'll torture us if they know what we know," he stage whispered.

Did the Nurian understand? None of the expressions on the bowmen's faces had changed, but an assessing mien narrowed the woman's eyes. Yes, she understood, and Rias must be counting on that, trying to pique her interest long enough to have a chance to do something.

Tikaya lifted one placating hand and stepped toward the woman. "I understand you have orders to kill me," she said in Nurian as she slipped her other hand into her pocket, "but I'm sure I can be of more use to you alive." She caught the other woman eyeing Rias and added, "As can he. We've just escaped our cells on the Turgonian ship; we've no allegiance to them—they kidnapped us against our will."

The practitioner seemed to be only half-listening. She stepped closer, peering up at Rias, whose head brushed the ceiling of the hold.

"You look familiar," she said in heavily accented Turgonian. "Who—"

Tikaya hurled a handful of sand, and the woman gasped, swiping at her eyes. Rias lunged past Tikaya, pushing her to the deck. His body coiled, then he sprang, whipping the sword through the practitioner's neck with a grunt.

He landed and charged, taking advantage of the startled silence gripping the hold.

For a stunned moment, Tikaya lay on her belly, staring at the decapitated head, the still-twitching body, and the blood. So much blood.

The Nurians recovered, and bows twanged. An arrow grazed Tikaya's arm and pinned her sleeve to the deck.

"Move," Rias barked. "Find cover." He was already attacking a third man.

Yes, cover, of course.

Tikaya tore her sleeve free and rolled toward the closest set of legs. An arrow thudded into the deck an inch from her ear. She kicked as hard as she could, and her heel smashed the inside of a man's knee. He yelped and collapsed on her.

Her first instinct was to shove him away, but another arrow slammed into the deck near her head. She tried to stay under him, to use him as a human shield. He drew back to punch her. An arrow lodged in his shoulder.

"Not me, idiot!" he screamed.

He thrashed, still on top of Tikaya as he clawed at the shaft. A wayward elbow nearly tore her spectacles from her face. His frustrated cries of pain reverberated in her ears. His face, eyes squeezed shut, mouth contorted with agony, loomed inches from her own. Fearful of more bows aimed at her, she wrapped her fingers into his shirt and kept him from pulling away.

Rias towered over the Nurians, head brushing the ceiling beams as he lunged about the space. He slashed bowstrings and pounded through the startled archers, who—after catching their own comrades in the cross-fire—were dropping their bows in favor of short swords and cutlasses. Howls of pain and rage bounced from the wooden walls.

The Nurians stopped shooting at Tikaya and focused their attacks on Rias, obviously finding him the greater threat. She spotted a bow within reach and grabbed it. The wounded man writhed, still trying to pull out the arrow, and she rolled away from him. She pried a quiver off a fallen archer and ducked behind a chest-high wooden contraption bolted to the deck.

Her hands shook, and it took three tries to nock the first arrow. She willed her fingers to still. She could do this. Human beings or not, they were trying to kill her.

Her first arrow went a foot wide of its mark, thunking into the frame by the hold's only exit. She wiped hands wet with blood and sweat on her dress and sucked in a deep breath.

A man with a raised hatchet drew up behind Rias as he squared off with two cutlass wielders.

Tikaya's nerves disappeared and she let an arrow fly. It struck the attacker between the shoulder blades, and he pitched forward, crashing to the deck at Rias's heels. The man lay still. She had found his heart.

She swallowed, mortified by the results of her reflexive act. Rias slashed his cutlass through the throat of the last man standing before him, glanced behind at the dead Nurian, and saluted her with the sword.

The rest of their attackers were down as well. Dead. A tremor coursed through Tikaya's body. She could not rip her gaze from the one she killed.

Muffled shouts echoed from deeper in the ship. Reinforcements who had heard the skirmish. Her mind processed what it meant, that more would soon burst in, that she would have to fight, but the tremor returned to her hands, and she shied away from the idea of shooting anyone else.

She was not a killer. If her family knew what she had done...

Rias stepped before her, blocking the view of the body and breaking her thoughts. He gripped her shoulder with a bloodstained hand. She swallowed and met his eyes.

"More work to do before we're safe," he said, voice calm and steady, commanding her attention. "You can react later. Right now, I need you to watch my back so we can live through this. Concentrate on that, nothing else, understood?"

Before she could nod, four men burst into the hold, swords leading. A flash of silver streaked toward Rias's head. He jerked back, and it split the air between them to land with a thunk in the wood wall. A throwing knife.

Rias leaped away from Tikaya and charged the Nurians.

"Curse me." She tore an arrow from her quiver. He had almost been killed because he was trying to keep her from falling apart. She nocked the arrow, forced her hands to still. React later. Yes. She could do that.

Rias led the Nurians about the hold, dodging behind crates and apparatuses, slashing to keep the men at bay, and evading their attempts to surround him. With agility surprising in someone so large, he kept them in each other's way and remained on the outskirts so he only had to face one at a time. More, he kept them from paying attention to her.

Good.

Tikaya lifted the drawn bow and selected the man farthest from Rias. She was not going to be the idiot who shot someone on her own side. The arrow took the Nurian in his chest, and he lurched backward, hands clutching the shaft. Horror and pain wrenched his face. Her own heart twisted in sympathy, but she smashed down the emotion. React later.

Her next arrow felled a second man even as Rias sliced the throat of the third. The fourth skidded to a stop, realizing he fought alone.

He backpedaled for the exit, and Tikaya had him targeted, but she hesitated. Even if he meant to run straight to his captain, how could she shoot someone fleeing?

Rias lunged after him, and the man jumped back. His heel caught on a downed comrade, and he pitched to the deck, cracking his head on a crate.

Rias dropped beside the man, gripping his throat, and Tikaya winced and looked away.

"Live or die?" Rias asked in accented Nurian.

Surprised, Tikaya looked back.

"Live?" the Nurian croaked, eyes darting with fear, as if he did not expect to be that lucky.

Rias glanced toward the door, then laid his sword on the ground while he tore pieces from the man's colorful clothing. With quick efficiency, he gagged the Nurian and started on ankle and wrist bonds.

"Who would answer with die?" Tikaya asked.

"Most of my people," Rias said. "To live when the rest of your team died would be an unacceptable disgrace to many."

With some vague sense that someone should be standing guard, she stepped over the bodies to watch the exit. Another hold stretched before her, lit by glowing orbs hanging from the beamed ceiling. No one else waited to charge.

Rias finished the bonds, leaving the Nurian wide-eyed on the deck, and snatched arrows from partially spent quivers. When he had a fistful, he joined Tikaya.

"I want to take control of the ship," he said.

"Take control?" She gaped at the audacity. Surely, the best they could manage would be to run for the upper deck and leap over the side. But, no, who would find them in the cold, dark waters? Even if the Turgonians spotted them, and that was unlikely, they had their own troubles.

"We'll have another fight when they realize what's going on." He held out the arrows, enough to stuff her quiver, and watched her face. "You've got my back?"

She guessed at what he was really asking: can you, a philologist from an island full of peace-loving academics, keep from collapsing in a weepy heap when I need your help?

Tikaya grabbed the arrows and jammed them into the quiver, angry with herself for that weak moment that made him question her. "I've had it so far, haven't I?"

"Yes." Rias gripped her forearm. "You've been magnificent."

She snorted. Right. He didn't know how lucky he was her trembling fingers hadn't loosed an arrow that turned him into a eunuch. "Will you still think that if I insist on taking a side trip?"

"What?"

"I want to search the captain's cabin for orders and find out why these people are trying to kill me." And maybe she could finally get answers about what this secret Turgonian mission was all about.

"We may not have time," Rias said.

Tikaya lifted her chin. "We'll make time."

His eyebrows flicked upward, but the surprise lasted only a second. He nodded once and gave her a Turgonian salute, a fist thumped over his heart. "Yes, ma'am."

"Jeela, is it done?" a tinny voice asked from the center of the room.

As one they stared at the dead practitioner. The voice emanated from within her black robe.

Rias pointed his cutlass. "Can you answer that?"

"Uhm." Tikaya knelt by the dead woman, trying not to look at the bloody stump where the head should have been, and patted the blood-sodden robe. She found a glowing opal pendant, the chain broken, just as the voice spoke again.

"Is the Kyattese girl dead? Jeela, do you need help?"

Though her education in the mental sciences was not ecumenical, she could sense the soft hum of a practitioner-made device. She held it up to her mouth, then waved at Rias and mouthed, "Make some noise."

She partially covered the device with her hand, hoping to disguise the fact that her voice would not match the practitioner's, and spoke in Nurian: "Yes, mission complete. She's dead." Then, fearing further conversation would only hurt her chances at pulling off the ruse, she dropped the device on the deck, so it clanked against the wood.

"I doubt that fooled anyone," she apologized to Rias as they exited.

The grim cast to his eyes suggested he agreed, but all he said was, "We'd best hurry."

CHAPTER 6

The Nurian captain's cabin offered a distinct contrast to Bocrest's quarters. Behind a desk painted with flowers and vines, lace curtains decorated a bank of windows. Velvet furniture and lush rugs covering the deck might have invited one to lounge, but the cannons booming in the distance suppressed the cozy parlor ambiance.

Tikaya and Rias slid inside, shutting the door behind them. For the moment, the Nurians were busy attacking—and defending against—Bocrest's warship, but sooner or later someone would figure out "Jeela" had failed her mission.

"Check those trunks." Rias jogged around the desk to the windows. "Let me know if you can tell if the captain is a wizard or not. If he is, he'll likely have wards protecting his orders."

Tikaya threw open the trunks and lifted a sword and a lacy brassiere. "I believe she's a warrior."

"Should be safe to search then." Rias tore his gaze from the windows and cocked an eyebrow at the lingerie. "Unless you want to model that for me first?"

Startled, she dropped the sword. The hilt banged onto her sandaled foot.

Rias winced and lifted an apologetic hand. "Sorry, I, er, two years, you know."

"It's fine." Cheeks warming, she threw the sword back in the trunk, relieved she had not cut off any toes. "I'll just, uhm, find those orders now."

Tikaya yanked open a desk drawer and rummaged through letters and supply receipts. Out of the corner of her eye, she caught Rias shaking his head, fingers splayed across his face, before he turned back to the window. A grin tugged at her lips.

A moment later, he found his fearless-soldier-in-charge tone and reported: "All four Nurian ships are even with the Emperor's Fist now, two on each side. Bocrest is doing damage, but...if we're going to help, it'll have to be soon."

Tikaya tried another drawer. She wanted those orders, and she wanted them to say something significant to justify detouring here. Rias helped her search, checking cupboards under the bunk, but she sensed restless energy emanating from him. He wanted to assist his people, though she could not imagine how he planned to take over the ship.

Under a pile of log books in the bottom drawer, she found a parchment displaying lines of gibberish. "Got it. Encrypted though." She tapped the nonsensical Nurian letters. "Given enough time, I can work it out, but it'd be helpful to have the key. The captain ought to have it, right?"

"Yes." Rias joined her at the desk and opened and closed all the drawers.

"I already looked in there."

He paused at the lower one, yanked it clear, dumped the contents on the deck, and ripped out the bottom. His vandalism revealed a secret compartment from which he plucked another sheet of parchment.

"Guess my looking skills need improvement," Tikaya murmured.

"I get suspicious when inside dimensions don't match outside ones."

"Ah." She laid both sheets on the desk and quickly memorized the key.

The clanging of a bell echoed through the ship. More footsteps pounded, this time on their deck instead of above.

"Alarm," Rias said. "They know we escaped. Take that with us. We're out of time."

"Wait, I've got it."

"Already? How could you..."

She skipped the introduction and translated the meat of the orders: "'Search and destroy the Emperor's Fist before it reaches the Northern Frontier. If any artifacts with strange symbols are found, sink them in the ocean. Use extreme caution in handling them. Do not bring them home and do not try to destroy them.'"

"Honored ancestors," Rias murmured. "What have my people uncovered?"

"'In addition,'" Tikaya finished grimly, "'the Kyattese linguist allied with the Turgonians must be killed at all costs.'" Allied? She was no cursed Turgonian ally.

The windows exploded.

Rias tore Tikaya off her feet before she knew what was happening. Wood cracked louder than thunder. Rias came down on top of her, protecting her with his body. Glass and splinters rained about them, tinkling as they hit the deck.

"What was that?" Tikaya asked when her heart left throat. Wind whistled into the cabin.

Rias pulled her up. He nodded to a cannonball lodged in the bulkhead perpendicular to the broken window. "Friendly fire."

She gulped and plucked a shard of glass out of the side of his neck. "Glad your reflexes are faster than mine. Thank you."

"Welcome." He shook more glass from his jacket, then headed for the door. "Still got my back?"

"Of course." Tikaya grabbed her bow.

They had reached the captain's cabin without trouble, but, with the alarm clanging, search parties clogged their deck. Fortunately, Rias seemed to know the layout of the Nurian vessel as well as the Turgonian ironclad. They hid in cabins and shadowy nooks to avoid men before slipping down a ladder to the deck below.

"How're we taking over the ship from down here?" Tikaya whispered, neck bent to keep from clunking her head on the ceiling.

Rias's shoulders brushed the walls as they crept single-file down a dim passageway. "This is a Nurian striker. Not a big vessel. I think I can handle the tiller by myself. It should be located...there."

He pointed at a door marking the end of the corridor. He jogged past a ladder well and charged inside, cutlass leading.

As Tikaya passed the ladder, movement stirred the shadows. A woman dropped from above, legs swinging out to wrap around Tikaya.

"Rias!" she called.

Steel rang out in the tiller room. He was busy.

The Nurian tried to pull Tikaya into the ladder well with powerful legs. For a woman, she had surprising bulk and muscle. Tikaya spread her stance and braced herself against the wall. She tried to maneuver her bow to prod the woman loose from the rungs, but it proved too unwieldy for the tight passage.

The Nurian woman released the ladder and threw her arms around Tikaya. The momentum slammed Tikaya back into the wall. A second form dropped into view in the ladder well—a black-robed man.

"Who's got *my* back?" Tikaya cried as the woman plucked a dagger from between her teeth.

She released the bow and tried to knock the blade away. Sharp steel bit into her arm.

The practitioner hanging on the ladder narrowed his eyes in concentration. The female fighter clung to Tikaya with one hand and raised the dagger again with the other.

Tikaya bit the arm wrapped around her shoulders. The woman hissed and her grip softened. Tikaya pushed off the wall and tried to shove her foe into the ladder well. The move jostled the practitioner. He cursed, his concentration disturbed, but the woman stuck to Tikaya like a tick. She raised her knife again.

A hand caught the Nurian's wrist, and Rias yanked her away. Tikaya stumbled and went down. Arrows spilled from her quiver.

The practitioner leapt on top of her, a dagger held aloft. Tikaya grabbed an arrow and rammed it into his gut. Luckily, it was the pointy end.

Eyes bulging, the practitioner reeled back. He dropped the dagger and clutched the arrow in his belly.

Before Tikaya could decide if she was safe, Rias loomed behind the practitioner. He wound up and swept the cutlass through flesh, muscle, and bone. The Nurian's head fell onto Tikaya.

"Errkt!" She shoved it off and scrambled away. Panting, she pressed a hand against the wall for support.

"I've got your back." Rias raked her with his gaze. "Are you injured?"

"Not...severely," she said numbly, staring at the decapitated practitioner. "How—why do you do that?" It came out more accusatory than she meant. Or maybe not. He had just saved her life—again—and she did not want to sound ungrateful, but, damn, it was chilling when the man on her side was more fearsome than those trying to murder her.

Rias turned her away from the decapitated practitioner and nodded toward the tiller room. "I've seen too many wizards I thought dead heal themselves and later come back after my men. As to how..." He ducked low to enter. "If you're ever in the imperial capital's war library, look up *Applications of the Kinetic Chain Principle in Close Combat.* I wrote it for Lord General Micacrest during my final year of studies, and parts are now used by the military training academies. Not scintillating reading, I'll admit, but it covers everything from breaking boards with a punch to—"

"Beheading people?" She trailed him inside, also ducking for the hatch.

"That's not listed in the table of contents, but, essentially, yes."

A pair of glowing orbs in sconces by the door illuminated the interior, though even without them Tikaya would have noticed the matching ragged holes adorning the exterior walls of the wedge-shaped compartment. A cannonball had gone straight through, leaving uneven gaps more than two feet in diameter. Wind shrieked, and water splattered the deck, pooling and running with the rocking of the ship.

"That doesn't look good," she muttered, before noticing a dead warrior on the deck, short sword still clutched in his grip.

"Actually..." Rias shut the door and peered out both gaps. He lingered on one side and kicked out a few broken boards to enlarge it. "It's fortuitous since there aren't portholes in here. There's the other Nurian vessel on this flank, and I see the Fist's smokestacks beyond it."

He strode to one of the block and tackles stretched from either side of the long metal tiller. They allowed manual access, though control ropes disappeared through the ceiling to connect to the wheel on the upper deck.

Rias grabbed one of the ropes and readied his cutlass. "They'll know right away they've lost wheel control, and half the crew will probably charge down here."

"I see, and how will we stop them from killing us?"

"Let me know when you figure it out." At odds with the seriousness of the situation, a mischievous glint warmed his eyes. "It's going to take all my strength to man the tiller."

He sliced through the control ropes even as she blurted, "You're crazy!"

Rias unhooked the end of the rope on the starboard block and tackle, glanced at measurements on the wall above the tiller, and sank into a low stance to pull. Inch by inch the great lever shifted, and the ship leaned, cutting across the waves in a new direction.

Tikaya hunted for something to block the door that she would surely be defending in a moment. Alas, there was no convenient beam for barring it shut—probably so people could not do what they were attempting.

She pushed a trunk full of spare rope to the door. Forcing queasiness aside in favor of practicality, she muscled the dead Nurian's body on top of it to add weight.

"Where exactly are you steering us?" she panted.

Rias was a statue, leaning back, arms extended, fingers wrapped around the rope, tendons taut with the strain, but he grinned at her nonetheless. "The closest Nurian ship."

"Oh, dear."

A fist hammered at the door.

"The Turgonians cut the ropes," Tikaya yelled in Nurian. "We're taking care of it. They ran to the hold!"

A long pause answered her, and, for a moment, she thought they might believe her. Then synchronized thuds struck the door.

"A nice try," Rias said, and she wondered how much Nurian he understood.

The chest skidded with each strike. She shoved it back in between blows.

"Get a ram," someone yelled.

"Better ready that bow," Rias said.

"If we're successful in crashing this ship, how are we getting out of here?" Tikaya asked.

Rias nodded toward the cannonball holes. "Hope you can swim."

She groaned.

For a moment, the thumps at the door stopped. Tikaya abandoned the chest and looked out the hole. They had halved the distance between themselves and the other Nurian ship, where a fire burned on the deck. People were scurrying to put it out.

"Are they tacking?" Rias asked. "Do I need to make adjustments?"

"Not yet. You're dead on, and they're busy. Not sure they've figured things out yet."

"Let's hope."

The hairs rose on the back of Tikaya's neck. Before she could shout a warning, a wave of power surged at the door. The trunk and body were flung into the room.

While nocking an arrow, Tikaya tried to shut the door with her shoulder. Warped hinges kept it from closing fully, and someone thrust it wide.

She jumped around and fired the bow, point blank, into the lead man's chest. Shocked eyes launched an accusation at her. She forced aside guilt and kicked him into others trying to surge forward. While they struggled to get around their dying comrade, she targeted a practitioner in the corridor behind them. Her arrow sailed over the heads of men shorter than she, but bounced harmlessly off an invisible shield. The practitioner never flinched.

The Nurians cleared the fallen man away, and their renewed push demanded Tikaya's attention. The corridor and door were too narrow for more than one to attack at once, but the seconds it took to nock and aim arrows let them push her back.

"Rias! I can't—"

Then he was there at her side, the slashing cutlass a wall of steel guarding the doorway. He had tied the rope to the other block and tackle. The lever wavered with the rocking of the ship, but hopefully they were close enough now that their course was inevitable.

"Get in there, you fools!" the practitioner shouted. "We're on a crash course!"

An arrow clipped the doorjamb and whizzed past Tikaya's head. Every time she found the opportunity, she shot around Rias, peppering their attackers. Her supply of arrows dwindled.

"This is madness," she yelled over the clamor.

"Yes!" Rias grinned at her, as if he loved every second.

A gifted swordsman made it to the front. Blade a blur, he forced Rias back.

Metal screeched in Tikaya's ears. She drew the bow, hoping for a clear shot. Two men slipped in behind the swordsman. Tikaya shot one, but more piled inside.

A thunderous crash buried the din, and the ship lurched and tilted on its side. Men scrambled and fell over each other, sliding toward the lower wall. Tikaya tumbled into Rias, but he grabbed the jamb and kept them from falling. Even in the stern of the ship, the cracks of wood breaking against wood were audible. Water gushed in from one of the cannonball holes, which was now submerged. Men flailed and floundered, struggling to get back to the door.

"I can't swim!" someone yelled.

"Time to go," Rias said.

Tikaya grabbed one of the glowing orbs from a sconce before he pushed her toward the upper wall. They had to pull their way along the block and tackle to reach the escape hole. Though the orb hampered her, she refused to release it.

Finally, with Rias's help, she clawed her way through the hole. The ragged wood tore a new gash in her beleaguered dress, but she wriggled free and slid down the hull into frigid black water.

The icy shock stole her breath. Salt stung her wounds, and she almost dropped the orb.

Rias plunged in beside her, spraying water.

The Nurian striker had rammed into the side of its sister ship, and water gushed into a great hole in the hull. Fire still burned on the deck, lighting up the night. Timber, from splinters to broken beams, littered the water.

"This way." Rias swam away from the ships, pushing the large pieces of wood out of the way.

"You sure you don't want to stay?" She was already swimming, side-stroking with the orb clutched against her hip. "You seemed to enjoy having people trying to kill you."

"You seemed to enjoy it less."

"Probably—" she spit icy salt water out of her mouth, "—an acquired taste."

They paddled away from the ships, rising and falling with the waves. Both vessels burned now and flames crawled up the sails of one. Neither would trouble the Turgonians again that night. As they swam out of the shadow of the Nurian vessels, the ironclad came into view. Only one of the two ships on its opposite flank remained, and both masts had been toppled, so it was falling behind. Tikaya and Rias, too, were falling behind. Her chest tightened at the idea of being left in the middle of the sea.

"Hope they see this." Tikaya lifted the glowing orb overhead, waving it in the air.

"Me too," Rias said.

The lookout in the crow's nest shouted something down to the deck. Tikaya's teeth chattered, and it felt as if hours, not minutes, passed before the warship dropped a boat.

"It's fortunate you're here," Rias said, bumping her arm as they treaded water. "I doubt they would have bothered coming for me."

"Not sure how fortunate I feel about going back to the Turgonians." Tikaya swiped water out of her eyes and grimaced at the cold drops tunneling into her ears. "I guess it's better being wanted than being wanted dead."

"Prevailing opinions agree with that sentiment."

Oars lifted and dipped as the craft neared. Lanterns at either end provided light, and Tikaya spotted Agarik leading the rowers. She smiled a bit, glad he had survived the chaos. He gazed at Rias with a wide-eyed, openmouthed stare of adulation and helped him out of the water first. She tried not to feel a twinge of envy. She *had* helped after all. At least Agarik managed to notice her second and gave her a hand into the boat. She collapsed on an empty bench between rows of burly, young oarsmen.

"Turn this dinghy around," Agarik yelled, and the men set to work.

Tikaya wrapped her arms around herself. The breeze needled her soaking dress, cold water dripped from her hair, and she had lost her sandals in the fall so the puddles on the bottom chilled her feet.

Rias settled on a bench next to her, and she pressed closer than she normally would have. Shivers coursed through her body. He put his arm around her, though he must have been just as cold and miserable. Their proximity caused raised eyebrows and significant looks between the marines. Agarik's jaw tensed.

"Here, sir." A marine handed Rias a blanket.

The use of the honorific made Agarik give the man a sharp look, though Tikaya was not sure if it was quelling or curious. Rias draped the blanket over his and her shoulders.

On the short ride back, the marines peppered him with questions. How had he gotten out of his cell? How had he and Tikaya gotten aboard the Nurian craft? Had they seen the Nurians on board their ship? Did they know what they wanted? Apparently, the Turgonian chain of command meant nobody not commanding had a clue was happening.

Tikaya thought Rias might share the story, but, back in the presence of the marines, he grew reserved and quiet. Was this the real man or had she glimpsed that person on the Nurian ship? Or neither? She liked the amiable fellow she had chatted with while target shooting best, though she suspected she could grow accustomed to the soldier she had seen tonight too. Not that it mattered. Certainly, she appreciated his help, but it was not as if she was going to develop feelings for some ex-officer from the military that had tried to take over her islands.

Still, when their knuckles bumped beneath the blanket, she gripped his hand.

"Thank you," she whispered, wanting to say more, but their hulking male onlookers stilled her tongue.

Rias smiled and squeezed her hand.

Back on the warship, Captain Bocrest waited, arms folded across his chest, a scowl accompanying his usual glare. Tikaya had not expected gratitude from the man, but the anger radiating from him surprised her.

As soon as Rias came over the railing behind her, that anger found an outlet.

"How could you make such an idiotic decision?" Bocrest snapped.

"He didn't do anything wrong," Tikaya said. "The Nurians teleported us to their ship. What was he supposed to do?"

The captain did not spare her a glance. His glare stayed pinned to Rias.

"What are you talking about, Bocrest?" Rias asked.

"You know what I'm talking about." The captain jerked his hand at a squad of marines standing by with pistols. "Take him back to his cell."

"Wait." Rias lifted a hand. "Did you find the assassins?"

"The dead men in the brig? Yes."

"No." Rias gave Tikaya a concerned frown. "There are two others, at least, who can skulk about invisible."

"They killed the man guarding my cabin," she said.

"We'll find them," Bocrest said.

"I can help," Rias said.

Bocrest scowled again. "You can go to your slagging cell and *stay* there this time."

"Captain." Rias stepped forward, staring down at Bocrest. "The Nurians want Tikaya dead and are making great sacrifices to ensure that happens."

"I'm aware of that." Bocrest did not back off, nor shrink away from Rias's glare. "I have orders to keep her alive until she decodes the runes, and I'll do that."

"She'd be dead now if she hadn't escaped on her own. You already botched your orders."

Afraid he would land himself in irrevocable trouble for her sake, Tikaya grabbed Rias's arm and tried to pull him away.

"I botched *my* orders?" Bocrest yelled, fists clenched. "If you hadn't screwed up two years ago, you could—" He cut himself off with an audible snapping shut of his jaw, and Tikaya sensed the 'idiotic decision' he accused Rias of had less to do with this night and more to do with whatever had landed Rias on Krychek Island. Bocrest glared around at the watching marines. "You men have duties," he roared. "Get this ship repaired. Now!"

Men sprinted from his wrath, leaving only Rias, Tikaya, Agarik, and the guards waiting to escort their prisoner below.

"Let me stay with her until the assassins are found," Rias said, as if he had not heard the captain's outburst. "Or stand guard outside her door. I've tangled with enough wizards to survive them."

"You're not her bodyguard, you're our guide. I thought I explained that to you when you were taking swings at me."

"A job for which you don't need me until we arrive at the tunnels," Rias said.

Tikaya's ears perked. Tunnels? Was that where the rubbings had come from? She still needed Rias to explain his history with the runes.

"No," Bocrest said. "You're a prisoner. You don't get your way."

Tikaya still gripped Rias's arm, and she could feel the tension in the knotted muscles beneath the damp sleeve. Though she hated seeing him angry, especially on her behalf, she had to wonder how much more might be revealed if she simply stood quiet and listened.

"Bocrest..." Rias tried again.

"Go. To. Your. Cell." The captain jerked his arm to wave the guards forward.

Rias tensed and dropped into a fighting crouch. He had not noticed when she grabbed his arm, so Tikaya stepped in front of him and planted two hands on his chest.

"Don't." She gazed into his eyes and made herself smile, though, she would have preferred Rias stay by her side too. "I'll be fine. You won't accomplish anything by getting beaten up."

He closed his eyes, seemed to struggle for his calm, and finally sighed, a deep long exhalation. "Be careful."

"I will."

Tikaya watched glumly as the guards surrounded him.

"This way, sir," one said.

Bocrest's head jerked up. "Don't you 'sir' him. He's Prisoner Five, and that's it."

The guard gulped. "Yes, captain."

Head lowered, Rias offered no reaction to the terse conversation. Surrounded, he trooped belowdecks. Bocrest stalked in the opposite direction, grinding his teeth.

"Ready to go back to your cabin, ma'am?" Agarik asked.

She shook her head but followed him. "Who is he, Corporal?" She had asked the question before, and Agarik had not known, but that was the second time someone sir'd him that night. Maybe it was out respect for what they had done aboard the Nurian ship, but somehow she doubted it. She wagered that shave and haircut had made him recognizable, at least to some.

"I wish I knew." Agarik led her down a ship's ladder. "It seems like he must be an officer at least, someone who fought during the war. But

I fought as well, and I don't remember hearing about anyone court-martialed and exiled to Krychek." They threaded through the wardroom, where furniture had toppled and slid against the wall, and stopped at her cabin. "He hasn't told you?"

"Just to call him Rias. Does that mean anything to you?"

The corporal's expression grew thoughtful, but eventually he shook his head. "No."

Tikaya stepped into her cabin. Thankfully, the bodies had been cleared, though a few bloodstains smudged the deck.

Before Agarik could close the door, she leaned back out, remembering something. "He did say..."

Agarik paused, eyes questioning.

"If I was ever at the war library in your capital I should look up a book called *Applications of the Kinetic Chain Principle in Close Combat*, because he wrote it."

Agarik froze. Utterly and completely. His mouth hung open, and he stared at her for a long moment before recovering. "I see. Thank you."

"Wait." Tikaya raised a hand as he started away. "You know, don't you? Is he somebody I would have heard of?"

"I don't—I can't. I'm not sure. I—"

A lieutenant passed through the wardroom on the way to his cabin, and he frowned at Agarik.

"I have to go." Agarik chopped a wave.

"Could you at least have someone bring me a towel?" Tikaya called to his receding back.

* * * * *

After dripping a puddle of water onto the cabin floor, Tikaya wondered if she should take off her dress and dry in the blanket on her bunk.

What were the odds the Turgonians would supply her with a change of clothing at some point? She plucked at the damp dress. At least the sea had washed out most of the blood.

When she reached for the blanket, her gaze fell across the desk. It was empty.

The rubbings, her notes, and the reference books Bocrest had provided were missing. She searched the tiny cabin, thinking they might have been knocked off during the scramble, but no. They were gone.

A shiver ran through her that had nothing to do with the wet dress. The assassins must have returned and taken them.

Tikaya eyed the corners of the cabin, all too aware that they could be right in front of her and she would not know it.

She opened the door, wondering if a new guard had been posted or if she could leave and find the captain. Sergeant Ottotark leaned against the wall outside, and she did not manage to hide her groan.

Briefly, he met her eyes, offering a hostile glare, but his gaze inevitably drifted downward. She shifted to the side to stand in the shadow of the door.

"The rubbings are missing," Tikaya said. "I think they stole them—the Nurians who attacked me in my cabin and killed the young man standing guard."

Ottotark's face frosted at the mention of the dead marine.

"Can you tell Bocrest?" she asked.

"The captain is busy directing repairs, cleanup, and funeral services, thanks to the flotilla of Nurian ships that showed up tonight looking for you."

"While I'm sympathetic to your lost men—"

He snorted.

"—you people kidnapped me," she continued. "I never wanted to be here, so don't blame that attack on me. If you could just tell the captain I'm not able to continue my studies unless he finds—"

The sergeant stepped forward, shoving the door further open. "I'm not your messenger boy."

She stumbled back, glancing around for something to use as a weapon if she needed to fend him off. The sparse cabin offered nothing.

"You'd do best to remember you're a prisoner here. Prisoners have no right to the captain's time, nor to an officer's cabin with a busy sergeant as your guard, a busy sergeant who's stuck on this duty because your presence here got one of his men killed." His low voice was gravelly, and tendons strained against the skin of his thick neck. "You haven't done anything useful since you got here."

Tikaya wanted to defend herself—she had helped Rias crash the ship that had allowed the Turgonians to sail away, hadn't she?—but Ottotark seemed to want her to argue, to incite his anger. He stepped closer, and she eased back until her calves bumped the bunk.

Rage boiled in the sergeant's dark eyes, but lust too. He had not looked at her face since she first opened the door. "The captain ought to chain you to that bunk and let you be of some use to the crew."

A throat cleared in the corridor.

The glare Ottotark snapped over his shoulder could have frozen lava, but Corporal Agarik merely lifted his arms, displaying boots, a parka, a stack of black uniforms, and a towel. Tikaya held her breath, aware the sergeant outranked Agarik, but hoping the corporal's presence would keep Ottotark in line.

"The captain said to bring her these and relieve you as guard," Agarik said.

Ottotark eyed the stack. "Now we're pampering the bitch with extra clothes? Why don't we invite her to dine in the officer's mess next?"

"Gonna be cold up there, sergeant." Agarik walked in, set the clothing on the bunk, and then stood outside the cabin, in full view of the door, which he left open.

Ottotark issued a low growl and a backward glance that promised "later" before striding out.

Even after the door banged shut, Tikaya could not relax. Her luck would not hold with that one. She would have to figure out how to abscond with a dagger from the exercise area and keep it on her at all times.

And hope it was enough against the powerful marine. And that she could use it on him. But then that should not be a problem now. Her lip twisted bitterly. She had killed. When she thought of how easy it had been, how accurate she was with that cursed bow, she had to steady herself with a hand on the wall.

React later, Rias had said. Well, it was later.

Tikaya curled on her side on the bunk, her head in her hands, her eyes shut. Images of her deeds flashed in her mind, the terrified and pained faces of the people she shot. She let them flood over her again and again, feeling the need to punish herself. What would Parkonis think if he were alive? Would he be shocked—disgusted—that she could release an arrow into someone's chest? He never would have killed a human being, probably not even in self-defense. He would have been horrified to see Rias beheading those practitioners.

She opened her eyes and stared at the polished wood floorboards. If she had been transported to that ship with Parkonis, she would have been dead in the first minute. She was no longer in his world, no longer in hers. She could adapt to this world—she had proved that to herself that night—but at what cost?

Tikaya wondered if she would ever see her family and her island again. More, she wondered if she would be someone her parents could still love if she did return.

CHAPTER 7

Ice stretched in all directions, an endless white blanket, unbroken save for a black trail of water stretching behind the ship. Tikaya gripped the frost-slick railing near the bow with gloved hands and peered over the fur trim of her parka, amazed by the heavy iron hull smashing through the inches-thick frozen crust. The pace was slow and the deck vibrated with the efforts of the engine, but their progress continued. Her people's wooden vessels could never do this and she admitted reluctant admiration for the Turgonian engineers and metallurgists who could build such a craft without help from practitioners.

For the first time during the trip, land stretched along the horizon, white, flat, and stark. To the south, a range of jagged snow-smothered mountains stretched inland. A settlement hunkered a few miles ahead, low buildings and ice-locked docks just becoming visible. On the ship, marines were hauling food and supplies out of the hold, preparing for a land excursion.

"Good morning," came a familiar voice from behind.

Tikaya whirled, smiling. "Rias."

Thanks to the captain's claim that his men were too busy with repairs to perform extra guard duty, she had not seen Rias for more than a week, not since the night of the attack. Her smile faded at the sight of shackles binding his wrists and guards trailing behind him. She clenched her jaw. How could Bocrest still treat Rias like a prisoner when he had risked his life—*their* lives—to save the warship?

He joined her at the railing. "I've missed you."

That simple statement warmed her far more than the parka. The captain had allowed Rias a shave, at least, and she had a nice view of the smile softening his face.

"Me too. I mean you. Er, I've missed you too." Tikaya stifled a groan, avoided his eyes, and reflected on the mortification her linguistics professors would feel at hearing her mangle language so. To cover her fumbling tongue, she nodded at the ice cracking beneath the bow. "That's impressive."

"Hm, the Emperor's Fist has a strengthened hull, but that won't be enough to get us all the way to shore. If you want to see impressive, you should see our dedicated ice-breaking ships. They have a double hull and a special steel alloy designed for peak performance at low temperatures. The bows are rounded instead of pointed, so the ship rides up over the ice, smashing it with its weight. And the engines! They..." He blushed. "Sorry, you probably don't want all that information."

Tikaya grinned. "I did ask."

He smiled sadly. "No. No, you didn't."

"Well, I expressed interest in the subject."

That seemed to mollify him. "I should have asked already: are the men treating you decently? Any sign of those assassins? Any nightmares after our adventure?"

"As well as can be expected for a loathed enemy of the empire, no assassination attempts, and nightmares..." Tikaya *had* slept poorly, reliving the killings on the Nurian ship, but she did not want to talk about it here, with guards looking on, so she pretended to misunderstand. "Why do you ask? Are women usually traumatized after an evening out with you?"

He blinked a few times. "No, but I don't usually take women into battle on first dates."

"Ah, I see. You save that until the relationship is more established."

"Exactly." He slid her a sidelong look, and she suspected he understood what she was not saying.

Tikaya propped her elbow on the railing and faced Rias squarely. Though she enjoyed chitchatting with him, she had been waiting all week to ask about the tunnels he mentioned to Bocrest. And how they tied in with the symbols.

"Will you tell me about these tunnels you're supposed to guide us through?" she asked. "You've asked me to help Bocrest, but you haven't explained what that will entail."

His face grew somber as soon as she mentioned the tunnels. This time, though, he nodded instead of retreating into himself. "The place we're going...the source of the runes... I've been there before. It was my first assignment as a raw sub-lieutenant, what we call a 'testing mission.'"

"What's being tested? You?"

"Yes. Every officer gets something early in his career, a deliberately challenging task that's meant to show whether or not he has the courage, intelligence, and command ability to go on to become a leader of men. I imagine this was...more than my superiors had in mind. I was attached to an army unit for the month because of studies I'd done on excavation engineering. Forty of us walked into those tunnels. A week later, three of us crawled out—through a ventilation shaft high in the mountains, in the middle of a blizzard. We barely made it back to Fort Deadend, and the major I'd been assigned to wrote a heartfelt report that stated we should never send men into the tunnels again."

"They were ancient ruins?" she asked. "With traps?"

"Ancient, perhaps. Not ruins."

Rias's shoulders hunched in an uncharacteristic slouch, his gaze toward the snapping ice. Tikaya thought of the man she followed through the Nurian ship, head up, alert, leading the way with confidence that should not have been there against such lopsided odds, and she regretted drawing him back to what was obviously a dark place for him. Still, she had to know.

"What happened inside?"

"The tunnels were in good condition. Too good. No dust, cobwebs, no signs of age other than damage from tectonic shifts. The men with me declared the place possessed by some powerful ancient magic. I thought... not. The 'traps' we kept stumbling into—I got the feeling they weren't traps at all but simply the workings of a place we were too ignorant to understand. We were like clueless rats drowned in the city waterworks when the level rises."

"But there was writing? These symbols?"

For the first time a spark of interest entered his eyes. "Not a lot, but things were labeled. If you could translate, perhaps that could keep us safe."

Tikaya feared the smile she offered was bleak. The rubbings were gone, and she had made zero progress with the language.

"Well, not safe." Rias's shoulders slumped again, independent of her thoughts. "There were strange and deadly creatures roaming those tunnels too. Nothing we recognized, nothing the archaeologists with us knew from the fossil record."

"You had archaeologists with you before?"

"A team of scientists, yes, and a linguist."

"Did any of them make it out?" The bleakness infused her tone now.

"No, and they weren't particularly helpful while they were alive."

Great grandmother's gray locks, what was she supposed to accomplish that a team of archaeologists had failed to do?

A worried expression creased Rias's forehead. He seemed to realize he had blundered. "But you're better than them."

She snorted. "That'd be more reassuring if you'd ever actually seen me do anything and could qualify that statement."

He bumped her shoulder and smiled. "I've seen enough."

Tikaya blushed.

"You two relax." Sergeant Ottotark glared at Tikaya and Rias as he stalked past carrying a massive bag labeled 'tent: medium.' "Enjoy the view. Have some rum. Those of us who aren't prisoners will handle all the unloading and loading."

"I hope he's not coming with us," Tikaya muttered after he moved out of earshot. Somehow, she did not think she would be that lucky.

"Despite his bite, I'm told he's intensely loyal to the emperor and the captain," Rias said.

"If he kept his bite out of my cabin, I wouldn't care one way or another."

Rias looked at her sharply. "What?"

"Nothing." Tikaya lifted a hand, realizing she had insinuated more than Ottotark was guilty of at that point. "He's just an ass. He hasn't done anything yet."

Rias's gaze did not waver. "Yet?"

What did he expect her to say? "I'm trying to stay out of his path."

"You shouldn't have to. Not on a Turgonian warship." Rias offered a jerky wave, hampered by the shackles. "I have to go." He stalked away, his guards hustling to catch up.

"Rias?" she called after him.

He paused, looking back over his shoulder.

"Did you pass the test?"

His lips twisted into a sour expression. "They gave me a medal."

He resumed his determined walk. Before she could consider his words or abrupt departure further, Agarik strode toward her, a full rucksack in his arms. He plunked it on the deck at her feet. He already wore a rucksack of his own with a rifle strapped to the back. His utility belt was loaded with a knife and pistol, ammo pouches, and powder tins.

"Are you ready to go, ma'am?"

"Go?" Tikaya glanced over the railing. The ship had ground to a halt against ice too thick to break, but marines still hustled about, piling gear next to a hoist. A gangly grinning private surged through a hatch leading—being led by—eight thickly furred gray and white dogs. "Now?"

"Yes, ma'am. You're part of the scouting party. We're expecting trouble, so you're going in first with me and a dozen others under Lieutenant Commander Okars's lead."

"You're *expecting* trouble?" Why would they include her if that was the case? Weren't they supposed to be keeping her from being killed?

Agarik pointed at the distant buildings. "No smoke. Fire is crucial for warmth up here. No smoke means the town's been deserted. Or worse. Might be the Nurians again, and if any are around, we'll need a translator to interrogate them."

Dread curled in the pit of her stomach. Not only did she not want to see any more Nurians, but she surely did not want to help with a brutal Turgonian interrogation.

"You've got to come at some point anyway, so the captain says now." Agarik gave her an apologetic shrug. "We'll protect you. We scouts are well trained."

"No doubt. You found me and dragged me off my parents' plantation without trouble."

He winced.

"Sorry," she said. Agarik was the closest thing she had to an ally amongst the marines, and if he had not found her, another would have, so she could hardly blame him.

He pointed to the rucksack. "Want to check that? I grabbed your clothes and some pencils and blank journals. Then there's standard issue gear for this climate: medical kit, snow goggles, crampons, canteens, blanket, and a hygiene and shaving kit."

"Shaving kit? As cold as it is up here, I'm not sure I want to remove any of the little body hair I have."

He did not smile at the joke. Instead he watched her with curious intensity, as if willing her to understand something. Then she got it. Shaving kit. *Razor.*

Agarik's gaze shifted toward Ottotark, who stood by the hoist, directing the lowering of a dog sled.

"I see," Tikaya breathed. "You won't get in trouble, will you?"

Agarik hesitated a second, then said, "Standard issue gear," which she took to mean he probably *would* get in trouble for doing something as stupid as arming a prisoner, but it would likely be seen as negligence rather than treason. A lesser crime with a lesser punishment, she hoped.

"Thank you, Corporal."

He saluted her, fist to chest. "Ma'am."

"I think you can call me Tikaya at this point."

"Yes, ma'am."

* * * * *

Powdery snow skidded sideways as wind scoured the ice field. The icy crystals needled Tikaya's neck as she crunched along behind the squad of marines. For the seventy-third time, she adjusted her wool scarf and cap, wondering why the secret to the gear's effectiveness eluded her. A wan sun burned in the sky, but its arc remained low on the southern horizon, and it provided no warmth. At least the bulky goggles smashing her spectacles against the bridge of her nose warmed her cheeks somewhat, though the main purpose of the darkened lenses was to protect from the sunlight glinting off ice and snow.

Despite her discomfort, determination kept her feet moving as quickly as those of the scouts. Even before Rias's story, she had daydreamed of translating the language and bringing awareness of it to the greater archaeological community. Now, she had a more compelling reason to learn as much about the runes as she could. Quickly. Since the Nurians had deprived her of the original clues, she would have to find new ones inland. It struck her as odd that she resented the assassins more for stealing the rubbings than for trying to kill her.

Tikaya peered over her shoulder. She still did not know if the Nurians had returned to their ships or had holed up on the Emperor's Fist somewhere.

Agarik, bringing up the rear, asked, "Problem, ma'am?"

"Just wondering how far back Rias and the others will be."

The ironclad, its black hull a dour blot against the stark white world, rose a couple miles behind, and she could no longer pick out the men and dog sled teams assembling in its shadow.

"An hour back or so for the main party. As for Five..." Agarik might know who Rias was now, but he was careful to use the number instead of a name. "I heard him and the captain arguing just before we left, and, uhm, Bocrest told him he could shove—er, he had to carry the blasting sticks, so he'll be in the rear."

Tikaya groaned, knowing that argument had been her fault. She should not have complained about Ottotark. "Blasting sticks? Are those practitioner-made or the unstable alchemical kind?"

"We don't use anything magical."

She groaned again. One thoughtless comment, and now Rias had to traverse the slick ice while carrying a heavy box of volatile explosives. While wearing shackles.

The image distracted her, and she crashed into the marine in front of her. An unstrung bow strapped to his rucksack clipped her jaw.

He glared over his shoulder but said nothing. At some signal or command she had missed, the queue of marines had halted. Two dogs the scouts had brought sniffed and romped, unconcerned by whatever caused the leaders to stop.

"Bones!" someone called.

Tikaya glanced at Agarik. Was that a name? Or a discovery?

Agarik said nothing. Every man in the squad stood still, apparently drilled to do so until a command came. Well, she was not a marine. She sidled out of line. Ten meters in front of the formation, two men stood around something pale half-covered in snow.

Would she get yelled at if she went up to investigate? Did she care?

Tikaya shrugged and walked to the front of the line. Men glanced at her as she passed, but no one stopped her.

She slowed as she approached, regretting her decision to leave the squad as soon as she identified the object on the ground.

It was a naked man. A *dead* naked man.

Snow mounded against one side of the body, and ice crystals gathered on limbs blackened by frostbite. He had died face down, an arm stretched out, fingers splayed.

"Nothing to translate here, woman." Lieutenant Commander Okars, a stocky man with eyebrows thicker than the fur trimming his parka hood, leaned against his rifle. He removed a plug of tobacco from a pocket and gnawed off a corner with stained teeth before handing it to the other man. "What d'you think?"

The second marine looked so similar to the commander that Tikaya thought them twins for a moment. The name tabs on both their parkas read Okars, but this fellow wore lieutenant's pins and had fewer lines on his face. He spat a brown stream into the snow by the body. "Looks like he was running from something."

"I called you up here for a more professional assessment than that, Sawbones."

"Oh, I'm sorry. Did you want me to inquire about his health and see what ails him? Perhaps if he'll give me a list of his symptoms, hm."

At that point, Tikaya realized 'sawbones' was slang for doctor. The connotations in that name disturbed her—she had never visited a healer who did not work as much with the power of his mind as with his hands—and she hoped she did not require this man's services any time soon, especially if he kept serrated metal tools in his kit.

"Bones," the commander snapped. Strange that he used the term instead of his brother's name. Maybe the staid Turgonians had regulations against familial familiarity.

"What?" Bones asked. "He froze to death. What do you want me to do?"

"Figure out what drove him to run out here naked and suicidal."

Bones levered the barrel of his rifle under the corpse and leaned onto the stock. Ice snapped, and the rigid body rolled over. Tikaya jumped, surprised at the irreverent treatment of the dead. That did not keep her from staring. The front half was no more illuminating than the back, but the face, eternally contorted in terror, made her shiver. The man had died afraid, very afraid.

Bones shook his head at the commander. "Nope, no clues."

Okars ground his jaw. "Curse the Headquarters desk-rider who thought it'd be amusing to put my little brother on the same ship as me."

"Exquisite torture, isn't it?" Bones grinned.

Tikaya stared at the brothers. They were joking. A corpse lay before them, a corpse probably belonging to one of their own citizens, and they were joking. Uncharacteristically intense irritation stirred within her.

"Animals," she blurted before she could still her tongue. "Where's your respect for the dead?"

The commander's bushy brows lowered, and a cold, almost predatory expression darkened his face.

Bones placed a hand on Okars's sleeve. "You'd best get back to your place, ma'am. Stay out of the way and let us do our jobs."

She nodded and backed away.

"Mouth shut, Tikaya," she muttered. "Keep your mouth shut around these warmongering fools."

Strange, she thought she had learned that lesson already.

CHAPTER 8

When Tikaya and the marines reached the shoreline, it differed little from the ice they had been marching across. The ground rose subtly, and she supposed a beach lay somewhere under all the snow. Two docks, embraced by ice, stretched away from a couple of wooden warehouses with drifts piled to the eaves along their northern walls. One of the dogs lifted a leg and yellowed a sign post promising the availability of alcohol at the *Rat Wrangler*.

The town itself, with a single snowy road running parallel to the waterfront, seemed more outpost than community. Unpainted wood dwellings hunkered against the elements. Three long rectangular buildings overlooked the town from the crown of a hill. No life stirred anywhere. A stiff northeasterly wind rattled shutters, and somewhere a door banged against a wall.

"Welcome to Wolfhump, ma'am," Agarik said, speaking for the first time since the discovery of the body.

"That's the name of the town?" Tikaya asked.

"It's a trade outpost for the miners working the mountains. I don't think there's a lot to do up here except drink and watch the wildlife, uhm, frolic."

Encrypted

At the head of the formation, Commander Okars made a few hand gestures, dividing men into parties for scouting. Marines checked rifles and a couple strung bows. Tikaya wondered if she might talk the commander into letting her borrow one. She thought of letting an arrow fly into Sergeant Ottotark's chest and his scream of pain as he pitched backward, sprawling on the ice. Tikaya jerked with surprise, startled her mind had conjured the grizzly image. Too much time spent with these Turgonians.

"As far as you know Wolfhump should be occupied?" Tikaya asked.

"Of course, it should be occupied," Agarik snapped. He twitched, seemingly as surprised by his tone as her. "Sorry, ma'am."

A growl rumbled up ahead. One dog dove at the other dog's neck. Fangs sank into flesh and the victim squealed, a heart-wrenching cry that halted conversations.

Tikaya gawked at the brutal attack. Marines jumped into the fray, grabbing the dogs by the ruffs of their necks and trying to pull them apart, but the attacking canine had gone berserk. Muscles surged, fangs flashed, and soon blood spattered the white snow.

"Get those dogs under control, private!"

"Trying, sir!"

"Idiots," Agarik muttered and strode forward to help.

Tikaya stayed back. The exchange had a bizarreness to it that left her uneasy. She glanced toward the icy sea again, wishing Rias was there to consult. Her gut lurched. The ship was gone.

Nothing to worry about, she told herself. It had probably just retreated to open waters to keep from being ensconced when the ice reformed. But that meant the group had nowhere to retreat to if they ran into trouble they could not handle. She squinted, trying to spot the main party, but the sun shone brilliantly on the ice. Even through her goggles, she could not make them out yet.

"Don't touch—"

"Get off me!"

108

She turned back in time to see two marines crash to the snow. They wrestled and thrashed, and men previously trying to keep the dogs apart now turned their attention to separating the human combatants.

"Satters, Choyka, stand down!" Okars raced toward them, his voice strained and angry. Where was the calm confidence one expected from a senior officer?

Tikaya pulled her goggles up as if a clearer view might enlighten, but the scene only stunned. The smaller dog lay still, its neck torn open, blood drenching the snow beneath it. The other raced across the ice field, yowling like a wolf. Three marines grappled on the ground, clawing and punching at each other. The commander tried to drag one of them away and took a fist to the jaw. He slipped and went down.

The sawbones stood back, a bewildered expression on his face. At least he was not brawling with anyone.

Tikaya jogged over to his side. "What's going on? Have you ever seen anything like this?"

He worked over the wad of tobacco in his mouth. "Nope."

"Could it be the Nurians again? Trying to keep us from resolving whatever is going on in those tunnels?"

He froze, mid-chew. "How do you know—how much do you know?"

"I know they tried to kill me so I couldn't help your people translate that unknown language."

"I suppose it's possible the Nurians have done...something. I can't think of anything natural that would explain this sudden aggressiveness."

The scuffles were dying down. Men's ragged breaths frosted the air. A couple marines still struggled against those restraining them, while others seemed embarrassed. Blood flowed from broken noses and split lips.

"Bones, come patch people up." Commander Okars did not appear wounded, but his eyes had a wild cast to them. "And tell me what's going on."

"No idea."

"No idea? Grandmother Hakstor was a better sawbones than you. For spit's sake, get your ass over here and figure this mess out."

Amusement flickered in Bones's dark eyes, and he gave Tikaya an irreverent salute, saying, "Nice talking with you, ma'am," before he trundled off.

She was not sure what to make of the man's odd humor or this situation. The fact that she was dependent on the marines out here rankled. She gazed down the flat coastline toward the mountains, wondering how many hundreds of miles lay between her and a town where she could find passage out of the empire. A lot, she feared, and she knew nothing about surviving in this climate.

"Corporal Dansk," Okars said. "Head back and warn the others. Corporal Agarik?"

Tikaya shook away her musings and turned her attention back to the marines.

"Yes, sir?"

"We're heading in. Stay here and guard the woman."

Irritation flattened Agarik's lips, and for a moment Tikaya thought he would question the officer. He kept himself to a glum, "Yes, sir."

One man trotted back the way they had come, while the others marched away in pairs, leaving Tikaya and Agarik alone with the dead dog.

"You want to go with them, don't you?" She lifted her eyebrows at Agarik, whose gaze remained fastened on the backs of the men. "To explore?"

He huffed a sigh. "No."

"You must not lie very often, because you're not good at it."

A slight smile quirked his lips.

Tikaya's gaze returned to the buildings overlooking the town. A giant cannon and a flag pole flying Turgonian colors stood before one. Military structures, she guessed. If there were any clues to this mystery, she wagered they would be in an office up there. Exploring the town might be hazardous, but, then, standing out here where anyone with a bow or a rifle could target them felt hazardous too. And if this strange aggression affected the main party... She thought of Rias holding a box of blasting sticks and shuddered.

"Why don't we ramble up that hill and see if we can figure out what's going on?" Tikaya suggested.

"We've orders to stay here."

"Actually, I believe your orders were to 'guard the woman.'"

"'*Stay here* and guard the woman.'"

A breeze gusted down the coast, icy fingers poking through Tikaya's scarf. "They don't encourage initiative in Turgonia, do they?"

"Not in the marines, no."

She curled her fingers in her gloves. Even if she did not want to explore, she would have appreciated getting inside out of the wind. "Suppose the woman runs off and you're forced to chase after her in order to guard her?"

"With respect, ma'am, I could catch you before you ran five steps."

"Rias would run off with me." It was a stupid argument, and she knew it. She felt like a stubborn five-year-old trying to wrangle an extra hour of play before bedtime. Unfortunately, manipulating men to get her way was not her specialty. No doubt her teenage years should have involved less time studying ancient tablets and more time flirting with boys at the beach.

"I'd rather he run off with *me*," Agarik said.

The comment surprised a laugh from her and reminded her flirting would probably not work on him anyway.

A gun fired in the town, stealing her mirth. Someone shouted. It sounded like Turgonian, one of the marines, but distance muddled the words. Agarik's grip tightened on his rifle and he took a step before he stopped himself. A scream of pain echoed from the dwellings, and it made Tikaya shiver.

"Something creepy is happening here," she said. "We should check the buildings on the hill. They're military, aren't they? That'd be the place to start looking for answers, you'd think."

"Tikaya..."

"Why are you being so frustratingly obtuse about this?" she growled. "You'd think I was asking you to—" She noticed Agarik's startled expression and caught herself.

"Something creepy *is* happening here," Agarik said softly.

"I'm sorry. I didn't mean it. I understand that you want to be the good soldier and follow orders, and I don't want to get you in trouble. But..." Rias's words flashed through her mind: *to live when the rest of your team died would be an unacceptable disgrace to many.* "Do you want to be the only one of your team left alive when the others catch up?"

His gaze jerked up, latched onto her. He closed his eyes for a long moment before sighing and asking, "When I get court-martialed and kicked out of the empire for following your suggestions, can I come live on your island?"

"Absolutely. Free lodging in my parents' guest bungalow overlooking the sea. I'll even introduce you to my cousin's handsome friend who surfs nude every afternoon. He was in one of my linguistics classes; he has a gifted tongue."

Agarik's eyes widened, and he clapped her on the shoulder, leading the way toward the hill. "If you'd promised me all that the first time we met, we'd still be on your island."

Tikaya peered down the main strip as they passed it, but she did not spot any marines. They must be exploring inside the buildings.

When she and Agarik rounded the back corner of a saloon, they jerked to a halt at the sight of skulls and bones half-buried in fresh snow. Human skulls and bones.

"Cursed ancestors," Agarik grunted.

The snow had obscured footprints but did not quite hide the tooth marks scoring the broken bones, the marrow prodded out by tongues.

"How long has it been since your people had contact with this town?" Tikaya asked.

"How should I know?" Agarik barked.

She peered at him, at the irritable frown creasing his brows.

"Sorry." He nudged a skull with the toe of his boot. Myriad fractures spun out from a ragged hole smashed into the back. No wolf had done that. "The fits of rage surprise you, don't they? You think you're fine, and then..."

"Yes," she said. "That's a concern, especially since the second group is bringing explosives."

"I've never heard of a Nurian plot like this," Agarik said.

She gazed thoughtfully at the mountains, the tundra, and the ice-coated sea. "Since I grew up around practitioners, I'm sensitive to when they're performing their science. I haven't felt any of the telltale signs of one at work."

"So, this isn't magic?"

"I don't think so."

"Then what?"

She could only shrug.

Tikaya and Agarik did not speak as they climbed the hill. Several minutes had passed since the last yell, scream, or shot that would have indicated the scouting party was still around. It was as if they had simply disappeared.

They reached the first of the buildings perched on the crown. The back two, one-story wood structures with narrow windows, were probably barracks and offices. The closest, a taller building with corrugated metal walls, lacked windows, though massive sliding doors marked entrances. Tikaya and Agarik stopped there first, heading for the leeward side, which was free of drifts, though shoveled snow piled high near a walkway. It could not have been too long since the living occupied the outpost.

Ice shattered and metal groaned as Agarik shoved a door open a few feet. Weak sunlight probed the interior, revealing an empty building with an earthen floor splotched with dark stains. The smell of engine oil wafted out.

"All the caterpillars are gone," Agarik said. "Guess we're stuck with dog sleds."

"Caterpillars?" she asked.

"Steam vehicles designed to handle the ice and snow."

"Ah. How many are there supposed to be?"

"There's room for five or six in there."

They crunched across the crown of the hill, sinking calf-deep into snow. Wind gusted, blowing powder off the roofs.

A three-foot long icicle sheared off an overhang and plunged into the snow a foot from Agarik's shoulder. Tikaya jumped to the side, tangling her feet, and toppled into the snow. Agarik raised his eyebrows, and she felt sheepish.

She clambered to her feet. It was chance that the deadly icicle had dropped then, nothing more. Regardless, Agarik took a couple steps to the side before continuing along his route.

Heavy shadows lay in the alleys between the buildings, and Tikaya glanced skyward in surprise. The sun had dropped well past its zenith.

"It's already afternoon." Feeling silly for blurting the obvious, she added, "I didn't realize how short days are up here."

"I was here once near the winter solstice. Day is about an hour then."

By the entrance to the next building, shoveled snow piled nearly to the roof. They followed a wide walkway with a couple of inches of fresh powder blanketing it. Paw prints marred the surface. Large paw prints.

A gnawed skeleton, not quite hidden by the snow, sprawled a couple feet from the door. A hammer protruded from the skull, its head caught where it had smashed a hole through the bone. Shreds of a black uniform were tangled amongst the ribs.

"I hope our scouting doesn't require us spending the night here," Tikaya said. "I doubt this town gets any less disturbing after dark."

Agarik nodded at the hammer. "Scavengers might have cleaned these corpses, but it looks like humans were responsible for the deaths."

"Of course. Killing people is what you Turgonians are good at." She regretted the words as soon as they came out.

Agarik slid a knife free of his belt and whirled, glowering at her. "We need answers, not sarcastic comments."

Lindsay Buroker

Tikaya skittered back, hands raised. He turned the knife so the afternoon sun glinted against the frosty steel. His breath steamed the air before his intense dark eyes.

"Agarik?" She shifted her weight, thinking of the razor in her rucksack. It would take a lot of rummaging to find it. She should have done that as soon as the other marines let her out of sight. "Put the knife away, please."

His cheek twitched and the blade trembled.

"Something here is affecting you, remember? They let it affect them..." Hands still raised, she nodded toward the bones. "And now they're dead."

Agarik forced his fingers open, and the knife tunneled into a snow drift. "Of course. I know." Eyes closed, he took a deep, shuddering breath. "Do you think... Are we making a mistake being here? Will whatever happened to these people happen to us?" For the first time that Turgonian fearlessness faltered.

Tikaya decided she preferred the fearlessness. "You know as much as I do, probably more." She picked up the knife and dusted it off. "Mind if I keep this for now?"

He flinched but nodded. "Go ahead. I have my rifle and pistol." He waved at the town. "Don't worry. I'm sure we can always leave if the situation escalates into something dangerous."

She bit back a comment about the townspeople apparently not being able to leave to save their lives.

Agarik pushed open the door, and Tikaya peered around him. A single corridor stretched to the opposite end of the long building. The far door stood ajar, and daylight slashed inside. Shadows in the middle stirred. Two dark furry shapes turned their direction.

Wolves.

They did not exist back home, but she had seen pictures. Tall and winter lean, the creatures growled, lips rippling, saliva gleaming on fangs.

The pair charged. Agarik raised his rifle and shot one, the boom thunderous as it echoed in the hallway. The ball struck the lead wolf in the shoulder, and it yipped in pain, but it kept running. Agarik fired his pistol, striking the second canine in the eye. This one faltered and flopped over, but the other kept racing toward them.

Tikaya backed outside and Agarik, needing time to reload, almost fell out beside her.

"Stay back," he barked.

She ignored him and lunged forward to slam the door shut. A heartbeat later, the wolf crashed against the wood. It shuddered but held.

Agarik already had his ammo pouches open. With admirable calm, he poured powder down the muzzle of the rifle, rammed a cloth-wrapped ball home, and slipped a percussion cap on the nipple. The wolf slammed against the door two more times, then claws scrabbled at wood. Tikaya gripped the knife and wished she had a bow. On a whim, she yanked the hammer out of the skull.

The clawing at the door stopped.

"I bet it's going around," she said.

"Stay back," Agarik repeated. "Stand against the wall."

Rifle loaded, he stepped away from the building, ready to fire either direction. Tikaya put her back into the corner between the door and the pile of shoveled snow.

Even expecting the wolf, she was startled by how soon it ripped around a corner. Agarik did not flinch as it hurtled toward him. He lined up the shot and fired.

The ball struck the wolf in the chest, and it missed a step, but amazingly it did not stop. A craziness lit its yellow eyes as the beast launched itself at Agarik.

He had not had time to reload the pistol, so he could only swing the rifle like a club. The wolf twisted in the air, and Agarik merely clipped it. The beast's fangs snapped inches from his neck. The snow hindered him, and he stumbled back against the wall.

Tikaya slashed at the wolf when it landed nearby, but it sprang again too quickly, and her blade sliced air. Agarik hammered it with the butt of the rifle, but the creature seemed not to feel pain. It readied itself to spring again.

Tikaya lifted the hammer, thinking she might get lucky if she threw it, but a new thought halted her. She turned her back to the fray and scrambled up the snow pile.

"Good idea," Agarik called. "Stay up there until..." He grunted as he swung at the wolf again. "Until I finish this."

Retreating was not Tikaya's idea. She crawled through the snow near the edge of the roof until she could peer down upon the skirmish. The eaves sheltered Agarik, but the wolf, needing room to run and leap, kept moving in and out of the overhang's shadow.

"Stay against the wall, and suck in your belly," Tikaya called.

She leaned over and grabbed an icicle as thick as her upper arm. Even with the hammer it took several cracks to free it from the edge. The wolf leaped. She timed it, then released the ice spear.

Tikaya did not expect to hit the creature on the first try, but her aim proved true. The icicle bludgeoned the top of its gray-furred head.

Agarik sidestepped, and the wolf smashed against the wall and fell, unconscious. "Throw me the knife."

She dropped it into the snow before climbing off the roof. Apparently taking no chances, Agarik sliced the beast's throat.

"Ma'am?" He fished in his pouches to reload his weapons.

"Yes?"

"Marines are very fit. We do *not* have bellies."

"My apologies."

"Thank you for your help." He lifted his fur cap and swiped away sweat as he looked back and forth from the roof to the wolf to her. "I wasn't expecting you to, ah, to be able to..."

"You're welcome." Tikaya felt insulted that he was so shocked she had done something useful. She supposed she should appreciate his protectiveness, but she found herself missing Rias and the way he had assumed her competent enough to help. She snorted. Actually, he had assumed her a little too competent, but they had both survived, so she could not fault his decisions. "Are wolves always that difficult to kill?" was all she said.

"No."

"I suspected not."

"Let's see what they were after." Agarik led the way inside.

This time, no creatures attacked when they opened the door. The second wolf lay dead where Agarik had shot it. The drab green paint covering the wood walls and the gray tiles lining the floor could not camouflage the dark blood spatters staining the hallway.

They passed doors, some closed, some open to utilitarian offices. Each contained identical military-issue desks, chairs, and bookcases. Some offices appeared untouched, as if the men had simply stepped away to make a cup of tea. In others, toppled chairs and scattered papers suggested struggles had taken place.

Agarik stepped into a messy room to investigate, and Tikaya chose a tidy one across the hall. She peeked in cabinets and drawers, not sure what she sought. The cause of this madness, but what would that look like?

She paused before returning to the hallway. She tugged her glove off and ran a finger along a bookcase by the door.

"No dust," she murmured.

That and the mostly cleared walkways outside implied things had been normal within the last week or two.

Tikaya returned to the hallway, passed an office where Agarik poked and clanked, and stopped before a closed door. Wood shavings dusting the floor drew her eye. Above them, claw marks ravaged the door and jamb.

Dread settled in the pit of Tikaya's stomach. "Agarik? I think we want to check this one."

Maybe it was cowardly, but she stepped aside when he walked out, gesturing for him to turn the knob. He took in the claw marks with a grim set to his jaw, then handed her the rifle.

"Uhm?" she asked, startled.

"Just in case," Agarik said. "It's loaded. Just point and pull the trigger if you have to."

"I've never shot a—"

"If you can make a bull's-eye with a bow and an icicle, you can shoot a firearm." He withdrew his pistol, turned the knob, and pushed. The door bumped against something and only opened a couple inches. Pistol leading, he leaned against the door, shoving to open it further. Furniture inside scraped, and something tipped over with a crack. He peered inside. "Cursed ancestors." He glanced over his shoulder. "Too gruesome for a woman. Wait here."

He disappeared into the dim room, and she waffled, torn between wanting to know what was inside and not wanting to see it. Considering they had tramped past human skeletons and a frozen dead man together, she did not want to know what qualified as too gruesome.

A few bumps drew her curiosity, and she decided to force aside her squeamishness and go in. Before she could, Agarik opened the door again.

"Sorry, ma'am, but I need you to look at something."

"It's fine."

Agarik lifted a hand first. "I want you to know... I know it won't help anything and won't make up for..." His gaze slipped off her eyes and settled on the wall past her shoulder. "I'm sorry I was the one to find you and let them know where to get you." The words came out in a blurted jumble, as if he had been trying to work up the gumption to voice them for some time. "This isn't your battle. It never was, and I hope...I hope you're able to live through it and get home. Somehow."

"Thank you, but don't feel guilty on my behalf, please." Tikaya rested the rifle butt on the floor and touched his arm. "If it hadn't been you, I'm sure it would have been someone else. I knew when I helped my people decrypt those messages that there might be consequences someday. Nothing remotely like this entered my thoughts, but..." She steeled herself. "Show me your something."

Agarik led her into an office with a broken barricade of chairs, bookcases, cabinets, and a desk cramping the area near the door. At first, she did not see the bodies, but they were there, in the middle, around an odd black object, that appeared half box, half table with an utterly foreign set of symbols glowing red in the air above it. A pipe rose from one side, and six slender legs attached the construct to the floor. The dead were strewn about it. Blood stained everything, even the ceiling. For the first time since they arrived, she was thankful for the freezing temperatures. In her climate, the decomposition, the *smell*, would have been overpowering.

Following Agarik, Tikaya shuffled through the clutter. He obviously wanted her to examine the box, but she could not get there without stepping over bodies. Cuts and punctures desecrated them, far more than would have been needed to kill. A dagger protruded from one man's burst eyeball. The whole macabre scene seemed too messy for the neat and efficient marines.

"I didn't touch it," Agarik said as she came even with the object. "I don't have any idea what it is."

Symbols formed neat rows on one side of the black box, and giddiness replaced the nausea in her stomach. They were familiar in style, probably from the same language as the glyphs on the rubbings, but arranged individually instead of in groupings. Each symbol marked an indention. In the center of the box top, a red light smaller than her pinkie nail glowed, projecting a set of symbols above.

Tikaya eased around for a better look, but her boot bumped a wood stick. Not a stick, the shaft of a shovel. It and a pickaxe lay on the floor near smashed tiles. The subfloor was torn up, with exposed dirt beneath. With a jolt, she realized the contraption's 'legs' stuck through the floor and into the earth.

"How the..."

"Looks like these men were trying to dig it out," Agarik said. "Probably wanted to get rid of it."

"Yes, but how would its legs have plunged through the floor and anchored down there to start with?"

His parka rustled as he removed his cap and rubbed a hand through his short hair. "I don't know. Magic?"

Tikaya turned her attention to the symbols again. She poked one, indenting it; it glowed red and a larger version appeared in the air with a ball spinning around it. The originally displayed image disappeared in favor of the new one. "Er." She had best be careful; this had probably all started with some idiot pressing buttons.

She glanced at Agarik, afraid he would chastise her for touching things, but he nodded encouragingly. Dear Akahe, he thought she could figure it out and fix things.

Underneath the box, she found a couple groupings of the more traditional symbols engraved in the cool black surface. She recognized a few from the rubbings. So, this might be writing. Directions? For operating the device?

In the air above, the symbol she had pressed faded and the original diagram returned. She poked the button again, then stabbed a couple others. They all appeared in the air. Something reminiscent of an equals sign formed between two while others dangled individually. Waiting. When she did not touch anything for a moment, the symbols faded, replaced again by the original.

"Numbers?" Tikaya wondered, though some two hundred symbols were there. She knew of one ancient language that had used a base forty math system instead of the nearly ubiquitous base ten most of the modern world preferred, but nobody had two hundred different numbers. "Numbers and mathematical symbols?"

"Eh?" Agarik asked.

"If that's what these are, then maybe operating the device involves punching in different combinations to create... I don't know. Equations for something?" Tikaya rubbed her jaw. "But how would that relate to whatever this device is doing to negatively affect the town? I don't know. Maybe I'm all wrong here. What do you think?"

"Uhm." Agarik's eyes were so blank he appeared hypnotized.

"Agarik, I don't mean to insult you, but can you see if Rias is here yet and bring him?"

Relief flashed across his face, but he hesitated. "I shouldn't leave you alone."

"I've got your rifle. I'll be fine."

"My orders are—"

"I know, Agarik, but I need to stay here, and figure this out, and if it's math-related, Rias could help. Please find him."

After another long hesitation, he sighed. "Yes, ma'am."

Though she had told him to go, she felt uneasy once she was alone. At least her irritability had disappeared. Agarik's had, too, she realized. Despite his lack of understanding, he had been calm and patient while she mulled over the strange artifact. Maybe the device was the thing responsible for people acting oddly, and maybe, in her random symbol touching, she had cut off whatever it was doing or emitting. She snorted self-deprecatingly. If it had been that simple the dead men on the floor would have figured it out before the end. Besides, thinking back, she had felt that return to normalcy before she started touching things, perhaps even out in the hallway.

She stretched and walked to the window, intending to open it and let some air in. Maybe she should have asked Agarik to drag the bodies out before leaving. Someone had nailed a couple boards across the window. So much for fresh air. Maybe she could still open it a bit.

A scream echoed from the building next door. Tikaya froze, her hand on the window lock. She drew back. Maybe she would leave it shut after all.

She dug a chalkboard out from behind a toppled filing cabinet. It was hard not to look at the bodies, but she could not remove the device to study elsewhere. The men had apparently tried to do that and failed.

Tikaya copied the writing from the bottom of the device and circled spots where the lone symbols on the side of the box appeared in the groupings. If they were numbers... No, she better not assume that yet. Just because something reminded her of an equals sign in her language did not mean anything.

Time bled past, the chalk clacking on the board the only sound in the building. Infrequently, gunshots in the distance interrupted. She found herself squinting at the chalkboard and realized twilight had come. The glowing symbols gave off some light, and she worried it would be visible through the windows.

A crunch sounded in the snow outside. She halted her work, chalk poised in the air. More crunches. Footsteps on her side of the building.

Tikaya eased past the bodies and grabbed Agarik's rifle. She wished he had left powder and balls too. One shot was all she had if someone attacked her, one shot with a weapon she had never used before.

She cracked the door. Deep shadows lurked in the hall, and she barely made out the dead wolf. At one end, the door thumped and banged in the breeze.

Shots fired beyond that door, and she jumped. "Stop—what—" someone cried. Then screams of pain and aggressive yells followed. A lot of them. Her mind conjured the imagine of a wolf pack chasing after its wounded prey. Not Agarik, she prayed.

"Where's the woman?" someone yelled.

Tikaya swallowed and closed the door. The voices still penetrated the walls.

"Find the woman!"

Someone cackled, and graphic descriptions of what could be done with 'the woman' followed.

Tikaya forced herself to return to the device. The same set of symbols glowed crimson in the air, taunting her.

There was an answer here; she just had to figure it out before time ran out.

CHAPTER 9

A boom rattled windows, shook the earth, and knocked Tikaya's chalkboard on the floor. Rias's group must have arrived, though she could not imagine him flinging blasting sticks wantonly.

Chalk still in hand, she ran to the window to peer between the sloppily nailed boards and through the frosted panes. Darkness had fallen, but flames burned in a building down the hill. Two figures with rifles ran through the light before turning down an alley.

She shivered, wishing for warmth in the office. The already frigid temperature had dropped noticeably after the sun had set.

Footsteps sounded at the end of the hallway.

Tikaya lunged for the rifle, but caught her heel on the downed chalkboard and skidded to her backside with a noisy thud. Great. If they hadn't known where she was before, they knew now.

She scrambled to her feet and grabbed the rifle. She hopped over the bodies and slid into the shadows thickening the corner across from the door.

Finger on the trigger, butt pressed into her shoulder, cheek against the stock, Tikaya waited. In the stillness, she could feel her heart pounding in her ears. The footsteps thudded closer, the steady pace of someone jogging.

The door bumped against the furniture barricade, eliciting a surprised grunt that sounded familiar.

"Rias?" Tikaya hazarded before she could think better. What if he was as crazy as everyone else out there seemed to be?

"Tikaya!"

Rias burst into the room, bringing lantern light with him. He did not seem to notice the artifact or bodies; he searched until he spotted her in the corner, started forward, but stopped, gaze dropping to her weapon. He was missing his cap, his hair stuck up in places, and blood trickled from a gash on his temple. A cutlass was strapped across his back, two bulges in his parka suggested pistols, and he carried a rifle as well as the lantern.

"Are you...you?" Tikaya asked.

"I'm not murdering people and trying to kick the ore out of everyone's cart if that's what you're asking. Just a little—" Rias cocked his head, almost like a dog listening. "Actually, it's strange but I feel normal in here."

Tikaya lowered her rifle. "Yes, I think the device creates some kind of normalcy field around it, probably so the operator isn't affected by whatever it's emitting that's causing everyone to be on edge."

"On edge, that's an understatement."

Rias closed the door and hopped over the upturned furniture. Tikaya joined him in the middle, intending to show him the device, but he dropped his rifle on a desk and wrapped her in a hug. Surprised, she found herself crushed against his chest. There was a desperate fierceness to the grip, but she managed to get one arm around to his back to return the embrace.

"I'm relieved you're not hurt or..." Emotion thickened his voice.

"I'm guessing you've had a worse afternoon than me," she said, relaxing against him. The fear that had tensed her shoulders since Agarik left disappeared, and she felt warm for the first time in hours.

Rias released her and stepped back. "Sorry, I just... I wasn't sure if you..." He cleared his throat. "It's dangerous out there. Half the people are mildly affected by whatever's in the air, and the other half are crazier than the bloodthirsty maniacs I left on Krychek." His gaze skimmed the bodies in the room, and he frowned thoughtfully as he took in the furniture barricade and the half-boarded windows.

"I'm glad you were able to get to me," Tikaya said. "I need your help. Maybe Agarik can stand guard while—wait, where *is* Agarik?"

"I don't know."

"I asked him to go find you."

Rias spread his arms, palms up. "I haven't seen him. When I realized what was going on, I worried that one of these lunatics would shoot you, so I escaped at the first opportunity. I've been hunting around, dodging packs of the more aggressive people, and just now found you."

Despite the situation, she smiled. Escaped at the first opportunity. By what creative means had he eluded his shackles this time? She almost felt sorry for Captain Bocrest.

"I hope he'll be able to stay safe." Tikaya tapped the box and nodded at the collection of symbols hovering in the air. "I need your help. I think this device is responsible for what's happening out there."

Rias walked around it, shaking his head and massaging the back of his neck before he even saw the side with the runes and indentations.

"If you press those, the representations appear in the air." She demonstrated as she explained.

"Oh, Tikaya," he murmured. "I'm sorry, but you've got the wrong person. We Turgonians may be good engineers, but students go to different nations if they want to seriously study alchemy."

Her breath caught. "Alchemy?"

He stabbed one of the indentions and a symbol flared to life. "That's iron, isn't it?" Another stab. "And copper." He shrugged apologetically. "I only remember the ones that we use in alloys. Since the Turgonians deny magic exists, we won't publish anything in our textbooks that was only discovered through the use of magic. Aren't your people the ones who first talked about atoms and electrons and such? We don't have a microscope that can see anything that fine. We've only got fifty things on our table of elements."

Scarcely breathing, Tikaya dropped an incredulous stare to the symbols. Was he right? Were they looking at the alchemical table of elements? If so, then this could be her Tekdar Tablet. She had to be sure before she based translations on it. "There are almost two hundred symbols. Are you certain? Our table has seventy-five, I think, and it's the most complete of any in the world."

"But your people are still finding new ones, right?" Rias ticked his fingernail on the top of the device. "You'll believe me when you see the tunnels, but for now just trust me when I say these people were more advanced than us."

"More advanced?"

He had hinted of that in his tale of the tunnels, but she had not truly thought it possible. Though, advanced technology might explain how this device had dug its legs into the earth, piercing tile, wood, and permafrost to do so. She clasped her hand over her mouth and stared at the runes. There was no existing evidence that a people more advanced than modern man had ever lived. This was rewrite-the-history-books kind of stuff. Incredible. If it was true.

"I just want to be certain. I don't see what you're seeing to make these identifications. Nor does the layout of the symbols look like the table I'm familiar with, but I've only had a cursory introduction to alchemy. It wasn't anything I thought I'd come across studying ancient languages." She realized she was making excuses and decided to still her lips before it grew more obvious. Rias had thought so highly of her intelligence; she hated to give him reason to think less of her.

"I've spent my life looking for patterns and trying to find the predictable in situations others see as unpredictable. If this odd skill can be of use to you now, I'm delighted." Rias slid next to her in front of the interface and poked one of the simplest runes and brought it to life before their eyes. "The atomic structure is incorporated into the symbol itself."

"Oh!" As soon as he said it, she saw it. "Hydrogen." She slapped herself on the forehead. "I thought these might be numbers. It never occurred to me that an ancient people might have this kind of scientific knowledge, with specialized symbols for..."

Rias tapped hydrogen again and another rune. The symbols appeared in the air. "How do you—" he started, but bonds formed on their own.

"Water." Tikaya grinned. The symbols were not nearly as simple as the diagrams her people used to represent the various elements—indeed, these reminded her of the bizarre perception puzzles a professor had distributed during a lesson on optics—but if one knew what to look for, the structures were there.

The water molecule flashed twice, then disappeared to be replaced by the far more complex image she had been seeing all afternoon.

"I guess that isn't the answer." Rias gave her a sad smile. "I'm afraid that's about the extent of my knowledge in this area. I haven't an idea what that could be." He swiped his finger through the dozens of linked symbols hovering in the air. The image did not waver. "Something we haven't invented yet, probably. I can look through the shelves in the offices. It's a long shot, but there might be a book that has our mediocre table of elements in it. Maybe that'll help you with translating. Sorry I don't have the answer."

"Sorry!" Tikaya grabbed his arms. "You have no idea how much this helps. I mean, this could be the key to translating this whole language. You're amazing!" She kissed him on the cheek, then danced back to her chalkboards. Now that he had pointed out the structures so cunningly crafted into the symbols, she could pick out ten or twelve she remembered from school. That was enough to get her started. Although...

"Actually, yes, I could use a book with your table in it." She turned back and was about to ask him to look, but he was staring at her, his fingers touching the cheek she had kissed.

"Yes, of course." He lowered his hand.

She bit her lip, tickled at his reaction. "Do you not get praised often?"

"It's been a while," he admitted. "And before Krychek, uhm, more often by men than women."

"Not even your wife?"

He snorted. "Especially not by her."

They shared a chuckle, and she admitted herself curious about the woman, though it should not matter. Rias's past relationships were none of her business, and they had more important things to worry about. Besides, he had left her anyway. Tikaya blinked. Or had he? Maybe she was something, like his land and his name, that the empire had taken from him as punishment. Still, he did not sound disappointed.

"Horrible woman?" she asked, fishing.

"No, but we weren't a good match from the start. It never would have lasted as long as it did if I hadn't been away at sea so much of the time. She had my home, my money, and the freedom to spend time wherever—" he winced, "—with whomever, she pleased."

Tikaya grimaced in sympathy. Like her, Parkonis had not been perfect, but he had always been faithful. "How'd you end up together to start with?"

"I was twenty, she was pretty, and our parents thought it would be a good idea." Rias laughed ruefully. "But mostly I was twenty and she was pretty." He waved away further discussion. "I'll get that book."

"Be careful."

He waved an acknowledgment on his way out, and Tikaya shifted uneasily, as worried for him as for herself. Agarik had walked out, and she had not seen him since. Rias was only going to search this building, she told herself, and settled into work.

A few moments later, Tikaya had three chalkboards lined up, all full. She listed the translations for the atoms she recognized. Also, she listed runes she remembered from the rubbings, those displaying what she now recognized as molecular structures. The elements came up surprisingly often in what she had assumed was normal writing. Perhaps the subject was always science. Or maybe these people—this race?—had a language specifically for scientific matters. The Herdoctans had a different written language for religion, so why not?

A hand touched her shoulder, and she jumped, dropping her chalk.

"Sorry." Rias held a book with his finger marking a page.

"No, don't apologize. My fault for not paying attention." Tikaya picked up the chalk and accepted the book. She glanced at the cover. "*Torture and Interrogation Methods Technical Manual?*"

Rias cleared his throat. "Yes, ah, just stick to the chapter on chemical applications."

"Oh, I will. I don't want to chance upon any Turgonian brutality secrets." Or pictures more gruesome than the bodies on the floor.

He surveyed the chalkboards with bemusement and scraped at dried blood on the corner of one. "You know, some women wouldn't be willing to work in a room full of corpses."

She had already started writing and almost missed the comment. "What?"

Rias chuckled. "Nothing. Continue your work. I'll stand guard."

* * * * *

Tikaya straightened, wincing at the ache in her lower back. She stretched her arms toward the ceiling and shook out a cramp in her hand. Midnight had to be near, maybe past. Her stomach growled. Fatigue numbed her brain, and her mouth battled unsuccessfully against yawns. Even if the lighting had been better, her notes and the symbols on the device would have blurred and swam before her bleary eyes.

Rias stood guard by the door, checking the hallway from time to time, but mostly staying silent and letting her work.

A scream raced down the street below the hill. What if she translated the writing too late? After the entire team killed each other? She eyed the bodies in the corner. Rias had dragged them out of the way, muttering something about funeral pyres in the morning, but she worried about getting to morning. If enough people attacked at once, she and Rias could end up like that before dawn.

No, she decided, watching him standing with his ear cocked. Despite the hour, he was alert, rifle across his arms, hand on the stock, finger near the trigger. Not tense but relaxed and ready. She imagined he could fight off superior odds for a long time, but he would not want to do so. He'd be shooting his own people, the very men they were supposed to help later on.

Rias saw her watching him and lifted his eyebrows.

Tikaya felt silly to have been caught gazing at him. "I was wondering if you could get my mind off this for a moment."

Rias joined her. He set the rifle butt on the floor and rested his forearms across the muzzle. He surveyed her, and she felt a self-conscious twinge. No doubt she had strands of hair sticking out in all directions and dark smudges assailing her eyes. And her baggy Turgonian uniform and parka did not flatter her form under any circumstances.

"A question." Rias's gaze rested on a chalkboard, though he did not seem to focus on anything. "If someone from Kyatt were to decide to marry a Turgonian, would they be allowed to live on your island?"

Tikaya was not sure what she had expected him to ask, but that was not it. "That wasn't a marriage proposal, was it?"

He coughed. "No, no, just hypothetical. If it were a proposal..." He offered his half smile. "There'd be soft music, excellent food, romantic ambiance..." He tilted his head toward the corner. "Fewer corpses."

"Ah, I wasn't sure how they did it in the empire. Given your people's reputation, I thought bloodshed and mangled bodies might be standard at social gatherings."

"Bloodshed perhaps."

Rias watched her, waiting for an answer to his question, she realized.

"The Kyatt Islands are major trade ports and learning centers, and we have numerous foreigners living there, either temporarily or permanently," Tikaya said. "I can think of numerous Turgonians who studied at the Polytechnic over the years. And there have been cases of foreigners marrying natives and staying on the islands."

"Turgonian foreigners?"

"Well, you would have been more welcome *before* your people tried to take over the islands." She smiled, but no humor lightened his expression. "The president might ask you to leave if he found out you were among those sinking our ships and slinging cannon balls at our harbor, but if you said you didn't take part in the war, I'm sure you'd be allowed to stay."

"So." Rias laid the rifle across his shoulders and draped his forearms over the ends, reminiscent of a man in a pillory. "Refuge, if one was willing to lie for the rest of one's life."

"Or just dodge questions about one's name and one's past. You're good at that."

She had not meant the statement to sound accusatory, but he flinched.

"Listen," Tikaya said, "I don't mean to insult you, but whatever you did, or whoever you are to those marines, you're probably less important than you think to the rest of the world. Chances are my people have never heard of you."

"Oh?" Leave it to the Turgonians: he looked faintly offended.

"You could tell *me* your name—" Tikaya wriggled her eyebrows suggestively, "—and then I could let you know whether or not you'd be welcome on my island."

She thought he might remind her that his original question had been hypothetical and that he was not asking about his own future, just some imaginary person's. He did not. He took a deep breath. "You're right. I don't know if we're going to survive the next couple weeks and, even if we do, I'm guessing Bocrest has orders to make me disappear afterward, but either way it's not honorable of me to keep truths from you. I—"

Glass shattered.

Tikaya whirled, grabbing the heavy book as if she could use it as a shield. A shadow moved at the window. Something long and small slid between the boards and rolled onto the floor. Flame spit and hissed on the end of a string. Not a string, a fuse.

Rias yanked her off her feet. The furniture blurred past as Rias leaped over it, arm clenched around her waist. He landed in the dark hallway, and shadows swallowed them.

He sprinted but only made it three steps before the explosion tore away the darkness. A great boom roared, and a concussion pounded Tikaya's back, ripping her away from Rias.

The wall filled her vision. She tried to bring her arms up to protect her head, but she crashed first. Something popped in her shoulder and agony seared her body. The book dropped from her hands. She landed on the floor, which sent a second jolt of pain rocking through her. She gasped, trying to stifle cries, not sure who might be nearby.

A door at the end of the hall opened, and lights swam in the darkness. Tears blurred Tikaya's vision. She gritted her teeth and blinked them away. Half a dozen men raced into the hall, lanterns swinging, swords and pistols waving.

The door at the opposite end flung open. They were surrounded.

Tikaya staggered to her feet. Her shoulder flamed with pain. She gasped and braced herself against the wall. Next to her, a shot cracked with a flash of orange flaring from Rias's rifle.

"There she is!" someone shouted, voice ragged and rough, almost inhuman. "Give us the woman!"

"This way," Rias whispered.

She grabbed the book and ran into a room after him. A return shot echoed through the hall behind them.

"Don't shoot us, you idgeets!" came a cry from the opposite end.

Rias shut the door. A hint of starlight came through the window, but darkness reigned inside.

"They sound drunk," Tikaya said, words broken as she gritted her teeth through the pain.

"Where are you hurt?" Rias snapped the lock, and furniture scraped as he shoved something in front of the door.

An image of the dead men in the other office invaded Tikaya's mind. They had been trapped in a room, and this was exactly what they had done. It had not worked.

"Dislocated shoulder," she said.

"Let me see—feel—it."

"Don't worry...about me. I'll—"

But he was already sliding her parka off. She clenched her teeth, trying not to whimper.

Footsteps thundered down the hall, and light slipped under the crack in the door.

"Which room?" someone barked.

Rias unbuttoned her uniform jacket and probed her shoulder. "Bite down," he whispered, putting something wooden in her mouth. Knife handle, she guessed. It was smooth and hard. He gripped her arm and shoulder, then jerked with one powerful motion.

Agony erupted. Tikaya clenched her teeth on the handle, panting to keep from crying out. Blackness encroached on her vision, and her legs gave way. Rias caught her and held her gently.

"You hear something?" someone asked.

"That room."

"No, that one!"

"It's whichever one's locked, you halfwits."

"Sorry," Rias whispered, cupping the back of her head. He leaned his forehead against hers, and even in the darkness she sensed his distress over hurting her.

"Not your fault," she said.

Someone rattled the doorknob.

Tikaya found the strength to stand again. Already the pain was fading to a manageable ache.

"I'm ready," she whispered.

"Strong lady." Rias squeezed her good arm before pressing a pistol into her hand. "Back corner. Find something to crouch behind, but stay where you can aim at the door. If they get past me, shoot them. Here, take this too." He loaded her up with the second pistol, a powder flask, and an ammo pouch.

"Shoot to kill?"

He hesitated. "Do what you have to do to stay alive."

She nodded, then, realizing he would not see it, added, "I understand."

Someone pounded on their door. "They're in here!"

Tikaya set the book on a chair and slid behind a cabinet where she could see the window and the entrance. She gripped the pistol. At least the wall had been considerate enough to mangle her left shoulder instead of her right. "Maybe we'll get lucky, the blasting stick will have destroyed the device, and everyone will return to normal any second."

"Maybe." Rias's tone made the possibility sound unlikely, and Tikaya wondered if he had seen explosives used on the strange technology before.

More pounding—louder pounding—hammered the wood, and something snapped. A crack of light appeared, but the desk kept the door from opening wide. Rias waited in the wall's shadows.

She glanced toward the window, wondering if they could escape that way. Lantern light danced past—men were out there, too, perhaps counting rooms to figure out which office she and Rias occupied.

The door opened wider, and the slash of light broadened, illuminating the corner of the desk and a coatrack.

A rifle barrel slid through the gap.

Tikaya tensed, expecting Rias to shoot first. Despite the chill, sweat dampened her hands.

The rifle slid in farther, and Rias burst into motion. He grabbed the barrel, yanked it into the room, and slashed upward with his cutlass. The attacker yelped in surprise and pain, releasing the weapon. Rias planted a foot, thrust the other man back, and slammed the door shut.

"One man disarmed, seven to go." He shoved the desk against the frame again.

Muffled voices came through the door—the sound of people plotting. The next attack would not be so easy to thwart.

"There are men milling around outside too," Tikaya said.

"You think I don't know that?" Rias snapped.

She stared at him, startled. He had never so much as looked crossly at her. Then she remembered: "I guess the protection from whatever the artifact is putting out was limited to that room."

After a silent beat, Rias said, "You're right. I'm sorry. I wasn't thinking. It's like before; something's making it hard to keep my equanimity."

"Your breakdown is a lot less disturbing than that of most of your countrymen."

He grunted.

"I feel it too," Tikaya said. "It's nothing you can see, nothing you smell or feel. Maybe I've been going about this the wrong way. Like a, well, like a philologist. But maybe I don't need to translate the writing on the bottom in order to cut the device off. If we can guess what its purpose is, maybe we can switch it to another purpose, something less troublesome. It has all those options you can put in—doesn't that imply you ought to be able to get more than one thing out?"

"What could it be putting out that would affect us mentally? It's nothing we've seen or heard or smelled."

"An odorless gas?" Tikaya guessed.

"Ah, being disseminated through that pipe, perhaps?"

"It'd have to be something invisible but heavy enough to float down and blanket the town. Something designed to irritate people, to outright anger them, even make—"

A shot fired.

Tikaya jerked her head up in time to see Rias slam the door shut again. The scent of black powder tainted the air.

"Only two in the hallway now," Rias said. "They've either lost interest or they're going to try another way in."

"We have to get back to the device," Tikaya said. "If we punch in another gas, maybe it'll change the output. Something innocuous that won't hurt anyone."

Thumps continued at the door, probably more for the purpose of distracting Tikaya and Rias than getting in. The lanterns previously visible through the window had disappeared, which made her think the marines had stopped planning and were now engaged in that plan. She shifted her stance, readying herself to fire toward the window if necessary. The last thing she wanted was to dodge another blasting stick.

"Innocuous gases," Rias said. "Oxygen? Hydrogen?"

"We tried those, albeit on accident. And you pressed in water, which should be deliverable as a vapor. Except the device didn't like any of those." Tikaya groaned. "Maybe my guess is completely wrong."

"Or maybe the machine is only designed to create synthetic or organic compounds," Rias said. "Though I don't know any molecular structures that might qualify. Do you?"

"No, but maybe there's something in your book." She tapped it with the pistol butt.

"There aren't many innocuous somethings in that book."

"I know it's a long shot, but—wait, no. When your people captured me, they knocked me out with something sweet-smelling in a rag. When I breathed in, I passed out. Do you know what that was? Would it be in there?"

Rias shifted away from the door. "Chloroform. Yes."

The thuds stopped.

"Let's try it." Tikaya had a feeling it would be better to find a light and check the book in a different room. "Can we get down the hall?"

Rias cracked the door. A rifle fired, and the ball smashed into the frame, hurling wood splinters. He closed the door.

"Not at this time."

Tikaya snorted. She pressed her nose to the icy glass window panes. At the edge of her view, shadows and lanterns moved.

"Not this way either," she said. "Unless we can—oh!"

"What?"

"Maybe nothing, but Agarik and I had to shove our way into the room with the artifact. The window was boarded, the door barricaded, so whoever killed all those men must have come in through—"

"Attic," Rias said. "There must be space to move around up there. Watch the door." He hopped onto the desk and thumped the ceiling. Wood scraped against wood. "Here."

Outside, the lanterns headed toward their window.

"I need help up." Annoyed to be a burden, Tikaya stuffed the pistol in her pants and joined him, book clutched against her chest. "I don't think I can lift my arm over—"

Still standing on the desk, Rias caught her by the waist and lifted her over his head as if she weighed nothing. Blackness waited above, though an icy draft touched her cheek. That meant a way out. She hoped.

"Hurry," Rias said, giving her a final boost.

Tikaya scrambled into the dark attic. Even with his help, she came down on her shoulder and had to stifle a curse. When she tried to stand, she bumped her head on a beam.

Below, glass shattered.

"Rias?" She started to lean over to check on him.

He jumped through and a thud sounded—his head hitting the ceiling—but he did not pause to acknowledge it.

"Go, go!" he barked, pushing her ahead of him.

Half running, half bear-crawling, Tikaya maneuvered past beams and supports.

Light flashed and an explosion rippled through the floorboards beneath her. The force sent her crashing into Rias, and they went down in a tumble.

"Ooph," he grunted, voice sounding odd.

Then her mind caught up to the situation. Rias had been behind her, not in front of her.

Tikaya tried to jump back, but the man grabbed her. She dropped the book. His grip kept her from reaching for the pistol. He unshuttered a lantern, illuminating beams, trusses, and his snarling face. One of the marines.

"Got her!" he yelled.

Rias charged past Tikaya and tackled the man. The lantern flew free. In a lucky lunge, she caught it before it hit the floor and went out. Though her shoulder protested, she held it with her left hand and yanked the pistol free with her right.

Rias needed no help though. He knelt over the marine, arms locked around his neck. The man's face turned purple, and he passed out.

A shadow moved behind Rias.

Tikaya reacted. She fired the pistol without thinking, and the ball hammered into someone's chest. Rias spun to look.

Only after the man collapsed did her brain scream that these people were her captors and aiming to kill one might get her into a mess of trouble.

"It's Lieutenant Commander Okars." Rias checked the officer's pulse. "It *was* Lieutenant Commander Okars."

"Oh, no," Tikaya breathed.

Rias picked up a knife. "Yes, but he was going for my back, so I must thank you for my life."

Tikaya closed her eyes for a moment. "Let's just get that horrible device cut off."

By the lantern's light, they found the source of the draft. The first explosion had left a ragged hole in the ceiling of the room with the artifact.

"Walk softly," Rias said as they neared it. "The structural integrity has doubtlessly been compromised."

"Thank you for that brilliant engineering assessment. Maybe when I fall through the floor, I can take out my other shoulder." Her grumbling made her wince and long for the sphere of protection around the artifact.

It would be easier to problem solve if she did not feel so cranky. She hoped. It could be worse; she could have become an unthinking aggressive lout who thought it was a good idea to throw blasting sticks at innocent—

Her boot went through the floor, and she pitched sideways. When her body struck, the footing deteriorating further. Rias grabbed her and tried to pull her free, but the floor had enough of them: it dropped away completely.

She smashed to the level below and landed on something cloth covered. Not cloth, she realized as she looked under her. Clothing. Clothing on dead bodies.

She lurched away, igniting pain in her shoulder. Rigid fingers tangled in her braid, and she pulled, trying to free herself without using her injured arm or touching the corpse again. A disheartened cry escaped her lips when the dead man's hand lifted with her, fingers fully snagged in her hair. Tormenting ancestors, this was too morbid, and too damned much. Why couldn't the idiotic Turgonians run a decent Polytechnic so they'd have their own philologists to kidnap for secret missions?

"Sorry," Rias murmured, crouching beside her. "As soon as we get this taken care of, we'll find the sawbones to check your shoulder."

"The problem is less the shoulder—though that is irritating me every three or four seconds too—and more the bodies. And the being attacked. And the part where I'm shooting people to death, and—" She brought her fist to her mouth and squinted her eyes shut, struggling to keep from breaking into sobs. Slow breaths, she told herself. This was not the time for wheezing and gasping and flirting with an emotional breakdown. React later. "I'm all right. I'm just... I'm better in a classroom, I swear."

Rias wrapped his arm around her back, and she leaned on him.

"I suppose you'll think I'm odd—odder—if I admit this is the most exciting my days have been in ages," he said.

She rubbed her eyes. "I'll forgive you for being a crazy odd Turgonian who probably has had a horrible life for the last couple of years, if you'll kindly disentangle that dead man's fingers from my hair."

"Oh." Rias released her to undertake the task, then stood. "We're back in the artifact room, but they'll figure it out soon. That new window doesn't hide much."

The blasting stick had blackened the floor, turned furniture to shrapnel, and torn holes not only in the ceiling and a side wall but in the building's exterior as well. In the center of the room, the device remained, unharmed, symbols still glowing.

Tikaya picked up the book, set her jaw, and strode over to it. There was not much time. Shouts on the other side of the building promised the men were still looking for her.

She flipped through the chapter on chemicals. "There."

"Find something?" Rias stood nearby, weapons loaded and ready.

Reluctant to speak too soon, Tikaya pressed the appropriate runes. The regular image blanked out to be replaced by the new symbols. They hovered until she finished. Then, by some alien consciousness, the artifact understood what she wanted, and it arranged them in a way eerily similar to the layout in the book. Even though it was what she hoped for, it sent a shiver down her spine.

A soft click sounded in the core of the device.

Tikaya arched her eyebrows at Rias who gave her an encouraging hand gesture. She gripped the edge of the device and waited. Nobody stirred nearby. She tried to decide if the distant shouts were diminishing. Minutes passed, and a deathly quiet fell over the town.

Rias walked to the door. He cocked his head, listening.

"What is it?" she asked.

Rias lifted a finger, cracked the door, and peered into the hallway. He leaned back in with a smile, and Tikaya heard the noise now too.

"Snoring?" she asked.

"The two men out there are sleeping, and the air has that sweet smell of chloroform."

Tikaya exhaled slowly. "Good. That should mean we're safe from being shot or knife-stabbed for the moment. Of course, now we have a lesser problem."

"How to wake everyone up, leave town, or even leave this room without succumbing to unconsciousness ourselves?"

"That's the one."

She dropped to her back on the floor to gaze up at the writing beneath the machine. Before, she had been trying to translate it. Now, she just thought about cutting the artifact off. Only one of the groupings did not have alchemical elements in it. The first one. Nothing so obvious as a switch stood out anywhere on the machine, so she poked and prodded that grouping. They sat flush and she did not expect them to move, so she nearly cracked her head on the bottom of the box when they did. By pushing and twisting, she could rotate them.

"What'd you do?" Rias asked. "The symbols are flashing."

She could rotate them further, but she paused and peered up at him. "You sure you want those people awake again?"

He smiled gently. "I'll possibly regret it later, but yes. We'll need help to tackle the tunnels."

"Or you and I could devise some kind of masks, gather as many supplies as we need, take a couple of those dog sleds down the coast until we reach a port, and then sail somewhere far away, leaving the empire to deal with its own problems."

Rias sighed and gazed into the night. "I cannot."

"Even though these people left you to die? Even though they probably got themselves into this situation?"

"Even though," he said. "But..." He took a breath and, with palpable reluctance, said, "If you want to go, I'll keep them busy long enough for you to do so. It's about three hundred miles south to Tangukmoo. If you grabbed a dog team and supplies, I'm sure you could make it in a couple of weeks. It's technically an imperial town, but it's eighty percent natives, and I suspect they'd hide you just to irk us. After the thaw, trade vessels come in to barter for whale oil and bone. With your skills, I'm sure you could bargain for passage and find a way home."

"Sounds like a lonely journey without any company," Tikaya said.

"Probably."

Encrypted

"Last week, you told me your people really needed my help. What's changed?"

He looked back and forth from her to the dead bodies. "This is only the beginning, Tikaya. It's going to get worse. I suspect this is also the only opportunity you'll have to leave."

That Rias offered meant a lot, but the journey he described would not be a speedy one. It was likely Bocrest would make it back to civilization first and send the order to have her family assassinated long before she reached home.

She rotated the grouping of runes as far as they would go. The crimson symbols in the air winked out. "When I'm complaining later about how horrible it is out here with your marines, remind me I had my chance and was an idiot who gave it up."

The glum expression on his face waned, and one side of his mouth curved up. He pulled her to her feet and wrapped her in a hug, mindful of her injured shoulder. His stubbled jaw brushed her cheek, and a pleasant shiver ran through her.

"Only if you remind me I was an idiot first," he murmured.

"Deal." Tikaya wondered if that talk of marriage had been inspired only by the moment, by the uncertainty that they would live to see dawn, or if it meant something more. She lifted her good hand to brush strands of hair away from the cut on his temple.

Rias drew back slightly, eyes flickering, watching her face. Soft breaths frosted the air between them, and some distant part of her mind announced that this was a ridiculous place and situation for a first kiss, but what if they didn't survive the coming weeks? What if there were no other opportunities to be alone together? What if...

Rias bent his head and kissed her gently, warm lips as welcome as the sun in this frozen wasteland. Forgetting about her injury, she started to wrap her arms around him, to pull him closer. Pain blasted her shoulder, and she gasped at the cruel reminder.

Rias drew back, wincing, eyes guilty. "Sorry, my fault. I'll go find the sawbones."

"No, it's all right. I was just..."

But he had already grabbed his rifle. He hopped through the broken wall with a quick wave before disappearing into the snow.

Tikaya wrapped her arms around herself. She already missed his warmth. And his last words sent a thrum of worry through her. The man who would come to deliver her medical attention was the brother of the man she had just killed.

CHAPTER 10

Something bumped Tikaya's foot, jerking her awake. She sat up and cracked her head on the bottom of the device. Her shoulder offered its own jab of pain as her journal and pencil clattered to the floor.

Bocrest and Bones loomed over her. The captain's presence surprised her. Surely the ship's commander usually stayed with his vessel, but then this was no ordinary inland excursion.

Thuds from the ceiling announced someone walking around in the crawl space. Probably retrieving bodies.

Beleaguered red eyes haunted the sawbones's stubbled face, and an invisible weight slumped his shoulders. He must already know his brother was dead, but he could not know she had fired the fatal shot. She hoped. He carried a black leather bag, and she swallowed, wondering if he truly kept a saw in there.

"Get up, librarian." Bocrest eyed the device. "Bones has a lot of men to tend."

After the battering she had taken, Tikaya expected more pains as she crawled to her feet, but she had not slept long enough for her body to stiffen. Only the shoulder throbbed. Darkness still smothered the snow outside. Given the icy temperature and the hard tile floor, she was surprised she had slept at all. She had painstakingly copied the two hundred alchemical elements into the journal and had been sketching the runes on the bottom of the device when she nodded off.

"Did Agarik make it?" Tikaya asked.

Bocrest prowled around the device, started to touch an indentation, but decided against it. "He got jumped by—it doesn't matter who by now—but he was cut up pretty bad and left to bleed in the snow. Bones stitched him up earlier."

Relief and regret mingled in her mind. If she had not asked Agarik to fetch Rias, he might not have been hurt at all. Would he resent her for it?

"Where's Rias?" she asked.

Bocrest scowled. "Prisoner *Five* is making some concoction in the vehicle house. Said we'll need it in the tunnels. After that, he'll be shackled again."

"Let's see your shoulder," Bones told Tikaya.

She eased her parka off under the cool gazes of the two officers. She was surely too old to want someone to hold her hand while a doctor worked on her, but she wished Rias had come back. Strange that he had disappeared so abruptly. Had he felt guilty about more than her shoulder?

Bones huffed and tossed her parka aside. Apparently impatient with her undressing speed, he unfastened the buttons of the black uniform jacket for her. Uneasy, she wondered how much disrobing she would have to endure for this medical treatment. Fortunately, Bones left her undershirt on. Icy but professional hands probed her shoulder. She tried not to wince.

Bocrest nodded at the device. "You figure out what this stuff says?"

"Some of it," Tikaya said. "I can only guess at the writing on the bottom, but the context gives me clues. If I get more samples, also in context, I'll be able to make some good guesses."

Bocrest's grunt did not sound impressed. Curse him, she and Rias had saved the marines—*again*. Why couldn't the captain acknowledge her usefulness?

Footsteps sounded above, and shards of wood rained from the biggest hole in the roof. Sergeant Ottotark slithered over the edge and dropped down behind Bones.

Tikaya groaned, but he did not look at her.

"Sorry, Bones. Your brother and Private Choyka are dead." Ottotark gripped the man's shoulder.

Bones's jaw clenched, but he did not otherwise react.

"I'll get a team to lower them down for the funeral pyre." Ottotark nodded to the captain and left.

Tikaya relaxed a smidgeon. Bones made a sling from a large square of cloth and secured her arm.

"You'll be fine in a few days," he said. "Sir, I'll attend the others if you don't need anything else here. I'd prefer to keep busy."

"Yes, go," Bocrest said.

Bones left, head down, shoulders slumped further.

"What's the purpose of this device?" Bocrest asked.

Tikaya rubbed her shoulder. "My best guess? Scientific experiments. They probably wanted to observe the somatic and neurological effects certain gases had on their specimens outside of a controlled environment."

"What kind of specimens?" Bocrest asked.

"Look in a mirror."

"Turgonians?"

Tikaya hesitated, almost tempted to play upon his paranoia. She had not yet figured out how she could ensure her family's safety while escaping with her life, but she would probably have more opportunities later if she convinced Bocrest her words were trustworthy now.

"Humans, animals." A cold gust blew snow through the broken wall, and Tikaya grabbed her parka. "I suppose Turgonian enemies could have brought it here and turned it on." She thought of the Nurian captain's orders; the Nurians were smart enough to not want anything to do with the artifacts. "Or your own people might have done it out of stupidity."

Bocrest's gaze grew frosty.

"Stupidity isn't a trait unique to Turgonians," Tikaya said by way of apology.

"Apparently not." Bocrest continued to glare. "Prisoner Five says Lieutenant Commander Okars attacked him, and he was forced to kill my officer in self-defense."

Unease trickled down her spine. Uh oh. Why had Rias said anything? Maybe the marines never would have thought to look for bodies in the attic, and, even if they did, in the craziness anyone could have fired at anyone. Rias could have feigned ignorance and no one would have known. But, no, he had felt guilty—or honor-bound—to explain the dead officer. She could not fault him for being an honest man, but his loyalty to these marines, to the empire, might prove disastrous for her. Or maybe not. He had covered for her, though she was not sure whether to be relieved or not. Surely his position here was as precarious as hers.

"I know who he is," Bocrest said, "who he *was*, and now that he's... himself again, I doubt he'd intentionally kill an imperial marine, nor do I believe he's inept enough to accidentally dispatch someone in self-defense."

"We were all under the influence of that device," Tikaya said. "Rias—"

Bocrest drew his arm back, and she turned her cheek, expecting a blow. He curled his fingers into a fist, but jerked it to his side. A vein at his temple pulsed. "I don't know what he's told you, but you will *not* refer to him as anything other than Prisoner Five. He lost his right to a name, and I don't want my men conflicted on who to follow out here."

"What did he do?" Tikaya whispered. And who is he, she almost added. But for the ill timing of that blasting stick, she might know by now. Someone who was Bocrest's equal, or maybe even a superior? Was Rias old enough to be an admiral?

Bocrest stepped back, and his eyes widened. "You don't know?"

She shook her head.

"Cruel ancestors, what a waste. He gave up everything, and your people don't even know."

"What?" She reached for his arm. "Please, tell me."

Bocrest scoffed and turned away. He grabbed the rifle and knife, making sure not to leave her any weapons. "Self-absorbed scientists," he muttered on his way out.

Tikaya dropped her arm. She thought back to the first conversation she had with Rias, when he asked if her president was still alive. Was that what Bocrest referred to? Had Rias done something for her people during the war, something that had turned the Turgonians against him? If that was the case, why hadn't he told her right away? If he had done a good deed for Kyatt, he might be allowed to come live on her island, and maybe he'd be someone her family could like, and...

She groaned and rubbed her face. When had he stopped being the enemy soldier and turned into someone she wanted to bring home to meet her parents?

* * * * *

Weariness plagued Tikaya's limbs as she marched after the squad of marines, her arm in the sling, her crampons replaced with snowshoes. The new footwear was almost as awkward to walk in as swim fins, and she struggled to keep up—and upright. There had been no rest after the funeral pyre. They traveled east, in the shadows of jagged white mountains that dominated the southern horizon. To the north, the flat icy tundra stretched until it blended into the pale blue sky.

Forty men remained, with fifteen dead back in Wolfhump, and many carried double loads. Dogs, too, had been lost and the teams pulling the sleds slouched along, as tired as she. A sergeant marched alongside the squad, singing a cadence that condoned plundering farm goods and stealing daughters from conquered nations. Or maybe it was stealing farm goods and plundering daughters. Tikaya tried to ignore the words, though she found her steps matching the encouraging refrains of left, right, left.

For the fortieth or fiftieth time, she glanced behind. Wrists shackled again, Rias walked with a small team tasked with carrying the boxes of

151

blasting sticks. A precautionary couple dozen meter gap lay between them and the main group, though, oddly, the captain walked at his side. She did not know what they spoke of, though his presence served as a deterrent to keep her from strolling back to walk with Rias. She had not seen Agarik since the day before, but his injuries must not be too severe, for he was ahead with the scouting team. Separate from the marines, separate from her two allies, she felt the loneliness and oppressive cold of the tundra. She was tempted to go back to walk with Rias even if it meant enduring the captain's sarcasm.

A dead arctic jaeger alongside the trail diverted her thoughts. The large bird's white-tipped wings were broken, its head smashed in, but no predators had sampled its flesh. Had it simply fallen from the sky? Two sets of snowshoe prints around it meant the scouts had stopped to look.

Long years had passed since her biology classes, so she left it without further examination, but she turned her attention to her surroundings as she continued on. Over the next few miles, she spotted other downed birds, all undisturbed by predators. An uneasy feeling shrouded her, and she wondered what would await them at the fort. More dead men? Another device?

"Prisoner Five, come back here!" Bocrest shouted.

Rias had set down his box of blasting sticks, and he churned across the tundra. Bocrest plowed after him, rifle in hand.

"Sir?" one of the marines in front of Tikaya called. "Do you need help?"

Bocrest waved, and the back two men stamped out of formation, flinging snow as they raced into the drifts with high-kneed steps. Tikaya veered after them, afraid they would think Rias was trying to escape and take violent measures—as if Rias would be dumb enough to run away with everyone watching. Unfortunately, her slog through the unbroken snow was less effective than theirs. Even with the snowshoes, she sank deep with each step, and she tripped twice before reaching the gathering.

Rias stopped, knelt, and picked up something. Bocrest and the others scrambled over, and Tikaya floundered up in time to hear the red-faced, scowling Bocrest speak.

"What are you doing, Five? Are you trying to get yourself shot? Prisoners don't get to take unannounced side trips."

Rias lifted his goggles to peer at his find.

"What is it?" Tikaya asked.

She attempted to slip past the other marines to join him, but one of them took a step at the same time and landed on the edge of her snowshoe. She sprawled, face heading toward the powder. Rias lunged, caught her, and even managed to keep from jarring her shoulder.

"Slagging librarians," Bocrest grumbled.

Face red from more than the cold, Tikaya got her snowshoes beneath her. "Thank you. It seems I'm always tumbling into your arms." She sighed, appreciative but a little envious too. Neither shackles nor snowshoes made *him* ungainly.

"I don't mind," Rias said. "Makes me feel useful."

Bocrest snorted. "Any excuse to grab a tit."

The two marines sniggered, and Tikaya stepped out of Rias's arms, her cheeks warm. Rias merely shook his head at Bocrest, like a father disappointed in a wayward child.

Bocrest scowled. "What did you find, Five?"

Rias held an empty, one-inch cube of glass, or what appeared to be glass, on the palm of his gloved hand. One corner was broken, though the evenness of the cut suggested the hole planned rather than accidental. He flexed his fingers upon the cube. Though the thin sides appeared fragile, they did not bend or crack under pressure.

"It glinted in the sun and caught my eye," Rias said.

"It looks like someone's trash," Bocrest said.

A dark shape loped across the tundra, and the two marines lifted rifles. A black wolf, so gaunt its ribs showed even at a distance. After her encounter with the berserk animals in town, Tikaya hoped the men shot it quickly, before it could attack.

"Hold," Bocrest said. "Why's it so scrawny when there are dead birds everywhere?"

She glanced at him, surprised by the perspicacious comment. He was right, though. It was odd. And this wolf, unlike the ones in town, gave no indication of aggressive behavior. Indeed, it did not seem concerned about the humans at all.

"It *is* the end of winter, sir," a marine said. "Maybe it was a rough one for the animals."

"That wouldn't explain why it's not eating those free meals," Bocrest said.

The wolf loped parallel to the squad, then paused at the corpse of a jaeger. It sniffed and pawed at the bird, and Tikaya expect it to take a chomp. Instead it lifted its muzzle and howled. The oscillating mournful sound made her shiver. Another wolf answered from the foothills, its howl just as forlorn.

"He seems to find the fowl unpalatable," Rias mused.

He turned his attention back to the cube, lifting it so the sun shone through the glass. Tikaya sucked in a startled breath. A familiar symbol etched one side.

She took it from Rias. "I recognize that. "It's one of the symbols repeated often in the rubbings the captain gave me." She nodded toward Bocrest. "Know anything?"

"Shit," he said.

"Very elucidating, thank you," Tikaya said.

"Where'd those runes come from, Bocrest?" Rias asked in a tone of command.

"That's top secret."

"If you want Tikaya to translate this for you, she needs to know everything about the symbols."

Bocrest ground his jaw. Tikaya had made that argument before, and the captain had ignored it, but he waved the marines to go back to the squad. When he, Rias, and Tikaya were alone, he spoke.

"Last month, a black box covered with those runes was delivered to the research department of the biggest university in the capital. No name, no identification. They should have buried it somewhere and forgotten about it, but scientists being scientists...they fiddled with it, let out some kind of airborne poison. It killed everybody on campus. It was late in the evening, so not as bad as it could have been, but hundreds still died."

Tikaya dropped the cube and stepped back. In her haste, she almost tripped over her snowshoes again. Rias's lips flattened, and he rubbed the fingers of his glove together, as if he could wipe off any taint from the cube.

"It's not the same thing, though," Bocrest said. "The bodies on campus were horribly mutilated, and these birds barely look dead. Maybe our people at the fort are fine."

"Those are carrion birds," Rias said.

Tikaya swallowed with grim understanding. "Not as bright as the wolves then, eh?"

"It seems not."

"What are you talking about?" Bocrest asked.

"We're just guessing at this point," Rias said, "but it's possible our people *are* dead by the means you're familiar with, and the poison was toxic enough that even the carrion beasts that tried to feed off them died."

Bocrest scowled at the dead bird. "Oh."

"Will it still be toxic if we get close?" Tikaya asked. "That cube wasn't covered by snow, so this couldn't have happened that many days ago."

"I don't know," Rias said. "It depends on whether we're looking at an area denial weapon or something short-lived, designed simply to kill." He faced Bocrest. "The scouting party. How far ahead are they?"

Bocrest's face froze, and a long moment passed before he said, "They'll be there by now."

Tikaya's gut twisted. Agarik. She had not even had a chance to apologize to him. She prayed it wasn't too late.

CHAPTER 11

The walled army fort squatted in the foothills, small and insignificant compared to the towering white mountains plunging it into shadow. Tikaya stamped her feet to keep warm and wondered if she was crazy for wanting to travel the last half mile to the gate. No soldiers manned the massive guns perched atop the ramparts, nor did any smoke waft from the chimneys inside. Rias's guess that everyone was dead seemed likely, but perhaps whatever weapon had done it waited within those walls. And such a weapon might be inscribed with language clues like those on the Wolfhump artifact. Now that she had made a little progress, the prospect of more tantalized her.

Rias meandered across the foothills, pausing to pick up something here and there. More of those cubes, she feared, not sure whether they were safe to touch or not. He carried a small notepad and scribbled something in it whenever he found one. He still wore his shackles, and two guards trailed dutifully behind him. Did Bocrest not know they were superfluous at this point? Rias had shown no interest in escaping since he learned what was at stake.

She hoped that loyalty to the empire would not result in his death. Or hers. She would much prefer to see him strolling on one of her island's beaches, picking up agates and sand dollars instead of vials that might have housed lethal poison. And in this vision, she saw him with less clothing on. She grinned. Or none. She thought of the scar that bisected his eyebrow and wondered what other battle wounds stamped his olive skin. He had filled out since she first saw him in rags in his cell, and she imagined broad shoulders and powerful muscles beneath that parka.

A guilty pang ended her thoughts. She believed Parkonis would have wanted her to go on and find love again—though not with a Turgonian, no matter how academically inclined—so it was not that. It was that she had never daydreamed about him with his shirt off. Parkonis had been boyishly cute with freckles and a mop of red-blond curls, but not the type to inspire women's fantasies. Of course, she was hardly the type to inspire men's fantasies. She hated to dwell on it, but feared she would not be able to compete with others if she and Rias survived to return to a world where she was no longer the only woman for hundreds of miles.

Snow crunched behind her.

A pair of privates approached, and she braced herself for insults or crude comments. Acne scarred one's face, and neither appeared older than twenty, though like most of the men here they were taller than she and no doubt dangerous.

"Ma'am, we're, ah..." The speaker glanced at his comrade, who gave an encouraging nod. "We're having rations."

Er, what did that have to do with her? "Yes?"

Behind them, marines sat in groups of four or five and shared lunch while the officers conferred in a cluster. More than one man snoozed against his rucksack, oblivious to the frosty environs.

"You could join our mess if you wanted." The speaker nodded to a knot of young men busy chatting, laughing, and stuffing crackers into their mouths. One waved. "We've got extra tooth dullers and—"

"Tooth, what?" Tikaya asked.

"Tooth dullers. You know, hardtack. It's right awful stuff, but Private Ankars has some taffy his mum gave him—his mum always posts him the *best* sweets—and anyway if you wanted you could come share with us."

"Oh, I..." After so much hostility from the marines, this kindness stunned her. The privates must know some of what had happened with the device, that she and Rias had been the ones to render it innocuous. "Thank you. It's considerate of you to invite me."

Rias strode their direction, brow wrinkled. The privates blanched when they spotted him.

"You're welcome any time, ma'am." The speaker waved to Tikaya, and he and his comrade scurried away.

"They bothering you?" Rias asked.

"No. They invited me to lunch."

"Ah?" His brow smoothed and a smile plucked at his lips. "That's an improvement."

"Yes." She nodded toward the pockets of men. "It's amazing they can sleep and laugh in the face of death and inexplicable alien horrors." As soon as she said it, she blushed. What about her? Fantasizing about Rias on a beach a few minutes earlier?

"That's a trait shared by soldiers everywhere. The officers handle the worrying." The grimness returned to his expression, and he held out his hand. A glass cube identical to the first rested on the palm. "I've found several now. The radial pattern and the distance from Fort Deadend implies..." He sighed. "I better see what's inside before jumping to conclusions."

"Are we going in?"

"Yes, good news there. The scouts are alive. The lookout has a spyglass and spotted them moving around inside."

Tikaya exhaled with relief. "Good."

Rias nodded. "Though you might want to wait until later for lunch."

"Why? Are there better rations inside?" Even as she finished the question, the meaning of his comment washed over her. They anticipated more dead bodies, right. She waved a glove to let him know she understood.

"Fort Deadend isn't known for its cuisine, no, but if I can escape Bocrest's guards, maybe we can share a meal?" He arched his eyebrows.

And another, less abbreviated, kiss? She smiled at the thought but couldn't resist the urge to tease him. "I don't know…. Those privates over there have taffy. Can you top that?"

"Ah, perhaps not." His expression grew wistful. "I fear I am a man with few resources these days."

She patted his arm. "You'll have to regale me with stories then. Such as why this place is called Fort Deadend. Are there more reasons than the obvious?"

"Not really. You've generally pissed in some general's tea cup if you get stationed out here. There's a pass through the mountains south of here, and the theoretical purpose of the installation is to guard against invasion from the north. But the route is as hospitable as an avalanche, so the likelihood of someone marching an army through it is close to nil. There's a lot of gold in the hills, though, and foreigners trespass to set up mining operations. Patrols watch for that, and I imagine the fort commander has orders to keep an eye on the canyon where the tunnels were discovered as well."

Tikaya thought of the invisible Nurian assassins. She was beginning to think they had transported back to their own ship the night of the attack, but that did not mean others with their skills were not out here. "Practitioners wouldn't have much trouble sneaking by this fort to get inside."

"They would have had to know about the place first, though I suppose after twenty years secrets are bound to get out. The Nurians obviously know."

Voices sounded ahead—the scouting group returning. Agarik came at the end, head bowed, shoulders drooped, though he kept his rifle crooked in his arms, ready to use. The leader headed straight for Bocrest and his officers, but she caught Agarik's eye and he tramped up the hill toward her and Rias.

A livid red gash dotted with black stitches ran from the side of his cheek to his nose, and the stiffness of his movement hinted at injuries beneath his clothing.

Tears pricked her eyes. She never should have sent him off alone.

Before he could speak, she stepped forward and hugged him. "I'm sorry. It's my fault you were hurt."

He seemed startled by the embrace, but rearranged his rifle to return it. "No, don't think that. I'm the idiot who let himself get ambushed."

His words did nothing to assuage her guilt. When she stepped back, she could not look away from that cut. It would be a permanent scar.

"Is there anything I can do?" Tikaya asked.

"Hugs are good." Agarik gave Rias a hesitant smile. "From anyone who wants to share them."

Tikaya glanced at Rias in time to spot a neutral expression shift to bewilderment.

"What?"

The word sounded harsh, and, though Tikaya suspected the tone more a result of surprise than anything else, Agarik's smile fell.

"Sorry, sir," he said. "I didn't mean, uhm."

"What'd you find at the fort, corporal?" Rias asked.

Agarik straightened, face composed. "Everyone's dead, sir. Ugly dead. Their skin and muscles were melted off like wax on a candle. You couldn't even tell who was who if they weren't wearing uniforms with name patches."

Tikaya shared that's-what-we-were-afraid-of glances with Rias.

"And there's something you'll want to see," Agarik said. "Both of you."

Before she could ask for details, an officer yelled, "Corporal Agarik, get over here!"

He saluted Rias before hustling off.

"You should hug him next time," Tikaya said.

That bewilderment returned. "Marines don't hug."

"Have you talked to him at all?"

"Not as much as you, apparently." He tilted his head and arched an eyebrow.

It took her a moment to match his concerned expression to the hug she had given Agarik. She almost laughed. As confident as Rias was about military and mathematical matters, she was surprised he did not share that confidence when it came to women. As if anyone here could offer notable competition.

"Pack it up!" Bocrest's voice floated across the hill. "We're moving out!"

Tikaya laid her hand on Rias's sleeve before he could turn away. "Agarik wants your attention, not mine."

Rias stared at her. "Oh."

"You two prisoners want to join the group or you going to stay out here and work on your sun tans?" Bocrest shoved a rucksack into Rias's arms as he stomped past.

"I can't imagine that man having a wife," Tikaya muttered as she headed off to retrieve her own pack.

"I've not met the woman," Rias said, "but I've heard she's as obnoxious as him and the undisputed master of the household."

Tikaya would have been content to march at the end of the squad— the going was a lot easier when numerous snowshoes had tamped down a trail—but Rias strode through the drifts with his long legs and overtook the men. Determined to keep up, she forced her own strides to unnatural lengths. Sweat soon plastered her clothing to her body and soaked the fur lining of her gloves. She removed her wool cap and stuffed it in a pocket.

Rias made it to the gates ahead of the marines, and Tikaya trailed close behind. The twenty-foot-tall wooden doors stood open, offering no sign that the fort had been attacked, but two men lay dead at their guard post. At least, Tikaya assumed they were men.

She thought the night spent with the corpses in Wolfhump would have inured her to death, but these were worse. Blisters and burns had seared flesh and muscle to the bone, mutilating the marines beyond recognition. Pustules even coated the bloated, protruding tongues. The eyes had popped like blisters themselves.

She was glad she had not had lunch.

Agarik caught up and walked between them. Sweat dampened his face too. "This way, sir, ma'am. Captain said it's all right to let you go first."

Tikaya snorted. As far as she could tell, the shackles meant little to Rias and it seemed he had already determined that he was going in first, captain's wishes notwithstanding.

Inside the fort, snow had been plowed into piles, so they unstrapped their snowshoes. Sand coated the icy cement. Agarik led Rias and Tikaya past wooden barracks, office buildings, and a couple of cavernous vehicle structures that housed plows, trucks, and other steam-powered transports. If not for the silence and the dead men, she would have guessed it a normal work day at the fort. People had been caught on errands, while practicing combat in an arena, and, in one spot, driving a snow plow that had subsequently crashed into a barracks building. No smoke wafted from the stack, but Tikaya paused to open the furnace door. The fire had gone out, but when she removed a glove and stuck her hand inside, a hint of heat remained in the ashes.

"People were alive here, no more than a day or two ago," she said.

But Rias, following on Agarik's heels, had gone on and did not seem to hear her. His head was tilted back, and she followed his gaze. A two-story office building rose ahead, a large corner of its roof sheered off. Splintered wood and sheet metal roofing shingles scattered the cement around a sleek black cylindrical object embedded in the walkway. Tikaya's step slowed. It was made from the same material as the artifact in Wolfhump.

She joined the men around the rubble. The landing had not dented or even scraped the cylinder, though it had gouged a hole in the cement, and jagged cracks radiated in several directions. Strips opened like flower petals on one end of the device, and dozens of square indentations lined the insides.

Rias produced one of the cubes and slid it into a slot. It clicked. Perfect fit.

"The delivery mechanism," he said.

Bocrest and a couple others approached, though the captain had the sense to keep most of his men from trampling around the artifact. He sent them off to secure the fort with a few terse orders, then stepped closer.

"What is that thing?" Glass crunched under his foot.

"Careful." Rias flung a hand up. "If some of the cubes didn't release their contents in the air, stepping on a full one could be deadly. For us all."

For once, Bocrest had nothing sarcastic to say. He gulped, lifted his boot, looked around, like he might set it somewhere else, then decided it was safer back where it had started.

"In the air?" Tikaya asked. "You don't think this is like the device in Wolfhump? Something that distributes its deadly load from the ground?"

"No," Rias said. "I think it's a rocket."

The only rockets Tikaya was familiar with involved fireworks, though she supposed Turgonians might have experimented with more sophisticated fuel-powered projectiles. Rias had studied ballistics in school, after all.

It took a moment for the ramifications to sink in. Tikaya's eyes widened when they did. "If this is a rocket, that means someone fired it, someone with the knowledge to do so."

"Yes," Rias said grimly.

Tikaya stared at the artifact. Was it possible the original builders were still around? Or—she eyed runes running down one side—had someone already been in the tunnels and translated the ancient language? Such strong disappointment flooded her that she sank to her knees. Surely she had not asked for this gruesome mission, but all along there had been the promise of being the first to translate a previously unknown language and share it with the world. A feat that would earn her a place in the history books.

Rias knelt beside her and put a hand on her good shoulder. "Are you all right?"

Aware of the others, she said, "Yes, just tired."

"Nurians," Bocrest growled. "Those cussed Nurians are responsible, have to be."

Rias arched inquiring eyebrows at Tikaya. She guessed his question and nodded permission.

"I don't think it's them, at least nothing sanctioned by their government." Rias explained the orders he and Tikaya had found on board the Nurian ship.

"Then who?" Bocrest demanded.

"The Turgonians have many enemies," Rias said.

Bocrest tugged off his cap and scrubbed his short steely hair. "This whole slag pile is giving me a headache."

"There's something else to consider," Rias said, tone grim. "We haven't hidden our approach to this fort, so it's very possible whoever did this knows we're here."

CHAPTER 12

Tikaya sat cross-legged next to the rocket and finished copying the runes into her journal. Coldness seeped through her trousers to numb her backside, and shivers made her pencil hand shake. As if writing with gloves on was not bad enough. She ought to move somewhere warmer. But, oh, there was another symbol she recognized from the table of elements. And interesting how each grouping on the rocket held thirteen runes. Could the different prime clusters alter the meaning of—

Light splashed across her pages, and Tikaya dropped her pencil.

Agarik stood beside her, holding a lantern. Only then did she realize twilight had descended on the fort.

"Thank you," she said. "When did you leave to get that? And where'd everyone else go?"

He stared. "You didn't notice people coming and going, ma'am? Talking? Arguing?"

"Er." She vaguely remembered Rias saying something about finding surveying tools. "Not really."

"Half the men are retrieving corpses for a funeral pyre while half are off on a mission Five concocted. Looking for people who might have died outside the fort and searching for more cubes and recording where they landed. Seeing how it's night, that sounds about as fun as hunting for a wrench in a scrapyard. He says he can figure out where the rocket was launched from, though, and Bocrest wants it done tonight, so he can take a team up there at first light."

In case someone was up there preparing another weapon to launch at the fort. Yes, that seemed wise.

Tikaya rose, an awkward movement with her shoulder in a sling, and her injury twinged despite her care. A noisy yawn escaped her lips. She thought of her bed back home, though right now she would be tickled with a blanket in front of a fireplace.

Agarik's jaw dropped in a noisy yawn of his own.

"Sorry," Tikaya said. "Are you tasked with watching me again?"

"I don't mind, ma'am. Of the jobs I could be assigned, it's not a bad one."

Men crossed a nearby courtyard, lantern light bobbing at their feet. They worked in grim silence, bringing wood for a fire. She looked away as others dragged a body from a building and laid it at the end of a grisly queue.

Though tempted to ask Agarik about sleeping arrangements, Tikaya wanted to search the fort for other language clues first. If the marines feared an attack imminent, they might march out at dawn. Somewhere, she hoped to find an artifact she could slip into her rucksack to take home for study—and to prove to her people this nightmare had been real.

"Mind if we find the fort commander's office?" she asked.

"I don't think the captain wants you wandering around."

Tikaya started to object, but Agarik smirked and spoke first.

"But since you'll doubtlessly make arguments until you get me to change my mind, we may as well go now."

"Good man."

Thousands of stars glittering like ice crystals blanketed the black sky above the fort. Tikaya almost felt she could reach up and stir them with her fingers. Here and there lanterns sputtered on lampposts or in sconces. Agarik hugged shadows barely dented by the flickering light as he led her beneath the ramparts and through an alley suffocated with piles of snow. They stopped at the back door of a two-story building. She had the feeling he was avoiding the other men and hoped he would not get in trouble for escorting her around. Her desire to poke through the commander's office kept her from asking.

They slipped into an unlit kitchen where copper pots and steel counters gleamed, reflecting the lantern's flame. Agarik led her around an island to avoid a body clad in bloodstained cook's whites. Tikaya ripped her gaze from the melted flesh, glad the lighting did not illuminate too many details.

They passed through a mess hall lined with tables. Plates of bread, carrots, and now-frozen meat waited for someone to finish them. Bodies, some fallen across tables, some sprawled on the floor, matched the place settings. One man had died tending the coal stove in the corner, and the door stood open, ashes spilled onto the wood floor.

"Surprise attack," Agarik said, disgust hardening his voice. "There's no honor in killing like this."

"I can't believe how quickly the poison acts," Tikaya said, chilled by the idea of something that could kill a man before he could even get out of his seat and wonder if something was wrong.

There were not any bodies at the tables nearest the far door, and wet footprints suggested the marines had started carting them out. Heavy footsteps sounded on the floor above. Tikaya doubted she would make it to the commander's office without being spotted. She hoped no one would question her for snooping about.

They entered a corridor, and Agarik led her to a stairwell. Broad steps rose toward a second floor, while narrow ones turned a corner and dropped into darkness. That made her pause. A basement in a land where permafrost hardened the earth inches below the surface?

Agarik headed upstairs, but voices came from the lower level.

"Wait," Tikaya whispered, cocking her head to listen.

"I think...a Nurian," someone said.

"...doing out here?"

They had found a Nurian? Had someone been caught nosing around in the carnage of the fort? Her breath hitched. What if it was the person who had fired the rocket? The person who knew enough of the language to know *how* to fire the rocket?

She edged closer to the stairs. The men were not whispering, so the discussion was probably not secret, and nobody had forbidden her from exploring.

Agarik gripped her forearm. "Tikaya..."

She frowned at him. "What do you know?"

"The cells and interrogation chamber will be down there. It's not...a fitting place for a lady to visit."

Tikaya almost laughed. Was he worried she would see something more macabre than the legions of bodies around the fort? She patted his hand before drawing her arm away. "I just want to see if they found someone who knows more about what's going on than we do."

If Agarik's frown grew any deeper, he would pop the stitches out on that gash. Still, he followed with the lantern when she eased down the stairs.

She anticipated a pitted rusty iron door streaked with blood at the bottom, but the bland wood was no different from any other door they had passed. Beyond it, gray stone lined a narrow hallway. At the end, light seeped through the cracks of a partially open door. The voices had dropped to murmurs.

On the way down the hall, Tikaya checked a door to the side, expecting racks filled with torture implements. Instead, it was a supply closet loaded with brooms, lye soap, lanterns, kerosene tins, and painting supplies. So far, this dungeon was not living up to expectations.

Chains rattled in the room ahead.

"Where's the slagging key?" a familiar voice growled.

Tikaya froze. Ottotark.

She started to turn, not wanting anything to do with him, interesting prisoners or not, but someone thrust the door open. Two marines tramped out, a body between them, but if it was Nurian she could not tell. It was as melted and featureless as the rest in the fort.

The marines halted.

"What's she doing down here, Corporal?" one asked.

Agarik shrugged. "Looking for language clues."

Ottotark leaned through the doorway, his eyes narrowing to slits when he spotted her. For a long speculative moment, he stared, and she fought the urge to race up the steps in retreat. He would not do anything with so many witnesses, and surely this was not the time regardless.

"Go on," Ottotark told the marines, "take the body out. Agarik, come help me get the other one. I expect the captain will want to see the Nurian, so we'll leave him here for now."

Tikaya stood aside for the men to pass. Agarik headed for the chamber, and she almost bumped into his back when he stopped in the doorway.

"What is it?" she asked.

But Agarik had already moved to the side so she could see. She wished he had not. The amount of human carnage from the last couple days should have numbed her to it, but this dead man was different. The naked Nurian hung from shackles on the wall. His fingernails and toenails were ripped out, flesh mutilated with blades and brands. Someone had gut his genitals off and dug both eyeballs out. The removed organs lay in a tidy pile next to the dangling body, and Tikaya had to gulp several deep breaths to keep from vomiting. Thank Akahe the temperature kept everything frozen, and no odor accompanied the visual horror.

"By the book," Agarik commented.

Ottotark nodded. "Professional job. I'll bet two weeks pay one of our people ran the torture session, but who? This is recent work, done by somebody—*to* somebody—who showed up after everyone else got their faces slagged like ore in a smelter."

"Unless..." Tikaya took one more deep breath to steady her gorge. "Unless the basement protected people here from the poison."

"Look around, idiot woman." Ottotark pointed past racks containing wicked metal instruments whose purpose she could only guess.

Steel bars in the shadows formed a pair of cells. A corpse in one had suffered from the same affliction as all those in the fort above. And, of course, she had seen the body those two marines had taken out.

"Sorry, yes, I'm not thinking." Odd that this deliberate cruelty affected her more than the mysterious otherworldly deaths. The marines, even Agarik, seemed to find this torture commonplace. Just when she was thinking some Turgonians might be normal people. "You must be right. So, one or more of your people got here ahead of us. And this fellow, I wonder if he's the one who launched the rocket. Or..." She looked past the damage to what remained of the man's features, and her stomach did a little flip. "I recognize him."

Ottotark stared at her. "What?"

"He's the bodyguard of the practitioner who attacked me on the ship."

"You sure?" Ottotark's forehead scrunched. "He's not looking too recognizable at the moment." He threw back his head and laughed.

Agarik rolled his eyes.

"Come, Corporal," Ottotark said. "Help me drag that other body up to the pyre. We'll leave the librarian to clue hunt, though I don't reckon this bloke was worrying overmuch about languages in the end."

He laughed again, and the inappropriateness ground on Tikaya's nerves.

"I'm supposed to stay with her," Agarik said.

Ottotark's humor evaporated. "That wasn't a request, *Corporal*. I'm sure the captain didn't mean for you to get out of all the physical labor with your special assignment. You can come back when we're done hauling bodies."

Agarik looked at Tikaya, and she gave him a quick nod. He had risked enough trouble for her, and she would give him up for a while if it would get Ottotark out of the room as well.

Though a troubled expression wrinkled his brow, Agarik helped Ottotark heft the other corpse, and they left. Tikaya did not wish to spend a lot of time alone down here, especially since the presence of the dead bodyguard implied the practitioner was around somewhere, probably alive, but she wanted a moment to think things through.

"So," she said in Nurian, as if the man's spirit might hear and help, "you've been following us all along, biding your time, is that it?" She thought of the hour or two she had spent alone in Wolfhump and shivered, for that could well have been an opportunity for the assassins, but perhaps they, too, had been affected by the gas. "You ran ahead here to lay an ambush for me? Or someone transported you here?" That was a hard skill to master, but not an impossible one. Someone familiar with the arrival area could have done it. "Either way, it seems you got here after the weapon struck, or you'd have been killed the same way as the others. Unless you launched the weapon yourself and came to check the effectiveness of your work. But, no, your people wanted nothing to do with these artifacts." She took off her spectacles and rubbed her face. "But when you got here, someone was waiting. Was it a Turgonian, or the person or persons who figured this rocket out? Or both?"

Not surprisingly, the dead man was not talking. Likely he had given up all his secrets to his interrogator. Tikaya glanced around, noting that the pliers, knives, and other implements she could not name had been meticulously cleaned after use and returned to the storage rack. Little else caught her eye, though, and she decided it would be wise to finish up and find a spot with people around.

She headed back to the stairs. Someone had shut the door at the bottom. She tried the knob, but it did not turn.

A kernel of dread formed in her gut.

She tried the door again. It could just be a flaky knob, but no. It was locked. She pounded on the door. Maybe someone working upstairs would hear her and let her out.

"Is anybody out there? Hello?"

No one came.

Tikaya leaned her forehead against the cold wood. Ottotark must have locked the door on the way out without Agarik noticing. Maybe he had even ordered the men clearing bodies to work in a different building. She swallowed. Odds were Ottotark could make sure Agarik stayed busy for a while too.

The rack of torture implements flashed into her mind. "Dolt," she cursed herself. Of all the places she could be trapped with that man, this had to be the worst.

She slipped the razor Agarik had given her out of her boot and unfolded the blade from the wooden handle. It seemed a puny tool compared to those in the other room. If Ottotark worried about her having weapons, he would not have chosen this spot. He obviously did not see her as a threat in close combat, and rightly so. This was no archery competition where she could stand back and plunk arrows into a target.

She needed to catch him by surprise. She hoped she had time to set one up.

Tikaya checked the supply closet. An idea came as soon as she saw the kerosene tins. Unlike the whale oil her people used, the vapors ought to be flammable. She grabbed a paint pan, a full tin of kerosene, and a box of friction matches. She would only have one chance. It had better work.

In the torture chamber, she closed the door part way. Footsteps thudded in the corridor on the floor above. She swallowed. If that was Ottotark, she did not have much time.

The safety lid of the unopened kerosene tin thwarted her fingernails, and her shoulder sent stabs of pain through her when she tried to brace the can with that hand. She huffed in frustration. Then she remembered the razor. Agarik's tool would help after all.

She gouged a hole in the top of the tin and, careful not to spill any on herself, poured kerosene into the paint pan. The fumes stung her eyes, but she dared not slow down. Footsteps thudded on the stairs. For once, she had reason to thank her height. Though the doors had been made to accommodate the tall Turgonians, she reached the top without trouble and balanced the pan. The footsteps reached the bottom of the stairs, and the lock clicked. The door creaked open.

Tikaya hopped into the shadows beside the door.

"I know you're down here, bitch," Ottotark said. "No point in hiding."

Tikaya's breathing sounded loud in her ears, and she tried to quiet it. She yanked her left arm out of the sling, ignoring the pain, and dug out a fistful of matches. In her right hand, she held a single one. The tremble to her fingers annoyed her. She eyed the pan atop the door, and doubts flooded her. It was too stupid, too obvious. Children did this as a prank; it was not a way to attack an enemy, a bigger stronger enemy who would probably only be angered by the attempt.

"I'm going to wipe that arrogant defiance off your face," Ottotark growled. A door creaked. He was checking the closet.

She swallowed. Would he notice the missing kerosene? Or would he smell it before he entered her room?

"You don't act like a prisoner, not like you should, and the captain's too lenient. You screwed us during the war. You gave our secret orders to the Nurians. They knew just how to ambush the *Crusher*. All those men—my *brother*—didn't have a chance." The heavy footsteps thudded closer. "I've been waiting to avenge him since you came on board."

Ottotark shoved the door so hard it cracked against the stone wall. Tikaya jumped back and almost didn't see the trap spring. Kerosene drenched him, and the pan clattered to the floor.

"What the—" He stumbled into the room.

She slammed a boot into his backside with all her strength. He pitched forward, though he turned the fall into a graceful roll and came up facing her. She kicked the door shut and scraped a match against the stone wall. The scent of sulfur stung the air.

Ottotark snarled and started to lunge. She almost threw the flame then and there, but she kept herself to holding it out and shouting.

"That's kerosene you're covered in!"

Ottotark paused, just short of springing.

"Ever wanted to be a human torch?" Tikaya asked. "You could look just like all the dead soldiers here in about three seconds."

He snorted. "You've not steel enough to kill anyone." But his gaze stayed on that match, and he did not advance.

"I've killed more people than I can count since this nightmare started. First on the Nurian ship and then in Wolfhump."

Ottotark's eyes widened. "The captain was right. *You* killed Commander Okars!"

Admitting that might be stupid, but it might convince him she was a threat. She needed to resolve this before Ottotark realized she would run out of matches eventually. She had to gamble. "Yes, and I liked him a lot more than I like you." She tried to put a manic expression on her face as she looked him up and down. "I can't imagine anyone would even miss you. Maybe I should just—"

"Wait!" He licked his lips. "What do you want?"

"Your word that you won't touch me ever again." It was another gamble. Just because Rias's word meant a lot to him did not mean every Turgonian shared that viewpoint. Still, there were several words for honor and promises in their language. Maybe it was not that big of a gamble.

And Ottotark winced. If his word meant nothing, he would have agreed quickly. He would not be thinking it over.

The first match was burning low. She lit a second from it, then tossed the discard into a puddle of kerosene at Ottotark's feet. The vapors ignited and flames roared, hurling shadows from every corner of the chamber.

Ottotark leapt away, slamming his back against the dangling corpse. "Shit, woman!"

"Your word or you're next." The confident steely tone of her voice surprised her.

"Fine, fine. I won't even touch you if you're dangling on the edge of a cliff, begging me to pull you to safety."

"Excellent." Tikaya stepped to the side of the door. "You first. We're going up to the others before I let you out of match range."

Teeth bared, he edged past her and sprinted up the steps. Tikaya would not have kept up, but he crashed into someone in the hall upstairs.

"Sergeant Ottotark, what are you doing?" It was Bocrest.

Tikaya stepped out of the stairwell, and both men turned. Ottotark thrust an accusing finger.

"That crazy bitch doused me in kerosene and threatened to light me on fire!"

"Because you locked me in the dungeon so you could rape me, you sadistic prick." The burning match had gone out, but she clutched the box in her hand, prepared to light another if need be. She eyed Bocrest, who lifted a lantern and eyed her back.

"Ms. Komitopis," he said, "we call it an Interrogation Station, not a dungeon."

Curse him, he sounded amused. At least he had used her name. That was a first.

"Ottotark, go get cleaned up and find a rack," Bocrest said.

The sergeant slunk away, muttering under his breath.

"What were you doing in here?" Bocrest asked with no preamble, no apology for his loutish man.

Tikaya thought about lying, but reminded herself she wanted the captain to trust her. For now. And she did not think her true purpose that condemning. "Looking for the fort commander's office. If anyone has more relics or rubbings, I figured it'd be him."

"I just came from there. It's been searched, probably by whomever tortured the Nurian. There's nothing, not even Colonel Lancecrest's orders."

"Colonel...Lancecrest?" Tikaya asked.

"Yes, usually we'd have a general commanding a fort, but this is a small outpost."

"It's the name, not the rank, that surprised me," she said. "There was a Turgonian named Lancecrest studying at the Polytechnic when I was a student."

Bocrest shrugged. "Probably one of the younger ones. There are nine or ten kids, and they've had to make their own ways. The family's poor as pond scum. Their lands were salted during the Border Wars, and you couldn't grow a weed there now."

"So, just a coincidence, you think?" As she recalled, that Lancecrest had been studying archaeology; he had shared a couple classes with Parkonis.

"The colonel's body is up there in his office. If he was plotting with some relative, don't you think he'd have figured himself up a better deal?" Bocrest headed for the stairs. "Get some sleep. I've got to look at this Nurian body. One cursed mystery after another up here."

"Captain?" she called, halting him on the steps. "Why is your team here, with me and Rias, instead of hunting for whoever sent that box to your capital? It might have originated in the tunnels, but surely the people who found it didn't stick around and post it from there."

The flickering lantern played shadows across Bocrest's face. Answering was probably a violation of orders, but he had already doled out some information when they discovered the cube. Maybe he would divulge more.

"Someone was sent to hunt down and kill the person who delivered the box," he said. "We are here to seal the tunnels."

"Oh?" Tikaya sensed a cover story. "Why would you need Rias or me if that's all you're planning to do?"

"We need to make sure we find all the possible entrances and exits. You two will ensure we don't stumble into the kinds of traps that devastated the last group."

The blasting sticks they were carrying were the only things that led credence to his story. Tikaya believed him about the attack on the university—something had started this wave crashing toward the beach—but, now that she'd glimpsed the potential for genocide these artifacts offered, she wagered sealing the tunnels was at the end of a list Bocrest received. Wouldn't the Turgonian emperor love to have some of these weapons for his own use? With which to utterly destroy anyone who defied the empire? She swallowed. Like her people?

She should to talk to Rias, see what he thought about this. She blinked. Or should she? Whatever had happened, he seemed loyal to the empire through and through. What if he merely shrugged and went along with the mission?

Bocrest was watching her through narrowed eyes, and she feared too many of her thoughts traipsed across her face.

"I understand." She smiled innocently. Nothing to worry about from her. "You mentioned something about sleep? Where would that be done here?"

"Officer billets are the single-story building across the courtyard, flag out front." Expression unreadable, he turned and descended the stairs.

* * * * *

As Tikaya approached the billets, she yawned so widely tears sprang to her eyes. They froze in her lashes. The air smelled of burning coal, and light brightened the windows on an end room. A marine stood outside the door, rifle crooked in his arms.

She paused. Only Rias would be under guard. What would he think if she strolled into his room at night? Would he assume she wanted... No, surely not. Neither of them had slept the night before, and her shoulder nagged like a cranky child.

"Help you, ma'am?" the marine asked, no doubt wondering why she lurked in the shadows.

"Can I, uhm, er..." Tikaya pointed to the door before her linguistic skills could fail her further.

Lanterns burned so it was not likely Rias would be in bed naked, though that thought made her blush.

The marine sniggered. "Captain just said to keep him in. Didn't say nothing about keeping anyone out."

"Thank you."

She slipped inside. A coal stove glowed cherry, spilling warmth into the room, and a narrow bunk piled with blankets awaited. Fortunately—or perhaps unfortunately—Rias was not naked. He sat at a desk, still wearing those shackles, though a pencil tucked above his ear destroyed the felon look. She grinned at the papers scattered across the desk and on the floor all about his chair.

Weariness darkened the skin under his eyes, but he stood and smiled. "Tikaya."

She strode to the desk, hardly noticing that her hip caught the corner, and wrapped him in a one-armed hug. Between her sling and his chains, it was an awkward embrace, but she did not care. After dealing with Ottotark and Bocrest, it felt wonderful to lean on someone pleasant.

Rias laid his forehead on her shoulder. "I've been tasked with pinpointing the origins of the rocket and estimating the area that was affected by the cubes. I figured you'd be too busy puzzling over those runes and I wouldn't see you for the rest of the night."

"Actually, I was busy almost turning Ottotark into a human torch."

His muscles tensed beneath her arm. He drew back to meet her eyes. "What happened?"

Tikaya shared the story, deliberately putting more emphasis on the mystery of the tortured Nurian than the sergeant's actions. She probably should not have mentioned Ottotark at all—no doubt Rias would worry about her—but she admitted to a little pride that she had handled the odious man herself instead of falling apart. Maybe Rias would be proud of her too. Dumping kerosene on someone was no feat of brilliance, but a month ago, she probably would not have had the wherewithal to think of anything while locked in a dungeon with a rapist on his way. A month ago, she had been hiding from the world because she was too much the coward to go back to work—to her *passion*—because she associated it so much with Parkonis and lost dreams.

"Ahh," Rias rumbled when she finished the story, and his muscles relaxed. "I feel remiss that I wasn't there to demonstrate the use of those torture implements on Ottotark. But you're clever and capable, and, alas for my ego, I don't think you need my help in these matters."

She absorbed his praise; it warmed her more than the heat radiating from the stove. "Don't worry. I need your help in other matters."

"Oh?"

"Someone has to catch me when I trip."

His eyes crinkled. "That has been a daily occurrence."

He held her gaze, and Tikaya was suddenly aware of the heat of his body. If not for the chains keeping his wrists close and his arms between them, she could have leaned against his chest and...

Rias cleared his throat and stepped back. "I need to finish those calculations. If there's someone out there with another rocket—"

"Of course," Tikaya said. "I shouldn't have bothered you. I can—"

"No!" Rias seemed to realize his objection too loud, for he shrugged sheepishly. "I'd like you to stay. I promised you dinner, remember? And..." He dragged a second chair to the opposite side of the desk and cleared a space. "You can work with me, or you can sleep of course too." He waved toward the bunk. "You must be tired."

Tikaya dug into the big pocket on the side of her trousers and pulled out the journal. "I wouldn't dream of sleeping before sampling a Turgonian dinner."

"Excellent. I've got a treat." Rias sauntered to a credenza. He slid a parcel wrapped in brown paper off the top, plopped it on the desk, then knelt before a cabinet. "I found the colonel's personal stash."

She unwrapped the parcel and crinkled her nose. "Salty fish? I don't wish to sound ungrateful, but isn't this from the same provisions we've been eating all week?"

"Yes. That's not the treat." He laughed and pulled out two small glasses and a bottle filled with amber liquid. "*This* is."

Reverently, he carried the bottle over and set it before her. Applejack.

"That's a thirty-year-old label." He uncorked the bottle and poured two glasses. "Since you're from the land of rum, I thought you'd like to sample a good Turgonian alternative."

Tikaya sniffed the subtle apple aroma and found it pleasant. She expected the applejack to burn her throat, but the liquid slid down smoothly, like her father's finest barrel-aged rum. "Nice."

Rias beamed, took a conservative sip from his own glass, and returned to his work. Though her eyes were gritty, and her muscles ached, Tikaya opened the journal to study the runes. More than once, she paused to watch him zip through calculations without the benefit of a slide rule. Despite the horrors all around them, she enjoyed the companionable moment, sitting there with Rias, him with his work, she with hers.

It occurred to her that this was an opportunity to ask him his real name, to find out who he had been during the war and what he had done. Except the very fact that he had not told her made her hesitate. Would the truth create an insurmountable obstacle between them? Maybe she should wait. It seemed a shame to ruin this first peaceful time together.

Maybe she was still a coward, after all. She sipped her drink. No, she *would* ask. Just not tonight. Tomorrow night. She would find a time tomorrow night and ask then. No matter what.

Comfortable with the decision, she leaned back in her chair. The applejack left her with a warm muzzy feeling. Her gaze drifted to the sleeping area where the furry blankets and pillows appeared far more comfortable than anything on the ship. It was not a big bed, but she supposed a couple of creative types would have no trouble...

No, that she would certainly not do without knowing who Rias was. "It's too bad. I've finally got you in a private room with a bed and—"

The pencil in his hand snapped, and he gawked at her.

Erp, had she said that out loud? Tikaya stared at the amber liquid, feeling betrayed.

"I didn't realize that was a goal of yours." Rias smoothed his face and slid out of his seat to pick up the pencil ends. One had flown all the way to the door. Impressive velocity. "If I had, I would have taken it upon myself to escape my cell and call upon you. In a gentlemanly manner, of course."

"I wouldn't have wanted you to get in trouble." Dear, Akahe, how was she supposed to explain the context of her comment?

"Oh, but I'm willing to make great personal sacrifices to help people achieve their goals."

Rias squeezed her shoulder, and a delightful shiver ran through her when his fingers brushed her neck. She sighed in disappointment when he returned to his seat without presuming to do more.

Tikaya set her glass down and pushed it to the side.

Rias chuckled and slid the backup pencil out from behind his ear. "It's a potent drink."

"You wouldn't think apples could get you caned."

"Apples are *the* Turgonian fruit. We make them into everything. I think I mentioned my family's orchard." Rias continued to work as he spoke. "I loved the trees as a kid. I was scrawny, so I'd climb them to hide from my older brothers. They loved to beat on me almost as much as I loved getting them in trouble."

Tikaya eyed him skeptically. "I can imagine you as young, but... scrawny? You're, what, six and a half feet? And broad."

"Oh, I was *always* scrawny because I was always the youngest. I was the youngest child in my family, and then I went to the university four years early, so I was the youngest there. I got smashed whenever I tried to join the sports teams, and I couldn't attract girls, because I was fourteen and they were at least eighteen and only interested in older men. Though I did finally bribe one gal to kiss me by volunteering to do her homework."

Tikaya smiled. So, he had also been the youth who did not fit in. Maybe more so than she, since it sounded as if there was less educational infrastructure for precocious children in the empire.

"Surely, you've long since outgrown those troubles." She yawned, folded her arms over her journal, and pillowed her chin. "I'm sure you could entice women of any age now."

The pencil paused, and he bent down to peer into her eyes. "Hm, I've been meaning to ask you about that. How old are you?"

"Thirty. Does it matter?"

Humor glinted in his brown eyes. "Just wondering if my fantasies have been downright scandalous or merely lacking in propriety."

If Tikaya had been less tired, she would have laughed at the idea of being someone's fantasy, but she smiled blearily, her eyelids half shut. The thought, like the applejack, left her with a warm contentedness.

"How old are you?" she murmured.

"Forty-three."

"As far as my people are concerned, it'd be more scandalous that you were a Turgonian military officer than that you're older than I am."

He had never told her he was an officer, but he did not deny it now. Glum acknowledgment replaced the humor on his face, and Tikaya wished she could retract the comment.

A knock sounded at the door, and the guard walked in. He blinked in surprise at Tikaya, probably expecting her to be naked, then focused on Rias.

"Skeldar's team checked that mining camp like you asked," the marine said. "It's ten miles out. The men there were dead, same as everyone here. Same time ago. And the lookout tower at the bottom of the pass seems the same. The scouts saw no fire, no one moving."

Rias scribbled a note. "Distance to the tower?"

"Fifteen miles."

"Thank you, private. Dismissed."

Grimness hooded his eyes, and he did not watch as the marine walked out. Tikaya shifted in her seat, waiting for him to finish, or waiting for an opportunity to ask him his thoughts. But she already sensed the problem. If people fifteen miles away had been killed by the same rocket...

"Ancestors help us." Rias sat back, eyes closed.

"What?"

"The rocket detonated in the air over the fort, sending those cubes in all directions where they opened of their own volition to release their contents. I can only guess at the exact nature of the substance, but based on all the data points I've received, we're looking at a weapon that can kill everyone within twenty miles of the detonation point. That's more than twelve hundred and fifty square miles." He stared at her. "Can you imagine what would happen if a weapon like this was launched in a populated area? Our capital city has more than a million people."

"Ninety percent of the Kyattese population lives on our main island, and it's smaller than that." Tikaya thought of such a weapon in the Turgonian emperor's hands. Why worry about subjugating her people when one could just kill them all and claim the deserted island for colonization?

CHAPTER 13

The door opened with a bang, and cold air flooded the room. Tikaya sat up. Wan morning light silhouetted Bocrest.

Confusion disoriented her for a moment. She remembered falling asleep at the desk with her cheek pressed against the pages of her journal, but now she sat in the bunk, a blanket pooled about her waist. Rias lay on the floor before the stove. He rolled his head toward the door, eyes slitted.

Bocrest looked from the nearly full applejack bottle on the desk, to Tikaya, and finally to Rias. "This is pathetic. You've got a private room, a bed, booze, and a woman, and you spent the night on the floor like a hound."

"Ass," Tikaya grumbled, wondering if she was too old to hurl pillows at people.

Rias yawned, stretched, and rolled to his feet. "Careful, Bocrest. You're starting to sound like your brutish sergeant. Officers are supposed to be an influence on their troops, not the other way around."

Bocrest snorted and walked to the desk. He picked up the top sheet of paper and scrutinized it, appearing as enlightened as a rock. "Did your big genius brain figure out where that rocket was launched from?"

"Yes."

"And?"

"I'll lead a team to the location, but I have conditions. I want ten men who have taken the mountaineering course. Give me a tracker too. I need a rifle, a pistol, a knife, and I want these chains off." Rias rattled them for emphasis. "Permanently."

Bocrest gaped at this list of demands. "Is there anything else this humble captain could lay at your feet, Master Prisoner? Perhaps I could grovel while I fulfill your wishes?"

"He wants me to come too," Tikaya said.

"Absolutely not," Bocrest said.

Rias arched his eyebrows at her. "Are you sure? It'd be difficult even without an injury."

Tikaya hesitated. She did not want to make more work for him, but what if they found a cache of weapons and needed help disarming a rocket poised to launch? "You may need me up there."

"As you wish," Rias said.

"Emperor's spit," Bocrest said. "She's got you leashed, and you're not even screwing her."

The manacles ensured Rias's punch was not pretty, but he got a fist on the captain's nose all the same. Bocrest saw it coming and partially blocked it, but the force still sent him staggering backward. His own fingers curled into a fist, but he snorted and released them.

"You'll have your team." Bocrest unclipped keys from his belt and tossed them to Rias. "But she should go with the main force to set up the base camp. What's she going to do up there besides be a liability?"

"She's found more ways to be useful than any of your men thus far." Rias beamed her a proud smile.

Tikaya smiled back, ignoring the captain's disgusted huff.

"What's she actually translated?" Bocrest asked. "Did that rocket say anything?"

"I'm still working on what appear to be instructions," she said. "I believe the simple phrases on the side say 'caution' and 'this side up.'"

Bocrest snorted. "That's as useful as goat spit. Great."

"Captain..." Rias warned.

"Whatever. I don't care. If she needs to be carried, none of my men are doing it. She's your responsibility." He stalked out the door, not bothering to shut it. "Team leaves in fifteen minutes!"

Tikaya slid her legs off the bed and grabbed her boots. It was the only thing Rias had presumed to remove before tucking her into bed. Her heart ached. Even if he had not leapt to her defense, she could have loved him just for being a gentleman up here in this savage land so far from the mores of civilization. She almost confided her suspicions to him, her fear that Bocrest's mission would prove less about saving the Turgonians and more about getting the emperor a stockpile of terrifyingly powerful weapons.

"Something wrong?" Rias sat beside her to put on his own boots.

How could she tell him? A man whose every choice proved he still felt loyal to the empire, even after they had taken everything and exiled him. "I'm worried I made a mistake," she said instead of bringing up the weapons. "I spoke hastily. I don't want to be a burden on you. Maybe you could just copy any runes you find for me."

"Do you want to go?"

"Yes." A self-deprecating laugh spilled from her lips. She had never craved field work; she'd always preferred to stay in the lab, letting agile adventurous sorts bring their finds to her. When had that changed? "I don't want to miss anything."

"I wouldn't want that either." He smiled, but it soon faded. "Besides, I'm concerned about your assassins. The bodyguard may be tortured and dead, but if the wizard is still around, he'll feel he's running out of time. It'll be dangerous on the mountain, yes, but I'd prefer you with me rather than with a bunch of men who don't care."

By now his admission that he cared was no surprise, but hearing him say it almost brought tears to her eyes. If only he weren't a Turgonian.

She leaned against his shoulder. "I care too."

"Good." He leaned back. "About me, right?"

She grinned and swatted him. She thought about doing more, but a pair of marines tramped past the door, pausing to peer inside. Then Bocrest hollered for his guide. Sighing, she finished tying her boots.

* * * * *

Tikaya eased along the narrow ledge, her metal crampons scraping and clinking against the ice. Sheer granite towered to her left while equally sheer rock plummeted on her right. A snowy canyon stretched hundreds of feet below. Though the white drifts appeared soft, she had no illusions of a landing being anything but deadly. Wind buffeted the face of the cliff, tugging at her thick braid and whipping stray strands of hair against her spectacles. Frost crystals glittered on the scarf snugged over her nose.

"We're close," Rias called, voice muffled by his own scarf.

He led the single-file squad of marines inching along the cliff face. Tikaya came second with Bocrest third. At first, the captain's presence had surprised her, but a few curt words here and there had given her the impression he was there to remind everyone 'Prisoner Five' was most definitely *not* in charge of the team, even if he led.

A shadow fell across the group as a black raptor as large as a man sailed overhead. This was its third appearance. The way it coasted past made Tikaya think it was scouting the group. Her imagination, no doubt.

The sun glinted off sharp ebony talons as it flexed its legs to land on a perch a couple dozen feet above the ledge ahead of them. It cocked its head to stare at her through a calculating black eye.

"I'm getting tired of that bird," a marine grumbled.

"We could make a meal out of it," another said, voice loud and threatening, as if the creature would understand and leave.

Tikaya caught Bocrest glancing at the bird, but he otherwise paid it little attention. He did, however, carry his loaded rifle in one hand, barrel leaning against his shoulder. Earlier, he had worn it strapped to his rucksack.

The hair on the back of Tikaya's neck rose as they walked under the creature's perch. She had not felt the tingle of the mental sciences being used since the night the Nurians attacked. She paused to study the bird.

"Quit gawking," Bocrest said.

"What species is that?" she asked. "Are they common?"

"How would I know? Do I look like I keep a summer estate here?"

"Ice condor." Rias turned and held up a hand to halt the squad. "They're predators but scavengers too. It's unlikely it'll attack a group of armed men. It's probably just waiting to see if one of us falls."

Lovely thought. "They're usually natural creatures, then?"

"Of course, it's a *natural* creature," Bocrest said. "What else would it be?"

Tikaya pointed at it. "This one's a—"

The condor dropped from its perch, plunging straight at her, beak agape, talons extended.

With nowhere else to go, Tikaya smashed herself against the cliff. The giant bird filled her vision, wings pressed against its body for speed. She raised her good arm to guard her face.

A rifle cracked. Someone pulled her up the path.

The condor squawked, clipped the edge of the ledge, and bounced away. Rock crumbled and fell into the canyon. The bird flapped its wings and recovered before tumbling far, but blood spattered the ice on the ledge. The condor sailed on a draft and disappeared from sight before Tikaya recovered.

"Thanks," she rasped.

It was Rias who held her, Bocrest's rifle that smoked.

"That was peculiar," the captain said.

"More than that." Rias checked Tikaya for injuries and released her. "A familiar?"

"That's..." She mulled over the Turgonian word options. "Close enough. I'm guessing it's a regular creature that someone is manipulating with thought control." She remembered the snatch of conversation she had overheard the night the Nurians attacked her; the practitioner had read someone's thoughts to find her. If he had studied telepathy on humans, controlling animals was not a stretch.

"How would you know?" Bocrest asked. "I thought you weren't a wizard."

"I'm not, but I've grown up around practitioners. I can sense when the mental sciences are being used nearby."

Bocrest scowled at Rias. "Get moving. I want to finish up and get off this mountain quick."

When they reached the top of the cliff, long shadows darkened the snowy plateau despite the early afternoon hour. They had climbed less than halfway up the mountain, and another granite wall rose to the rear, blocking the sun. Nothing on the plateau caught Tikaya's eye, but the fantastic view to the north made for a memorable perch. Miles of unbroken tundra stretched to the horizon with ridges and swirls roaming like striations in stone.

Though nothing but drifts adorned the plateau, Rias strode across it as if he expected to find something. He stopped at a protruding edge and pointed.

"Perfect view of the fort from here," he called.

"But there's nothing here." Bocrest gestured for his troops to fan out and investigate.

Tikaya floundered through deep snow to join Rias. He held a thermometer and a round bronze device she had seen him consult a few times. She had thought it a compass, but the numbers on its circular face did not represent degrees.

"Barometer?" she guessed.

Rias nodded once, though his eyes rolled upward as if he were busy with some calculation. Bocrest shuffled up behind them.

"Worried about a storm coming in?" she asked when Rias's attention shifted to her.

He chuckled. "No, calculating our elevation. As long as you know the temperature, the air pressure at sea level, and the air pressure where you are, you can—"

Bocrest jerked his hand up. "Nobody cares, Five. Is this the spot or not?"

Rias's sigh had a long-suffering quality, and, as he turned to face the captain, Tikaya wondered how many times in his career he had been cut off by officers with Bocrest's temperament.

"We're either here or we're very close," Rias said. "I was expecting a launching platform, but I suppose it's possible the rocket was self-propelling."

"You brought us up here to find nothing?" Bocrest demanded.

While the men debated, Tikaya removed her spectacles to clean them. She tilted them toward the sky to check for specks and almost dropped them when she spotted a sliver of familiar black metal on the cliff top above.

"Gentlemen." She pointed, ending their argument.

"Ah." Rias put away his tools. "Another fifty feet."

"Thought your math was better than that." Bocrest smirked.

Rias's eyebrows disappeared under his wool cap. "My math is impeccable. The tools are imprecise."

Tikaya grinned, always amused when his Turgonian arrogance peeped out.

Bocrest only snorted and called to his men: "Get some grappling hooks out. We're climbing."

"We'll go first." Rias pointed to his chest then at Tikaya. "I don't want overeager young men thundering around up there before we've ascertained the danger."

"I'll go first," Bocrest said. "You can come after and pull your wounded librarian up."

Tikaya grimaced. She held her own on the walkable terrain, but even without a shoulder injury, she would have needed help up the cliffs. Already, Rias had pulled her up two, while she scraped and pushed with her crampons, trying use her legs and burden him as little as possible.

"Doing all right?" Rias patted her on the back as Bocrest stomped away.

"I'm fine. Do you always volunteer women to lead the way with you into potentially dangerous situations?"

He winked. "Only if I know they can handle it."

Not for the first time, she wondered if he thought too highly of her.

* * * * *

When Rias pulled Tikaya over the edge, she knelt to catch her breath. Even with his help, the climb had been taxing.

The first thing she noticed was the dead man. The second thing she noticed was that he had not died the same way the marines in the fort had. An enormous amount of blood spattered the snow around him, and methodical cuts marked the body. Bocrest already stood over it, arms crossed, lips dragged down in a scowl.

"Tortured," he said. "Same as the one in the fort."

"Nurian?" Tikaya asked.

Bocrest was too busy cursing under his breath to answer.

The ledge, similar to the one below, offered another ideal view of the tundra—and the fort. A second cliff to the rear shadowed a tent and a fire pit. The source of the black metal Tikaya had spotted rested near the edge: a flat circle mounted on tripod legs. A shaft tilted upward from the disk and appeared the right size for cradling the rocket. The launching apparatus was not large, but it would have taken more than one man to carry it up there. Or a telekinetics practitioner.

Tikaya walked over to look at the body. "Uh."

"Uh?" Rias asked.

"I recognize this one too."

"Can't be a practitioner," Rias said. "He looks Turgonian."

"He is Turgonian. That's Lancecrest."

"The fort commander?" Bocrest asked. "He's too young."

"No, the Lancecrest I told you about. And actually I think he *did* study the mental sciences at the Polytechnic. Along with archaeology." She filled Rias in with the information she had given Bocrest the night before.

"Huh," Rias said. "That he's here is not wholly mystifying—Colonel Lancecrest could have taken command, found out about the tunnels, seen an opportunity for the family to improve its fortunes, and told his little brother to prepare for a relic hunt. But why would the younger Lancecrest have launched a rocket at his older brother's fort? And why is he now up here tortured and dead? This is...unexpected."

Bocrest spat. "If something *expected* happens at any point in this mission, I'll shit myself in shock."

Tikaya shook her head at the lurid speech. "Is he truly married?" she asked Rias.

"Last I heard." Rias knelt to examine the body more closely. "The empire has failed to keep me apprised of the latest gossip surrounding its officers."

"It's hard to imagine that tongue wooing a woman." Tikaya headed for the launch pad.

Bocrest dropped his arms. "Was that an insult? Did she just insult me?"

"I believe she did," Rias said.

"I never know with her. She gives insults in the same tone as a scientist analyzing an experiment."

Tikaya dug out her journal. "You do remind me of the lab rats they keep in the science wing of the Polytechnic."

"That was definitely an insult," Rias said.

"I know," Bocrest said. "It's hard to be offended, though. She's so civilized when she delivers them. Tidy job on Lancecrest. Whoever ran the torture session was experienced."

Tikaya scratched her head at the abrupt topic shift. Only Turgonians could go from casual chit chat to analyzing dead people in the same breath.

"Body's stiff but this doesn't look like it happened long ago," Rias said. "Yesterday maybe."

"There's a mess in the tent," Bocrest said. "Like someone searched it, same as the colonel's office in the fort."

Rias leaned over the ledge. "Koffert, come up. We need your tracking skills."

Bocrest frowned at this presumptive order giving. Tikaya wondered when Rias had found the opportunity to learn people's names and skill sets.

Long before the tracker reached the top, the launch device swallowed her attention. Runes ran down the tripod legs, giving her plenty to study. She sat in the snow with her journal, gloves off. Not knowing how much time Bocrest would give her, she risked the cold to make copying the symbols easier. The men's conversations faded from her awareness as she worked. She brushed her fingers along a complex grouping of seventeen symbols, and a faint hum teased the edge of her mind. It startled her, and she dropped her journal. Surely the sensation did not come from the launch pad. The artifacts had not yet made her suspect the mental sciences were involved in their creation. Yet something here teased her sixth sense, reminding her of the communications pendant on the Nurian ship. The residual tingle of a practitioner-made device.

"Tikaya?" Rias touched her shoulder. "The tracker is done. Are you ready to leave?"

She blinked and stood, surprised by the stiffness in her limbs. How long had she sat? Rias removed his gloves and held her hand in his warm ones, and she noticed white tipping her fingers.

"Frost nip." He rubbed her hands and raised an eyebrow. "Keep your gloves on. You'd have a hard time taking notes if you lost your fingers."

"Sorry, that was dumb. I needed to use the pencil, and, uhm." She blushed. Of all people, he could probably understand an absent-minded streak, but she still avoided his eyes.

"What I don't understand is how someone else found this ledge," Bocrest said, apparently resuming a conversation she had missed. The tracker stood before him, a sergeant with a lined face and beaky nose. "How many math geniuses are roaming around up here?" Bocrest added.

"Perhaps our mystery man saw the rocket being launched," Rias said.

Despite his suggestion that she keep her gloves on, Rias had not released Tikaya's hands. Calluses hardened his palms, but his touch was gentle as he rubbed her skin. She made no move to pull away.

"Wouldn't he have died from the gas, too, then?" she asked. "And how do you know our torture-loving person is a man? The Nurians have female warriors."

"Walks like a man, pisses like a man," the tracker said.

"Uhm. All right." Tikaya knew nothing about tracking, but supposed squatting and standing would indeed leave different yellow-snow signatures. "But what about the gas?"

Rias gazed east. "The pass is that way and at a higher elevation. The rocket released its load in the air above the fort, so perhaps that means the gas—or whatever it is exactly—was heavier than air and wouldn't have affected someone above the detonation point. This camp, after all, is well within the twenty mile radius."

"Perhaps?" Bocrest asked. "You're just guessing?"

"Yes," Rias said.

"Good steel used for the torture," the tracker said.

Rias and the captain nodded, though it took Tikaya a minute to follow. Right. The good steel and the possible entrance through the pass implied a Turgonian. And hadn't the men in the dungeon suggested the same thing? That the torture was done by the book? The Turgonian book?

"So, you've got an ally up here?" Tikaya asked. "Maybe he'll show himself, and we can share your applejack with him."

She smiled. The others did not. Rias and Bocrest appeared more grim than anything.

"Ally," Rias murmured, then found Bocrest's gaze. "Did the emperor say anything about sending help?"

"He made it clear he wanted the mission accomplished."

Tikaya wondered if Rias derived more from that answer than she did.

"You find anything useful on that rocket, Komitopis?" Bocrest asked.

"I'm getting some fantastic data. If we find more samples in this scientific vein, I believe the shared contexts will allow me to—"

Bocrest hissed in frustration and jerked his hand up, much as he had to halt Rias's explanation of the altitude calculations. "When I ask you a question, I want a yes or no response."

"Then, yes," Tikaya said.

Rias chuckled and squeezed her hands.

"Although if you'd listen to all I had to say, you'd learn that there's some science about the device."

"Science?" Bocrest's expression blanked.

"Magic," Rias said.

"Oh," Bocrest said. "How?"

"I'm not sure yet," Tikaya said. "Give me a moment."

She started to bend down again, but Rias stepped in front of the launch pad. He picked up her gloves and handed them to her. Not until she stuffed her numb fingers back into the fur-lined interiors did he move aside.

"Thank you," she said.

Rias saluted her with a wink. Bocrest heaved a sigh.

She touched the launch pad again, checking several spots. It was weak, but she did sense something, especially close to the ground. On a whim, she tried to lift one of the legs. She expected the black metal to weigh too much, but she raised it with relative ease, revealing a leather-bound book flattened into the snow. Her heart sped up in anticipation. Rias grabbed the leg, so she could retrieve her find.

A pen was stuck in the spine, and it felt warm beneath her fingers. That was it: the practitioner-imbued item, probably crafted to never run out of ink or some simple thing. As far as she could tell, the book—no, journal—was mundane. She flipped it open, but had scarcely read the first couple words when someone tore it from her grip.

"Our people will vet this and decide if it's suitable for a foreigner to read," Bocrest said.

"Bocrest..." Rias started, but Tikaya lifted her chin and spoke.

"Then I hope you brought someone who reads Kyattese, because the writing isn't in your tongue."

Bocrest flipped through a few pages and his lip curled into a snarl. "Kyattese?" His eyes narrowed. "Why would there be a notebook up here in your language?"

"He spoke Kyattese." Tikaya nodded at Lancecrest's body.

"Is it possible that journal is what our 'ally' was searching for?" Rias asked.

Bocrest jerked his head down, eyes scouring the pages as if he could translate them through will. With a disgusted grunt, he thrust the book at Tikaya.

"You tell us," he said.

She skimmed the opening pages and practically bounced at the massive number of the language samples within. Notes, mostly speculation, surrounded drawings of symbols she had not yet seen. No firm translations yet. "I'll need time to read over everything, but it's definitely Lancecrest's journal, and it looks like he's been in your tunnels a while. There are hundreds of pages here and dates go back almost a year."

She turned to a dog-eared page, and her hand froze. Launch instructions for the rocket. It appeared Lancecrest had discovered how to operate the weapon through trial and error rather than true understanding of the language. Nonetheless, the instructions were there. And suddenly she knew: this book was exactly what their mysterious stranger was searching for, here in the tent and perhaps in the colonel's office as well. It could explain the torture sessions too. He had been trying to locate these very instructions, but the Nurian had not known and Lancecrest must have held out to the end.

"Find something?" Rias asked.

She flinched, knowing she had been silent too long to brush it off. "Just an interesting take on what the prime groupings imply." She hated lying to Rias, but she was not going to hand Bocrest directions for launching the rockets. She could only assume there were more of the devices in the tunnels.

"Find something *useful?*" Bocrest asked.

Since shadow covered the ledge already, Tikaya received little warning when the ice condor approached for the second time. Movement teased the corner of her eye, and Rias yelled, "Get down!" just as she was turning to check.

The condor swooped toward her head, talons outstretched. She flung her arms out.

Rias smashed into her, taking her to the ground. Her shoulder flared with pain, but the talons meant for her eyes grazed her forearm. They cut through her parka and stung flesh.

Bocrest and the tracker fired, but the condor banked before the balls hit. It swooped out of sight over the cliff above the tent.

"Are you injured?" Rias asked, eyes locked on her as he shifted to let her up.

Tikaya pushed up her parka sleeve. "Just a couple scratches."

Rias removed a glove and brushed his finger across one of the wounds, which had started to well blood. A green pasty substance mingled with the crimson drops.

"What is it?" Dread hollowed her stomach.

"Poison." Rias jumped to his feet. "We have to get to the sawbones."

Tikaya stared at her arm. She knew nothing about poison. "Is this a lethal dose? How much time do I have?"

He started to respond, but the condor swooped toward them again.

"Someone shoot that slagging bird!" Bocrest shouted to the men below. He and the tracker were still reloading.

Rias had dropped his rifle to shield Tikaya. The bird landed on the launch pad as he grabbed the weapon. Unconcerned, the condor cocked its head, black eye studying Tikaya.

"Yes, you got me." Bitterness choked her words.

"Sh." Rias aimed the rifle, but hesitated. A calculating flash crossed his face, and he raised his voice. "Don't worry, Tikaya. You're not going to die. We've got the antidote in camp, and you've got plenty of time."

Bocrest, the first to finish reloading, lifted his rifle. The bird flapped away. Several shots fired, but it weaved and banked with preternatural speed, and disappeared unscathed.

Rias lowered his weapon. He had not fired.

"I'd like to be reassured by your words," Tikaya murmured, "but I suspect that was for the benefit of the bird."

"Will whoever is controlling it understand our speech through its ears?" Rias asked.

"I'm not sure. Maybe." She might have stopped to consider what he hoped to accomplish with his words, but other thoughts stampeded to the front of her mind. "How much time do I really have?"

"Plenty," Rias said.

She had come to know him too well; she could tell he was lying.

CHAPTER 14

Tikaya woke to the sound of pained wheezing. Her own. Air. She couldn't get enough air.

She opened her eyes to a green canvas tent ceiling supported by slender steel bars. Confusion muddled her mind. The last thing she remembered was Rias and another marine carrying her down the mountain on a litter. Now she lay on a cot, blankets pulled to her chin. Somewhere behind her head, a lantern provided illumination that failed to reach the shadowy corners.

They must have reached the base camp, but if the sawbones had applied some antidote, she could not feel it. Her breath rattled in her ears, and she could not pull in enough air to satisfy her lungs. She tried to wriggle her toes. If they moved she could not tell.

Still alive, she thought, but still poisoned. And alone. Rows of empty cots stretched into the darkness. Where was Rias? Why hadn't he stayed with her? And what about the sawbones?

"Akahe, please don't let me die alone," she mouthed.

She blinked away tears, but it was hard to keep the wheezing breaths from turning into sobs. With no one to witness her torment, why bother being stoic? And why hadn't she written a letter to her parents? Rias might be slated for a return to exile, but Agarik would have found a way to post it. But now her family would forever wonder what happened.

The tent flap swayed, and icy air gusted inside.

She could not lift her head to peer into the shadows at the entrance. "Is someone there?" she tried to ask. It came out weak and garbled.

She saw no one, but soft footfalls trod across floor mats. A man coalesced before her—a familiar man. The Nurian practitioner from the ship. She tried to move, to roll away, but her body did not respond. When she had begged the Divine One to keep her from dying alone, this was not the company she had meant.

"The Turgonian lied," he murmured in his native tongue, his gaze flicking over her supine form. "I see no evidence that an antidote has been applied. They probably don't even know Irkla Root when they see it." He withdrew a knife and met her eyes for the first time. "I'm sorry, Ms. Komitopis."

She groped for something to say that would save her, but only a wheezy gurgle came out when she tried to speak.

"I regret the need for this task," the Nurian continued. "After the help the Kyattese—you—gave my people during the war, it's unfair to kill you, but I can*not* let the Turgonian military get their hands on that kind of weaponry. Nor am I going to let those archaeologists sell it to the highest bidder. I can't let your talents be used against my people, but I'll show mercy and end your suffering now."

He leaned forward and lifted the blade. Tikaya tried to thrash, to fight him off, but her limbs were already dead.

A shadow moved behind the Nurian, and a dagger appeared at his throat. His weapon was wrenched from his hand.

"You move, you die," Rias growled in his accented Nurian.

The assassin's eyes widened. He reached for his throat, but Rias's blade bit into flesh, drawing blood.

"Most of your people who work with poisons carry the antidote in case they infect themselves," Rias said. "You've five seconds to produce it, or you'll suffer the same fate as your bodyguard."

Rias's head was right next to the Nurian's, and rage burned in his eyes. Tikaya wanted to yell, to warn him that a practitioner did not need a weapon to kill. Only a strangled wheeze came out.

Surprisingly amenable, the Nurian reached into his parka and withdrew a handful of fingernail-sized clay vials. "The gray one."

"Sample it," Rias said.

The Nurian blanched.

Rias shoved him to his knees and smashed his face into the mats. The two men dropped below Tikaya's line of sight.

"You're justifying killing the one person who saved your asses in the war over paranoia," Rias snarled.

"You saw your fort. Your people would destroy the world with weapons like that. I can't—"

"Quiet." Rias slammed the man into the ground again. "*Which* vial is the correct antidote?"

"The clear one," the Nurian rasped, his airway restricted.

Did Rias have a hand around his throat? She struggled to turn her head, but could only move it an inch.

Rias sat back, kneeling on the man's chest, and pulled the cork out with his teeth. He forced a drop down the Nurian's throat. The man made no attempt to elude it, and Rias seemed satisfied.

As he started to reach for Tikaya, the hairs on her neck stood.

"Spell," she blurted, praying the word would come out intelligible.

Rias growled and drove his dagger into the Nurian's chest with a crunch of bone. The pained grunt sounded final.

He leaned close to Tikaya and rested a hand on her forehead. The rage was gone, and an uncertain desperation haunted his eyes. He held up the vial.

"I don't know for sure, but I have to try it, all right?"

She tried to nod vigorously, though she was not sure her head moved. He propped her up to slide the liquid down her throat. It burned like cheap rum, and tasted like resin, but she was not about to reject it.

Rias never shifted his gaze from her face. He stroked her hair gently. When his hand brushed her cheek, it felt cool against her fevered skin. The lantern light reflected in the moisture pooling in his eyes. Tears blurred her own vision again, though this time they came from knowing someone was there with her, someone who cared.

Utter weariness overcame her, and she closed her eyes.

Rias was still with her when she woke. He had removed the body and knelt on the ground with his head next to hers on the cot, his hair touching her cheek. Her breathing seemed smoother, less labored. Somewhere beyond the tent, voices rose in argument. She listened, but could not make out words. That she even noticed the goings on outside seemed a good sign.

She wiggled her fingers experimentally. They responded. Her toes did too. Yes.

She eased her arm from beneath the blanket before she could think to favor her shoulder, but no blast of pain accompanied the movement. Perhaps the antidote had healed the injured joint as well. She would test it later. For now, she gave in to the urge to slide her fingers through Rias's hair. It was thick and black, save for those silver strands at his temple, and surprisingly soft.

He lifted his head, and she let her hand drop. The shaman's concoction might have healed her, but weakness weighted her limbs. He winced as he adjusted his position—falling asleep on one's knees could not be comfortable—but the pained expression turned to a pleased smile when he saw her watching him.

"It worked," he said.

"I think so," she rasped, voice rougher than Sergeant Ottotark's manners.

Rias held up a finger, moved away, and returned with a canteen. He slid his arm behind her shoulders and propped her up to drink.

"Not so bad being sick," she said, "when someone's willing to carry you around and take care of you."

"Well, don't make getting poisoned your new hobby. It's hard on—" He cleared his throat. "It's hard."

Tikaya leaned against him and tried to recall the events of the day. What had brought the Nurian into the tent? Then she realized: "When you spoke so the bird could hear, talked about an antidote, that was a trick? To make the Nurian think he needed to come personally to finish the job?"

"A trick, yes, also known as a hopeless stab at making something happen. I feared the sawbones didn't have antidotes in his kit, and, as it turns out, I was right."

"Ah." She shuddered to think how close she had come to dying. "Rias, if someone does succeed in killing me up here, and you make it out, will you do me a favor? Please find a way to let my parents know what happened."

He placed his palm alongside her face, traced her cheek with his thumb. "I'm planning on making sure you live, but, yes, of course."

"Thank you." Weariness dragged her lids down again. "I love you," she murmured before falling asleep.

* * * * *

The next time she woke, darkness still wrapped the tent, and Rias was gone. Agarik sat on a nearby cot, whittling a piece of wood.

"Is it still the same night?" she asked.

"Yes." Agarik lifted his head. "Near midnight, I think." His fresh scar appeared garish by the lantern light, but he smiled and said, "I'm glad you made it."

"Thanks. Me too. Is Rias around?"

His lips flattened, and he looked down, fingers gripping the carving too tightly.

"I'm sorry," she said. "I didn't mean to imply—I appreciate your company too."

He snorted. Agarik's annoyance surprised her since she had only seen him irritated in Wolfhump and *everyone* had been irritated there.

"Is this about..." She thought about the number of marines who knew she and Rias had shared a room in the fort. If Bocrest had said nothing of their sleeping arrangements—and why would he gossip with his subordinates?—everyone likely assumed they had slept together. "Agarik, I'm sorry, but he was married so...even if it wasn't me..."

Agarik waved a hand and met her eyes. "It's not that. I mean, of course a fellow dreams, but...it's just unfair that you don't even know who he is and you get to be his friend." As soon as the words came out, he winced. "Rust, that was pitiful. I sound like a child. And I should be sorry, not you." He scrubbed a hand through his hair. "You almost died today, and I'm sulking because the only time my boyhood hero speaks to me is to inquire about you."

"Your...*boyhood hero*?" Tikaya caught herself gaping and closed her mouth. "How old are you, Agarik?"

"Twenty-three."

He was younger than she had thought, but that still meant Rias had to have been someone of note for at least ten or fifteen years. Not just an officer, someone distinguished enough to have been known and discussed all over the empire. The night before she had resolved to ask Rias his name. She was tired of being in the dark. She had to know.

"To answer your original question," Agarik said, "last I saw him, he was heading off to a meeting with Bocrest. The captain's finally given up trying to keep him at prisoner status. He told the men to treat Rias like an officer for the duration of the mission."

Tikaya found herself gaping again. "Er, how long was I asleep?"

"While the captain was up on the mountain, the marines setting up camp down here had some time to chat. Things came out." The mischievous glint in his eyes suggested the source of those 'things.' "Not that many men were surprised. Most of us had pieced together who he is and started deferring to him anyway. Ottotark about shi—had an accident, though."

She flexed her fingers and eyed her nails. "And he's who, again?"

She hoped Agarik would let it slip, but he shook his head. "He should be the one to tell you."

"Of that I have no doubt, but he hasn't." He almost had, the night in Wolfhump, probably because he had not been sure they would live to dawn.

"Have you asked him?"

"Yes."

"Oh."

Agarik scratched at his scab, caught himself, and scratched around it instead. A breeze buffeted the side of the tent. She would get the answer from Rias as soon as she saw him. No more waiting. In the meantime, there was little point to dwelling on it. She should rest, or study Lancecrest's journal. The notes would help her along on her translations. She would love to be the one who—

Love! Her memory triggered. She had told Rias she loved him before falling asleep. She bit her lip. Had he responded? She could not remember. Had he felt awkward? Alarmed? Dare she hope—pleased?

Tikaya swung her legs off the cot. "I need to talk to him."

Agarik lifted a hand. "You can't go anywhere. You were almost dead a few hours ago. You need to rest."

"I did rest. I'm done now." She stood and promptly fell back onto the cot, betrayed by straw legs.

"Really," Agarik said dryly.

"I just need to get my muscles moving." She stuck her legs out. Maybe a few ankle rotations and toe wiggles would improve the blood flow.

"Rias will be back by morning, I'm sure. You should rest."

"I need to talk to him now. It's, uhm..." Tomorrow they would be surrounded by squads of men again. She needed to talk to him tonight.

Alone. And she was not about to explain that to Agarik. "I need to see if he has the journal I recovered," she said instead. "I want to study it further before we go into the tunnels."

"It's the middle of the night, Tikaya."

"Night is eighteen hours long here. It's *always* the middle of the night."

"You've a point there." Agarik stood, head brushing the rafter of the tent. "I'll get the journal for you if you stay here and rest, all right?"

She smiled at him but did not answer. Whatever got her nanny out of the tent so she could leave.

Agarik unfastened the flap and slipped out. An icy draft reminded her to dress fully before venturing outside. Fortunately, someone had piled her gear at the end of her cot where a portable stove burned. She checked for the journal in case Rias had tucked it in there, but he probably placed it elsewhere to make sure the Nurian would not find it.

Outside, stars and a half moon brightened a wedge of sky framed by steep canyon walls. They must have arrived at the canyon where the tunnels began.

A bonfire blazing in the center of camp snapped and launched sparks into the air. Five tents, large enough to hold cots for all, stood back from it. The sleds lay between her tent and the next, and the dogs had burrowed into the snow and slept with their noses tucked under their thick, fluffy tails. A surprising number of men were still awake and chatting fireside. Or perhaps they were awake again. Rias must have kept the camp quiet and had the men feign sleep to draw in the Nurian. A ceramic jug passed from hand to hand, and laughter gave the atmosphere a jovial feel, though some of the chortles sounded strained. No doubt rumors abounded concerning the tunnels, and, after the deaths they had seen, the men must suspect not all of them would make it out again.

Tikaya stood, breath fogging the air before her eyes, wondering where to find Rias. She considered the other tents. Three stood dark, but light seeped from beneath the flaps of hers and one other—might that be a command tent?

She padded to the entrance and debated whether to peek inside or wait for him to come out. If Bocrest led the meeting, he would not appreciate her interruption. She lifted her hand but let it hang as she considered how one knocked on a tent.

The flap peeled back, and one of the sergeants almost crashed into her.

"What're you doing?" He lowered his brows and glared at her. "Spying?"

"Huh? I mean, no, I—" She looked at her still raised hand as if that would explain her intent.

"Who is it?" Captain Bocrest asked from within.

"The woman," the sergeant said over his shoulder. "Standing outside, spying."

"I'm not spying!"

"I got to piss." The sergeant shoved past her. "Out of my way, girl."

"It's Tikaya," she informed his back.

He threw a rude gesture over his shoulder. No one called to invite her into the tent, but she walked in anyway. Six marines, Bocrest and his senior ranking men including a scowling Ottotark and the sawbones whose brother she had killed. No Rias. She swallowed.

"Sorry, for interrupting," she said, "but I'm looking for...that journal. I thought it'd be useful to finish translating it before we head in."

The glowers facing her seemed more suspicious than her presence called for after what she had been through with these men.

"For our benefit?" Ottotark growled. "Or so you can deliver it to the archaeologists inside?"

"I don't know what you're talking... Oh." She recalled the Nurian's speech before he had tried to kill her. Those moments when she had been so close to death were fuzzy, but she did remember archaeologists being mentioned. Rias must have relayed the information. "I don't know who's in there. There are a lot of archaeologists in the world." Though she had to admit that at least half of the renowned ones came from the Kyatt Islands and most of the other half had studied there at one point or another. "Chances are I don't know any of them, if that's what you're worried about—the folks I know aren't the types to go hunting for ancient weapons caches. And, anyway, I wouldn't betray Rias."

"*You*, the cryptomancer who slagged us all in the war, wouldn't betray '*Rias*?'" one of the sergeants asked.

"Quiet, Karsus," Bocrest said. "He hasn't told her."

"No? Oh, yes, that relationship's going to work."

The ire in the room evaporated and was replaced by sniggers. Tikaya set her jaw. She preferred the hostility. This was one more reason for her to talk to Rias tonight. She was damned if she was going to be the only one in camp who did not know.

Bocrest reached into the rucksack beside his cot and pulled out the leather journal. He tossed it to her. "Go. Figure out what's in there that's worth torturing people over."

Naturally, she bumped into the returning sergeant on her way out. He growled at her, and she skittered away with an apology. She stopped a few paces beyond, bent over, hands on her knees, fatigue making her limbs heavy.

What further cane fields would she have to harvest for these Turgonians to prove she was sold on working with them? Then again, was she? She cared what happened to Rias and Agarik, but she would not cry over the rest if an avalanche swallowed them. What if she did encounter scholars she knew and respected inside? Men and women—how she missed having female colleagues to talk to!—with a ship anchored somewhere, a way back home. What if she *did* have a chance to switch sides?

"Tikaya?"

She straightened and turned toward Rias's concerned voice. She hoped the darkness hid the guilty flush that heated her cheeks.

"Is something wrong?" He wore parka, cap, scarf, and he even carried snowshoes and a rifle. Where had he been? Scouting the tunnel entrance? "I thought you'd sleep until morning."

"I, uhm, wanted to talk to you." She had been looking all over for him, but had not given much thought to what she would say.

"Of course."

Rias leaned the rifle and snowshoes against the side of a tent, and she joined him in the shadows, wanting to be out of eyesight if anyone else from the meeting came out to relieve himself. He wrapped her in a hug, and she slid into his arms, though the amused eyes of the men in the tent nagged her mind. She had to know. Tonight. She waited for Rias to release her, but he held her in silence for a long moment, arms tight. She breathed in the tang of weapons cleaning oil and black powder mingling with his warm male scent. Men laughed around the fire, trading jokes, boasting of brave feats.

"I'm sorry," he finally whispered.

Sorry? Was that in response to her proclamation of love? He was sorry he didn't love her back?

Then he added, "I used to be faster. You shouldn't have been—I should have seen the condor sooner." He sounded so distraught. It brought a lump to her throat.

"Oh, Rias." Tikaya wriggled her glove off and laid her hand on the side of his face. "That's not your fault."

"I should have sent you with the main party." His own glove came off and he laid his hand on hers.

"I'm sure that condor could have found me down there as well as on the mountain."

His sigh came out as more of a grumble. "I'm tired of people trying to kill you."

"I'm not an enthusiast of the trend either."

Rias's other hand slid under her scarf to rub the back of her neck. She closed her eyes, letting those strong fingers knead her flesh, even as she lamented the layers of parkas and wool uniforms between them. The voices of the marines faded from her awareness. Soft breaths tickled her cheek, and she opened her eyes to find his face close. Shadows cloaked his eyes, but she sensed his intent and leaned into him, head tilted back.

His lips brushed hers, questioning at first. Tikaya parted her lips, invited more. His kiss grew firm, confident, and she thought of the experienced warrior she had followed through the Nurian ship. Heat flared through her body, and she forgot about her questions, the camp, and the freezing air. She might have forgotten a lot more if someone had not crunched around the tent and stopped to stare.

"Well, well, well." Ottotark.

She winced and drew back. Of all the people to stumble upon them.

"Ignore him," Rias breathed, nuzzling her ear.

A small grin stretched her lips as it dawned on her that she could. If Bocrest had told the men to treat Rias like an officer, that would mean he outranked the sergeant. As much of an ass as Ottotark was, he seemed loyal to his uniform and the chain of command. Surely, he would leave them alone if Rias ordered it.

Tikaya probably should not have looked so smug as she cast a dismissive glance Ottotark's way, but she could not resist, not after all the torment he had thrust upon her. She slid her hands under Rias's parka and kissed him deeply. Let the bastard watch.

Ottotark guffawed.

Startled, she broke away. That was the last reaction she expected. She looked at Rias, eyes questioning, but Ottotark spoke first.

"The captain really needs to let you live." He was pointing at her, laughter punctuating his words, but his tone seemed designed to carry to the whole camp. "I'd love to accompany you back to your island so I can tell your mom and pop that you were out here fucking Fleet Admiral Saskha Federias Starcrest, the man who *personally* recommended taking over your islands to the emperor." Now it was Ottotark's turn to be smug. Very smug. "But don't let that stop your plans for the evening. I can see you're enjoying yourself. Carry on." There was far too much pleasure in the cruel sneer he launched at them before walking away.

Tikaya felt lightheaded. She had to remind herself to breathe. All she could do was stare at Rias's shoulder.

"I'm going to kill that man," he said.

No denial. No explanation about how Ottotark was wrong. No claim that it was a lie.

"You were right," Tikaya choked. "My people have heard of you, and you'd never be welcome on my island."

She stepped back.

Rias grasped her arm. "Tikaya, please. Let me—"

Shaking her head, she pulled her arm free. She had to get away. She had to think. She had to—she didn't know.

"I'm sorry," Rias called after her.

She stumbled, not sure where to go. Not back to the fire and the marines. If she returned to her tent, Agarik would be waiting to yell at her for leaving. She definitely did not want to go anywhere she would have to look at Ottotark. But neither could she go out where yetis and wolves and grimbals waited to devour silly girls thousands of miles from their homes.

Tikaya finally sat down behind the sleeping tent. She drew up her knees and buried her face in them. She ought not be so stunned. There had been clues all along. She just hadn't wanted to see them. Had she really thought someone who so readily took command and led the way into battles was an *engineer*? That love of mathematics made him the best cursed strategist of his generation. Starcrest. How often had his name come up in the documents she decrypted? The youngest fleet admiral in the history of the empire. The man who, as a captain, had been responsible for the sinking of a hundred Nurian ships. And the man who, as an admiral, had guided every battle, every skirmish that allowed the Turgonians to again and again best the preeminent mental scientists in the world, with only mundane technology on their side. It was not until after his death that the tides had turned, ending in a stalemate. Yes, his *death*. She vividly remembered decoding a note that said a Nurian assassin had killed the admiral. He was supposed to be dead, not exiled. That was why she had never considered her Rias might be the legendary admiral.

Still, who could she blame but herself? She should have known. She certainly should not have fallen in love with him. If he was nobody important, nobody who would matter to her, he would have told her his name. This was exactly why he had kept it from her. He had known she wouldn't want anything to do with him. How could she? If what Ottotark said was true, and Rias had been the one to suggest taking over her homeland, then every death was indeed on his hands.

Her stomach writhed, and she choked on a sob. Every death, including Parkonis's.

CHAPTER 15

Tikaya did not know how long she sat in the shadow of the tent, but shivers and a frozen nose finally convinced her she had to find a warmer berth. She put a hand down and started to rise. The crunch of boots stopped her. A tall figure with a rifle strode between the tents and into the darkness before her. She could not make out features but had an inkling. She remained still, cloaked by shadows.

A long moment passed with the figure scanning the dark canyon beyond the camp.

"Tikaya?" he called.

She closed her eyes. Rias. No, Fleet Admiral Starcrest.

She did not want to—*could* not—talk to him. Not then.

He called twice more.

"The bitch is gone." Ottotark strode into view from another direction. He passed within a couple feet of her and stopped a few paces from Rias.

"Ottotark," Rias growled. "I ought to twist your head off your slagging neck and shove it up your ass."

"It's not my fault you didn't tell your girlfriend your name. Admiral."

Rias had no answer for that, and even the darkness did not hide the slump to his shoulders. "Where is she?"

"Off to the tunnels to join her friends and leave us hanged."

Tikaya clenched her jaw. Damn these men. She did not want to deal with either one, but she could not let Rias believe she had run off. She opened her mouth to say something, but Ottotark spoke first.

"You should thank me," he said. "It's pathetic the way you were hanging all over the bitch. And why? She slagged us in the war. If you want her, tie her down and screw her, but don't—"

Rias threw down his rifle and charged. Between one eye blink and the next he covered the distance and crashed into Ottotark, taking him down so hard they flew backward.

Tikaya drew her knees in tight, too startled to speak. The attack may have surprised Ottotark, but he recovered and fought back like a cornered badger. Grunts and snarls accompanied the smack of fists striking flesh.

In the darkness, she lost track of who was who as the men thrashed and writhed on the ground. Clumps of snow flew, spattering her cheeks. Something cracked, and one of them—Rias?—yelped in pain.

Tikaya held her breath. Ottotark was younger, bigger, and without any morals as far as she could tell. She tried to tell herself that Rias—Starcrest—was no longer her concern, but her fingers clenched into a fist, and she silently rooted for him.

One man maneuvered on top and straddled the other. He punched down, and a head hammered the snow. The bottom man bucked and twisted, and a moment later the positions reversed.

"Traitor," Ottotark snarled.

Both men panted, breaths rasping. They switched positions again, legs tangling as each tried to pin the other.

Metal rang, a knife being pulled.

As furious as he was, Rias would not pull a blade. Tikaya knew he wouldn't. She almost yelled a warning, but stopped herself. A distraction could prove fatal.

One man found the top again and raised an arm, the knife silhouetted against the night sky. The blade plunged down at the head of the other.

Movement halted. Ragged breaths assaulted the still air, and Tikaya could not tell whether they belonged to one man or two. The top person lurched to his feet and staggered back, a hand to his belly.

Her heart hammered in her ears, and she could not bring herself to call out. If it was Ottotark, who knew what he might do to her? If it was Rias, and he had just made good on his promise to kill the sergeant...

But, no, the supine man groaned. Weakly.

Tikaya could not identify him by the sound. She forced her limbs to unlock and she rolled to her knees. She crept to the fallen man's side and hesitantly reached toward the face. Her glove bumped something hard.

The knife.

It wasn't lodged in an eye after all. The attacker had sunk it to the hilt in the snow a hair from the other's ear. That told her what the shadows did not: of the two, only Rias would have shown mercy.

She jerked her hand back as the man—Ottotark—groaned again. She lunged away from him and looked for Rias. He might be injured and need help. She spun slowly, searching the shadows, but he was gone.

Maybe he had gone to find a cot. She trotted into camp. The number of people awake had dwindled, and the fire burned low. She tore open the flap to the sleeping tent and crashed into someone coming out.

"Tikaya," Agarik blurted. "We've been looking all over for you."

She grabbed his parka. "Is Rias with you? Have you seen him?"

"Not since he went to check the perimeter." He must have read her distress. "Why? What's wrong?"

"Ottotark told him I'd gone to the tunnels. I'm afraid he might have gone after me." She explained the fight, all the while cursing herself for staying silent during the men's confrontation. Why hadn't she answered when he first called out? If he got in trouble because of her stung feelings...

"He shouldn't go in there alone," Agarik said, tone terse, worried. "Come, we've got to tell the captain."

Glad to have him leading the charge, Tikaya followed him into the command tent. Heat and faint light emanated from the portable stove in the center, and she could pick out shapes amongst the shadows. The meeting had dispersed, and only Bocrest and a couple lieutenants remained inside, all flat on cots. Tikaya stopped near the stove. Certain the captain would blame this on her, she did not want to be close enough for him to grab easily.

"Sir?" Agarik asked.

Bocrest jerked awake, hand finding a pistol.

"It's Agarik, sir. The admiral's missing."

Bocrest growled and lurched to his feet. "Explain." He must have had a suspicion, for his eyes skimmed the darkness and found Tikaya. He cursed. "No, *you* explain."

While Agarik had listened to the story patiently, she had to suffer curses and hurled gear while reciting it for Bocrest. He managed to get dressed despite his preoccupation with throwing things and was stuffing his feet into his boots by the time she finished.

"*This* is why women aren't allowed in the military." He cursed again, but shifted to efficiency after that.

By now, the lieutenants were awake and dressing, and he snarled orders at them. Less than five minutes later, the entire camp stood in formation outside. The last to show up, Ottotark limped to the head of one of the lines. Several men held lanterns, and the flickering light revealed bloody and swelling contusions on the sergeant's face. A dark part of her wished he *was* dead, though Rias probably would hate himself if he killed someone out of sheer rage.

Bocrest stalked over to face Ottotark. "Did you draw the knife or did he?"

"Sir?" Ottotark asked in a tone that sounded like he was trying to play dumb, or maybe buying himself time to think.

"You heard me!"

Ottotark licked his lips. The marines in formation apparently knew better than to turn their heads and watch, but their eyes flicked toward the confrontation.

"I did, sir," Ottotark finally said.

"I told you—I told *everyone*—to treat him like an officer. The punishment for drawing a weapon against an officer is death."

"Sir! He's not an officer any more. He's a traitor, you said so. The emperor—"

"Isn't here," Bocrest said. "We'll discuss punishment when the mission is over. For now, do your job and don't talk to our guide or our translator. Is that understood?"

"Yes, sir," Ottotark said so softly Tikaya almost missed it. If only the captain had issued that order a few hours earlier.

The tracker strode out of the darkness, and Bocrest shifted his attention.

"There are footprints at the tunnel entrance and it looks like someone walked in, at least a few steps. The floor is that hard black material, and there's no way to track further."

"Slagging women," Bocrest said before raising his voice. "Gather your gear, men. We're going after him."

* * * * *

The marines marched in step, and the echoes reverberated through the wide black tunnel. No dead skeletons had marked the entrance, no piles of rubble scattered the floor, nor did water drip eerily in the distance, but the place made Tikaya uneasy nonetheless.

It was too clean, too perfect. No cobwebs obscured the distance, no chips or scratches marred the dust-free floors, and no decoration adorned the walls. The cool dry air reminded her of the lava tubes meandering beneath her father's plantation, but no familiar earthy smells accompanied it. No smells at all. The lanterns the marines carried went unused. A soft glow emanated from all around, illuminating the tunnel as clearly as the midday sun. She had visited several ancient catacombs, qanats, and subterranean cities, and she had studied dozens more. This sterile tunnel was like nothing in the archaeology books. Nothing in the world.

"Who made this place?" someone muttered.

She walked behind Bocrest, second in a queue of thirty men. A handful of marines had stayed in the base camp while Agarik and a couple others scouted ahead.

"Ancient people," someone answered.

"How?"

"Magic."

No telling tingle stirred the hairs on Tikaya's neck. "I don't think so."

"Magic," another said, his tone brooking no argument. Others murmured assent. "Evil magic made this place, just like the rocket and the thing in Wolfhump."

"No talking," Bocrest snapped over his shoulder, saving Tikaya from launching into a lecture that would doubtlessly not be well received.

Rias must have a lot more patience than she to have commanded such men all his life. It must have been lonely for him with so few peers. She shook the thoughts from her head. It was none of her concern. Even if she could forgive him for his lie of omission, Admiral Starcrest was nobody she could have a life with, not without betraying her people, her family, and everyone she loved. Especially those fallen during the war. She could want him found and safe, but she could not want him. Not any more.

She swallowed a lump and fished the journal out of her pocket. A challenge. Her mind needed a challenge, and she needed to learn as much as she could before her services were needed. If ever there was a place she could walk and study at the same time, it ought to be these flat, terrain-free tunnels. The worst thing that could happen is she would trip. An animal screeched in the distance.

Well, maybe not the worst thing.

Rias had mentioned strange predators in the tunnels. Predators that would probably find a single man an appealing target. Best not to dwell on that. Tikaya turned her attention back to the journal.

A mile or two passed with no side rooms or cross corridors forcing decisions. With her mind and her eyes locked on the pages, she failed to notice Bocrest stopping, and she crashed into his back. The journal slipped from her fingers as he spun and scowled.

"Didn't you see the sign?"

"Sign?" Tikaya blinked and glanced about. They had come to a six-way intersection, where the scouts had stopped to wait. Large symbols in groupings of threes glowed a soft red above eye level at each corner. "Oh, yes, signs. I just read about those."

Bocrest sighed noisily, while she picked up the journal.

"Not those signs, the hand signal." He demonstrated by raising his hand, fingers spread. "That means 'squad halt,' not 'librarian run into the captain's back.' You need to pay attention in here."

"Do you want me to pay attention or do you want me to be able to translate the writing on the walls?" she asked.

Bocrest folded his arms. "Yes."

She snorted but pointed to each sign as she relayed them: "Biology labs, alchemy labs, physics, animal experiments, labs for something Lancecrest didn't recognize, and living quarters."

"What is *that?*" A marine pointed to a calf-high scat pile in the middle of one of the corridors.

"Sorry," Tikaya said, "I don't translate poo."

"Koffert." Bocrest gestured for the tracker.

The man knelt to examine the pile. He rubbed some between his fingers and sniffed it. "Predator, unknown. Large. Passed this way less than an hour back." He stood, wiping his hand on his trousers, and Tikaya made a note not to share meals with the man.

Bocrest faced the scouts. "Any sign of Starcrest?"

"No, sir," Agarik said. He met Tikaya's eyes, and they shared a grimace.

Bocrest grunted and waved toward the symbols. "Komitopis, which way?"

"Which way do I think Rias would go if he was wondering which way I would go?"

Agarik smiled faintly. Bocrest did not.

"Alchemy?" she guessed.

"Fine. Someone mark the wall." Bocrest waved the scouts forward. "Go. You boys in the back, stay alert. Watch for monsters creeping up on our asses."

As the squad headed the new direction, Tikaya cast a longing gaze at the corridor that led to the living quarters. If any personal affects remained after all this time, she could learn much about the people from studying them. After they found Rias, perhaps they could go back.

Soon, doors marked the passage, taller and wider than normal, and without knobs or latches. Symbols denoting laboratories adorned some while others remained plain.

Someone walking closer to the wall than the center of the tunnel triggered a door to slide upward of its own accord. The man cursed and lurched back into line. Tikaya glimpsed a landing overlooking what she guessed to be lab stations—all the furnishings were oversized by human standards. A hand on her back encouraged her to hustle forward and catch up with Bocrest.

"Should we check some of these?" she asked.

"I'm not exploring anything until we catch up with our lovelorn guide," Bocrest said.

Up ahead, the scouts stopped before a closed door. Agarik and another knelt to check something on the floor while the third man stood guard. After a moment, Agarik jogged back to the group.

"What is it?" Bocrest asked.

"Blood." Agarik glanced at Tikaya. "A lot of blood."

Her hands tightened around the journal. If Rias was hurt—or worse—because he had charged in here to look for her, it would be her fault.

When they reached the spot, the size of the dark puddle only increased her dread.

"Human blood," the tracker said after a taste. "Plantigrade print over there, but definitely not human."

He pointed to a second puddle halfway under the door. A bloody print more than twice the size of Tikaya's foot lay beside it. Dots at the end of the toes suggested claws.

"Bear?" Bocrest asked.

Tikaya, remembering Rias's tale of the tunnels, said, "I doubt it."

A man screamed somewhere beyond the door. Rias? She lunged for the door, triggering the opening mechanism, but Bocrest caught her before she crossed the threshold.

"We'll get him," he said. "You wait here."

He waved two fingers, and the scouts slipped in first, fanning out on a landing with their rifles raised, ready to fire. Tikaya shifted her weight from foot to foot and eyed a bow stave and quiver attached to a rucksack. The man carried a rifle and pistol too; surely, he could spare the weapon so she could—

"Clear on the landing," Agarik said.

"Sergeant Karsus." Bocrest nodded for the man to take over the lead.

Without words, and faster than Tikaya expected, the marines shucked their rucksacks and split into two teams. They filed down stairs on opposite ends of the landing and disappeared from her sight. Only Bocrest remained with Tikaya.

Ignoring his hiss of annoyance, she twisted free of his grip and stepped inside. The landing overlooked a cavernous room that stretched a hundred meters or more. Thick thirty-foot-high columns supported the unadorned black ceiling. Empty floor dominated the front third of the room, and she could only guess at the furnishings beyond. She decided to think of them as lab stations and storage cabinets, though even the lowest counter rose taller than the approaching marines. The height and arrangement blocked much of the floor view as the stations created a maze of sinuous yet symmetrical aisles, some wide, some surprisingly narrow. As with the tunnel, light from an indiscernible source illuminated everything.

A cry of agony echoed from the center, and she glimpsed a blur of black before it disappeared behind a row of twenty-foot-tall cabinets.

"Sprites-licked idiot," she cursed, whirling to look for a bow amongst the discarded gear. She was not sure whether she meant Rias or herself. If, after all he had lived through, he died to some random animal attack...

Tikaya spotted the bow stave she eyed earlier. The marine had left it in favor of the rifle. She stuffed the journal into her rucksack, then untied the bow with fingers too irritated to fumble with fear. She yanked the quiver free as well. Stringing the weapon was a struggle, and she prayed the draw wouldn't be too heavy for her.

"Let my men do their job, Komitopis." Rifle crooked in his arms, Bocrest leaned on the wall by the door, which had slid shut again. His voice was more sympathetic than she had ever heard it, and he did not try to take the weapon from her, but he did add, "You're staying with me," in an implacable tone.

She succeeded in looping the string over the limb of the bow. "I'm not going to—"

"I'm not going to lose you as well as Starcrest. We need someone to read this grimbal shit."

Noise in the corridor made them spin toward the door. Tikaya nocked an arrow while Bocrest raised his rifle. In the lab behind them, the men stalked in silence, and she had no trouble hearing the fast, heavy footfalls outside as they grew louder—closer.

Bocrest cursed, probably regretting that he had sent all his men below. The footfalls thundered to a stop outside the door. Tikaya drew the arrow, ignoring the strain between the backs of her shoulders. At least her shoulder no longer vexed her.

The door slid open. She held her breath.

The tunnel was empty.

The tip of her arrow wavered as her muscles quivered from the effort of holding the draw. She glanced at Bocrest, a question on her lips.

Then a head popped around the jamb and disappeared again. It happened so quickly she doubted her sight. Then a familiar voice spoke with wry humor.

"Can I come in?"

"Rias!" she blurted, even as Bocrest shouted, "Curse you, Starcrest."

Rias slid out from behind the wall. "I hope that's a yes."

They lowered their weapons as he joined them on the landing. First Tikaya noticed a garish black eye and fingermarks bruising his neck, then saw the sweat bathing his face, saturating his hair, and dripping from his chin. His chest, framed by the straps of his rucksack, rose and fell with rapid, deep breaths. He wore all his weapons too—in addition to the rifle he carried, pistol, cutlass, and knife challenged the ammo pouches and powder tins for room on his belt. He must have been back to camp since the fight.

"I can't believe you left without me," Rias said, eyes darting as he took in the lab.

"But I saw you with Ottotark," Tikaya said. "He said—I thought you went in the tunnels looking for me."

Rias dragged a sleeve across his brow, not quite hiding a grimace of shame. "No, I didn't believe him. I just had to... I almost lost it with him. I needed to get away, to think."

Tikaya sagged against the railing with relief.

Disgust curled Bocrest's lip throughout their exchange, and he finally jabbed his rifle toward the lab below. "If you were behind us, who in the empire are my men trying to rescue down there?"

"I don't know." Rias glanced at Tikaya. "Maybe someone we can question if we recover him alive?"

Bocrest raised his voice for the benefit of the men below. "Starcrest accounted for. Continue with retrieval operation."

"Treat them like grimbals," Rias called. "It takes a cut to the neck or shot to the eye to kill. And, above all else, do *not* break anything in here."

The last command seemed strange when a man's life was at stake, but the grimness in Rias's mandate kept Tikaya from questioning it.

A shot fired, and a roar came from the center of the lab. Something crashed against a cabinet, and Rias winced. "Not good. Wish I'd had time to do a briefing."

He glared at Bocrest who in turn glared at Tikaya.

"This is your childish sergeant's fault," she said, "not mine."

"Why couldn't the cryptomancer have been a man?" Bocrest glowered at Rias. "Though after all that time on Krychek, you probably wouldn't have cared."

Rias raised an eyebrow. "I am armed, you realize."

Another roar answered the first, and Bocrest's head snapped back toward the lab. "There's a second?"

"Back corner." Rias headed for the stairs. "Who's coming with me?"

"You're not going anywhere," Bocrest said.

"I've fought these before. Better me than them. But I could use backup." He offered Tikaya a tentative smile.

More gunfire and a spatter of curses sounded in the lab, but she stared at him for a long moment. "You want me? After last night?"

"Nothing's changed for *me*," he said with a sad smile. "Besides, you're a better shot with that bow than my other option."

Bocrest sniffed. "I am armed, you realize."

But Rias was already heading down the stairs. "Third team advancing along the south wall," he called.

A strangled groan of pain whispered through the aisles. Before she could think better of it, Tikaya slung the quiver across her back and followed Rias. She could figure out her feelings later.

They descended floating steps too deeply spaced for human comfort. Bow at half-draw, she trailed him across the open area toward a narrow gap along the south wall. As they approached, claustrophobia tightened her chest. The backs of cabinets and lab stations loomed in the same black as the wall, with the counters well above Tikaya's head. She and Rias would have to walk single file.

Sweat dampened her grip and slithered down her spine. She had been ready to throw herself into the fray for Rias's sake. Going on a monster hunt for uncertain stakes was another matter. Why had she followed him down the stairs? Surely he would have been better off with Bocrest. Despite her trepidation, she kept following. It should not matter, especially now, what Rias thought, but she could not bring herself to complain or back out.

He pressed himself against the wall and gestured for her to go ahead. "Since I can fire over your shoulder, you can lead."

Just when she thought it couldn't get bleaker.

"You know," Tikaya said, struggling for nonchalance as she slid past, "some men protect the women they care about by keeping them *away* from danger."

Rias raised an eyebrow. "Sounds stifling."

"Perhaps so."

"Military officers like to challenge people to encourage growth."

"I've been six feet tall since I was thirteen; growth hasn't been my goal for a while."

"You could grow a bit more before you got too big for Turgonian tastes."

She smiled a bit at the double meanings, her mind distracted from her fear. As on the ship, his steadiness calmed her. She could worry about whether it should or not later. In the meantime, she wiped her palms dry, and padded forward, bow ready.

As they traveled deeper into the lab, new higher pitched growls grew audible. They came from somewhere near the back wall. The second creature. Tikaya hoped some of the marines were moving that way too.

They eased closer. Twenty meters, fifteen, ten. Around the corner, claws clacked, teeth snapped, lips smacked, and a tearing sound ripped the air. Tikaya hesitated, certain she did not want to see the source of those noises—or what it was eating. Rias's hand rested on her shoulder briefly. She nodded to herself and peered around the corner.

Fifteen meters away, in a wide aisle, a huge bipedal creature crouched over a ravaged human corpse. The beast lacked fur, and powerful muscles rippled beneath oily black skin that gleamed under the light. The only thing soft were full breasts that swayed as it tore at flesh.

Tikaya slipped out and raised her bow.

The creature snorted. The head that came up appeared simian except for the long fangs flecked with blood and tissue. The arms and hands, too, were disturbingly human, though claws flashed at the ends of those fingers. The creature reared on its hind legs, powerful thigh muscles bunching. It sprang and sprinted toward them.

A rifle fired over her head, the report deafening. Tikaya expected it and did not flinch. Rias's shot grazed the creature's jaw. She loosed her arrow at the neck. It sunk in, and the beast cried out, its scream eerily human. But neither shot slowed its advance.

Rias's pistol fired, hammering the creature between its breasts. Tikaya had time for one more shot and aimed for an eye, but the beast was closing fast. Her arrow skimmed its temple instead.

Tikaya flattened herself against the wall, hoping she could dodge if those claws flashed. She thought the beast's momentum would carry it past her, but it halted with amazing athleticism.

It whirled on her, claws raised. Rank breath washed over her. She ducked even as Rias yanked her out of reach. She almost lost the bow as he charged past, cutlass raised. She recovered and stepped back to nock another arrow. Rias ducked a swipe and darted in, but the muscled torso deflected his blade like armor. He nicked a vein, drawing blood. Claws gashed his arm before he could leap out of reach. Its speed was mesmerizing, but she forced herself to focus.

With the creature sparring with Rias, she could wait for a chance at a critical target. There. She fired, and the arrow plunged into its eye.

The beast staggered into a counter, gashing its own face as it clawed at the arrow. It stumbled, then pitched backward. Still.

Tikaya leaned a hand against the wall for support and let her bow droop. "Next time we attack a twelve-foot-tall monster, we probably don't need to worry about me seeing over your head."

"Conceded." Rias rotated his arm to check the slashes below his shoulder, but dismissed them. "One down. Let's see if the other is still alive."

A rifle cracked in the center of the lab.

"I'm guessing so," Tikaya said.

Rias jogged along the wall toward a cross-aisle where he could cut over. He paused when he reached the half-eaten man. It was wearing the black uniform of a Turgonian marine. Though the neck had been torn out, the chest smashed and ravaged, the face remained mostly intact.

"That's not one of ours, is it?" Tikaya asked.

"No."

"Somebody from the fort?"

Multiple rifles fired.

"Later," Rias said, already disappearing around a corner.

A bestial screech reverberated through the lab, and men shouted orders. Tikaya raced after Rias, careening around the corner to face another melee. A second creature, larger and more muscled than the first, fought in the center. This one was male.

Marines attacked from both ends of the aisle, cutlasses and daggers struggling to pierce the resilient skin. The creature whirled, slashing forward, then back, its wild actions enraged, and Tikaya wondered if it knew its mate had fallen. Blood streamed from its sleek flesh, but it batted men away without faltering. As tall as the Turgonians were, they had little chance of reaching the neck or head with their blades.

Rias charged into the fray. Tikaya drew the bow, waiting to glimpse an eye, but the beast chose that moment to escape. It sloughed off its attackers and charged her direction. Her heart lurched. She loosed her arrow, but she lunged to the side too soon, and her shot only struck muscle.

She glanced at the cabinets on either side of her. There was no time to climb out of reach. She smashed herself to the side again, hoping this creature would run past. Though, even if it did, all it would have to do was rake her on the way past and—

Steel zipped through the air from the aisle behind her. A knife lodged in the creature's eye.

It tripped and tumbled, skidding past her. The prone form crashed into a cabinet, jolting it. The door flung open, and trays of bones spilled out. Human bones, tagged and marked with colored dots. Smaller ones, fragile with age, shattered.

Tikaya found Rias's eyes, thinking of his admonition not to break anything. Chest heaving, he stood amongst the other marines. He shook his head slowly.

"Everyone back to the entrance," he said.

Before following the men, Tikaya tossed a glance toward the back wall. Someone had thrown that knife, yet no marines filed in from that direction.

A clunk echoed through the lab.

"Hurry," Rias urged.

He led a sprint to the stairs where Bocrest twitched an eyebrow at Tikaya and said, "Nice shot."

She did not answer. It had not been her attack that brought the second creature down.

"Let's go," Rias said. "In the hall. We don't want to be here when the cubes arrive."

"Cubes?" Bocrest asked.

Tikaya thought of the square vials from the rocket, but surely he could not mean those.

"No time to explain." Rias pushed past and into the corridor. Leaving the lab without exploring it seemed an abandoned opportunity, but Tikaya did not question him, not when such grimness haunted his face.

Before they took three steps down the tunnel, a door ahead of them slid open. A black one-foot-wide cube floated out at chest level. Tiny red and yellow lights flashed on its top, and a one-inch hole glowed red on its front. A few symbols ran along the sides, and she leaned forward, squinting.

"Back," Rias said. "Back into the lab."

"What does it—" Tikaya started, but the glowing hole brightened and a red beam lanced out. Rias yanked her to the side, and it caught the edge of her sleeve. The beam burned a hole through the material.

She half ran and was half dragged back into the lab. Marines crowded the landing, but Rias shoved his way to a panel on the wall. He waved his hand over a pale square. The door slid down from the top of the jamb.

Tikaya stared at smoke wafting from the hole in her sleeve and swallowed.

A beeping started, soft but audible throughout the lab. It came from the walls, the ceiling, everywhere.

"Two more of those cubes coming from below," Bocrest said.

"If I can get close enough to read what's on the sides, maybe I can figure out how to stop them," Tikaya said.

"If you get that close, you'll be dead," Rias said.

"There're two more in the back." Agarik pointed. "Shooting, burning, er, incinerating the dead creatures."

"Yes." Rias rummaged in his pack. "They do that to everything. And everyone. Also, I don't know how to lock the doors. The one outside will be in soon."

Tikaya bent to examine runes lighting the wall by the door. She recognized one that had indicated "up" on the rocket. When she pressed the symbol it indented, but nothing happened. She found she could rotate it. A soft thunk came from within the wall. "I think that may have—"

"We've got to split up, or we'll be surrounded," Bocrest said.

"Actually, I want·them all in one spot." Rias had opened his rucksack and knelt, mixing a liquid and something else into a bottle. Caustic fumes stung Tikaya's eyes.

A red beam from below splashed against the wall on the landing. It adjusted, lowering, and marines ducked out of the way.

"Forget that," Bocrest said. "Karsus, get these men under cover, and shoot at anything that moves."

"Bocrest!" Rias barked.

The squads were already running off, Bocrest included this time, leaving only Tikaya and Rias on the landing. Below, a pair of cubes, which had been floating languidly toward the stairs, split and increased speed. One chased after each group of men. Before one of the squads reached cover, a beam shot out, taking the last man in the back.

He screamed. Tikaya gripped the railing, unable to take her eyes from the scene.

The rear two men from the squad shot and rifle balls clanged off metal. At the least, the force should have propelled the cube backward, but it never moved. The beam continued, piercing the marine's body and coming out the other side as it incinerated flesh, muscle, and organs. Even when he dropped to the ground and curled into a ball, it stayed with him. It cauterized as it burned an ever-widening hole in his torso. The marine stopped moving, eyes glazed in death. The cube's beam kept breaking down the body, even burning blood away.

Tikaya, thunderstruck by the ghastly scene, almost did not notice Rias racing down the stairs with nothing but a jar of orange liquid in his hands. At first, the automaton ignored him, busy finishing its incineration of the dead man. Rias kept sprinting, one hand gripping the jar, one on the lid. The cube abandoned its task and rotated toward him.

"No!" Tikaya grabbed her bow, though she did not know what good she could do if rifles had not damaged the device.

Rias flung some of the liquid on the cube, then ducked under it as the beam shot. It sizzled past, missing him. It struck the stair railing, but the beam did not affect the black metal. The viscous liquid on the cube smoked red. Pungent fumes gagged the air as it oozed down the sides.

That did not stop the automaton from rotating toward Rias, its ominous red hole glowing. Before its deadly side disappeared from sight, Tikaya fired, aiming for the orifice shooting those beams. Her shot flew true, and the shaft lodged inside. But the red glow flared and a beam incinerated the arrow.

Rias found cover behind a column.

A hiss sounded behind Tikaya.

"Look out!" Rias yelled.

She whirled. The door she had tried to lock opened, revealing two cubes on the threshold. Their holes glowed.

Tikaya leaped over the railing. The floor came quickly, and she landed with an ankle-jarring jolt. Two beams zipped over her head. Off-balance, she skittered into the shadows beneath the landing.

Gunfire echoed elsewhere in the lab. She sensed rather than heard the cubes floating down the stairs.

"Over here." Rias beckoned with an arm. "Zigzag your path."

With a wary glance at the cubes coming down—they were only a few steps from the bottom—Tikaya raced across the open space toward Rias.

"Zag!" he barked.

She angled left. A beam splashed the floor inches from her feet. After a few more steps, she veered right.

Something crashed behind her, but she did not slow to look. She skidded behind Rias's column, nearly jabbing him in the face with her bow.

He gripped her shoulder and started to speak, but an agonized scream echoed from the back corner.

"Curse Bocrest for not listening," Rias growled. He pointed at the cube he had doused with the goop. It lay on the ground, part of its exterior burned away to expose silvery innards. "It's working. I made it in the vehicle garage in Wolfhump. I wasn't sure it'd be the same as— "

"Those two are coming," Tikaya said.

"Right, yes. We have to get some of this on them, too, but I don't have a chance unless they're distracted."

"You want me to do that?"

"Not ideally," Rias said.

The cubes floated closer, no urgency to their movement, but an eerie inexorableness marked their flight.

"This way." Rias led Tikaya down the aisle to find cover behind the next column.

"I thought you wanted to challenge me," she said.

"You saw how lethal one can be, and we've got two to deal with. I don't want you to get hurt."

More likely killed, Tikaya thought. She smiled bleakly. "If not me, who else?"

"I'll do it," an emotionless unfamiliar voice said from behind them.

A young man—he could not have been more than seventeen or eighteen—stood there, wearing fitted black clothing and soft black boots. Several sizes of daggers adorned his belt, and a set of throwing knives was strapped to his right arm. He carried nothing else.

"Go," Rias said, hefting his jar.

If the boy's appearance surprised him half as much as it did Tikaya, he did not show it. She lifted a hand, intending to protest sending someone so young on a suicide mission, but the youth had already jogged from concealment.

Two beams lanced toward his chest, but he anticipated the attack and dove, rolling beneath the cubes. They rotated to target him. This time he jumped to avoid the shots. Next, the mechanical assailants teamed up, showing a disquieting ability to work together. They tried to surround him, but the youth proved too quick. He darted away, keeping both cubes to one side of him.

"If I get killed," Rias said to Tikaya, "get the jar and finish them. It's an acid, so don't let *any* of the liquid touch your skin."

Before she could say how little she thought of his get-killed option, he left. Tikaya nocked an arrow. The bow might not do damage, but perhaps it would help distract the cubes. Though the boy was doing a good job of that on his own. He dodged, darted, jumped, and rolled with the fluid ease of a well-trained natural athlete. Who was this ally who had shown up just in time to help? Even when a beam washed the floor inches from him, his face held no expression, though the intensity of his dark eyes promised nothing would break his focus.

Rias neared the closest cube, keeping its backside toward him. Tikaya fired at it. The arrow clanged off, and the cracked head clattered to the floor. Despite the distractions, the cube somehow sensed Rias' approach. It rotated toward him.

He flung some of the liquid and dodged just before the beam struck. Red smoke fumes plagued the air. The second cube remained focused on the youth who led it around columns and over lab stations. Rias zigzagged back to a column adjacent to Tikaya's with the tagged cube shooting after him. Smoke drifted from its surface, and the corrosive liquid burned through the casing.

"What is that stuff?" Tikaya asked, shifting to keep the column between her and the cube as it approached.

"A variation on royal water," Rias said. "The black metal is particularly susceptible to it. We were trapped in a room with all sorts of chemicals, and I tried several things last time. I couldn't read any of the labels, and I'm lucky I didn't kill myself. It took too long, though. A lot of men died before I figured it out."

The smoke thickened, inflicting the air with an acrid tang. It was nothing like the scent of burning wood or coal or anything else Tikaya had ever smelled. Before the cube reached them, it ground to a halt, then plummeted to the floor, innards exposed.

"Next." Rias headed toward the gunfire and shouts in the rear of the huge lab. "We lost ten men to these things last time. We have to hurry."

"Shouldn't we get the one attacking the boy first?" Tikaya asked.

"He's the last one who needs to be rescued."

They ran through the aisles toward the chaos. When they passed the spot where they had killed the creatures, there was no sign of the remains, not even a blood stain on the floor. The corpse of the marine was gone too.

Rias picked an aisle parallel to the gunfire and shouts of Bocrest's squad. He jumped, caught the edge of a counter, and pulled himself to the top of a lab station. He knelt, his jar poised to pour when the mechanical assailant came into range.

Tikaya thought to wait on the floor, but the youth came into their aisle from the other end. His cube sailed in a few seconds later. Tikaya tossed her bow up, then climbed to Rias's side, hoping to avoid the path of fire.

"Admiral," the youth said as he ran past.

Tikaya blinked, almost as shocked at the calmness of the boy's voice as the fact that he knew who Rias was. Rias leaned over, prepared to pour his concoction on the cube following the young man. It seemed to detect the trap, for it slowed several paces back. Its glowing orifice rotated up, toward Rias and Tikaya.

"Rust," he muttered and prepared to jump.

"Wait." Tikaya jabbed the tip of an arrow into his jar, nocked it, and fired. The dripping missile spun into the red hole. A flash later, a beam incinerated the arrow. The cube floated closer.

"Double rust," Tikaya said.

"It was a good idea," Rias said.

They crouched to jump down into the aisle behind, but the cube slowed, then halted. Smoke wafted from the beam hole. The cube sputtered and thunked to the ground.

"It *was* a good idea." Rias clapped Tikaya on the shoulder and gave her an appreciative smile that warmed her soul, despite the dire situation.

Enemy of the islands, she reminded herself. She was not supposed to be pleased by his compliments anymore.

"Think you can hit that target again to help these men?" Rias pointed to the marines scrambling in the other aisle. They were so busy dodging beams of a cube in their midst they had lost their usual cohesiveness. Every man was busy trying to stay alive. "Make it quick, though," Rias added. "The acid will eat away your arrowheads."

Tikaya waited until the orifice faced her before dipping into his jar. Her shot flew true and made short work of the remaining cubes.

The relieved party met in the open area before the stairs. Tikaya picked up one of the mostly intact cubes so she could work on translating the writing.

Bocrest counted heads and scowled at the loss of two men and injuries of several others. He glowered at Rias. "Why didn't you tell me you had something to battle them with?"

"You didn't give me a chance," Rias said.

"We had to act quickly, and you were digging around in your gear. If you want to override my orders, you need to give me a reason for doing so. Fast. You don't have the right to make decisions and keep the reasons to your..." Bocrest gaped as the youth stepped out of the shadows to join them.

He was smaller than many of the big marines, standing only an inch taller than Tikaya, but, after seeing his grace in evading the beams, she doubted he lost many fights.

His dark-eyed gaze pinned Bocrest. "Admiral Starcrest is giving orders?"

He had short blond hair, a color unusual for a Turgonian, but he did have the olive skin, and he sounded like a native speaker. From the dialect, Tikaya guessed he came from one of the satrapies around the capital. When her gaze fell on the throwing knives on his forearm, she realized he was the one who had killed the creature chasing her earlier. Where had he come from?

"I...uhm..." Bocrest noticed his men watching him—they seemed as confused by the young man's appearance as Tikaya— and straightened, lifting his chin. "Given his helpfulness thus far on the mission, and his familiarity with these tunnels, I deemed it wise to listen to him. I am aware of the emperor's wishes for him, and they will be complied with in the end."

"I see," the young man said, voice cool.

Bocrest shifted uncomfortably under that steady gaze. His men murmured to each other, surprised at their blustery captain's deference.

"What are you all looking at?" Bocrest barked. "Let's get the wounded patched up and set up a camp. And for the emperor's sake, someone figure out where in this blasted maze a man is supposed to piss and drop cannon balls."

The marines scurried off to do his bidding. The youth produced a small sealed envelope and handed it to Bocrest, who accepted it and walked away to read the message.

Tikaya edged closer to Rias. "I'm perplexed. Who is this boy?"

"That is Sicarius, the emperor's personal assassin."

Rias's voice was low, for her only, but the young man looked at them, as if aware of their discussion.

"Is he as young as he looks?" Tikaya asked even as she wondered why he was there. Why had he not traveled with Bocrest from the beginning if he meant to help the captain accomplish his mission? Her eyes widened. Could he be the one responsible for the tortured men?

"I believe he was fifteen when I met him two years ago," Rias said. "He smashed my face into the deck and held a knife to my throat."

Tikaya stared at Rias. "Did he catch you by surprise?"

"No. As I recall, I was trying to catch *him* by surprise."

"Why? What happened?" She frowned, wondering why the emperor would send his assassin to harass his star fleet admiral. Something to do with Rias's reasons for ending up in exile? She tried to read his eyes.

He opened his mouth, but he shut it again and shook his head. "No, I fear you'd suspect my motives if I told you the story."

"Suspect your..." She scowled at him. Now what was he hiding? "I suspect your motives in *not* telling me."

He closed his eyes. "I'm sorry."

"Why are you so elusive about these things?" Her throat tightened. Now that she knew who he was and that she could have no future with him, his choice to keep things from her should not hurt, but it did. "Afraid to share imperial secrets with the enemy?"

She clutched the cube to her chest and stalked toward the lab stations, intending to find some nook where she could be alone to study the language.

"Tikaya..." Rias said.

"Stuff an apple core up it, Admiral Starcrest."

She caught the boy assassin watching, and almost snapped at him too, but the dark impassive gaze stole the heat from her ire and left her chilled. She stalked by without comment.

Several marines sniggered behind her back. Cheeks flushed, Tikaya slipped into the aisles, glad for the concealment.

CHAPTER 16

Few runes adorned the cube, and it did not take Tikaya long to translate them. Automatic cleaning machine. She could have laughed if not for the unsettling realization that the people who created this place had considered human beings something to be incinerated to keep the labs tidy.

With that mystery solved, she itched to work on the next. Weariness plagued her body, and probably would for days in the aftermath of the poisoning, but her mind churned, so she could not think of sleep yet. There was so much to study.

She wished she had Lancecrest's journal, but she would have to return to her gear to grab it, and she did not want to face Rias or the snickering marines. Instead, she explored the back half of the lab. Most of the finds were innocuous—alchemical liquids and powders, equipment and containers—but others were as disturbing as the bones that had scattered when the beast fell. The human organs sealed in jars and slides with blood samples made her wonder if the race who had created this place had come for the distinct purpose of experimenting on people. But, if so, to what end?

She probably should have been horrified by her discoveries, but the labels on the identifiable substances helped her resolve new nouns, and that kept her too busy for squeamishness. A few days wandering this place and she would have an impressive dictionary. If the marines gave her time.

Agarik rounded the corner and approached, his rifle crooked in his arms. He quirked an eyebrow at the rows of open cabinets in her wake.

"Exploring?"

"Yes, this place is perfect. If I had a few weeks here, I bet I could decipher the whole language. Or the science aspects, at least. Of course, this entire language seems to revolve around science and mathematics. I keep wondering who these people were, what happened to them. Where could such an advanced civilization—"

He was frowning, so she stopped.

"Problem?" Tikaya asked.

"No. Yes. I don't know. We've lost so many men out here. Your enthusiasm for such a deadly place is... Well, I can't share it."

"But don't you see? Everything here is labeled. If I can learn how to read it all, this place won't be deadly. We're bumbling into things. Those cubes, they're the maids. Not some malicious security system, a cleaning device to take care of messes in the labs."

"And the poison rockets," Agarik said. "Are they also not malicious if only you know the words? And the gas that twisted our minds in Wolf-hump? Was that not malicious?"

The sobering words squelched her enthusiasm. He was right. It was very likely this place had been created, at least in part, to build weapons. Weapons far deadlier, and ghastlier, than anything humanity currently knew.

Agarik sighed at the expression on her face. "Forgive me, I don't mean to judge. Besides you're not the only one fascinated with the place."

"Oh, what's Rias doing?" Tikaya asked, certain of her guess.

"He's taking apart one of the boxes."

"Figures."

"Uhm, about him..." Agarik watched her, and she had a hunch he had brought up Rias to gauge her reaction.

"Did he send you over to talk to me?"

Agarik's head shake did not surprise her. Tikaya had a hard time imagining Rias sending a minion—or admirer—off to solve problems for him. No, he would likely suffer in silence.

"No, ma'am. He, ah..." Agarik set the butt of his rifle on the floor and polished a smudge on the barrel. "He forbade me from bothering you."

"Oh? And you're going to disobey your boyhood hero?"

"If there's a chance of fixing things, yes." Agarik blew out a long breath. "I got the story about the assassin, if you want to hear it. I think it might influence your feelings for Rias."

Though curious about the story, she hesitated to ask for it. Now that she knew Rias was safe, she needed to put aside her 'feelings' for him, figure out how to thwart the weapons-acquisition mission, find a way home, and warn her family they were in danger. She could not bring herself to send Agarik away, though. "Is that actually what he calls himself?"

"What?"

"Rias. I thought it might be something he made up because he didn't want to tell me his real name."

"He told me to use it. He goes by Federias and said his friends have always shortened it. Apparently, he's never liked his first name. Got teased about it as a boy and told it was girly." Agarik grinned, probably delighted to have been trusted with this secret information.

"Does 'the story' explain his exile?" she asked. "Why he was stripped of everything and declared dead?"

"Yes."

She nodded for him to continue.

"He says he *did* recommend the Kyatt Islands as the place for a strategic outpost, on account of its location right in the center of the sea between Turgonia and Nuria, but he wasn't planning on bloodshed. I don't know if you remember, but a couple of imperial ironclads showed up in your harbor a few years ago. He went in with a diplomat to talk to your president."

Despite her resolution to put aside feelings for him, a flutter went through her stomach. To think that Rias had been so close years before. She had been working at the Polytechnic then, and she remembered the hubbub around those ships arriving. If she had looked out the window at the right time, might she have seen Rias striding along the docks, straight and proud in a dress uniform, flanked by dozens of men who respected him?

"They offered your people entry into the empire as an imperial territory and protection from the Nurians in exchange. Your president said no. They negotiated, tried to get the right to build a naval base on one of your islands. Your president was adamant that your people would remain neutral, and he denied it all. The emperor was not pleased. He ordered Kyatt be conquered, and you know what happened after that."

"Yes." All too well.

"Rias was busy managing the entire Northern Eerathu Theater, and the skirmishes with your people were just a tack on his busy map, but he says he was impressed with your president's backbone and how hard your people fought, especially considering the odds were all against them. The emperor was more annoyed than impressed. Particularly so after you started decoding messages and sending them to the Nurians."

"I'll bet," Tikaya murmured.

"The emperor sent this Sicarius out to Rias's flagship with orders—and don't irk that fellow, by the way; he's apparently been groomed from birth to be the throne's assassin. All Rias was supposed to do was take his vessel into port and let Sicarius kill your president and his advisors."

Tikaya stood statue still. She did not remember any personal attack on the president.

"Rias was angry that the emperor even *had* an assassin. We've always been an honorable warrior people, and sneak attacks are considered cowardly."

"What'd he do?"

"He refused to take the assassin to your island and, when he learned Sicarius was trying to make other arrangements to get there, Rias tried to incapacitate him."

That explained his earlier comment about attacking Sicarius.

"It didn't work," Agarik said. "Fortunately, Sicarius was loyal enough to the emperor not to take it into his own hands to kill a fleet admiral. Rias had time to send warning to your president and describe the assassin so your people could watch for him—that's a part of the story you could verify when you get home, I imagine."

A spark of hope kindled. If the president knew Rias had tried to help him, maybe it would make a difference someday if...

Tikaya shook her head. Was she truly still thinking of bringing him home?

"Sicarius took word back to the capital," Agarik continued, "and the emperor about shi—, er, he was livid at Rias's disobedience. He stripped him of his name, his rank, his ancestral lands, everything, and ordered him taken to Krychek Island. The story passed around is that Rias was assassinated by Nurians."

"Why the story?" Tikaya wondered. "Why tell everyone he was dead?"

"He's a hero to our people and well-liked. He had scads of loyal men who would have made rescue attempts if they knew he was alive."

"Then why not actually kill him?" Could the emperor have known he would need Rias again?

"My guess," Agarik said, "is the emperor wanted his best military strategist somewhere he could get to him again if needed. Though that's quite a gamble."

Tikaya raised her eyebrows.

"Krychek Island isn't a place you put someone for safe keeping," Agarik said, tone bleak. "I remember newspaper stories over the years about some of the men who got sent: cannibals, serial murderers who defiled their victims, molesters who tortured children. Crazy people who aren't right in the head." Agarik ran a thumb along the muzzle of his rifle. "I reckon Krychek Island is like a Harvest Moon War."

Tikaya had heard the Turgonian expression a couple times, but had not stopped to think about the meaning. "As in the war goes so late in the season that even if you win, there's no one at home to bring in the crops, so your family starves over the winter?"

"That's the gist of it. When Rias first came on board, he didn't talk to anyone. He was just the unpredictable monster locked away in that dark cell, and it seemed to suit him. You'd catch him in the light, and you'd see this crazy haunted look in his eyes. The captain was scared of him, and all those guards following him around in the beginning weren't for show. That's why I was so startled when he spoke out on your behalf. He hadn't said a word to anyone up until then. But I guess having a woman present made him want to be more civilized. To pull himself together, you know?"

Tikaya closed her eyes. Rias had never spoken of his time on the island. What demons might it have left cavorting in his head?

"I would hate to see him like that again," Agarik said, eyes sad. "Are you irrevocably mad at him? It's hard to tell with you. Today you worked together as if nothing stood between you, and you saved us again. You're a good team."

Though there was nothing accusing in Agarik's words, they made her gut twist with guilt. Everyone thought she was mad at Rias, him too most likely.

"I'm annoyed that he blindsided me," Tikaya said, "but mostly I'm frustrated with the cosmos. I can forgive him for being born on the other side and for being an officer—*the* officer—in the enemy army, but I can't see having a life with Fleet Admiral Starcrest. It would be a huge betrayal to those I love—I loved."

"It wouldn't be any sort of betrayal to turn your back while they return him to Krychek?" Agarik said.

"He wouldn't let them do that."

"He won't have a choice. That assassin outfought him before, and...I'm not sure he'll care enough to worry about escaping if he doesn't have anything to live for."

Tikaya stared at the floor. His words shamed her. She had been thinking only of herself and how Rias might fit into her life.

"I better get back to my rounds," Agarik mumbled.

"You're a good man, Agarik. I never expected you to play matchmaker for us."

His lips curled wryly. "Me either. But I reckon if you care for someone and you can't have their love, you can either be a spiteful bastard about it or you can try your damnedest to make sure they're going to find some happiness in the world."

* * * * *

Tikaya yawned, a great face-tilting-up kind of yawn that made her crack the back of her head on a cabinet door. That, and her bleary eyes, forced her to concede that she needed sleep. She, fearing the marines would move on too quickly, had spent several hours learning as much as she could from the lab, scrawling notes at top speed. Agarik had been nice enough to bring her food and her notebook so she could avoid the camp for a while longer, but he claimed not to have seen the journal. She thought that odd since she had tucked it into the same place in her rucksack as the notebook, but she had been in a rush to grab a bow at the time, so perhaps it slid to the bottom.

Tikaya picked her way past snoozing bodies toward her gear. Aside from Agarik and a man perched at the top of the stairs, the rest of the marines slept. She did not see the assassin.

She spotted Rias on the edge of the camp, sprawled on his parka amongst a pile of disassembled machine innards. She grinned. Just like a child fallen asleep on the floor amongst his toys. But, as she stepped closer, she noticed his eyes moved beneath his lids, and some dream turned his lips to a grimace. Agarik's words about Krychek Island came to mind. She sat on the rucksack next to him and stroked his hair.

Rias's eyes opened and, for a moment, confusion creased his brow.

"Where were you?" Tikaya murmured.

He rubbed his face. "Nowhere pleasant."

"Should I feel bad about waking you, or is this an improvement?"

Though he did not lift his head, his eyes roved, taking in the bleak black ceilings, black walls, and snoring marines. He smiled though. "Nobody was fondling my head in the dream."

Careful to avoid his bruised eye, Tikaya brushed a lock of hair back from his forehead. "I translated the symbols on the cubes." She recited the lines from memory, and he made the same conclusion as she had.

"Cleaning devices? That's amazing."

"More disturbing, I'd say, since humans are something to be incinerated along with the trash."

"Actually, I was talking about you. You just got your first real clue about the language in Wolfhump, what, three days ago? And now you're reading it." Rias gripped her hand and gazed up at her, dark eyes full of pride. "When you get home, you'll be the main story in the next volume of Archaeology Monthly."

The lump in her throat made her laugh more of a hiccup. Rias's words reminded her, not for the first time, how different he was from Parkonis, who had always envied her language gift. His congratulations had been grudging when she had been selected by the president to work on decryptions during the war. She had not even wanted the dubious honor, made even more dubious by the predicament it had landed her in, but he had envied her the recognition. Maybe there was good reason to love someone who had so many accolades of his own that he could never feel jealous of a bright philologist. Of course, she reminded herself, Rias had nothing now except a trip back to a savage island of deranged criminals. And still he was proud of her.

"Something wrong?" he asked gently.

"No." She wiped her eyes. "I'm sorry I snapped at you. I've—"

His eyes widened. "Tikaya. You don't need to—"

She pressed a finger to his lips. "Let me finish, please?" When he did not nod, she left her finger there. "Before I met you, before Parkonis died, before the war, I knew what I wanted from life. I dreamed of sharing a little house near the beach with someone, close enough to town to walk to the market and the Polytechnic. I'd teach in the mornings and work in the labs in the afternoon, studying relics and data our field people brought in. And I'd have two children, a boy and a girl, of course. Blond hair, blue eyes, freckles." She smiled wryly, acknowledging the unlikeliness that life would ever turn out exactly as she dreamed. "When Parkonis came along, I knew he was the one who could give me that dream." Her smile faded, and her voice dropped to a whisper. "Then the war came, and Parkonis died, and my dream died too. It's hard for me to admit it, because it's so selfish, but I think I've spent the last year mourning the loss of my dream as much as I've been mourning his death."

She felt silly holding her finger to Rias's lips. He was watching and listening. She turned her hand over and brushed her knuckles along his jaw.

"And then I met you. Of course I knew you were a Turgonian as soon as I heard you speak, and you admitted to being in the war, but I imagined you were just some ship's engineer following orders, some simple soldier who none of my people could blame their troubles on, and I had all these ideas about how you could come home with me, and...maybe my dream could live again." She shook her head. "It's not your fault you don't fit into the fantasy I made up. It's not as if there weren't clues to the contrary. I was just set on my theory, because I thought I could work you into my life somehow that way. Like I said, it's selfish. And I'm sorry."

Rias sat up abruptly, and her hand fell away. "Tikaya—"

"Emperor's bunions," Bocrest growled. He lay a couple of men away with his arm flung over his eyes. "If you two are going to wake people up with your relationship crap, you could at least be fucking, so we'd have something to watch."

Rias winced at the crude words. Tikaya's cheeks warmed, but she kept her tone light when she said, "Is he really one of your emperor's most trusted officers?"

"Only because of his parents."

Feral noises emanated from Bocrest's throat.

Rias stood up, took Tikaya's hand, and led her away from the sleeping men. Her heart sped up, and she wondered if he had Bocrest's suggestion in mind. He went to a corner, out of earshot if they talked quietly, but within sight of the camp, so she supposed not. Too bad.

They sat, backs against the wall, shoulders touching.

"Tikaya," Rias said, staring at the floor. "I appreciate your words, but hearing you apologize to *me* is like getting a dagger in the chest. I'm the one who... I need to say..." He snorted, or maybe it was a laugh. "My men used to call me courageous because I'd lead the way into battle and take risks others thought ludicrous. They didn't know that it was just arrogance. I thought I was too good to get myself killed. I knew I wasn't immortal, but I won often enough that I always thought I'd come out on top. So, it wasn't really courage." He continued to look down, avoiding her eyes. "Courage is the ability to do the right thing when you're terrified of the consequences. I've only recently realized that I'm a coward."

For a moment, the only noise was the snoring of the marines. She could hear herself breathing.

"You asked for my name, more than once, and I could have told you. You deserved the truth. If I'd *wanted* you to know, I wouldn't have let Bocrest's threats sway me, but I knew as soon as I told you, that your willingness to spend time with me would be over. I wouldn't be able to dream that somehow, someway..."

He fiddled with his hands. "Tikaya, I'm not a young man. I've been in love before, infatuated with beauty or taken by a sympathetic shoulder, but no woman has ever asked me to explain my papers on mathematics." That familiar half smile tugged at his lips. "And, dear ancestors, the fact that you were the cryptomancer too?" He chuckled. "I fell for you that first day we shot together on the exercise deck."

She watched his face as he spoke and tried to memorize every word. Her heart soared at his naked admission.

"But I knew you could never love Fleet Admiral Starcrest, the man who—Ottotark is correct—pointed out to the emperor the strategic value in having a base on your islands, and helped try to make that advice a reality. Even if you could somehow forgive that person for hurting your people, I'm sure they—your family—would never understand. I wouldn't want to be the cause of your ostracism. I kept trying to convince myself to keep my distance, to figure out a way to make sure you walked away at the end of this, and to just accept my fate. It didn't work. I was afraid to tell you, afraid to lose you, and so I made the wrong choice." He finally looked up, forced himself to meet her eyes. "I've been a coward, and, in being so, I've hurt you. I'm sorry."

Emotion welled in Tikaya's throat. She had fallen in love with him every bit as much as he had with her. The thought of going home by herself, never to see him again, brought tears to her eyes.

She wanted to hug him, to kiss him, but she caught the marine on guard watching them. She settled for leaning her head against Rias's shoulder. "I forgive you."

He rested his head on hers, and neither suggested returning to camp to sleep. She thought about bringing up her suspicions about Bocrest's mission. If Rias had risked his career because he thought assassinating her president dishonorable, surely he would not knowingly help the emperor obtain weapons that could wipe out millions of innocent people. She trusted him more after his confession, but she still hesitated. His first questions to her came to mind, the way he had asked if her president was a good person, if the people liked him. Now she realized he must have had regrets during his time on Krychek, that those questions had been a damaged man asking if it had been worth it. If he had those moments to live over, would he make the same choice? Could she trust him now to make the right choice over one that might gain him the emperor's favor once again?

Rias lifted his head. "Is that the journal you found?"

Tikaya looked toward camp. It *was* the journal. And the assassin was reading it. She could have smacked herself on the forehead for not hiding it. If Sicarius was the one who tortured Lancecrest, he was also the one who had been looking for the journal.

She jumped to her feet and hustled toward the camp while trying not to *look* like she hustled toward camp. If she seemed desperate to keep it to herself, it would arouse suspicions, but she had to get it away from him.

Sicarius flipped through the pages. The way his dark eyes skimmed the columns from top to bottom and left to right made her believe he could read Kyattese. He lifted his head as she drew near, and Tikaya's determined step faltered when that cool gaze landed on her.

"Uhm, that's mine. I mean, I'm the one who found it, and I've been translating the runes drawn in there. The owner's guesses are largely incorrect, so you wouldn't want to..." She stopped talking since he had already turned his attention back to the journal.

To make sure her concerns were founded, she switched languages and asked, "Can you read Kyattese?"

His eyes flicked up briefly, but she received no answer. She took another step, toying with the idea of seeing if he would let her take it out of his hands. An arm slipped around her waist from behind.

"Yes," Rias said near her ear. "He can. Among other languages." He put a hand on her arm and guided her to her rucksack. "Is there something in it you don't wish him to find?"

Her uncertainties about Rias's regrets and loyalties made her hesitate, but she needed an ally, and he was still the most likely one. She did not see how she could fool the Turgonians and eliminate the threat to her people—to the world—by herself. "Instructions on how to launch the rockets."

His grip tightened on her arm. "Why didn't you tell me what was in there?"

Tikaya watched his face. "I didn't know whose side you were on."

"That's..." Rias closed his eyes, "understandable. Get some rest. We'll look for an opportunity to get it back tomorrow."

Tikaya found her bedroll, but her earlier weariness had disappeared. For a long time, she lay on her side, watching the assassin read.

CHAPTER 17

Water trickled somewhere in the distance. After the monotonous black walls and tomb-like silence of the tunnels thus far, Tikaya would appreciate some dripping stalactites, striated walls, bumpy columns—proper cave appurtenances. As of yet, though, no end of the alien passages lay in sight.

The marines marched ever deeper with Bocrest and Rias leading, and Tikaya walking behind them. Sicarius came and went, sometimes padding soundlessly alongside the captain, other times exploring on his own. That morning, Rias had given a briefing highlighting the dangers of the tunnels. Admonitions had included "no touching things" and "don't wander off on your own." The assassin apparently did not believe rules applied to him, and she could not even wish him to get lost and fall off a cliff, not as long as he had her journal.

"You've been here longer than us, right?" Bocrest asked when Sicarius returned from one of his roaming stints. "Do you know where the archaeologists are?"

"No."

"Do you know where the weapons are?"

"No."

"Do you know what other dangers we'll face?"

"No."

The assassin's cool monotone never changed, though Bocrest's pitch grew more agitated as he failed to hear the answers he wanted. He was probably used to flogging kids this age for not cleaning the head sufficiently.

"What *do* you know?" Bocrest asked.

Tikaya, walking behind them, had a good look at the frosty gaze Sicarius slid the captain. She glanced at Rias who merely raised his eyebrows. He might pull her away and keep her from doing something stupid to annoy the young assassin, but he did not appear inclined to watch out for Bocrest.

"I crossed the mountains on foot and arrived only a day before you," Sicarius said.

He withdrew the purloined journal, and Tikaya's fingers twitched. She strained to see over his shoulder as he opened it to a dog-eared page. The instructions. He ripped them out. He turned to another page in the back of the journal and tore the bottom third off.

"What are you doing?" Tikaya blurted.

Sicarius ignored her, showing the scraps to Bocrest. "Operation instructions for the rockets and the sequence of runes Lancecrest pushed to get into the weapons chamber."

Tikaya cringed. She should have hidden the journal. Assuming no one else could read her language had been foolish.

"Lancecrest claimed the sequence only worked once," Sicarius said, "and his team has been stymied since."

"Give the book back to Tikaya now that you've got what you wanted," Rias told Sicarius.

Bocrest glanced at Rias, startled eyes wide. Even the captain had not dared give the emperor's assassin a direct order. But Sicarius handed the journal back to Tikaya without missing a step.

"Thank you," she said, though it seemed obsequious to thank him for returning something he had stolen out of her rucksack. He was going to be a problem—as if she did not have enough problems already. She needed more allies out here, not more enemies, and her only option was the team that waited within. "Why did Lancecrest fire the rocket on your fort?" she asked Sicarius.

He did not respond or even glance her direction.

"I'm just wondering why one of your citizens would turn on your people like that. Is living in the empire that bad? Are people disaffected and eager to fight back against the oppressive rule of your emperor?" She hoped to goad the assassin into speaking, but it was Bocrest who responded.

"There's nothing wrong with living in the empire," he snapped. "If that Lancecrest brat was motivated by anything, it'd be money."

"I didn't know slaying marines in remote outposts could be profitable," Tikaya said.

Rias's lip twitched. He was staying silent, but she decided it did not represent disinterest or annoyance at her sleights toward the empire. In general, he was not as garrulous around the marines as he was alone with her, and she imagined all but the closest of his men had known him as a quiet, enigmatic leader.

"I only bring it up," Tikaya said, "because it might be useful to know why Lancecrest was attacking your people and whether those left inside are out to get you, too, or if he was the leader and now they're rootless."

"I'd like answers to those questions too," Rias said when Sicarius did not respond. "What happened on that ledge?"

Sicarius glanced at the squad of marines following them, men who had grown silent as soon as the conversation started. Rias nodded to Bocrest, and the captain called a halt. He, Rias, and Sicarius walked ahead to speak privately. Tikaya followed. She'd asked the questions, and she intended to get the answers.

The assassin watched her walk up, his gaze cold and unwavering. He didn't want her there. She folded her arms and leaned on the wall. Too bad. Rias's eyes crinkled.

"I was too late to stop Atner Lancecrest," Sicarius told Rias and Bocrest. No remorse or angst colored his tone. He spoke it like a simple fact. "But I learned much from questioning him. He originally heard of the tunnels from Colonel Lancecrest, who disliked his assignment and wanted to retire. He told Atner about the possibility of ancient valuables and asked for a split of whatever profits were made.

"So they intended to be relic raiders from the start," Tikaya said.

"Atner Lancecrest started assembling a multinational expedition of archaeologists and linguists a year ago, and they've been inside for several months. They came for relics. They found the weapons. Atner revised his plan. He decided to figure out how to get the weapons so he could hand them to the emperor and gain favor for his family. Some of his team, which included a handful of Nurians, were against that. A pair of them slipped away with a box. They warned their government, and—"

"The box that was delivered to the capital?" Bocrest asked. "The one that killed hundreds?"

"Yes," Sicarius said. "The Nurians delivered it, and, after the deaths, they sent a message telling the emperor to seal the tunnels forever or more killer artifacts would be delivered."

"Your emperor doesn't seem the sort to heed threats," Tikaya said.

"No."

"Nor," Rias said, "does he suffer fort commanders who share top secret orders with little brothers. Or little brothers whose actions result in the deaths of hundreds."

"But he didn't know about the Lancecrest involvement when he sent you," Tikaya said to Bocrest, "did he?"

"No," Bocrest said. "But Lancecrest—both of them—would have known they'd be in an ore cart full of shit as soon as their roles came out."

Rias nodded. "It would have been more than their deaths. For a disgrace like that, the emperor could take away the entire family's warrior caste status and wipe their ancestors' deeds from the history books."

Tikaya raised her eyebrows at Rias, wondering if his act of disobedience had created a similar backlash for his family. He seemed to guess her question, for he hesitated, then shook his head. She took that to mean not as drastic a result, perhaps, but some backlash, yes.

"I don't get it," Bocrest said. "The family's wrecked, but why make things worse by killing everyone in Wolfhump and Fort Deadend?"

"To delay your party?" Tikaya guessed. "If Lancecrest knew he was dead if he stayed in the empire, maybe he wanted to get the weapons out so he could sell them to the highest bidder. Maybe his family would forgive him if they could all live the life of luxury in some remote paradise."

"But he got himself killed." Bocrest nodded to Sicarius. "So, now all we're dealing with is a confused bunch of science twits with no leader." He appeared pleased at the prospect.

"And possibly Colonel Lancecrest and an indeterminate number of his men," Rias said.

Tikaya nodded, thinking of the half-eaten marine they had found in the lab with the creatures.

"What?" Bocrest asked. "He's dead. I saw his body."

"Are you sure it was him?" Rias asked. "Or was the skin melted by the gas?"

Bocrest opened his mouth, shut it, then spat. "You're right. I saw a body in his office and a jacket with his name on it on the chair, but it could have been anybody. Bloody ancestors, he'll be a pain to deal with if he's in here. Pissed his little brother slagged things up so badly and left him to endure the aftermath."

Tikaya listened bleakly. She had been hoping for fellow archaeologists to ally with; instead she might have another cursed Turgonian military commander waiting. She looked to Rias, hoping for some comfort there, but his face was inscrutable. She still had no idea what he thought about his emperor's desire to obtain these weapons.

"But his team is stuck, right?" Bocrest said. "If they could get to the weapons, they'd have taken them and disappeared by now."

"Correct," Sicarius said. "They lack what we have." His gaze came to rest on Tikaya again.

Her bleakness increased. When this had started, she had worried her skills would not be enough to keep her family safe. Now she worried her skills *would* be enough.

"Valuable intelligence," Rias told Sicarius. "Good work."

Tikaya jerked with surprise. Was he actually complimenting an assassin on the bounty his torture session had yielded?

"Yes," Sicarius said, apparently unaffected by the praise.

* * * * *

The tunnel opened into a cavern with a ceiling that disappeared into darkness. A chasm over a hundred feet wide yawned across the center, cutting through walls as well as the floor. A multistory building perched near the edge on their side, and eagerness quickened Tikaya's step—finally, a chance to see something more than a lab. A plant for distributing water, she guessed. Pipes ran vertically and horizontally from the structure, and a smokestack rose as far as the eye could see. A reservoir adjacent to the building held driftwood-littered water, which trickled over the edge on one side, flowing into the chasm.

Tikaya peered over the edge. Darkness and distance cloaked the bottom—if there was one. The black floor ended at the lip and started again on the other side. The tidy cobweb-free tunnels made Tikaya forget how much time had passed since this place had been created, but this chasm, which appeared to have formed after the complex was abandoned, reminded her that thousands of years, maybe tens of thousands of years, stood between then and now.

"Looks like we've caught up with the other team." Rias pointed at a tunnel entrance on the far side. Tikaya froze. Two men stood in it, and one had shaggy red-blond hair and a scruffy beard. She could not make out features at the distance, but they reminded her of Parkonis and sent a painful jab through her mind. Though her islands did not have the only blonds in the world, that hair coloring combined with the likelihood this was an archaeologist made her suspect this was one of her people. The second figure, dark-haired and dark-skinned, wore black and carried a musket. He could have been one of Bocrest's men. The pair stepped back into the darkness when they noticed the marines watching them.

"How'd they get over there?" Bocrest asked. "And how do we follow?"

"Assuming they have a practitioner studied in telekinetics, they could have floated across," Tikaya said.

Bocrest's expression turned sour. "Starcrest, you know any other tunnels that lead over to that side?"

"No. I don't know what's over there. We were desperate to escape by the time we got here. We climbed those pipes and got out through a vent mountainside."

Bocrest growled and gazed about. Two other tunnels left the cavern on their side.

"Karsus," the captain said, "take your squad through that one and see if there's a way across the gulf. Everyone else with me. We're checking this one."

"I'd prefer to stay here and study the journal," Tikaya said. "Not to mention there's probably much I could learn in that building." And maybe, if she was alone, those archaeologists would come visit her and she could find out more.

"You're not staying alone," Bocrest snapped.

"I can stay too," Rias said.

"Oh, yes, I'm going to leave you two alone to conspire."

"Bet they want to do more than conspire." Someone snickered.

Bocrest silenced the commenter with a glare.

"It's possible there's something in the pumping house that could get us across," Rias said.

Bocrest's gaze landed on the assassin. "Will you keep an eye on them?"

"Yes," Sicarius said.

Tikaya grimaced. A babysitter who was young enough to be Rias's son. Lovely.

Before the marines reached the tunnels, Rias was already checking out the reservoir. An underground stream fed the pool, and the current had pushed logs and branches to the nearest side. He gazed thoughtfully at the wood.

Though eager to explore the building, Tikaya dropped her rucksack and joined him at the edge. She could not remember her last bath, but dipping a finger in the icy water stole her fantasies of immersing herself. Maybe she could heat some up for washing later.

"Getting an idea?" she asked as Rias pondered the driftwood.

"Perhaps."

"You don't think the marines will find another way around?"

"If that rift is a result of a fault line, it could run a long way." Rias tapped a finger in the air toward the building. "The last time I was here, I found a fantastic cutting tool in there. It burned through stone, wood, and metal like a knife slicing apple custard. If those archaeologists didn't find it..." He dragged one of the logs out of the water and nodded to himself.

Tikaya waited for him to explain further, but the assassin appeared at Rias's shoulder. Tikaya jumped. She had not seen or heard the youth's approach.

"Ah, good," Rias said, less discombobulated. "I'll need some more muscle."

Sicarius had to be curious, but his expression never changed.

"What do you think, young man?" Rias asked. "Ever want to fly?"

Sicarius gave the faintest hint of an eyebrow twitch.

"Let's get this wood out of the water," Rias said.

"Can I help?" Tikaya wondered what he planned.

"How are your carpentry skills?

"Er. I helped my father build a birdhouse once."

"An impressive project." Rias smiled and pulled another log out. "But don't you want to explore the pumping house and look for language clues?"

"Yes." Though her curiosity would have to wait for satisfaction, she would rather translate runes than hammer nails anyway.

"Be careful in there. Touching things is how my team got in trouble. Multiple times."

"I won't touch anything," she said. "Unless I can read the label and know what it is."

With journal in hand, Tikaya headed to the structure. Though dwarfed by the cavern, it rose more than fifty feet and sported three rows of windows along each side. She paused inside the threshold, patting down pockets until she located a pencil. Before she headed deeper, Sicarius spoke to Rias.

"I bring you a message from the emperor."

Her ears perked.

"Oh?" Rias said.

"He believes you've been sufficiently punished for your transgressions and is willing to return everything to you—your name, your rank, your land—if you cooperate with Bocrest and myself and we're able to accomplish this mission."

Tikaya pressed a hand against the wall. She barely saw the vast room she had stepped into as she waited for Rias's answer. When it came, it was so soft she almost missed it.

"My ship? My command?"

"Yes," Sicarius said. "You can return with Bocrest, in command of the Emperor's Fist until you can be transferred to the *Raptor* and resume your full duties."

Say no, Tikaya urged. Tell him and your sprite-licked emperor to fall on their swords.

"What *is* the mission exactly?" Rias asked.

Tikaya clenched a fist around her pencil. What was he doing? He couldn't possibly be considering this offer. He had to know it was only coming because the war had gone badly after he disappeared. Disobeyed orders or not, the emperor must have realized he overreacted and come to regret ousting his star admiral.

"Kill the terrorists mucking around in here," Sicarius said, "obtain the weapons for our use, and seal the tunnels."

There. All her suspicions confirmed. She wished she had been wrong.

"And what of Tikaya?" Rias asked.

"She's only here to help with the translations."

"Bocrest has orders to kill her."

Tikaya nodded to herself, thankful Rias cared enough to be concerned. He might be tempted by the promise of getting his command—his *life*—back, but she did not believe he would throw her to the wolves on the way. She might even be the sticking point in this insidious proposition.

"Bocrest's orders were to ensure her cooperation by whatever means necessary," Sicarius said. "If we complete the mission, you'll outrank him again, and you can choose who lives or dies. If you own her loyalty, perhaps you could convince the emperor that it would be more desirable to employ a gifted cryptographer than kill her."

Own her loyalty? Presumptuous ass. But he was good. Curse him, he was good. Bocrest never could have swayed Rias, but this seventeen-year-old kid had all the right answers.

"I will consider your offer," Rias said, giving away nothing of his thoughts. "For now, let's get working."

"Agreed."

Tikaya headed into the room. Her interest in exploring had diminished, but she did not want to be caught eavesdropping. She forced herself into work mode. If the others came in, they would expect her to have made progress.

Tanks and pipes dominated the back half of the vast room, but she gravitated toward rows of black panels where more symbols than she had seen in one place marked the faces. A large oval glowed softly, displaying what she guessed were schematics or diagrams monitoring the station. She copied symbols, but her mind dwelled on Rias's conversation with the assassin, and she struggled to concentrate.

"Focus," she muttered to herself.

She tilted her head back to massage her neck and noticed only two rows of windows. There were three outside, so there had to be another story up there. No stairs, ladder, or anything similar led upward. Turgonians had steam-powered lifts in their taller buildings—might this advanced race have something like that too?

She circumnavigated the interior, finally spotting a pale blue circle glowing on the floor in one corner. Thinking it might mark a place where a lift would descend, she waved a hand above it. Nothing happened. She pressed her boot into it and pulled it out. Nothing. Finally, she stood in the center with both feet planted.

Air whooshed around her.

"Errkt," she blurted, dropping her journal.

A platform of air thrust from below, propelling her upward. A circle in the ceiling slid aside, and the force raised her through a hole. As soon as her feet cleared the aperture, the floor slid back into place, and she stood on a second blue circle. It felt solid, but she jumped to the side anyway.

A cozy space spread before her. Though she could identify little at first glance, she had the impression of living quarters and furnishings. Perhaps the caretaker for the pumping house had dwelled there. If so, she had a chance to see beyond the weapons-building, experimenting-on-humans side of the ancient people.

Tikaya roamed the space, repeatedly reminding herself not to touch things. Furnishings included cubes, octagonal structures, high tables, and a large hollow sphere open on two sides. No knickknacks or artwork decorated the surfaces, nor could she find practical tools such as eating implements, but perhaps all that had been taken when the occupant left for...wherever these people went.

There was one exception. In a storage area, she found a rack designed to hold spheres slightly smaller than her fist. The rest of the concave slots were empty, save for one. She slid the smooth black sphere out. A few groupings of runes ringed the center. She did not recognize them, but eagerness suffused her. Here was an artifact she could take with her to show the world. She pocketed it to check against the runes in Lancecrest's journal later.

She was about to peer out the window to check on Rias's progress, when her gaze snagged on a clear tank against the far wall. All the furnishings were made from the usual black material, but that piece was as clear as Tenesian glass. An inkling that it might be a bathtub enticed her further. Why settle for washing in front of marines and teenage assassins in the reservoir when she had this private room? And with the men off exploring, what were the odds anyone would stumble upon her? Hammer blows started up outside, so the two remaining men were busy on Rias's project.

Wary about making assumptions and touching the wrong thing, she puzzled over a small plaque near the ledge. She recognized the symbols for water and animals, but who would bathe animals? Then the pieces clicked into place: not animals, fish. It was an aquarium. Perhaps the plant siphoned off aquatic life from the stream for saving or for studying, or perhaps they simply liked observing fish for the same reasons as humans. Either way, Tikaya grinned. She was not above bathing in an aquarium.

She fiddled with the controls, and soon water flowed from an overhang around the inside of the tank. Her grin widened when she discovered she could change the temperature. Not only could she have a bath, but she could have a hot bath.

She snorted at herself. Such a female characteristic to be so tickled at the idea of a warm bath. She shrugged, removed her boots, and unbuttoned the Turgonian military jacket with relish. How she missed her sandals and loose hemp dresses.

There was no place nearby to set the clothing, so she folded it and crossed the room to leave everything on something octagonal, flat, and chest-high she decided to call a table. She skipped back to the tank and slipped over the side. Warm water embraced her, and she shivered with delight. She unbraided her hair, submerged everything, then draped her arms over the sides and laid her head on the ledge. Bliss. The bath reminded her of the volcanic hot springs near her family's property. She wondered how everyone back home was doing. The harvest would be over by now. She had missed her nephew's birthday and her parents' anniversary celebration. She closed her eyes, lost in memories of home.

"Tikaya?" Rias called sometime later.

She sat up, and water sloshed over the side. When had the hammering stopped outside?

"Tikaya, are you all right?"

"Fine!" She scrambled out of the tub. "I'm fine up here."

Naked and dripping water, she peered about for something to use as a towel.

"You didn't touch anything, did you?" He sounded like he was right below the lift.

She darted for her clothes even as air whooshed.

Rias appeared on the platform before she made it half way. Worry furrowed his brow, and he clutched her journal. That expression changed to a wide-eyed gape when he spotted her.

Frozen mid-step, Tikaya felt ridiculous—and guilty at being caught relaxing while everyone else worked.

"I, uhm, sorry." She stood, dripping, not sure where to put her hands or how to explain. "I found this tub, you see, and it's been so long, and, well, one does get sort of dirty tussling with tunnel monsters and marching across the tundra, and..."

Rias was just staring. She really ought to shut up and put some clothes on.

He closed his eyes and clenched a fist, looking very much like a man trying to control his temper. With rigid, precise motions, he walked to the table, placed the journal on it, and turned his back on her.

"Take your time," he rasped, then stepped on the platform and disappeared.

Belatedly, she realized it was not his temper he had been struggling to control. Her first thought was that she should have hopped into his arms and invited him to join her in the tub. Her second thought was to remember he was on top of the Kyatt Islands enemies-of-state list and that she had no idea what kind of seeds Sicarius's promises had planted in his head. The third thought ran the way of dismissing the second and seeing what might come of the first.

"Tikaya, you think too much," she muttered, grabbing her clothes.

Outside, she found Rias and Sicarius building the frame of something that promised to be large. While the assassin dragged wood over, Rias knelt, his back to her, and hammered. Hard.

"Rias?" she asked between whacks.

His shoulders tensed, and he hunched his neck. "Yes?"

She took a couple steps toward him. "May I speak with you?"

He fiddled with the hammer. "I should keep working, try to get this done so we can cross as soon as possible."

Tikaya hesitated. Maybe she had guessed incorrectly. Yet he had never lost his temper with her, and it was hard to imagine a midday bath truly irking him.

"Please?"

Rias's head drooped. He stood, gave Sicarius instructions, and finally faced her. Tikaya led him out of the assassin's earshot.

Rias stared at the ground, avoiding her eyes. She was about to speak, but he did so first.

"I'm sorry. I didn't mean to stare. I wasn't expecting you to be, ah..."

She resisted the urge to hug him—that would probably make him more uncomfortable—and gripped his forearm instead. Corded muscle lay beneath her hand. "I don't mind. You can stare." Though so many differences stood between them, she could not feel anything but delighted that he would want to.

Rias lifted his eyes. "Oh? I had the impression that your parents wouldn't approve of Fleet Admiral Starcrest ogling their daughter."

"They're not here."

He arched his eyebrows. "I didn't think you were particularly enamored at the notion either. Something about a nation's war enemies not being easily inserted into dreams involving beach houses and blond children."

She blushed. "Originally, I was rather distraught at the dishevelment of my dreams, but I must admit I can't think of anyone else in the world I'd rather have ogling me."

"Really." His eyes gleamed with humor but intensity too. He brushed his fingers down a lock of damp hair dangling by her cheek.

Tikaya considered the construction site and the assassin who, through tact or disinterest, was ignoring them. "Almost private around here at the moment." She arched her eyebrows and stepped closer, placing a hand on his chest. "I haven't figured out which piece of furniture up there is a bed, but I'm willing to conduct research."

"I wouldn't think it'd be a problem. You found the tub after all." Rias slid his arm around her, drawing her against him.

"Actually, that's an aquarium."

She felt the soft rumble of laughter in his chest, but it ended with a sigh. She tilted her head back, searching his face.

"Trust me, I'd very much like to research the furniture with you, but..." He smiled and brushed his thumb along her lips. "I suppose it'd be rather irresponsible of me."

She barely managed to avoid blurting 'huh?' Instead, she guessed, "Because you're supposed to be building a, er, whatever that is you're building?"

Rias snorted. "Rust what I'm building—and it's a counterweight trebuchet, by the way." His inability to dismiss his project without at least a short explanation almost made her laugh, despite her confusion over the rejection.

"I'm aware of what is, and what isn't, included in a standard Turgonian field kit," Rias went on, "and I wouldn't want to put you in the awkward situation of explaining to your family how you came to be pregnant with an enemy admiral's child."

"Oh." She laughed with relief. He wasn't rejecting her.

Rias frowned at her reaction. "Tikaya, I know what the world believes about Turgonians, and the Kyattese have every reason to think the worst of me. I fear that if you intimate that we're even friends, your people will believe I've tortured and brainwashed you into giving that response."

He looked exasperated that his words didn't drive the grin from her face, and his concern touched her.

"What you say may be true," Tikaya said, "but that's something to worry about after we both get out of here alive. As for the other, getting pregnant wouldn't be possible until I returned home to see one of our doctors to have the..." She groped for words to explain it in Turgonian—as far as she knew, their women took their chances drinking egata tea for contraceptive purposes. "It's a procedure, performed by a doctor—who is, in our culture, a practitioner specializing in the psychological and somatic aspects of the mental sciences. Anyway, it's not irreversible. You just go see the doctor again when you want to have children."

During her explanation, his expression changed from consternated to perplexed to enlightened. "There is no...danger?"

"No. After certain incidents during the war, it was recommended by our government that any women at risk of being captured have it done."

His face darkened. "Were there many? 'Incidents?'"

"I was sheltered by the fact that I never left the island, but from the folks who went out, I heard...there were some ships you really didn't want to find yourself aboard."

"I see." His jaw was tight, body rigid. "I'd ask for the names of those ships, but there's nothing I could do now. It's hard to know—I don't mean to make excuses, but men present a vastly different face to their superiors than they do to their prisoners."

"I doubt you ever did."

He grimaced, apparently not in the mood for praise, and she wished she had never brought up the subject. Except, she reminded herself, that bringing it up meant disavowing him of the notion that he could send her home a mother. Which actually was not a horrifying concept, though he was right in that it would be easier to deal with further down the line.

Still, a smile curled her lips at the thought of a passel of precocious toddlers scurrying around the house, getting into mischief and cutting down heirloom fruit trees to build play forts.

"What are you thinking of?" Rias's muscles relaxed as he watched her.

"Furniture research." She rose on her tiptoes, marveling that her eyes still weren't level with his, and kissed him.

Her explanations resulted in one pleasant outcome: he did not hesitate to return it.

The moment ended abruptly. Rias pulled away, annoyance flickering across his face. Before she could ask why, she heard the clomp of boots. One of the squads of marines had returned.

"What, by the emperor's eternal warts, is this mess?" Bocrest bellowed as soon as he entered the cavern and spotted the fledgling frame and the heaps of wood surrounding it.

Rias sighed and dropped his head on Tikaya's shoulder.

"Tonight?" she suggested.

He released her with a hand squeeze and a promise in his eyes. Please don't let monsters, machines, or annoying marines ruin the night, she thought.

"We need help, boys," Rias called. "Grab a hammer."

"About this catapult..." Tikaya said, a question occurring to her as her gaze skimmed the chasm.

"Counterweight trebuchet," Rias said.

"Yes, of course. How will one land without breaking every bone in her body?"

"Parachutes, naturally." Rias help up a finger. "That reminds me." He turned to holler at the approaching men. "Anyone who isn't able to find a hammer and work on this is on sewing duty."

Without glancing at the captain, the marines hustled over, prepared to dive into the construction work to avoid a stitching task. Chuckling, Tikaya returned to the second-story retreat to examine the sphere that had piqued her interest earlier.

CHAPTER 18

The sphere proved amazing. With the journal's help, she deciphered the runes on the outside, which were a proclamation of ownership and instructions for firing it up. Once she did that, a hole smaller than a grain of sand projected a display above the sphere. It appeared solid but she could wave her fingers through it as with an illusion. Plenty of practitioners who studied optics could make them, but she could not fathom how it was done with technology. She did not care either. It was the images and runes within the three-dimensional display that enraptured her. She found herself reading someone's diary, and she could look up symbols and terms she did not understand, as if a dictionary and encyclopedia underlaid the journal. This was the type of artifact every philologist dreamed of finding, something that held the keys to unlocking an entire language. She marveled that the other team had left it. Maybe they had not been up here, or maybe they had not realized what they passed up.

"How do you turn the water on?"

Rias's voice startled Tikaya so much she dropped the sphere. It slipped from her fingers and clunked on the high table where she sat. She caught it before it rolled off the edge, though she almost dropped it again when she spotted Rias.

He stood by the tub, his weapons, boots, and shirt already on the floor next to his rucksack, and a towel and bar of soap on the ledge. She stared at his muscled chest. If he had been on the gaunt side when she first met him, that was not the case now. Hard to imagine someone filling out on that abysmal military food, but perhaps it suited him. Scar tissue scored his torso and arms: several old gashes and two dense knots where he must have been shot. Some of those wounds had been life-threatening and represented a lot of pain. As with Krychek, he never spoke of it, never complained.

"Should I be feeling self-conscious under this scrutiny?" Rias asked. "Or are you only looking this way while thinking about translating runes?"

Heat flushed her face. She decided his first question was safest to answer. "Push on that symbol and slide it up, then rotate it for hot or cold."

"Hot? Excellent." He turned on the water and hopped up to sit on the edge facing her. "You're engrossed there. You must have found something good."

She brightened, taking this for an invitation to share her findings. "Yes! It's a journal someone kept. You must be wondering about this place, these people. It's all explained in here, though if I wasn't sitting here I'd think it the stuff of a storyteller's imagination. These people—they called themselves the Orenki—they came from another planet. A group was persecuted for their scientific research methods and driven out of their homeland. They came here and experimented—this is chilling by the way—experimented on primitive humans because we were biologically similar to their people. They wanted to come up with devastating weapons so they could return to their home world, use them on their own kind, and take over."

Rias opened his mouth to speak, but she barely noticed. She still had to tell him the best part.

"You're going to love these instructional, uhm, illusions—sorry, no better word for it in my language or yours. The first one I found shows how to repair and maintain this pumping facility. It looks like there are thousands of sets of instructions on all sorts of mechanical things, though I haven't quite figured out how to search through them. They're organized by codes. But I *will* figure it out. It's just a matter of..."

Rias turned off the water, and Tikaya realized she had been talking for a long time. And that she had cut him off. She smiled sheepishly. "Sorry, did you want to speak?"

Rias chuckled. "From another planet, you say?"

Tikaya, deciding she should let him talk for a while, offered an encouraging, "Mmhmm."

"I'm too ignorant of astronomy to even ask how that'd be possible, but given what I've seen here, I can't claim to be utterly surprised. I'm hoping they weren't ultimately successful, because I'd not be comfortable knowing beings capable of making such weapons were still out there."

Yes, that was an unsettling idea, but Tikaya was more concerned about human beings learning how to use those weapons. She could *not* allow the Turgonian emperor to have this technology. Or a disaffected marine colonel. Or anyone.

"Rias?"

"Yes?"

Tikaya wanted to tell him, ask him for his help going forward. But when she gazed at him, at the scar on his eyebrow and the war wounds on his torso, she stopped herself. He might share her passion for academics, but she could not forget he was a soldier. He had been loyal to a totalitarian government his entire life, and his one disloyal act had cost him more suffering than anyone should have to endure. Would he truly choose such a road again? "You should bathe before the water gets cold."

He watched her with sad eyes, and she wondered how much of her thoughts he read.

"After all," she said, "you've seen me naked. It's only fair I get to see just how much of a Turgonian legend you are."

That drew a self-deprecating chuckle, but not the repartee she expected. He slid his trousers off and climbed into the tub. Despite her words, she dropped her gaze to the sphere to give him privacy. She glanced up a few times, but Rias seemed lost in thought. He was considering Sicarius's offer, she knew it. Probably trying to figure out if he could work her into his life once he had everything back together. She supposed, in some less than ideal scenario, she could see living in Turgonia with him, but slaving for the emperor, creating ciphers her own people would never crack if there was another war? That was *not* going to happen. And even the rest made her grimace. He would be off at sea most of the year, and she would be alone amongst strangers, thousands of miles from her friends and family.

"That bad of a show, huh?" Rias leaned against the tub wall, arms folded on the ledge, chin resting on them.

She tried to disguise her blank stare but doubted she succeeded.

"The show—me," he clarified. "Nude. Never mind. I can see you're busy with the sphere. I understand the appeal of a puzzle, though I fear your enthusiasm means I'll be ogling only myself tonight." His smile was wistful but accepting.

"Oh." She shoved the sphere into a pocket and ran a hand through her hair, which still hung loose. "That wasn't the puzzle I was pondering."

Rias cocked an eyebrow. "No?"

Better to bring it up for discussion than guessing at—and maybe misinterpreting—his thoughts. For all she knew, he was musing over ways to remove a wart from his toe. "I heard Sicarius talking to you."

"Ah." He nodded with understanding, but did not say anything. No words to assure her she had nothing to worry about.

"I couldn't fault you for being tempted, but..." She searched his face, but his eyes were cast down, thoughts apparently turned inward. "Rias, I love you, you know that already. But I'm not going to do anything to hurt my people, and I'm definitely not going to work for your emperor."

"I thought not," he murmured.

"And..." She drew a deep breath, "I'm not going to let Bocrest, that assassin, or anyone else walk out of here with weapons that could destroy millions. I don't know how I'm going to stop them yet, but you'll have to kill me to keep me from trying." She lifted her chin. There, she had said it. Maybe it would have been smarter to lead him to believe otherwise, but she did not want to lie to him, even a lie of omission. Maybe that made her naive, but, so be it.

"Good."

"Good?" She rapped a knuckle on the table. "Would it be possible to get more than one-line responses? Do I need to posit my statements as math problems?"

Rias chuckled. "Oh, you're hard on me, Tikaya." He dunked his head under the water, ruffled his hair dry, hopped out of the tub, and grabbed the towel. "I was proud of myself for baring my feelings to you last night. I'd been pacing through the hills rehearsing that while the camp was conspiring to leave me."

Even frustrated with him, she had a hard time ignoring the 'show.' He wrapped the towel around his waist and padded over, rivulets of water snaking down the gullies between his muscles. He sat on the edge of her table, and she reminded herself to look at his face.

"I'm not used to confiding in people," he said. "Being a captain or an admiral, it's a solitary vocation. You're expected to be infallible, even omnipotent. Sharing your thoughts, showing any kind of fear or hesitancy, might crumble that facade, and that's something men need to believe in when chaos is erupting around them and odds seem impossible."

"I'm not in your chain of command, Rias."

That drew a smile. "I know. And I'm thankful for that. I'm glad you're here to remind me... Yes, of course, the weapons need to be destroyed. That's too much power for one man to wield, too much temptation. The easier we make it to kill, the less time there is to master the art of knowing when not to."

Tikaya nodded—it was everything she had hoped he would feel—but his earlier thoughtfulness made her suspect more remained unsaid. "But?"

"But..." Rias combed his fingers through his hair, spraying flecks of water. "You're right: I *am* tempted by the emperor's offer. I can't help but wonder if I could have it both ways. Help them with their mission, get my life back, and figure out how to make the weapons disappear later on." He picked at the hem of his towel. "They're selfish thoughts, not honorable ones, but dear ancestors, Tikaya, I've missed this." He waved to encompass the tunnels and the marines camped outside the pumping house. "Command, purpose, a challenge. When I'm not Admiral Starcrest, naval strategist, I'm not sure who I am or what else could be out there for me." He turned his eyes toward her, the question in the air.

Me. That was her first thought, but she kept it to herself. She was not fool enough to believe that she could dump herself in his lap as the answer—a man like him needed more stimulation than a relationship offered—but her second thought offered a neater solution. She hoped. "Do you know what the prime groupings in this language mean?"

His brow furrowed. "No.... Did you figure it out?"

"I haven't an idea." She tapped a fingernail on the sphere. "I've learned that what we've seen is one of four languages these people used, and this one is all skewed toward mathematics and science. I may be able to translate it eventually, but the numbers are beyond me. Figuring it all out, finding useful applications for our own world, it'd be the work of a lifetime. For someone interested enough to stick with me for that long."

"Ah?" A hint of speculation entered his eyes. "But you made it clear I wouldn't have a place on your islands."

"There are other countries in the world. Maybe we could find one where you're not wanted dead on sight."

"That might be a challenge. Doubly so, since I'm a penniless vagabond with nothing to offer you except myself."

"I'm rather fond of yourself." Tikaya scooted to the edge of the table to sit closer to him. "And..." She laid a hand on his bare arm. "Did you not say you appreciate a challenge?"

His gaze dropped to her hand, then returned to her face, and he smiled, the quirky half-smile that made her insides tangle. "This is true."

She leaned into him, breathing in the scent of lye soap. His bare thigh touched hers, warm even through her clothing. Too much clothing. She really ought to...

Rias slid his fingers through her hair, and she forgot her thought as goosebumps rose across her flesh. He removed her spectacles, and set them aside.

"So, have you decided?" He bent and kissed her neck, warm breath tickling her skin. "Is this thing the bed?"

"Uhm." Tikaya laid her hand on one of his broad shoulders, then slid it down his arm, tracing the dips and rises of the muscles. "What?"

He drew back, eyes narrowed in mock accusation. "You're not thinking about runes, are you?"

"Furthest thing from my mind."

"Really?"

"Well, it's definitely a distant second place to something more prominent."

"Oh, good." He tilted his head. "I *am* the something, right?"

She grinned. "Let me answer your first question. I think our current seat is the human equivalent of a coffee table. I believe that sphere over there is the bed. You get in and warm air floats you up and supports you. You can just lay there or there's an option for, ah, undulation."

"Sounds fascinating."

He slid off the table, faced her, and slipped his arms around her waist. She leaned into him, lips parting, and invited in his warmth. She tangled her fingers in his damp hair, pulling him closer even as his arms tightened around her. Where he had been hesitant before, asking permission, he was sure now, and she felt his need. And her own. It had been a long time for both of them, and she could never remember wanting someone so much. Not just for now, but forever.

His grip loosened, and she voiced a muffled protest, but his lips smiled against hers, then he knelt. He gazed up at her as he unlaced her boots, and her breath caught at the adoring tenderness in those gold-flecked eyes. She recovered and dug into the buttons of her uniform jacket. Her fingers didn't seem to work as well as they should.

"I miss my dress," she muttered.

"Me too." Rias's eyes crinkled as the first boot clunked to the floor.

She shucked the jacket, annoyed when her arm caught in the sleeve. By now, he knew she was no graceful gazelle, but it would have been nice to undress competently.

She started to tug the shirt over her head, but hesitated. It was silly—he had already seen her naked and was clearly interested—but a self-conscious twinge stilled her hands. With Parkonis and those scattered few before, she had shared bench space in the cute-but-not-beautiful part of the arena. Even before Rias turned into some legendary Turgonian hero, she had known he belonged up front, in the I-could-have-anyone-I-want seats. Tonight, he wanted her, but if by some miracle they made it out of here, would that change? When there were more attractive options available?

"Tikaya?" Rias asked gently, concern in his tone. The second boot had joined the first, along with the scratchy wool socks, but he still knelt, face tilted up, watching her.

"Sorry, it's nothing." The future was a murky incorporeal place; best to enjoy what was real, what was now.

Rias stood, body solid and warm between her legs, but tense. "Please, tell me. I don't want any more secrets, any more misunderstandings. I'm on your side out here, above all others." His eyes probed hers. "Do you trust me?"

She blinked. "That wasn't what I was doubting. I mean, I wasn't doubting. I was just wondering if...if you saw me, back when you came to Kyatt to talk to our president, if I'd been in your path somewhere along the way...would you have noticed me?"

"Ahhhh." Rias grinned and the tension melted from him. "Indeed so." His eyes grew hooded, sultry, and he leaned into her. "Especially if you'd been wearing that dress that so nicely accents your curves."

He slipped his hands beneath her shirt and massaged his way up from her waist. She shivered at the sensations those callused but gentle fingers stirred. He kissed her mouth, her jaw, and down to her neck, and she closed her eyes, arching into him.

"You do know..." he murmured against her throat, lips sending spirals of heat to her core. "Those dazzling blue eyes are rather rare in Turgonia. Exotic." He spoke slowly, lazily, kisses punctuating his words. "And it's always a challenge to find a lady of sufficient height."

She would have laughed, but his mouth returned to claim hers, and she met him with equal intensity, humor forgotten. He broke away only long enough to say, "You're a beautiful woman, Tikaya, and I love you."

She gave him a fierce hug before turning to other matters. There was not much talking after that, and fortunately he proved more adept than she at removing military uniforms.

* * * * *

Tikaya woke with a start. The soft light of the room left her confused as to the time. She was in the sphere, with its shelf of air acting as a mattress. Though she had no blanket, a cocoon of warmth kept the alien bed cozy.

Rias sat next to her, head cocked, ear toward the window.

She touched his bare back. "What is it?"

"I think I heard a scream."

"Not one of mine?"

"Not this time." He smiled and kissed her before crawling past her and out of the sphere. He reached the window before she maneuvered off the air cushion.

"Better get dressed." Rias jogged to their piles of clothing and tossed hers on the bed.

"What's going on?" She tugged her shirt over her head and tied her hair back.

"I can't see. There's some kind of fog out there."

As soon as Tikaya had trousers and boots on, she hustled to the window. A gray-blue haze made it impossible to see more than a few feet. She could not make out the reservoir, the walls, or the ground where the marines camped.

Rias belted on his sword and checked the rifle.

"Wait," Tikaya said as he headed for the lift. "What if it's poisonous? What if everyone is already..."

Rias hesitated, one foot on the blue circle.

A yell of pain pierced the walls and was cut off.

"They're not dead yet," he said.

But he did retrace his footsteps and find the towel he had used earlier. He tore it lengthwise, handed half to her, then wrapped the other half around his head to cover his nose and mouth. She tied hers and followed him down the lift.

Rias slid the door open and paused to listen before venturing out. "Stay close," he whispered.

They slipped outside. The haze stung Tikaya's eyes. Even through the cloth, she smelled an odor reminiscent of burnt coconut.

Rias led her toward the camp. Visibility ran only a few feet in the dense fog. They reached the first prone form, Agarik, still under his blanket.

"Is he..." she started.

Rias knelt and checked for a pulse. "He's breathing."

"Sleeping?"

Rias shook Agarik's shoulder, which elicited a snore, but nothing more wakeful.

"Not the type you can be roused from apparently," Rias said.

They crept farther and found more sleeping marines. None of them could be shaken awake, and Rias stopped trying.

At the edge of the fog, a hint of green clothing appeared on the ground to the right. Tikaya stepped over a marine to find herself staring at an unknown face with blood still streaming from a slashed throat. She struggled for detachment—and to keep from stepping in the spreading crimson pool. The dead person was small and thin-boned with a green shirt and brown trousers that lacked any hint of military uniformity. Definitely not Turgonian, but she was not sure of the nationality.

"Rias?" she whispered.

He had disappeared in the fog. She walked in the direction she had last seen him, but tripped over one of the marines. Her reaction was too slow and, almost as if she floated in water, she toppled face-first to land on the man. He grunted but did not wake.

Confused at the heaviness of her limbs, she pushed herself up. It felt as if a hundred pound rucksack burdened her. The cloth covering her face might delay the fog's effects, but she would be snoring alongside the marines soon if she did not get away from it.

"Rias?" she called a little louder.

"Tikaya?"

She nearly tripped again. That wasn't Rias. That wasn't any Turgonian. It sounded like...

She put a hand to her chest. It couldn't be.

"Tikaya?" the voice came again. "Are you here?"

She closed her eyes. The voice, so familiar, was speaking in her language.

"Over here," she said. She did not say his name. She still did not believe it could be him. How could it be? He was dead, his ship sunk over a year before.

She held her breath as the fog stirred. A shape coalesced.

"Parkonis," she croaked, lifting a hand.

He was a slight figure in comparison with the Turgonians, and he looked even thinner than she remembered. His curly red-blond hair, always a mess, had grown and stuck out in every direction, much like the beard hiding his chin and neck. Anxious blue eyes looked her up and down. He was the one who had watched from the opposite side as the marines entered. Oh, Akahe, if she had been close enough to identify him earlier, would she have...

She glanced behind her shoulder. Where had Rias gone?

Parkonis started toward her, arms wide, a white toothy grin escaping the beard. But his toe bumped against the fallen green-clad man.

His smile faltered. "Tatkar, no." His gaze darted a dozen directions. "One of them escaped the gas. We have to—"

A dark shape slipped out of the fog behind him.

"No!" Tikaya shouted before she even saw the bloody dagger.

She lunged forward, knowing she could never stop the assassin in time. He, too, wore a cloth across his face, but it did not hide the intent in his cold, dark eyes.

Rias stepped out of the fog behind Sicarius and dropped a hand on the assassin's shoulder. The dagger froze.

Parkonis whirled, took in the tableau, and stumbled back. Eyes still fixed on the assassin, Tikaya stepped forward and gripped Parkonis's hand.

"I have no idea how he's here," she said, talking to Sicarius who seemed to be deciding whether to finish what he had started or not, "but this man is a gifted archaeologist, and if anyone can help you get your weapons, he can."

Parkonis's Turgonian was as good as hers, and she had no trouble reading the incredulous look he gave her—helping the empire was the last thing he wanted to do. She squeezed his hand, hoping he would recognize the don't-say-anything signal. Rias's gaze fell to the hand hold, and guilt washed over her at his pained wince. He closed his eyes for a long moment.

Tikaya lifted her free hand and spoke as much for him as for the assassin. "Let's figure out what's going on before we do anything else."

Rias pulled a mask over his face, but instead of responding he released Sicarius and disappeared into the fog.

"Brace yourself," Parkonis whispered in Kyattese.

Tikaya opened her mouth to warn him the assassin understood their language, but the hairs on the back of her neck leaped to attention. A heartbeat later, blinding whiteness engulfed the cavern, and a thousand cannons roared in her ear. Her feet floated from the floor, and some-one—Parkonis?—wrapped his arms around her. She had the impression of weightlessness, of her body moving toward the chasm.

"What's going on?" she yelled, but she could not hear herself over the clamor in her ears.

With her senses overloaded, it took a moment to realize what was happening: Parkonis was rescuing her. And she did not want to be rescued, not if it left Rias to wonder if she had scurried off with her old lover.

She thrashed. She had to escape before they reached the chasm. Her elbow caught Parkonis in the gut, and she felt rather than heard his pained exhalation. Regret mingled with desperation—she did not want to hurt him.

Parkonis shouted in her ear, but she could not hear words above the roar. She squirmed again, determined to free herself. He let go with one arm, and she thought she had her chance, but something cold and coin-sized pressed against her temple. The world blinked out, and she knew nothing more.

CHAPTER 19

Tikaya woke slowly, mind groggy. She lay on her back, her head in someone's lap. Rias? No, concerned blue eyes peered down at her. Parkonis.

She struggled to sit up. A woman and a man in marine blacks stood above her. Colonel Lancecrest had not bothered removing the name tag from his wrinkled jacket, though she would have guessed his identity without it. Greasy salt-and-pepper hair stuck up in spicules, bags haunted his dark eyes, and furrows creased his weathered face. He looked like a man with nothing left to lose.

The woman had straight blonde hair and pale skin, so she might be Kyattese. Crow's feet lined her cold green eyes, and her thin lips flattened further under Tikaya's scrutiny.

"Where are Tatkar and my men?" Lancecrest asked.

"Dead or captured," Parkonis said. "Sorry, we—"

"Idiots." The colonel clenched a fist and stalked away, back rigid.

"Hate that man," Parkonis muttered.

Tikaya rubbed her face and tried to clear the wooziness from her brain. Another cavern stretched around them, this one with cracks and buckles marring a floor decorated with bat guano. Its pungent smell tainted the air. Stalactites hung from a ceiling far overhead. No sign of a camp or recent habitation marked the cavern, but her spine tingled with the telltale sense of nearby practitioner work.

A fifty-foot-high butte rose in the center, a natural formation with a steep, jagged face. A single chamber with transparent walls took up the space on top. Lit from within, the bright interior revealed dozens, maybe hundreds, of bristling rockets. Similar to the one in the fort, they stood upright, their outsides loaded with dense strings of colored cubes. Larger black cylinders stood in the middle, and Tikaya had no idea what they might do, but she doubted anything up there existed for a purpose other than devastation.

There was no obvious way to get to the chamber. Two broken pillars and the remains of a ramp had crumbled and collapsed. A cool draft whispered against her cheek. If bats were living in the cave, there must be access to the outside nearby. Several tunnels led from the cavern.

"Thank you for your help, Gali," Parkonis said, addressing the woman. "I thought that sleeping gas would be enough, but you were right: one of their guards was too alert."

"Tatkar was my colleague for years." Gali turned icy green eyes on Tikaya. "You better be worth it."

How nice. Tikaya had found people as amiable as Bocrest to be her new captors.

"She is." Parkonis rested a hand on her shoulder.

A thousand questions for him burbled in her mind, chief among them how he was alive and what he was doing with relic raiders, but she would wait until she could get him alone to ask. As long as he was here to vouch for her, she might have the freedom she needed to investigate those weapons and plot their demise. Maybe she could even destroy them before the marines showed up.

Colonel Lancecrest returned, his face composed, though frustration still tensed his body. "You Starcrest's ally or his prisoner?"

"She'd *never* ally with that monster," Parkonis said.

Tikaya climbed to her feet, pushing back dizziness. She touched her temple. Whatever Parkonis had used to render her unconscious was gone.

"Captain Bocrest is in charge." She decided to give them information that didn't matter. Maybe she could gain their trust if she seemed to hold nothing back. "He kidnapped me from my parents' plantation and threatened to kill my family if I didn't translate these runes for him. I have no loyalty to him."

"And can you?" Lancecrest asked. "Translate this gibberish?"

Parkonis turned curious eyes toward her.

"Some," she said. "I'm learning more every day."

Lancecrest jerked his chin at Gali. "Test her, witch. See if she's telling the truth."

Gali scowled but stepped forward. She cracked her knuckles and flexed her fingers. Lancecrest closed in on Tikaya.

"Test?" she asked.

She had never failed an academic test in her life, but somehow she doubted these people wanted to assess her ability to categorize vowels. Lancecrest stepped behind her, reinforcing her supposition by taking her arms in a viselike grip. An inkling of what they meant to do stirred in Tikaya's gut, and she tried to pull away from him. He held her firmly.

"Telepath?" Tikaya asked Gali.

"Yes."

"Just in case the oath you took matters to you, I do *not* grant you permission to poke around in my thoughts." Numerous people on the Kyatt Islands had a knack for telepathy, but it had never concerned Tikaya since back home there were strict laws against intruding without permission.

"We're not on Kyatt," Gali said. "No one here to enforce oaths."

"That's when they matter the most, then, isn't it?"

The woman stepped forward without answering and raised her fingers. Tikaya tensed. Cursed sea, she did not want someone rooting around in her mind, reading her memories, maybe replacing them with more acceptable ones.

"I'm sorry, Tikaya," Parkonis whispered behind her.

In other words, he was abandoning her. He must not have much power in the group. She could not help but think about how Rias had started out with no power amongst the marines and he had never failed to fight for her. She pushed thoughts of him from her mind. They could only get her in trouble here.

Gali's cool fingers prodded Tikaya's temple. Something itched inside her mind, like stitches being pulled out. Panic gripped her. These bastards had no right to her thoughts. She yanked her head back.

"Hold her still," Gali growled and reached again.

Tikaya kicked her in the gut. The woman doubled over, clutching her stomach and gasping for air.

Lancecrest forced Tikaya to the ground, leaned a knee into her back, and shoved her face to the floor. She tried to twist free, but he wrenched her arms until she gasped with pain. Her cheek smashed against cold rock.

They were too strong. Her fate was unavoidable.

Gali's hand came down on the back of her head, nails gouging skin. Tikaya felt the other woman's annoyance, not just in those tense fingers but in her mind.

Images from the last month were dragged into her surface thoughts. Tikaya tried to fight it. She thought of cutting cane on the plantation, her family, school, childhood escapades, anything but—

Rias.

The foreign presence in her mind focused on him, tearing into any thought related to him. And there were a lot. Tears formed in Tikaya's eyes at the pain the invasion brought, the disdain she felt through the woman's link. The experience was bad, maybe worse than Ottotark's attack back in Fort Deadend. For the first time in her life, she regretted not studying the mental sciences. A practitioner would have known how to block a telepath.

After minutes that felt like hours, the presence in her mind dissipated. The hand left Tikaya's head.

Awareness of her surroundings returned. The weight on her back. Her labored breaths. Gali's boots before her face. Parkonis's silence. A hot tear ran down her cheek and splashed on the floor.

"Well?" Lancecrest asked.

"You can't trust her. They've duped her into working for them."

Tikaya focused on their words, groped for equilibrium. And she frowned. Duped? What in her thoughts had suggested that?

"They must have known she would never willingly help Turgonians, not after they decimated our islands in their war. Admiral Starcrest made her believe he was a prisoner, too, and gained her trust." Gali snorted. "He tricked her into thinking he loves her, and—this is lush—that the two of them are going to destroy the weapons together. Dear Akahe, Tikaya, I'm embarrassed for you. I could see it if you were eighteen, but you're not young enough to be that naive."

Stunned, Tikaya said nothing. The woman had been in her head, read all her thoughts, and *that* was the conclusion she had come up with? How could she possibly think Rias's friendship—his love—had been a ruse after all they had gone through?

The weight on Tikaya's back lifted, and she pushed herself to her knees. Gali stood before her, arms across her chest, pity and annoyance wrestling for room her on face.

"Love?" Parkonis asked in a soft, stung tone.

Tikaya winced. She would have told him about Rias, but not like this. Maybe the woman would have the humanity not to share everything. But she was shaking her head.

"You would lecture me on my oath when you're sleeping with that man?" Gali looked over Tikaya's shoulder. "Sorry, Parkonis, but your faithful fiancée has been sheet wrestling with Fleet Admiral Starcrest."

Tikaya remembered an earlier thought where she had lamented having no females to talk to out here. She decided to rescind it.

When Parkonis said nothing, she risked a glance at him. He was staring at her, mouth hanging open, eyes bulging. Not angry, not yet. Still in shock.

"Parkonis," she said quietly, trying to ignore Gali's cold stare. "As far as I've known, you've been dead for more than a year. The Eagle's Spirit went down at the end of the war. You never wrote, never sent word. I had no idea I'd ever see you again."

He closed his mouth, turned his back, and walked away.

"Leave us, Gali," Lancecrest said.

The woman shrugged and headed for an empty stretch of cavern. Between one step and the next, she disappeared. An illusion shrouding a camp, Tikaya guessed.

"Come." Lancecrest offered a hand.

Tikaya eyed him, surprised he had not simply grabbed her and yanked her to her feet. She got up on her own, but she did follow him as he walked away. He led her past bat guano piles and to a portion of wall engraved with a column of symbols.

"I've only been here a few days," Lancecrest said, "but I gathered from my little brother that Parkonis wasn't as good of a translator as he'd hoped. Atner actually wanted you on his team from the beginning. Can you tell me what this says?"

Tikaya hesitated, but it was such a basic sign that she saw little reason to withhold the information. "Lights."

"What?"

"It's a panel to control the lighting level."

"The lighting? You're sure? Parkonis thought these panels might have something to do with the web."

Tikaya slid one of the symbols up, and the lighting level in the cavern increased. Down and it decreased.

"Damn," Lancecrest said.

"What's the web?"

Lancecrest turned toward the invisible camp. "Lork, show her the web!"

A gaunt, wispy-haired man appeared. He lifted his gaze toward the ceiling, and Tikaya felt the tickle of the mental sciences being used. A bat flapped down from the shadowed stalactites and soared toward the weapons room. Before it flew anywhere near the glass, a small explosion lit the air like a miniature star exploding. The bat did not have time to squeal in pain. Its charred body fell, causing three more explosions on the way down. Nothing but ashes remained to trickle to the floor.

Tikaya stared at the fine pile.

"The kill zone starts about twenty feet up," Lancecrest said, "and extends to the walls. You see that door in the chamber up there? And the symbols by it? My brother has—*had*—goggles that make it easy to see them. He got in once by randomly pressing them with that wizard shit he learned on your island."

"Telekinetics?" Tikaya suggested.

"Yes. He lowered a rocket out, but the code changed before he could get back in, and he wasn't able to find another combination that worked."

"How could you let him use that weapon on the men in your fort? The men who trusted you to command them?"

Lancecrest's jaw clenched. "I didn't *know*. Atner just sent a note to get out of the fort with my best men and meet him at the canyon. I still can't believe he—I know why he did it, but I can't believe he made that choice."

"Why'd he do it?"

"Keeler." Lancecrest waved toward the camp, and she guessed he meant the practitioner who had come out to bestir the bat. "Keeler can see what's happening elsewhere. He found out Starcrest was coming and my brother panicked, figured he had to do anything to delay you all."

"Rias isn't even in charge."

"Doesn't matter. He's there. And the other man—a captain, isn't he?—doubtlessly had orders to requisition half the fort to help flush the archaeologists out of the tunnels and get the weapons. Atner probably figured I wouldn't disobey those orders, even for him."

"Would you have?"

"I don't know. It doesn't matter now. Come." Lancecrest led her to another panel. "What's this one say?"

"Temperature and..." Not water, but similar to water. "Humidity," she realized. "Controls for modifying the cavern atmosphere."

He sighed. "I was hoping for more from these panels."

"I doubt the instructions for disabling the security system are going to be on the wall in the same room *as* the security system."

Lancecrest grunted and strode to the last panel of symbols, this one on the backside of the butte and situated fifteen meters from a tunnel entrance. Tikaya did not have to ponder long, for she had translated these exact symbols just a couple days earlier. Her stomach clenched. Rias was not here with his acidic concoction this time.

"Don't let your people touch anything on this one," she said.

"Security?" Lancecrest perked up. "Weapons?"

"Cleaning service. What's down that tunnel?"

"Labs. What do you mean, cleaning service?"

Tikaya nodded. "We've seen them so far near the labs."

Despite her own words, she prodded an "open" symbol. An invisible door swung outward, and her breath caught. Four stacked cubes waited inside, their deadly orifices pointed her direction.

Lancecrest cursed and jumped back. Tikaya stood frozen a long moment before her thoughts could push past her first instinct of fear. The cubes were dormant for the time being. A complicated drawing on the inside of the door caught her eye. A schematic? A label on top, a grouping of numbers and symbols, nagged her mind. There was something familiar about the arrangement. Oh, it looked like the codes on the instruction sets in the sphere.

"Can I get some paper and copy this?" she asked.

"If it'll help. I can get you the goggles, too, if you want to take a good look." He pointed at the top of the butte.

If she wanted to take a look? Strange, Lancecrest was treating her better instead of worse since Gali blabbed.

"Do I have a choice?" Tikaya asked. "I'm used to Turgonians threatening me or my family to ensure my help."

Lancecrest studied her for a moment. "Starcrest's a tricky devil on the water, but he's no asshole who would play mind games with a prisoner. If he says you're his woman, you are."

"And that means something to you?" she asked, not sure whether to be hopeful or not.

"I respect him. If he's between me and getting out of here alive, I'm still going to shoot him, but I'm not going to torment you."

"Is that a Turgonian tenet? It's fine to shoot a man you respect, but you don't mess with his lady?"

A faint smile stretched his lips. "Something like that. My little brother...destroyed things for our whole family. All I'm hoping to do at this point is get out of here alive with some weapons to sell. Ideally, I'll get those weapons and get out of here before Starcrest shows up."

"What happens to Parkonis and the other archaeologists? I assume selling weapons isn't what most of them signed on for."

Lancecrest's jaw tightened. "This isn't what *I* signed on for either, but we're all stuck in this together now. My brother didn't make his choices alone. Everyone here is going to be wanted for crimes against the emperor. We're all working for a split of the profits. And if you want Starcrest— and Parkonis—to walk away from this unharmed, you'd best get to work opening that weapons chamber up there. *You* can make sure there's no bloodshed."

No bloodshed. Right. Until whoever he sold the weapons to used them.

Better to let him think she would go along with him though. "Get me the goggles."

"Lancecrest!" someone called from the other side of the butte. "The Turgonians are over the chasm!"

"Already?" Lancecrest cursed and jogged toward the speaker.

As he trotted away, Tikaya eyed the tunnel near the cube cabinet, wondering if she could slip away before someone caught up with her. But, no, it would not take Lancecrest long to notice she did not follow, and for all she knew the tunnel dead-ended. Besides, she wanted to copy that schematic, examine the door symbols, and talk to Parkonis.

She jogged after Lancecrest. He disappeared ahead of her, but she expected that by now. She kept going and between one step and the next, the camp appeared. Crates, backpacks, bedrolls, muskets and bows, and food sacks sprawled about her. The scent of stale sweat mingled with the pervasive guano stench.

Twenty people, several wearing marine uniforms, stood around the wispy-haired fellow, who hunkered over a bowl of water. A clairvoyant, she realized when she spotted images of Bocrest's men moving on the still surface.

"How'd they get across?" someone asked.

"Built a catapult."

A marine whistled.

"I wouldn't have joined this team if I'd known we'd be against Admiral Starcrest," a woman muttered.

"Isn't he dead?"

"We'll be dead if we tangle with him."

"He's just a man," Lancecrest growled. "We've laid your wizard traps, and we know the terrain best. The advantage is ours."

Tikaya edged closer to the bowl, hoping to catch sight of Rias. She wished she could communicate with him somehow, let him know everything that mattered. For the moment, the clairvoyant showed them Bocrest and Ottotark as they removed their parachutes and gathered their gear.

"Find Starcrest," Lancecrest said. "Let's see what they're planning."

The image shifted, focusing on Rias and Sicarius. Tikaya wrestled with the urge to kick the water bowl over. Even if she did want to see Rias, it was better if Lancecrest did not know what he planned. She took a step toward the bowl. Lancecrest gripped her forearm to keep her back.

"How was the ride?" Rias asked.

"Exhilarating," Sicarius said in a monotone.

"I thought we might get a yell of excitement or at least a smile out of you, but I see the emperor has trained you well."

"Yes."

It was like conversing with a rock. Tikaya wondered why Rias bothered, especially when he ought to be worried about her. Not that she wanted him to fall apart, but a little agitation would have been flattering.

"Scouts will go ahead," Bocrest said, somewhere beyond the edges of the vision. "See what we're up against."

Rias took a step.

"Not you, Admiral. We need you back here planning brilliance, not wandering around looking for your misappropriated camp follower."

Rias's jaw clenched and the tendons sprang out on his neck. There was her agitation. And then some. He looked like he might tear Bocrest's head off.

Sicarius stopped whatever might have come next in the conversation, raising his hand and saying, "Hold."

He tilted his head, as if listening to something, but his cool eyes stared straight through the water. The clairvoyant flinched, and the image evaporated.

"What is it?" Lancecrest asked.

"That young one has unexpected perception for a Turgonian."

"He knows we're watching? So, what? Get them back. I want you on their every step, so we know when they're coming."

The clairvoyant closed his eyes and draped his arms across his knees, palms up. Nothing happened. "I can't. He's blocking us somehow."

Lancecrest's fists clenched and unclenched. "Who is that boy?" he asked Tikaya. "He's not in uniform, and he's too young to be giving orders."

She shrugged. "The marines didn't tell me much."

Lancecrest considered her, and she thought he might call Gali over, but the marines and relic raiders were watching him, and he turned to them instead.

"Time to get ready for company, people. Morrofat, take your squad out. Your job is to delay that team." Lancecrest dug in a rucksack and pulled out a clunky pair of goggles that reminded Tikaya of the eye protection she had worn on the tundra. He tossed them to her. "You know what your job is. We've found dangerous relics that we can throw at Starcrest. If you care about him, you'd best get me those weapons before he gets within range."

CHAPTER 20

Tikaya stood near the spot where the bat had been disintegrated. From there, the door to the weapons chamber was visible, and the runes glowed beside it. No ropes bound her hands—Lancecrest had decided she needed them for writing—but she had a guard. Gali. The woman huffed and sighed as she paced about, fiddling with a pistol. Her telepathy worried Tikaya more than the weapon. She wanted to copy the cube schematic on the chance Rias could do something with it. And she could escape the raiders long enough to meet up with him.

"You're not looking at them," Gali snapped. "I imagine that'll make the translation difficult."

"I'm ruminating," Tikaya said.

"On how to escape, I know." Gali slapped the pistol across her palm. "Ruminate on getting through that door."

Tikaya held the goggles before her spectacles and peered through the magnifying lenses. The symbols grew crisper, the nuances easier to make out. They were numbers. Four rows of four, each different. She only recognized a few, but she could look up the others with the sphere if she could find a private place to take it out.

She pushed the tool from her mind. Better these people did not know about it.

With the enhanced vision, she examined the rest of the weapons chamber. A cuboid contraption hung from a ceiling and was attached to a large pipe disappearing into the cavern depths far above. Some kind of fan or ventilation system to suck away fumes if there was a break or accident? Probably not fast enough to save the life of the person inside, but if the door shut and that fan activated perhaps destroying the weapons would not prove deadly for everyone down here.

"What does one do with the symbols?" Tikaya asked. "Push them?"

"I wasn't there," Gali said, "but I heard Atner stood down here and moved them around with telekinetics."

Gali stretched a hand toward the butte. One of the numbers indented and glowed red. She twitched her fingers, and it slid one place to the right. The number on the right edge disappeared and reappeared on the left.

"How'd you do that?" Tikaya asked.

"A bit of sideways pressure. The runes glide around naturally, as if they've been greased. Atner fiddled around for days and finally got lucky. But he only got in once and the symbols changed after that."

"But he got a rocket out. How was he able to get it down without the web destroying it in midair?"

Gali shrugged. "The web didn't attack it."

"So, the defense system won't attack what it's supposed to defend?" Tikaya wondered if there was anything else it would not attack.

The symbol winked off, though it did not return to its original slot. Three red beams lanced out of the clear door. Tikaya jumped, nearly dropping the goggles. The beams scoured the air in front of the door. After a moment, they cut off.

"I guess if you don't punch in the correct code while you're standing up there, you get incinerated." She chewed on the side of her mouth. "Your telekinesis does offer a workaround the original builders probably didn't consider. If they were here as long ago as I suspect, humans wouldn't have had the skill yet. Relatively speaking, our command of the mental sciences is a recent development in civilization. It's not something that started appearing until after we developed agriculture and became more agrarian rather than hunter-gatherer. More free time, creation of a leisure class, and—"

"We didn't bring you here for a lecture," Gali snapped. "Figure out how to get in before your cursed Turgonian lover gets here."

Tikaya turned her attention back to the numbers. The ones she recognized were prime: three, five, seven, eleven, thirteen, seventeen, nineteen. Could the whole series just be the first sixteen primes? She had not learned numbers beyond twenty yet, so she would have to look them up. Presumably, the sixteen digits had to be arranged in a specific order to open the door. If Atner Lancecrest had pushed them randomly, he truly had gotten 'lucky.' Rias could no doubt give her the exact odds of guessing correctly, but what she remembered of studying permutations in school suggested a ridiculously high number of combinations.

She did not have time for guessing. If the code changed regularly, it was probably a puzzle of some sort. If one knew the goal, one had a better chance of solving it. Could it be as simple as placing them in order? No, too obvious to someone who spoke the language, and the scientists who had built this place had surely had their own people in mind as potential trespassers, not the cave-dwelling humans who had occupied the world at the time.

There had to be more to it. Tikaya dug a sheet of paper out and copied the numbers for later perusal.

A distant clanking started up. She cocked an ear, trying to identify it. The noise had a muffled quality and did not sound like it came from within the cavern. A few men ran out of the camp and into a tunnel.

"I want to take rubbings of the panels too," Tikaya said.

"Whatever," Gali said.

Relieved, Tikaya pretended no more than vague scientific curiosity as she copied the panels—and the schematic on the inside of the cube cabinet.

"Can you work those?" Gali asked suspiciously.

Encrypted

"No." Tikaya closed the cabinet and tucked the rubbings into her pocket along with the numbers.

"Tikaya?"

She turned to find Parkonis standing a few feet away. The remaining marines and relic raiders carried bows or firearms. Parkonis had nothing more offensive than a utility knife. The last year had apparently not turned him into a fighter.

Gali backed away a few paces, giving them a semblance of privacy.

"Parkonis," Tikaya said, not sure what else to say.

He pushed a tangle of curly hair out of his eyes. "I'm sorry I ran off."

"Earlier today?" she asked. "Or a year ago?"

He grimaced.

"What happened out there, Par? You obviously got off your ship, but why couldn't you come home?"

"The Turgonians sunk us, just as you heard, but Atner Lancecrest happened by and rescued those left alive. There were only four of us. He showed us the runes from this place, and I was intrigued, of course. He swore us to secrecy before telling us anything about them, then asked if we wanted to join his team, to travel to the source and work on translating a previously undiscovered language. He was leaving right away to recruit others from Nuria and the islands. There was no time to come home. It was a dream opportunity, Tikaya. I couldn't refuse."

"You don't find it suspicious that he just 'happened by' right after the Turgonians attacked you? He was Turgonian himself. Maybe he wanted to appear a benevolent rescuer, but actually set up the whole thing. Maybe he had a deal with the captain of the ship that sank yours. All so he could get his hands on a handful of grateful archaeologists. Are you sure you had a choice about coming?"

"That's far-fetched, Tikaya. Atner wasn't a bad fellow."

"Wasn't a—he killed everyone in that fort out there. In a ghastly way. And those were his countrymen!"

Parkonis winced. "He was desperate at that point. We didn't... I didn't have anything to do with that. I swear. I didn't know about the weapons when I agreed to come. We were just looking for relics, and in truth I only cared about the language."

Yes, Tikaya could understand that temptation. She stepped toward him and softened her voice. "Even if you joined voluntarily—*especially* if you joined voluntarily—why didn't you write, Par? How could you let us believe, for a whole year... We had your *funeral.* I stood next to your weeping sister and parents. This devastated them. And me too. I spent months trying to get over..." Her voice broke. She was still struggling to resolve this new reality with her memories.

Parkonis avoided her eyes. The distant clanking continued, like metal beating against rock.

"I should have written," he said. "I just didn't know how to without explaining everything. I was heading off to Turgonian territory, and I knew it'd be dangerous. I didn't want you to worry."

"Worry! I thought you were dead. How could worrying for your safety be worse than believing you dead?"

"I know, I realize that now. I was a fool. You were always the smart one. You weren't going to marry me for my brains, were you?" He grinned, a disarmingly boyish grin that she knew well. And she knew when he was using it to cover something.

She folded her arms over her chest. "Did you not want me to worry or did you not want me to find out about the language?" She watched his eyes as she spoke, waiting for—yes, there was a wince. "Colonel Lancecrest said his brother wanted me on the team from the beginning. Are you the one who talked him out of recruiting me?"

Parkonis looked away. "I told him you wouldn't work for relic raiders, yes."

"You wouldn't either, at least I didn't think so. But we do funny things for a chance at history, don't we? I'll wager you wanted to be the first to translate this new language, something you wouldn't be able to lay claim to, not solely, if I came along and helped."

He opened and closed his mouth several times, and she knew she was right.

"I didn't think we'd be gone that long," he finally whispered. "I thought, when we got back, we could pick up where we left off..."

"I understand." Tikaya sighed. And she did. Hadn't she been enticed by that language too?

"You do?" Hope widened his eyes.

"I understand, but I wouldn't have made that choice. I would have wanted you to come along, to be a partner in the translating, even if it meant you got the credit."

"But I wouldn't have gotten credit. You were always first." He shrugged helplessly. "It was always you."

She rubbed her face and wondered if that clanking was in her skull. He was missing the point. Or she was. Maybe she couldn't truly understand what he felt, always being second best. Either way, she was beginning to think it would have been too much between them, even if Rias had never come along. She thought of him, of all he had lost, and of the temptation Sicarius had laid at his feet. So much more than accolades. But he had rejected it because of her. At least, he had before Parkonis showed up and kidnapped her. What if Rias believed he had lost her? Would he no longer have a reason to say no to that temptation?

"Tikaya?" Parkonis asked.

She tried to focus on him, though a new urgency fueled her intent. She had to escape and find Rias before he made a choice he would regret.

"Whatever happens here..." She squeezed Parkonis's arm. "I want you to know that I love you, and I'm beyond relieved that you're alive, but I can't go home with you. I can't marry you."

"What?" He reeled back. "Because of that Turgonian?"

"No." She did not want to get into that now, but Parkonis grabbed her arm before she could step away.

"Don't be a fool, Tikaya. You don't love that monster. How could you? It's a clear case of captive complex. No matter how badly you're treated, you start sympathizing with your captors, even wanting to please them, because you're grateful they're not killing you."

"I know what the term means, and that isn't the case." If anyone had captive complex, it was he. Even after hearing how he had come to be here, she could hardly believe Parkonis would be a party to this weapons-selling scheme.

"It's not your fault. I forgive you. You were just trying to stay alive. Who knows what that monster would have done if you'd fought him?"

"He's not a monster. I know our people have no reason to like him, and you even less, but he did save your life from that assassin. We can trust him. He disobeyed orders two years ago, and he refused to have our president assassinated. He's been exiled since."

"Exile?" Parkonis snorted. "Is that what they told you?"

"He's only here because of his familiarity with these tunnels—he was part of the original mission that found them. He's been as much a prisoner as I. He was the only ally I had."

"Tikaya, don't you see? It's all an act. That man outranks a captain. If he's been pretending to be a prisoner, it's only been to fool you, to win your sympathy. He's insidious, they all are. They've been tricking you."

"I'm not a fool, Parkonis."

"It's not your fault. They say he's a genius. He's probably a master of manipulation."

Tikaya groaned and dropped her forehead in her hand. Why couldn't he just be jealous? Instead, he thought she was an idiot who had been brainwashed. This was a glimpse of what going home would be like. Torture. Her heart cringed at the idea of never seeing her family again, but maybe her notion of sailing off to some obscure port with Rias was a better idea than she realized.

"You have to come back with me, Tikaya. We'll take you to see a doctor, someone who can heal your mind. You just need distance, some time to return to your old life. If—"

The lighting flickered and went out.

Tikaya whirled, but blackness swallowed everything. As with the marines, the raiders had been relying on the alien lighting and nobody had lanterns lit. Timorous voices called out questions while others cursed in irritation. The symbols at the weapons door and on the panels still glowed, but they did not provide enough illumination to diminish the darkness.

"Tikaya?" Parkonis's hand bumped her chest, then found her arm.

She gripped him back. With the light gone, she abruptly grew aware of how many thousands of feet of earth lay above their heads. Since she had been unconscious for the trip to the raiders' cavern, she did not know the way back. Half a dozen tunnels exited this place, so one could wander forever in the darkness.

A distant roar sounded. Or one could wander until one was eaten.

"Not them again," Parkonis whispered.

She recognized it too. The humanoid creatures they had fought the first day.

Parkonis's grip tightened. It did nothing to reassure her, not like Rias's would have. She started. Could Rias have manufactured this? As a distraction?

Light appeared at the edge of the camp. Lancecrest strode toward them carrying a lantern, and she felt silly for her panicked concerns about not finding a way out. Of course, the raiders would have kerosene and lanterns, just as the marines did. Enough to last many days, she was sure. The roar came again. Closer this time.

"Come." Lancecrest waved an arm. "Return to camp until we figure out what's going on."

"Gladly," Parkonis muttered.

Tikaya glanced over her shoulder. She could no longer see the tunnel Lancecrest had said led to labs, but she wondered if this might be her opportunity to disappear. Had Rias created this for her sake? Or did he think she wanted to be here, with Parkonis?

Gali stepped out of the shadows, her pistol aimed at Tikaya.

Right. It would take more of a distraction to escape, and sprinting into dark monster-filled tunnels without a lantern and a means of defense would be unwise.

Inside the camp, more lanterns had been lit. People hustled about, grabbing weapons. An unclaimed bow and quiver rested on a crate, and she weaved through the clutter toward it. If those creatures were coming, maybe Lancecrest would not object to arming her.

A heavy hand landed on her shoulder.

"You're sitting here out of trouble," Lancecrest said.

Before she could protest, he grabbed her arms and drew them behind her back.

"Wait," she said. "I can help fight. I know how to use a bow."

"I'll keep that in mind."

A moment later, Tikaya knelt with her wrists tied behind her. She endured it with no more than a sigh until his hands fumbled at her ears.

"No!" She ducked her head.

Too late. Lancecrest removed her spectacles. Everything more than a few feet away grew fuzzy.

"I doubt you'll wander far without these."

Tikaya craned her neck, trying to see where he was putting them. He stuffed them in a pocket without any concern for protecting the lenses.

"Bastard," she growled.

A shot fired, echoing from the closest tunnel. Everyone in camp dropped behind cover, but no squad of marines burst into the cavern. Three more shots followed, along with a distant angry yell. Still, no one entered. The raiders shifted uneasily.

Tikaya could not imagine the Turgonians tipping their hand before attacking, but maybe they had run into the creatures. Or Lancecrest's traps.

She could not stay here and wait for something to happen. A nearby lantern gave her enough light to see, and the white and green fletching on the arrows in the quiver caught her eye. She edged closer. Maybe if she could filch an arrow, she could use the head to cut her bonds. That would be easier if her hands were in front of her, but she had to try.

Something fluttered above the tunnel entrance. It was too far away for her to identify, but someone fired. Black powder smoke wafted into the air.

"That was a bat, you lummox," Lancecrest said. "And you just confirmed to the Turgonians that we're in here."

"Sorry."

"Scientists with guns," Lancecrest muttered. "What was my brother thinking?"

As the smoke rose higher, slowly dissipating, a faint white beam appeared in the haze. Tikaya blinked, wondering if she imagined the light. But, no, even with her spectacles off, she could see a beam. It reminded her of those emitted by the cleaning machines. Maybe that was all the "web" was, a pattern of beams crisscrossing the cavern, invisible under regular illumination. But if smoke revealed them, one might avoid them.

Ideas percolated in her mind. But first, escape.

Staying low, she crawled toward the crate. Though men and women crouched all around her, their focus was outward. Why worry about the tied, half-blind philologist?

A couple more feet brought her to the quiver. Gali glanced at her and frowned, a what-are-you-doing expression stamping her face.

Tikaya attempted what she hoped appeared a guileless smile. "Can you help me find my spectacles?"

The woman scowled.

"Incoming!" someone barked.

All eyes turned toward the closest tunnel. Tikaya rose, turned, and slipped an arrow out of the quiver.

No noticed. She dropped to her knees, putting her back to the crate. She found the sharp metal head and maneuvered it until the edge slipped between her wrists. Careful not to cut skin, she eased it up and down against the rope. The awkward position made it impossible to apply much pressure. She held back a scowl, knowing this would take a while.

It was not marines but two black bipedal creatures that burst into the cavern. Even without her spectacles, she recognized the towering muscular beings. The illusion spell did not fool them; they barreled straight for the camp.

Muskets fired and bows twanged.

Tikaya rubbed the arrowhead against her ropes.

The practitioners threw up an invisible barrier, and the creatures bounced back while men and women fired through it. The scent of black powder permeated the camp. Smoke stung Tikaya's eyes, but, in the rising haze, she spotted more beams in the air. They crisscrossed irregularly, nothing symmetrical or predictable like a spider web. None had more than a foot or two of open—safe—space between them. Even if they were visible, climbing past them might not be possible.

The rope snapped, and her wrists came apart.

She eyed the back of the cavern, trying to guess the distance to the cleaning cubes and the tunnel next to them, but, even if she had her spectacles, darkness would have thwarted her estimates. On the other side of the camp, Lancecrest stood, reloading a rifle. The creature battle had him distracted, but she did not see how she could retrieve her spectacles without him noticing.

In front of the camp, blood streamed from the beasts' dark flesh. Their muscles flexed and strained as they hammered the invisible barrier. Roars of pain and anger echoed through the cavern. Sweat gleamed on the practitioners' faces. One flexed his fingers. A pulse of power hammered the beasts. They flew backward, and landed hard, but they came up roaring with anger. Another volley was fired at them.

Everyone appeared busy.

Tikaya grabbed a lantern and slid bow and quiver off the crate. She turned the flame down so it would not make her a target as she ran, then slipped toward the back edge of camp.

Someone shot one of the creatures in the eye, and it toppled to the floor. A ragged cheer went up.

Tikaya eased around sacks of corn meal and rice. A couple steps and she would be out of the camp. She resisted the urge to hop the few couple obstacles and sprint for the wall. That would likely draw someone's eyes. Stealth would serve her better.

"The linguist is escaping!" someone yelled.

So much for stealth.

She bolted. Her boot caught on the uneven ground, and she slammed to her knees even as a shot fired over her head. They would rather shoot her than let her escape back to the others?

Gulping, she leaped to her feet and sprinted to the wall, lantern and bow banging against her legs with every step. That was the first time her clumsiness had saved her life—she could not count on it happening again.

Tikaya plunged into the darkness, using the blurry crimson runes as a guide. She reached the wall and stood to the side, not wanting to be silhouetted against them for the shooters.

Footsteps hammered the floor behind her.

She jabbed the symbol that opened the cabinet, but nothing happened. Growling, she slowed her movements and added a rotation. The cabinet popped open.

The footsteps neared. Lancecrest. She didn't have enough time.

Then a black shape blurred in from the side, crashing into him. The remaining beast.

Lancecrest yelled and flung his arms up.

As soon as it finished him, it would be on her. Tikaya pulled out a cube, praying it would not activate while she held it. Arms laden, she started toward the tunnel.

"Over here, you ugly pisser!" someone cried and a psi wave pulsed through the air.

It struck the creature full on, hurling it twenty feet. The edge of the wave caught Tikaya and smashed her against the wall.

Lancecrest patted the floor for his rifle. His men poured out of the camp and moved to surround the creature. And her.

She sprinted for the tunnel.

An arrow clipped Tikaya's sleeve and shattered against the wall. Fear surged through her, and she ran faster.

Someone conjured a yellow orb of light, and it spun her direction, illuminating her, making her an easier target.

"Stop!" A man pointed a pistol as he ran at her, his face a rictus of determination.

She had to keep going, hope his aim was poor.

A shot fired, and Tikaya dove, knowing it would not be fast enough. But no blast of pain came. The man's musket hit the floor with a clatter, and he collapsed a heartbeat later. Tikaya scrambled into a crouch and squinted into the gloom behind him. A tall blurry figure in Turgonian black stood in a tunnel entrance on the far side of the cavern. Rias?

She stepped in that direction, but he waved her toward her closer tunnel.

"Starcrest!" Lancecrest fired his rifle.

Rias flew back with a grunt. Tikaya gaped. It looked like he had been hit, but, curse her eyes, she could not tell. He ducked back into the tunnel. Lancecrest raced after him.

Tikaya took a step that direction, but an explosion roared, and the ground heaved. She was thrown onto her side, and the lantern flew from her grip. The cavern filled with confused yells and cries of pain.

A stalactite plunged to the floor where it shattered and hurled shards everywhere. A second explosion ripped through the earth. A sinkhole opened up in the floor, and rock poured in like water over a fall.

Tikaya scrambled for the nearby tunnel, hoping the alien walls would hold up better than the cavern. She had no idea where the lantern had gone. Even as the floor pitched, she clutched the cube and the bow, determined not to lose anything else.

Blackness smothered the tunnel. Three steps in, another concussion boomed, hurling her against a wall. Her breath whooshed out with a pained grunt. The bow and cube flew from her hands. She crumpled to the floor and barely had the presence of mind to curl into a ball with her hands protecting her head as further booms rocked the tunnel.

Nearby, rock shattered and cracked like gunfire. Tikaya cringed, expecting the ceiling to collapse at any second. Finally, the explosions ended, but rubble continued to pelt the floor. She kept waiting for rocks to hit her, but her tunnel seemed secure. Secure, but dark. Lifting her head to peer about was worthless since blackness pressed in from all sides. Worse, dust clogged the air and invaded her throat. She coughed and wheezed as fine particles smothered her tongue.

Distant, muffled yells made it to her ears, but she could not pick out words. She shifted to get to her feet. Her fingers bumped a hard edge. She jerked back. The cube. If ever there was a mess, surely an earthquake—or whatever that had been—qualified. She held her breath, expecting the cleaning device to flare to life, for the orifice to glow red, the beam to lance out.

But the cube remained inert.

Whatever the reason, she thanked her luck and hunted for the bow. She found it wedged under a pile of rubble. Rubble that blocked the mouth of the tunnel from floor to ceiling. Cave-in.

She hoped there was another way back to the cavern. And that she could find it in the dark.

Tikaya stood and started to brush herself off, but a new concern made her freeze. How far did the cave-in extend? What if it covered part, or all, of the cavern? And the tunnels beyond? Her heart lurched. What if Rias or Parkonis had been caught? She still didn't know if Rias had been shot. Damn, damn.

She clawed at the rubble, trying to dig a hole. She had to get back in and check.

A minute later, her fingers were bleeding and she had made no progress. Breath rasping in her ears, she backed away. She would not get in that way. She needed to find another way around. She needed to—

No. Tikaya wiped sweat from her face and forced herself to calm down, to think. Rias would want her to continue with the mission, not tear off, hunting for him. For all she knew, he might have set this all up. She remembered the clinking. Had the marines been crawling around in passages beneath the floor, placing blasting sticks?

She turned around and felt her way along the wall, trying not to feel guilty for walking away from Parkonis and Rias. She had to ensure those weapons were destroyed, and she could not assume the cave-in had done that. In fact, she would be shocked if it had.

The darkness made the trek feel longer, but she doubted she had walked far before she came to a four-way intersection labeled with glowing runes. Three possible directions, three labs. Biology, alchemy, and... She touched the last one, a new combination of symbols. Mechanical? That sounded promising, but she ought to let Rias know which way she had gone. She dropped her hand and snorted because her bloody fingers had already smeared a sign on the runes.

She padded down the hall. A door whispered open, and she stepped onto a landing. She expected darkness inside, but low blue lighting pulsed from the walls. Some kind of backup illumination, perhaps.

This lab was larger than others she had visited and had an upper level as well as a lower. She chose the upper, less out of any notion of what she might need, but because it would not be immediately visible to someone walking in.

Upstairs, blurry cabinets lined the walls and high stations dominated the center. She had to wander close for the edges to sharpen. They reminded her more of woodworking benches than alchemy stations. Intricate black tools she could not identify were mounted to the table tops and hung from the ceilings on articulating arms. Rias would probably be fascinated by them.

Her gut twisted with concern at the thought of him, but she forced herself to focus on the one thing she could accomplish here. She dug her notes, the sphere, and a pencil out of her pocket.

Tikaya put more obstacles between herself and the landing before stopping at a countertop that was not too high for her purposes. She thumbed the sphere on and identified the rest of the numbers from the door pad. More primes, but not the first sixteen as she had guessed. The sequence skipped a few: three, five, seven, eleven, thirteen, seventeen, nineteen, twenty-three, twenty-nine, thirty-one, thirty-seven, forty-one, forty-three, sixty-one, sixty-seven, and seventy-three.

"All right, Rias," she muttered. "Where are you? I've translated them and done my half." As soon as the words came out, she snorted at herself. Yes, they made a good team, but she *had* done this sort of thing before she met him.

There had to be some significance in the missing prime numbers. Maybe these were the first sixteen that could be turned into a combination that allowed one particular thing. She drew a bunch of four by four boxes, mimicking the layout on the door pad, and scribbled the numbers in. Four rows, four columns, sixteen numbers. She added and multiplied. She looked for patterns.

The door hissed open.

Rias? Tikaya lifted her head and almost called out, but could not see the landing and caught herself before she could give away her position. She waited for the sound of footfalls, thinking she might be able to identify his tread, but there was no sound at all.

The door hissed shut.

Quietly, oh so quietly, Tikaya picked up her work. It was possible someone had looked in, not seen anything interesting, and left, but she doubted it. That cursed assassin was the only one who walked without making a sound, and she had no idea what his intentions might be for her, especially now that she had, from the Turgonian viewpoint, escaped with the enemy. And if Rias had run off, too, Sicarius would know he had no intention of accepting the emperor's offer.

Tikaya twisted the symbols to open a couple of cabinets beneath a nearby workstation. One was empty enough she thought she could fit inside.

She stuffed the cube in one cabinet and knelt before the larger one. Careful not to make a sound, she slid boxes and tools out of the way. She could barely breathe, but she fit.

She pulled the door most of the way shut. Since the cabinets had to be opened with a turn of the symbols, she assumed she could not get out if she locked herself in. Terrifying thought that. No one would ever find her, and the cabinet would be her tomb. The assassin might spot the door slightly ajar, but she had to risk it.

Silence reigned in the lab. Tikaya could hear her heart beating in her ears, her shallow breathing. The awkward position cramped her diaphragm. Minutes dragged past.

She closed her eyes and rearranged digits in her head. The four-by-four box reminded her of a Skiltar Square, those puzzles where the goal was to arrange the numbers so that every column, row, and diagonal added up to the same sum. It seemed unlikely an alien race would have the same math games, but she rearranged and totaled the digits in her head anyway, seeing if she could find a combination that worked from all sides. It surprised her when she found an arrangement where each option added up to one hundred twenty. Could that be the way into the weapons cache?

Her fingers tingled with excitement. Or maybe numbness from sitting scrunched up in a cabinet. Her tailbone ached. She longed to crawl out and check her math with pencil and paper. Maybe Sicarius had left, or had never been there to start with.

Tikaya lifted her hand to the door, about to push it open. Then someone glided past the crack.

Black clothing, blond hair.

She held her breath and closed her eyes, as if the assassin might feel her stare through the crack. He had sensed the clairvoyant watching him, after all.

A minute later, the door hissed again, and she spilled out of the cabinet. Sitting on the floor beneath the pulsing blue light, she checked her math with pencil and paper. Every row, every column, and even the diagonals added up to one hundred and twenty. Maybe it meant nothing. Or maybe it was the solution to the puzzle.

She hopped to her feet, longing to go check it, but thanks to the cave-in she was not sure how to get back to the cavern.

The door hissed again. Tikaya cursed to herself. Now what?

Footsteps sounded on the landing. She reached for the cabinet door, ready to hide again.

"Tikaya?" Rias.

Relief swarmed her. "Up here!"

She skirted the workstations and almost crashed into him at the top of the stairs. He wore his rucksack and carried a rifle, but he managed to envelop her in a fierce hug. She clamped onto him just as fiercely, burying her face in his neck. He smelled of black powder and blood, but it didn't matter.

"You came for me," she whispered.

"Of course."

"The explosions... I was afraid you were..."

"Me too," he said, voice hoarse. "I feared you'd been caught in that cave-in. Bocrest was too quick to light the charges. He was supposed to wait until—it doesn't matter now. If I've succeeded, they think the weapons are buried and I'm dead."

She lifted her arms, intending to hook them over his shoulders, but her fingers encountered dampness. A torn section of uniform wrapped his biceps like a bandage. She drew back, staring at blood on her hand.

"You're wounded!"

"Lancecrest got lucky." Rias twitched a shoulder. "It's just a scrape. It'll be fine. Besides, it was worth it. He was carrying something you might find useful." He unbuttoned a pocket, withdrew her spectacles, and draped them over her ears.

Tikaya slumped against his chest. She should have been elated to have her vision back, but a lump of guilt lodged in her throat. "You got shot trying to help me. I'm sorry."

Rias took her face in his hands. "I'd risk a lot more than a trifling arm to help you."

Comforted by his words, she tilted her head back.

He seemed on the verge of kissing her, but he cleared his throat and glanced around. "Are you...alone?"

"Yes, though Sicarius was here a few minutes ago." She realized he had probably been wondering about Parkonis, but his eyes widened at the mention of the assassin.

"He was? Rust, he's not supposed to be on this side of the cave-in. He must have found a way through." He scrubbed his face. "Maybe we'll get lucky and be able to avoid him."

"I haven't seen Parkonis since before the explosions," Tikaya said. "Do you know if he... Did any of the raiders make it?"

"I didn't see him amongst the dead." Rias took a deep breath. "Tikaya, I'll help you find him, but I need you to know... When he appeared and absconded with you I... My first thought was to hurl myself into that chasm. But there's a stigma against suicide in my culture, and regardless it's always seemed like giving up, which isn't something I've ever strived to master. I fully intend to fight for you."

"Rias—"

"I know he represents your dream, the life you always wanted, and I know its selfish of me to want you when it could alienate you from your family, but... How is it he's been alive a year and never found a way to let you know? I would have toppled an empire to get back to you."

"Rias—"

"I can't walk away and let him have you, Tikaya. Not if there's a chance..."

"Rias."

He opened his mouth again, but she flattened her palm over his lips. His shoulders slumped, and wariness hooded his eyes.

"I appreciate hearing those things very much." She grinned at the idea of him toppling an empire—for most people, that was just an expression, but she wouldn't put it beyond his means. "But there's no need for you to go on." She lowered her hand, brushing his lips with her thumb. "You have me."

He gaped at her in stunned silence.

"You have me for a lot of reasons," she said quietly, "but especially because you're willing to give up everything to be here at my side, plotting against your people to destroy those weapons. The definition of a good man is someone who makes the moral choice when temptation invites him to do otherwise. The definition of a hero is someone who makes that moral choice even when temptation, threat of reprisal, and the mores of his culture invite him to do otherwise." She considered her words and issued a self-deprecating smirk. "That was preachy, wasn't it?"

"Oh, no, I liked it. Especially the part where you're calling me a hero." He grinned, eyes sparkling, and her heart danced.

"I'm sure I'm not the first, Fleet Admiral Starcrest."

"In Turgonia, you're a hero if you sink more ships than anyone else." He tucked a stray lock of hair behind her ear and laid his forehead against hers. "I like your definition better."

"Good. I hope you like this too: I don't want you worrying about being selfish because you want to have a life with me. I want one with you too. Some people are worth changing your dreams for." She kissed him, wishing there was time for more. "I want to be with you. Always. Even if it means we're both exiles on your forsaken prison island."

Rias's grip tightened. "Cursed ancestors, don't say that."

"It's the truth, though I'm going to be terribly disappointed if the preeminent military strategist of the era can't outsmart a teenage assassin in order to avoid that fate."

Whatever Rias's retort was going to be, it was lost when the door hissed open.

Before Tikaya could do more than think of hiding, Sicarius strode in. His gaze swiveled upward to lock on them. The pulsing blue light painted his face in eerie shadows. Blood stained his short blond hair, spattered the side of his face, and painted his hands. As those dark hard eyes raked her, she had an unsettling hunch none of it was his. Two pistols were jammed into his belt, and he carried a dagger. A drop of blood fell from the blade and splashed on the landing.

"Sicarius, good," Rias said.

Good? The assassin looked like he was about to kill both of them. Tikaya stifled the incredulous expression that wanted to waltz across her face.

"Do you have the door symbols from the journal?" Rias asked.

"You assured Captain Bocrest you were placing the blasting sticks to provide a distraction, but the tunnels came down in such a way that he believed the weapons cavern had been buried and you with it." Sicarius spoke in such an emotionless monotone it was almost possible to miss the accusation in those words. "I informed the captain that it was unlikely you would miscalculate so badly. The marines are searching the tunnels for you and her." His cool eyes flicked Tikaya's way.

She groaned inwardly. The plan would have worked if the emperor's perceptive henchman wasn't here. She glanced at Rias, almost expecting him to dive behind the railing and rip his pistol free for a shot, but he did not.

"Demolitions are dangerous and sometimes unpredictable," Rias said. "We can, of course, rejoin the others now, though why not get through the locked door and finish the mission while the relic raiders are too scattered to guard their cache? Do you have the symbols?"

"Yes," Sicarius said, no sign on his face of whether he believed Rias's lies. "I already tried them."

"How?" Tikaya asked.

No doubt, he was agile enough to scale the side of that butte, but not with those invisible beams waiting to slice off limbs.

"Bow and arrow," Sicarius said.

Rias lifted an eyebrow toward Tikaya. He probably had not had as good a look at the entryway as she had. She nodded thoughtfully. If Gali had used telekinesis to nudge the symbols around, she supposed something thrown—or shot—against them could do the same job.

"You lined them up?" Tikaya had assumed the numbers she copied were a different set than the ones that had appeared the day Lancecrest got in.

"As close as I could. Not all the symbols matched those in the journal."

"Maybe you misread them," Rias said.

Those dark eyes turned a shade cooler. "I did not."

"I've been told the symbols change periodically," Tikaya said. "It was probably designed so people who knew the secret to the puzzle could always get in, providing they had the math skills, whereas others would have, well, the trouble Lancecrest's team has had."

"You know the secret?" Sicarius glided up the stairs, eyes locked on her.

Rias dropped to the step in front of her, blocking the assassin's advance. Sicarius halted.

"I'm close," Tikaya said. Or not even remotely close. It was one of the two. "It would help to see the symbols you have that worked before, even if they don't now."

For a long moment, Sicarius stared past Rias's shoulder at her. Finally, he wiped the dagger, sheathed it with the myriad others he carried, and handed her the torn scrap of paper, neatly folded.

"Thank you." Half the numbers were the same. She would have to check the sphere to translate the others. "I have some ideas about how to get through the web." Maybe pretending to include Sicarius in their plans would make him more likely to believe they shared the same goal. She put a hand on Rias's shoulder. "Can you make something that causes smoke? A lot of smoke?"

"With the right ingredients, yes." Rias snapped his fingers. "Sicarius, can you get us some bat guano from the cavern?"

Tikaya almost choked. Bat guano?

Sicarius's eyes narrowed. "There is no potassium nitrate in these labs?"

Of course. Potassium nitrate—salt peter—was harvested in bat guano-rich caves, and it was one of the core ingredients in black powder. The kid was bright. They would have to be very careful—and probably lucky—to trick him into helping.

"I haven't seen any," Tikaya said. Which was true. With her spectacles missing she had not bothered examining the lab closely.

"I'll prepare the vats and put together the rest of the ingredients to make some smoke bombs," Rias said. "And Tikaya will work on the entry code for us. We can finish your mission before Bocrest even misses you."

"Bat guano," Sicarius said. "Very well."

As soon as the door shut behind him, Tikaya and Rias grabbed each other's arms and started to talk at the same time.

"You first," Rias said.

"First, I think it'll be a lot easier to find potassium nitrate in one of these labs than making it from scratch, but I assume you're just trying to keep him busy."

Rias nodded. "Yes."

"Second, can you look at this and tell me what you think? These are the translated numbers from the door pad." She fished out the page with her solution for the puzzle, wincing as she handed it to him. It had seemed a logical guess during her in-cabinet mulling, but now that she had to share the hypothesis with someone else, she feared it a foolish one.

"A Skiltar Square?" Rias asked. "It looks like you solved it. In Turgonia, you can get books full of them to entertain your precocious children."

He smirked, and she wondered how many his parents had foisted on him. Her amusement at the idea faded quickly.

"This can't be right then," she said. "Too simple for these people. And surely they wouldn't have had similar puzzles to what we have."

"Why not? In your studies, haven't you found that the fundamental properties of numbers are the same in every language, amongst every people? Mathematics surely transcends humanity, existing whether we do or not, so it doesn't seem odd to me that another species would play the same sorts of games with numbers. And why wouldn't this entrance code be simple? Do you think someone carrying a toxic weapon up a ramp would have wanted to stand outside the door for three hours making calculations? What if he dropped one of those poison-filled vials and it broke at his feet? Big oops, eh?"

Tikaya laughed. She had not considered that.

Encrypted

"Besides," Rias said, giving her an appreciative smile. "Those squares aren't *that* easy to solve. Why don't you translate the combination from the journal and see if it's a solution to one." He thumped a fist on the railing. "We still need a way to destroy the weapons. I was thinking we might find a formula for a powerful alien version of naphtha or kerosene, because even gas is flammable, right? At a high enough temperature... Tikaya, where are you going?"

Halfway through his spiel, she had charged to the cabinet where she left the cube. She raced back with the contraption clutched in her arms, and Rias lurched back a step at the sight of it.

"It's not active," she said. "I'm not sure why, but it gives us the chance to experiment."

Rias recovered, though he eyed the device warily. "Experiment?"

"The cubes already clean things by incinerating them, right? All we need to do is add those weapons to the list of items its programmed to burn, throw it in that chamber, and close the door. You took one apart, right? Do you think you could alter its parameters? Like a punchcard in a steam loom?"

"I... Tikaya, that thing is so far beyond a steam loom I wouldn't have any idea where to start."

"Even if I can translate the schematic?" She thrust the blueprint she had copied toward him. "Give me a moment, and I might be able to find repair instructions in the sphere's library too."

Though his eyes darted, devouring the schematic, his wary frown did not fade. "All before Sicarius returns or the marines stumble upon us or angry relic raiders burst in?"

So, that's what daunted looked like on him. Huh.

"We can do it." Tikaya slapped him on the backside.

He blinked. "What was that for?"

"I'm encouraging growth."

CHAPTER 21

Gunfire cracked in the distance. Again. Bent over a table with Rias, Tikaya did not lift her head. The cube, one side removed, sat between them. Several parts she could not name lined the table in the order Rias had removed them. A three-dimensional display of the inside of one of the cubes hovered in the air, courtesy of the sphere. The blue lab lighting continued to flash, providing poor illumination for such detailed work.

A yell of rage—or pain—sounded in the tunnels. Rias grumbled something under his breath about how he ought to be out there, helping the men. He had set the situation up so everyone would be running around in the tunnels, distracted dealing with each other and the darkness, creating just this time they needed, but it clearly did not sit well with him.

"The screwdriver thing," he muttered.

Tikaya handed him a long tool with a magnetic hook on one end and a tiny flat-tip head on the other. She had finished her work, gathering supplies for Rias's smoke bombs and translating the schematic and the numbers Sicarius had given her. The latter had proved to be another Skiltar Square. Now she handed Rias tools and tried not to feel useless.

"Close," he said. "It's just a switch that modifies the level of 'cleaning' to be done, so it's easier than I thought, but reaching it without taking everything else out is the problem. Also...I'm afraid if I take everything out, I won't be able to get it back in correctly without breaking something. The insides are much more fragile than the outside."

"Take your time," she said, wishing it didn't sound so inane.

She was not sure how many minutes—hours?—had passed since Sicarius had left the lab, but she was beginning to think he must have run into a distraction. As uncharitable as it was, she hoped for a nice arrow or pistol ball to the chest.

Rias grunted and held out his hand for another tool. The kit of precision implements they had found ranged from knives and scalpels to repair gizmos, most of which she could only guess at. Some were too large for human hands, but all were well-made, the craftsmanship amazingly sturdy for such fine tools. A pair of black knives, in particular, had caught Rias's eye, and he had stuck them into his belt.

"There," Rias whispered. "I think I got it."

"Is there a way to test it?"

"Not here." He started replacing the innards. "We'll have to get into the tunnels on the other side of the cavern. That's where I found the panel to cut off the lights. I'm guessing that whatever powers them powers these cubes and that's why they're inert."

Tikaya realized how lucky she had been when the blasts brought down all that rubble. If power had been running to the cube, it might have cut her down after all.

The door hissed open.

They spat silent curses at the same time.

"Distract him," Rias mouthed, waving at the mess still on the table. If Sicarius caught them with the cube, he would figure out their plan right away.

Tikaya grabbed the sphere and her notes and sprinted to the top of the stairs. Sicarius was halfway up. No bag of guano dangled from his grip.

Though her instinct was to keep space between her and him, she jogged down several steps so she could stop him before he could see Rias.

"We figured out the code," she said, waving the pages. "It's a puzzle with numbers."

"Where is the admiral?" Sicarius asked.

"We made smoke bombs, and he's packing them. We did find some potassium nitrate, so we won't need the guano after all. Which is good, since you seem not to have gotten any." She winced at her inane babbling. "What's going on outside?"

Sicarius watched her, impassive eyes betraying nothing of his thoughts. He knew they had sent him on a useless errand. He had to. And he probably knew they were not on his side. They were going to have to kill him or incapacitate him somehow.

"Cat and mouse," Sicarius said. "I killed one of the wizards. Some of Colonel Lancecrest's men are proving elusive, and they've set traps. Captain Bocrest's team has split them up, brought a few down, and taken others prisoner."

Down. Dead. "Parkonis?"

"What?" Sicarius asked.

"The man who...kidnapped me against my wishes. Do you know if he's alive?"

"He dropped to his knees and begged for his life when we came upon him. He bore no weapon, so the captain took him prisoner."

Tikaya closed her eyes, thankful Parkonis was not the heroic type. He had no weapons training, and bravery only would have gotten him killed. Being a prisoner was no guarantee of safety, but there was still a chance she could help him.

"Where is the admiral?" Sicarius asked again.

"Here."

Rias appeared at the top of the stairs, rucksack on his back, and what looked like ceramic globes with fuses in his hands. She had been busy with the translations and had not watched him assemble the smoke bombs. She thought of the vast cavern and hoped four would be enough.

He did not give her a wink or nod, not with the assassin watching, but she thought Rias's rucksack appeared lumpier than before. He slipped two globes into pockets and handed the other two to Sicarius.

Tikaya wondered how they would detour to the lighting panel with Sicarius tagging along. And would the cube fly up to the weapons room of its own accord, or did they need to get it up there and lock it in somehow? For that matter, would their modifications even work?

Footfalls sounded in the corridor, and gear jingled.

Rias reached for his pistol, but Sicarius's hand blurred, landing on his wrist in a firm grip.

Rias twitched an eyebrow, the only indication he felt things might not be going according to plan.

"The captain sent reinforcements." The steely gaze Sicarius leveled at Rias was far too knowing for comfort. "To watch you and guard our backs while we retrieve some rockets."

"Watch us?" Tikaya asked innocently. "Why?"

Sicarius did not bother to look at her.

Agarik strode through the door, and Tikaya lifted her head. Maybe this wouldn't be so bad.

Then Ottotark and Bones clomped in. She tried not to let her chagrin show. Even before Ottotark spotted her, he wore a self-satisfied smirk. Bruises from his fight with Rias still mottled his face, and a bandage wrapped his head, but he appeared delighted at this new turn. Bones ignored Sicarius and Rias in favor of glaring at Tikaya, an angry jaw-clenched glare. No delight there. She guessed Ottotark had buzzed in his ear, letting him know who killed his brother.

Tikaya looked at Agarik, but he avoided her eyes.

"Evening, Admiral," Ottotark drawled. "We'll relieve you of your weapons now." The smirk widened. "Captain says you're back to prisoner status." He ambled up to the step below Rias and held out his hand.

Rias neither moved nor spoke.

Ottotark launched a punch at his belly. Rias blocked it and slammed his knee into the sergeant's diaphragm. Ottotark's heel slipped off the step, and he nearly tumbled to the landing, but he caught himself on the railing. Tikaya started to back away, to give Rias room to fight, but Sicarius stepped in. He held a knife she had not seen him draw in one hand and splayed the other against Rias's chest. His eyes were icy in warning.

Rias froze.

Ottotark found his balance. Fury contorted his face, and he snarled as he snatched Rias's weapons. He lifted the musket, as if he might slam the butt of it into Rias's head. Tikaya stepped down with a vague notion of grabbing the weapon, but Sicarius stopped Ottotark with a word.

"Enough."

The men dropped their arms. While punching Ottotark had won Rias nothing, it concerned Tikaya that none of that defiant spirit came out against the assassin. Had his last meeting with Sicarius disillusioned him so much that he would not move against the youth again? If so, that did not bode well for their success.

"Lead on, Admiral," Sicarius said. "You two will get us into the weapons cache."

And then what?

* * * * *

The pair of kerosene lanterns the marines carried did little to push back the darkness in tunnels that had fallen silent. Eerily so. Tikaya began to feel as if their tiny group represented the only people left alive in the stygian passageways.

She and Rias walked side by side, leading the others. Ottotark and Bones kept their pistols trained on their backs. Agarik walked behind them, and Sicarius ghosted along in the shadows, rarely seen, rarely heard, always felt.

Tikaya checked symbols and peered down dark cross tunnels, hoping for inspiration. As soon as the marines had the weapons, they would likely shoot her. She wondered if Rias was expendable at this point too. At best, he could expect a trip back to Krychek. He would probably prefer death.

Rias caught her eye. "Sorry." He spoke in Kyattese, which she had not realized he knew, though the words that followed proved he was far from fluent. "I was engineer. Picked where explosives go. Had chance."

The slowness with which his words came out gave her time to puzzle over the meaning behind his choice of language. Bones, Agarik, and Ottotark probably knew no Kyattese, but hadn't Rias warned her that Sicarius did? He had certainly seemed to be reading that journal.

"No talking in codes." Ottotark jabbed Rias in the arm.

"Had chance," Rias repeated, brow furrowed as he groped for words. "To drop roof on my people. End it all. Could not." He shook his head and sighed.

Tikaya glanced between Ottotark and Bones, probing the shadows for Sicarius. Yes, he was there and close enough to hear. Maybe Rias wanted Sicarius to know he had spared the team. Tikaya could not imagine that or anything else winning sympathy from the stony assassin. Maybe Rias just wanted her to know without opening himself for sneering commentary from Ottotark.

Tikaya gripped Rias's forearm. She could not condemn him for being unable to murder his own people, though it would have been convenient if he had arranged an accident for Sicarius when the men were catapulting over the chasm.

In the darkness ahead, four sets of symbols glowed, marking corners of an intersection. Rias tried to walk straight through it.

"Right," Sicarius said, voice cold.

"I can turn the lighting back on if we go this way," Rias said.

"Darkness is tactically preferable."

Tikaya shook her head; the kid didn't even sound human. She and Rias had no chance if they couldn't get the cube powered.

"What if the door on the weapons room won't open without the same power that operates the lighting?" Tikaya asked.

"The lab doors are opening," Sicarius said.

Good point. She sighed.

"But it'll be easier to see what we're doing in that weapons room if it's lit." Rias turned to face Sicarius. "You were in Fort Deadend. You saw what happened to those people. Do you want to risk dropping something? A single broken vial could kill everyone in the cavern."

"Turn right," Sicarius said.

"Why are you so against turning the lights on?" Tikaya asked.

"Because you two wish it." Sicarius jerked his chin to the right. "Lead."

In other words, he did not trust them. No news there.

A long moment passed before Rias headed right. Even as a prisoner with everything going wrong, he remained outwardly calm, and Tikaya reminded herself there was still time.

Lantern light played over piled rock ahead. This was a different tunnel than she had fled the cavern from, but it, too, had been partially blocked. They clambered over the waist-high rubble. When Agarik hopped down from the pile, Tikaya tried to catch his eye again. But he seemed to be deliberately avoiding them. In plotting to betray the marines, had Rias lost Agarik's respect?

Boulders and shattered stalactites cluttered the cracked and uneven cavern floor. The illusion hiding the camp was gone, revealing a mess of smashed gear and broken crates. A pair of legs stuck out from a boulder, and Tikaya tore her gaze away. Above, darkness sheathed the rockets, though the number panel glowed, faintly illuminating the door area.

Sicarius detoured into the camp and grabbed a coil of rope and a bow. He plundered quivers, some still strapped to dead people, for arrows.

Tikaya waited to the side, not in a hurry to be helpful. Rias too, wandered into camp, though he looked less certain about what he sought. Inspiration, probably. Ottotark and Bones followed him, pistols cocked. The expression on Ottotark's bruised face promised he would love to use his.

Agarik bumped Tikaya's shoulder as he came up to stand by her. He pointed his pistol at her, though his finger did not touch the trigger. While Sicarius collected arrows and the other two men guarded Rias, Agarik chanced a whisper.

"Ottotark and Bones are planning to kill you as soon as you open the door."

It wasn't unexpected, but hearing how little time she had unsettled her nonetheless.

"Does Rias have a plan?" Agarik murmured.

Sicarius glanced their way. Fortunately, Agarik still had the pistol aimed at her.

Rias bent to pick something up. "Ah, these might help."

Sicarius turned back to him as Rias hefted Lancecrest's goggles.

"We *had* a plan," Tikaya whispered back to Agarik. "You people weren't a part of it."

"Rias will have a backup one," he said. "If I act against the others to help you, I can't go back, or it's the end of my career, probably my life."

She feared they needed his help, but this was their cause, not his. As far as the marines were concerned, getting those weapons was a good thing. How could she ask Agarik to risk his life when it meant betraying everyone dear to him?

But he had already made his choice: "Just wanted to be sure your offer is still good."

She wished she could hug him, but all she dared was a slight nod. "Beach house," she whispered. "As long as you want it."

A slight smile stretched Agarik's lips. "Surfer with the talented tongue?"

"I'll do my best."

A rifle boomed in a nearby tunnel.

"It's time, Admiral." Sicarius pinned Tikaya with his gaze as he strode to the base of the butte beneath the door. "Bring the ordering for the numbers."

Tikaya wanted to bring a dagger to stick in his gut, but she kept the thought to herself and the sneer from her face as she walked over. Best not to give him any warning that she would make trouble.

Rias joined her, deliberately turning his back on Ottotark and Bones. "What's your plan, Sicarius? There are only a few of us and a lot of weaponry up there. Getting it out will be a challenge."

"We don't need that many rockets to satisfy the emperor's needs," Sicarius said. "If your smoke reveals a safe path, I'll climb up with one other person. We'll press in the correct code and lower several of the weapons to the floor. Once the captain has cleaned up the raiders, he'll be here, and we'll have plenty of men to transport the weapons out."

"Over the chasm?" Rias asked.

"There are other ways out."

He sounded certain. An image came to mind: Sicarius gathering information by torturing captured raiders—Parkonis. She winced.

"Who's going up with you?" she asked. If Sicarius climbed to the top with Ottotark or Bones, that would leave her, Rias, and Agarik with only one hostile man to deal with.

"Starcrest," Sicarius said.

Tikaya fought back a curse. She was beginning to wonder if the assassin had telepathy training, Turgonian or not. Or maybe he just wanted Rias up there because he was expendable at that point. Her hackles rose. "I'm not certain we have the puzzle right. You're *not* making Rias push the numbers for you. Have you seen what happens if someone gets it wrong? Instant incineration."

Sicarius lifted his stuffed quiver of arrows, and she blushed. Wrong conclusion. Of course, he intended to test it from below or he would not have bothered gathering the arrows.

Rias touched his index finger to his lips. To silence her? Or warn her not to irritate the assassin? She scowled at him. Somebody had to do something, and he was just going along with these brutes. He gazed back at her, steady and imperturbable.

Above their heads, the door panel pulsed three times.

"What does that mean?" Bones asked.

"The numbers are about to change." Tikaya had no idea if that was true, but it sounded plausible, and if the marines feared they would need another translation, they might keep her alive a little longer.

"Give me the solution," Sicarius said.

Tikaya showed him the order of the numbers. He stared at it a moment, nodded, and nocked an arrow. Rias handed him the goggles. She expected Sicarius to regard them with suspicion, but he looked them over, then tried them. He lifted the bow and shot, untroubled by the bulky eyewear. The first arrow passed through one of the invisible beams and sizzled to ashes before it reached the target.

"Shit," Ottotark announced.

Unflappable, Sicarius took a step to the side and loosed a second arrow. This one found the target, bumping one of the symbols a slot to the left. The arrow did no damage to the durable alien technology. It bounced away, where another beam incinerated it.

"No need to worry about trash collection here," Bones muttered.

While Sicarius continued moving the numbers around, she gauged the distance to the corridor they had exited, the corridor that eventually led to that panel Rias wanted to visit. She would not consider running with Sicarius on the ground, but if he was busy climbing, the odds improved. Ottotark and Bones were no doubt proficient with their firearms, but she judged them far more fallible than the assassin. If she just had a distraction....

A final arrow clattered off the panel after shifting the last number into place. A chime sounded and the door slid open. It was hard to feel triumphant given the circumstances.

Sicarius removed the goggles and returned them to Rias with a single nod.

"Light a smoke bomb," Sicarius said, apparently unwilling to trust the ones Rias had given him until he had seen them used.

Rias held out the goggles, glancing around as if looking for a place to put them, then shrugged and strapped them around his head. He pushed the lenses above his eyes so they were not in the way as he lit one of the globes. He laid it on the floor at the base of the butte. Soon, plumes of grayish blue smoke wafted into the air. They diffused quickly, spreading over a greater area than the haze from a pistol firing. As Tikaya had seen before, an asymmetrical pattern of white beams grew visible in the smoke.

"Those kill you if they touch you?" Ottotark asked.

"Yes," Tikaya said.

"Glad I'm not trying to climb past them."

Sicarius gave him a cool stare, then laid down the bow and jogged to the bottom. Tikaya eyed the weapon. It would not take many steps to reach it.

"Come, Admiral," Sicarius said.

Rias strode to Tikaya first. He gripped her hands. "Whatever happens, you've been the light that's driven away the darkness in my life." He did nothing so obvious as putting special emphasis on the word light, but she understood anyway: he wanted her to try for the panel.

She squeezed his hands. "I love you too. Be careful."

Ottotark groaned. "Can we shoot them now?"

"Wait until we have the weapons out. If the symbols change, we'll need her again." Sicarius handed his two globes to Bones. "Light one of these if the smoke dies out before we reach the top."

Rias widened his eyes slightly before releasing Tikaya's hands and heading for the base of the butte. Tikaya tried to guess at the meaning in that look; had he done something with the other smoke bombs? The current haze tickled her nose and teared her eyes a bit, but had no significant side effects.

Overhead, the door slid shut. It had only stayed open a couple minutes before locking again. She wondered what happened if someone was on the inside when it closed.

Sicarius was already ten feet up the wall. Though natural, with protrusions and crevasses, it did not look like an easy ascent, even without the beams. They touched it in myriad places, and no easy routes awaited the climbers.

After considering the rock face, Rias removed his rucksack. Tikaya tensed. No, no, if he did not take the cube with him, how would they get it up there? He met her eyes and shook his head faintly. She grimaced. He must not think there was enough space between beams to climb with the rucksack on his back. After watching Sicarius, she reluctantly agreed. As soon as the assassin reached the level of the beams, he had to start sidestepping, twisting and contorting his body. For every two feet he ascended, he ended up dropping a foot somewhere else.

Rias started up, and worry gnawed at her before he even reached the beams. He was taller and broader—and older—than the agile assassin. Dodging those beams would prove a difficult feat. Not impossible, she hoped.

Tikaya eased toward the bow. Agarik remained near her, and he shuffled forward too. They froze when Ottotark eyed them.

"Agarik," he said. "Go hold the lantern for Bones in case he needs to light another smoke thing."

Ottotark slapped his pistol across his palm as he strode over to stand by Tikaya. Agarik glanced at her. She nodded infinitesimally. Better to comply now and wait until Agarik's side-switching might accomplish something.

Light pulsed at the door. The symbols changed.

"Is that what I think it is?" Rias asked, cheek pressed to the rock, a laser less than an inch from his eyebrow.

"Yes." Tikaya slipped the sphere out of her pocket.

Ottotark grabbed her arm, pistol digging into her ribcage. "What's that?"

"Not a weapon," she said, then raised her voice for Rias. "Give me a minute, and I'll translate the new numbers. I know some of them."

"How often does it change?" Bones asked.

Once a day, she guessed. "At random," she said.

Ottotark stepped back, startled when the display flared to life. She manipulated it to find the number symbols.

"You want me to read them to you?" Tikaya called. "Or try to solve the problem and shoot the numbers into place from here?" She had to try, though she doubted Sicarius would be foolish enough to let her have a bow much less authorize her shooting it in his direction. He would probably laugh and say nice try.

"Give Starcrest the numbers," Sicarius said with no sense of humor or annoyance. "He'll figure it out and he'll push them."

Rias grunted. Pebbles clattered down the cliff face. One bounced into a beam's path and was vaporized. The dwindling smoke made the sweat beading his forehead visible. Be careful, Tikaya urged.

The pistol bumped her ribs.

"Get to work," Ottotark snapped.

"I've got the numbers," she said a moment later and read them aloud to the men.

She hoped Rias would wait until he reached the top, or some place safe, to mull over the solution. He was about halfway up now. In a couple feet, Sicarius would reach the ledge.

"I could use more smoke," Rias said.

Bones and Agarik lit one of the globes. Tikaya checked on Rias, hoping he would wait until the smoke thickened before trying to climb farther. She caught him pulling his shirt over his nose and tugging the goggles over his eyes.

As soon as smoke curled from the globe, Bones and Agarik dropped it and stumbled back. They threw their arms over their faces, gagging.

Tikaya sucked in a deep breath and held it. Even then, she still caught the first whiff as the smoke disseminated. More pungent than rotten eggs, it invaded her nostrils and teared her eyes. Ottotark leaned forward, grabbing his nose.

This was her chance.

She drew back her arm and slammed the sphere into his temple. It was not big, but it was blunt and solid. He reeled sideways and stumbled to the ground.

"My eyes," Bones shouted, then retched.

Agarik clutched at his belly and vomited.

No time to check on Rias or Sicarius. Tikaya lunged for the bow and quiver, grabbed them, and wheeled. Agarik had dropped the lantern. She snatched it as well. By then, her lungs burned, demanding air, but she sprinted for the tunnel.

Tears blurred her vision, and she tripped over a rock. She sprawled, almost losing the bow, and her breath whooshed out. Before she could catch herself, she sucked in a mouthful of air. Distance stole some of the potency from the smoke, but it still made her gag. She staggered to her feet, forced her legs into motion, and clambered over the rubble pile and into the tunnel before retching.

As soon as she could, she raced toward the intersection. The air was clearer here, and she sucked it in. She rounded the corner, hoping to run straight to the panel without encountering a maze of tunnels to guess at. A T-section came first. She lifted the lantern and peered both ways. There. A faint crimson glow in the distance.

Tikaya sprinted to the panel, a column of symbols and five vertical lines that glowed solid blue.

Shouts echoed from the cavern. She shuttered the lantern and set it down, plunging the tunnel in darkness. The men would not be distracted for long, and the light would make her an easy target. She could only hope Sicarius would not take his irritation out on Rias, who she had left in a vulnerable position. Second doubts assailed her. She should have stayed and used the bow on the men, shot the cursed assassin, not run away. But, no, the lights were what Rias wanted, and her eyes had been too tear-wracked to aim at anything anyway.

She examined the symbols. Not all were familiar, and there were more than she expected, but she understood the gist. Lighting, power levels, and water controls. Right spot, but what to touch?

In the still tunnel, she felt her rapid heartbeat reverberating through her body. She started to reach for the sphere, but feared she had no time for research. Rias had guessed. She would have to as well.

Boots pounded into the tunnels. The marines would know right where she had gone.

Tikaya slid a finger across one of the horizontal stripes labeled with illumination. Nothing. There was no switch or knob. She slid her finger the other way. Nothing. She waved her hand before it as she had seen Rias do once to close a door.

The stripe pulsed once, and something thunked inside the wall. Had that done it? The lighting did not come on, and she waved her hand before the other stripes. More thunks, and a faint hum from behind the wall.

The footsteps hammered closer. She grabbed the bow, nocked an arrow, and flattened herself against the wall. The corridor offered no cover, but she could not run until she knew if her hand-waving had accomplished the goal. Besides, darkness stretched behind her, and she did not know if more tunnels lay that way or only a dead end.

The footsteps stopped near the intersection, and lantern light bobbed on the wall. She drew the bow, but no one burst into sight.

More footsteps, these ones softer and slower, reached her ear. She tensed. They were coming from behind her somewhere. Trap. And she had only the darkness to hide in.

Then the lights blinked on. It happened so abruptly, she squinted, half-blinded. She almost missed the movement ahead—someone slipping around the corner and dropping to a knee.

Tikaya loosed an arrow without waiting for her vision to clear. As soon as it flew free, she dropped to the floor. A pistol cracked.

She rolled to the side, cursing herself for getting caught in such a bad spot. She scrabbled for another arrow.

"Tikaya, this way," Agarik urged, not from behind but from ahead.

She cursed. Had she just shot at him?

By the time she lunged to her feet, her eyes adjusted enough to see the intersection. Bones lay on his belly, blood pooling beneath his head. Agarik waved for her to hurry.

"What the—" Ottotark blurted, a hundred meters or more down the tunnel behind her.

Tikaya sprinted for Agarik. His pistol, not her bow, had felled the doctor. He pulled her around the corner as another shot fired. The pistol ball clanged off the corner and ricochetted down the tunnel.

"Traitor!" Ottotark screamed.

"No time to reload," Agarik said as they ran toward the intersection that could take them back to the cavern. "You'll have to shoot if he catches up."

"Understood," Tikaya said grimly.

She glanced back to see if Ottotark had rounded the corner yet and missed the reason Agarik skidded to a stop, cursing. He flung his arm out to halt her as well.

A cube hovered in the intersection ahead.

She slammed a fist against her thigh. She should have known—the whole reason for turning the lighting back on had been to power one of the cubes. With the mess from the explosives, all of them would probably respond.

"Maybe it'll go on to the cavern," she whispered.

It rotated, and its crimson orifice came into view.

"Back, back." Agarik spun, taking her with him.

Tikaya ran at his side. They would have to take their chances with Ottotark.

"Zag," she barked on a hunch.

She pushed Agarik one way and ducked against the opposite wall. A red beam seared the air between them.

As soon as it faded, they sprinted off again. Tikaya nocked the bow as she ran. Any second—

Ottotark lunged around the corner, pistol pointed at them. She fired without slowing, and it threw off her aim. The arrow skimmed past his head, stirring his hair, but doing no damage.

He must have seen the cube coming, for he looked between them and cursed before choosing a target. Tikaya.

Agarik hurled a knife at Ottotark. It bought them a second as the sergeant dodged the projectile. She yanked another arrow from her quiver, but Ottotark recovered before she had it nocked.

He fired. There was no room to dodge, no time to duck. Agarik leaped in front of her, grunting as the pistol ball slammed into him.

"No!" Tikaya cried.

She jumped around him, took the split second to aim, and shot. The arrow spun into Ottotark's eye.

She dropped the bow and whirled back to Agarik, catching him as he slumped. His hand gripped his chest, and pain ravaged his face. The cube continued its inexorable advance, but she tried to pull him down the aisle.

"Leave me." Blood spilled from his lips. "Help Rias."

"It'll get you," she choked, refusing to accept the inevitable.

"Yes," Agarik rasped. "Give you...time."

Out of the corner of her eye, she saw it: that cursed glow intensified. She stumbled away as the beam fired. It burned into Agarik and started its deadly work.

"Go," he gasped.

Tears blurring her vision again, Tikaya grabbed the bow and sped away. She leaped over Bones's body and kicked Ottotark on the way past. She should have lit that bastard on fire when she had the chance. Agarik's death was her fault.

She found the corridor Ottotark had used to circle around behind her and cut over toward the cavern. It would take time for the cube to clear away all three bodies, but she recalled the multiple units in that cavern closet and knew others would be about.

Tikaya slowed at the cavern entrance and tried to peer out without revealing herself. No shadows remained, though, and the assassin was already looking down at her when she spotted him. He crouched on the ledge, his shirt off and tied about his nose and mouth. His back was to the closed door. None of the symbols had been moved. He dropped his head to focus on the floor at his feet—or something on it. Paper and pencil, she guessed from his movements. He was trying to solve the new Skiltar Square.

But where was Rias? Smoke still wafted from the noxious globe, but it had thinned, and she would have seen him on the cliff if he remained there. His rucksack lay on the floor where he had left it. Dread crept into her as she continued to search the area without spotting him. If he had fallen, the beams could have incinerated him before he reached the ground.

Two cubes worked in the cavern, eating away the piles of rubble. They reminded her of the one in the tunnels behind her. As soon as it finished with the bodies—she forced herself not to dwell on Agarik, not now—it would head this way.

Tikaya eased out of the tunnel and kept her back to the wall. Sicarius kept track of her as he figured. Her hand ached where she gripped the bow. If Sicarius had killed Rias, he was not getting off the cliff. Agile or not, he could not dodge arrows while he climbed down past those lasers. She removed an arrow and nocked it with steady hands. Cold controlled anger made her movements sure, free of fear. Even if he had not killed Rias, he was the Turgonian emperor's assassin, someone who had tried to murder her president. The world would be better off with him dead.

She drew the bow. No sense of alarm widened Sicarius's eyes, but he stood. Balanced on the balls of his feet, arms relaxed, he appeared unconcerned by the weapon pointed at him. Even on that small ledge, he could probably dodge an arrow. But if she bumped one of the numbers, and he could not solve the problem on time, he would either have to climb down, where she could shoot him in the back, or he would be incinerated.

Yes, then why hadn't she fired yet?

Killing Ottotark in self-defense was one thing; shooting someone in cold blood... Could she do it?

Motion across the cavern saved her from having to answer the question. Rias burst from a tunnel, diving and rolling as a red beam lanced the air over him.

"Rias!" she shouted.

He scrambled to his feet and zigzagged toward the butte. He chopped a wave her direction, but lifted his head to shout a stream of numbers at the assassin.

The solution to the door. Sicarius's head tilted, and he gazed upward—calculating. Not trusting enough to enter them without checking for himself. And why should he be? Rias had no reason to help, to get the assassin inside with the weapons. What was he doing?

"Is that..." She thrust her bow toward the cube chasing him.

Rias dove over a fallen stalactite. A beam struck the rubble, and rock and dust flew. He came up, racing toward the camp this time, and a wild grin lit his face. He pressed a finger to his lips and mouthed something. Distract it?

Sicarius was punching in the door code. Tikaya cut toward the cube from the side. As soon as she was closer to it than Rias, it rotated toward her. She ran toward a pile of rubble and ducked behind it without any of the grace Rias had managed. Her shoulder clunked against a boulder with a painful jar. She peeped around the edge.

Rias reached his rucksack and tore open the lid. He dug out the cube, still inert, the lid still off. So the one following him—her now—was an extra.

She circled the pile to avoid its approach. A beam bit into the rubble, and shards of stone rained upon her.

Overhead, the door slid open. Rias thumbed something inside his cube. Sicarius entered the chamber. Rias hurled the cube toward the top of the butte.

The one at ground-level was nearing Tikaya and she had to sprint to the next pile of debris. She glanced upward as she ran, fearing pieces would fly out of the open cube or the beams would incinerate it, but it reached the top unharmed. It caromed off the transparent wall, and Tikaya thought it would bounce away from the butte, but it righted itself. Hovering in the air, the cube approached the door.

Inside, Sicarius whirled at the noise and dropped into a crouch.

"Get out!" Rias called.

He dug a familiar jar out of his rucksack and raced at the cube stalking Tikaya around the rubble pile. She let it get dangerously close to keep it occupied.

She risked another glance upward. If the modified cube started destroying rockets while the door was open, they would all be dead in seconds. But it focused on Sicarius first.

A beam shot out. Tikaya held her breath. Sicarius ducked, and the beam splashed against the wall without hitting a rocket.

Her own cube almost skewered her when her heel caught a rock, and she ripped her attention back to the closer danger. Rias scrambled over the pile from the side and splattered the air with his concoction. He and Tikaya split and raced away while the cube was deciding where to focus its beam.

As they met on the other side of the pile, an earsplitting shriek echoed from all around. The weapons chamber door started to shut. Sicarius dove under the cube and rolled through the entrance. The door sealed. His momentum took him to the edge, and Tikaya thought he would fly over the side, but he twisted and caught the overhang.

Smoke rose behind Tikaya. Their cube was out of action. She leaned forward, willing the one caught inside the chamber to do what they wanted.

Rias gripped her hand. He had lost the crazy grin and stared at the chamber, as if he could will the cube to work with the intensity of his gaze.

Then the first beam shot out. Tikaya could not see the target from where they stood, but a green haze filled the air in the weapons chamber. A bone-shaking rumble emanated from the butte—the ventilation system firing up. Smoke whirled and rose, drawn into the ducts at the top.

Sicarius hung on the cliff, his chin over the edge, staring at the display. A blue gas joined the green, mingling and merging as it too was sucked upward. Tikaya hoped some sort of filter existed, so everything in the mountains at the other end of that vent did not die.

"It's working." Rias smiled and wrapped her in a hug.

She could not bring herself to return the smile, not with Agarik's death haunting her thoughts, but she did return the embrace. She smashed her face into his shoulder and hugged him with all her strength. And then released him. She would cry later, when they were safe.

A pebble clattered down the cliff. Sicarius was climbing down.

"We better get out of here," she whispered.

Rias nodded, grabbed his rucksack, and jogged to the camp. She followed him, but when he started gathering food and gear, she shifted from foot to foot.

"Do we have time for that?" She jerked her head toward Sicarius. Even with the beams to navigate, his progress going down was faster than it had been climbing up. "He's going to be irate."

"I know," Rias said, but he continued his preparations, unhurried. Black powder tins and ammo pouches went into his rucksack. "It's weeks to get across the mountains and back to civilization. We'll need supplies to survive the trek."

"I need to find Parkonis and make sure he can get away from the Turgonians," she said. "And, Rias? Agarik didn't make it."

His jaw tightened, but he kept himself to a curt nod.

"He saved my life," Tikaya said, "so I could come back to help you."

Rias grabbed a second rucksack and started filling it for her. She glanced at Sicarius.

"He's almost down," she murmured. "If we want to take him out, this may be our last chance." That weeks-long trek would be arduous enough without an assassin hounding them. "If he comes after us...after you... We can't waste the gift Agarik gave us."

Rias finished packing. "We won't."

Sicarius jumped the last ten feet, landing lightly. Even in defeat, that same stony mask hid his thoughts, his feelings.

Rias handed Tikaya her pack and a fresh quiver of arrows for her bow. He picked up a rifle but did not bother to load it.

"Ready." He pointed to a tunnel, a tunnel they would have to walk past the assassin to reach.

Metal rang softly as Sicarius pulled a dagger from his belt and stepped into their path.

Tikaya grabbed Rias's elbow when he did not slow. "Are you mad?"

Rias removed her hand gently and strode toward the tunnel. Tikaya nocked an arrow, but did not fully draw the bow. Rias had to know what he was doing. Didn't he? Shaking her head, she followed him.

Sicarius's grip tightened around the dagger hilt. "You never intended to help. You had the chance to redeem yourself, but you betrayed the emperor again."

Rias stopped a few feet from him. "Yes."

Sweat dripped down the sides of Sicarius's dust-streaked face and dampened his pale hair. For the first time, he seemed uncertain, frazzled. Young. "Why?"

"I couldn't let him have those weapons. There's no honor in destroying one's enemies like that. Nobody should have that kind of power."

"That wasn't for you to decide."

"Yes, it was. Sometimes the only person capable of such a decision is someone who stands on the outside, someone who has nothing left to lose, nothing to gain, by the outcome."

"Nothing to gain?" Sicarius asked. "You could have had your life back, your lands." The faintest hint of longing entered his voice. "You could have been a hero again."

Tikaya lowered the bow as it dawned on her that Sicarius had yet to point the dagger at Rias. Not here and not at any point since he had shown up.

"That's never been a goal of mine," Rias said. "The definition of a hero changes depending on the needs of the person with the dictionary. And of late I've become more aware how much being a hero to the empire means being a war criminal to the rest of the world." Rias smiled sadly at Tikaya before turning back to Sicarius. "For twenty years, I served Turgonia. I think it's time now to see if I can serve the world."

"I see," Sicarius said, and Tikaya had a hard time telling if he truly did or not.

Rias unsheathed a dagger, flipped it in his hand, and held it hilt-first toward Sicarius. It was utterly black, one of the tools they had gathered for working on the cubes. The keen edge would probably never dull.

Sicarius considered it for a long moment before accepting it. Peace offering, Tikaya guessed.

"Are you returning with Bocrest and the others?" Rias asked.

"Yes," Sicarius said.

"Parkonis is no threat to the empire. Will you see to it that he escapes when the ship docks in Port Sakrent?"

Tikaya's eyes widened, not in surprise that Rias would care enough to make the request, but that he was asking Sicarius for a favor. After they had defeated him.

"If that is your wish," Sicarius said, stunning Tikaya even more.

The kid was going to be in trouble already for not completing his mission, for letting Rias go. Earlier, she had been thinking of shooting him, but now she found herself hoping the emperor had invested too much in his education to dispose of him over a failure.

"Thank you," Rias said. "And one last request: will you relay a message to the emperor for me?"

Sicarius tilted his head.

"Though I may never see them again, I have family and friends in Turgonia. It is not my intention to make trouble for the empire. But I want him to know that if he bothers them or—" Rias angled toward Tikaya, directing Sicarius's eyes to her, "—if he sends anyone after her or her family, I *will* become trouble."

Tikaya thought she detected bleakness in the assassin's usual mask. Yes, all Fleet Admiral Starcrest would have to do to make the emperor's life unpleasant would be to show up on the Nurian Chief's threshold, offering to help war against his former nation.

"I will tell him," Sicarius said.

"Thank you," Rias said again, and he put a hand on Sicarius's shoulder. "You would have made a good officer."

"Not the road fate paved for me," Sicarius said, but something in the soft exhale that followed his words made Tikaya wonder if he wished things were different.

EPILOGUE

As the light faded from the mountains, Rias placed the last block of snow on the top of the igloo. There was no wood to make a fire, though a kerosene lantern provided a pool of light.

He stepped back, brushed off his gloves, and quirked an eyebrow. "What do you think?"

It had taken two days to find a "back door" out of the tunnels, and it had brought them out above the tree line with only a couple hours of daylight remaining. Icy wind gusted along the ridge, and the first stars glittered in the clear sky. The night would be long and cold, very cold. Though she had helped build it, Tikaya eyed the igloo dubiously.

"You're sure we won't freeze to death?" she asked.

They had enough gear, Rias assured her, to make it out of the mountains and to the nearest town. Still, the lack of firewood and the plummeting temperature made her nervous for this first night.

Rias flattened his hand on his chest. "Are you questioning my engineering skills?"

"No, I'm sure it's structurally stable. I'm questioning the wisdom of sleeping inside a box of snow."

He chuckled, ambled over, and kissed her on the forehead. "Snow is insulating, my dear. Once our body heat warms up the igloo, you'll be able to sleep naked if you want."

"Sleep naked, huh?"

His eyes twinkled. "The sleeping part is optional."

A distant boom echoed through the mountains. The marines had apparently found a different way out and were following their orders to seal the tunnels. She hoped they were treating Parkonis well. Leaving him felt like a betrayal, but the reality was he would probably make it home sooner and less eventfully than she. And though Sicarius ranked at the top of her list of People She Never Wanted to Meet Again, Rias trusted him to keep his word, and she trusted Rias.

She wished she had been able to keep her word to Agarik. Leaving him there to be incinerated by that machine... Another betrayal. She wondered what the marines would tell his family. If he even had family. It shamed her that a man had given his life to save hers and she knew so little about him.

Rias shoved their weapons and gear through the igloo's low entrance, then belly-crawled after. Tikaya grabbed the lantern and managed to get snow down her pants following him. She hissed in frustration as she dug it out in the tiny confines. She could not wait to walk again on a tropical beach.

Inside, there was room enough to lie down if one did not straighten too many limbs. Rias shoved a rucksack in front of the tunnel, leaving them entombed with only a few air holes. The snowy walls gleamed next to the lantern. The single flame brightened the space surprisingly well.

Tikaya lay down, head propped against her pack. "Not bad."

"Easy," Rias said, "your lavish praise will inflate my ego."

Tikaya pulled him down beside her, hoping to shake the gloomy mood that shrouded her. "I'd rather inflate other things."

"I'm always amenable to that."

She slid her arms inside his parka. If body heat was the way to warm up an igloo, then she was all for hastening that process along.

Sometime later, and with fewer clothes on, she asked, "How did you know Sicarius would let us go?"

"That was always my plan," Rias murmured, his lips brushing her ear.

Tikaya chuckled. She lay snuggled in his arms "And how did you know he would go along with your plan? Especially after we betrayed him and destroyed the weapons before his eyes."

"I read him."

"You *read* him? The kid emoted less than a rock."

For a moment, Rias did not answer, and she wondered if she had offended him. But, as she formed an apology, he spoke, his tone somewhere between amusement and bemusement.

"What do you think a military strategist does?"

An image filled her mind: Rias, leaning over a map-filled table surrounded by his officers. They pushed miniature battleships back and forth while debating numbers of troops, cannons, practitioners, and the like. Then she realized those battleships and troops were commanded by people. People he had never met face-to-face but that he had to analyze and out-think. She thought of the time Rias had spent working with Sicarius on the trebuchet, talking to him when no one else did, treating him like a promising young officer. As worldly and educated as the assassin seemed, he was still a seventeen-year-old boy, one who had doubtlessly grown up hearing of Rias's exploits. Whether he showed it or not, Sicarius must have felt a little hero worship for the distinguished veteran. Tikaya smirked. All that time, she had thought Rias was succumbing to his fate. He must have seen Sicarius as the one person he could not escape or physically force his way past, and the one person he needed to befriend.

"I see now," Tikaya said. "I was being obtuse. Military strategist isn't a career option where I grew up."

"Sounds like a lovely place."

"Yes...about that." She had told Rias she would follow him anywhere, and she would, but—

"You need to go home and let your family know you're safe," he said.

"Just for a week or two. Do you want to come or..." When she had learned his name, she told him he would never be welcome on her island, and she suspected that true, at least not until people's memories of the war faded, but if he had saved the president from assassination, surely Rias could finagle visitation rights. The president owed her too. He had said as much after her decryption work proved so valuable. But maybe she was being presumptuous. "Or do you need to visit your own family? Let them know you're alive?"

"I'll write them a letter from some distant port. The emperor will be irked when he finds out about this, and I don't think it'd be auspicious for my life expectancy to linger on imperial soil."

Yes, the Turgonian emperor had never come across as the magnanimous type in the orders she decrypted.

"Besides..." Rias found her hand and linked his fingers with hers. "I have little interest in going home. I seem to have fallen in love with an exotic foreigner, and I have the urge to follow her wherever she wants to go."

Flutters stirred in her belly. She had hoped that would be his response. "Well, we'll have the sphere to work on, and as far as places to go, I know of all sorts of ruins around the world with unsolved puzzles and mathematical oddities. Of course, many of them are surrounded by dangerous aborigines, crocodile-filled swamps, and pistol-toting relic raiders, all ready to end your life if you let your guard down for an instant."

"My dear," Rias breathed, "if you're trying to seduce me...it's working."

<<< >>>

Also by the Author

the Emperors Edge Universe

Novels:
The Emperor's Edge, Book 1
Dark Currents, Book 2
Deadly Games, Book 3
Conspiracy, Book 4
Book 5, coming soon
Encrypted

Short Stories:
Ice Cracker II (and other short stories)
The Assassin's Curse

THE FLASH GOLD CHRONICLES

Flash Gold
Hunted
Peacemaker

THE GOBLIN BROTHERS ADVENTURES

Connect with the Author

http://www.lindsayburoker.com

http://www.facebook.com/LindsayBuroker

http://www.twitter.com/GoblinWriter

Made in the USA
Lexington, KY
18 February 2013